THE DEAD, THE DYING

AND

THE DAMNED

JOHN HOLLANDS
MC

Quill Publications
Devon

Quill Publications,
2, Orchards Farm,
Buckerell,
Nr. Honiton,
Devon,
EX14   3GJ.

Email: hollands12010@hotmail.com
Website: www.johnhollandsbooks.co.uk

Publishing history:
Since **The Dead, the Dying and the Damned** was first published in 1956 there have been over 30 printings in various languages.   There have also been two 'pirate' editions, one printed in India and the other in Hong Kong. Additionally, there was a case of plagiarism. This was duly exposed and compensation paid out of court.

This new edition is shortly to be released as an e-book in all major formats, worldwide. In some countries, notably the United States, **The Dead, the Dying and the Damned** was published under the title, **'Able Company'**.

Reissued edition, published in 2013.
Reprinted before publication, July 2013
Third reprint August 2013
Fourth reprint September 2013

Book cover design: David Chapman-Andrews.
Printed and bound in the United Kingdom by:
Imprintdigital,
Upton Pyne,
Devon.

Also by John Hollands:

Able Company (America only)

The Gospel According to Uncle Jimmy

Never Marry a Cricketer (as Eileen Hollands)

Never Marry a Rugger Player (as Eileen Hollands)

Not Shame the Day

The Exposed

Blundellian Writers

Poetry of the Korean War (contributions)

Black Rain

The Court-Martial

Memory and Imagination Series

Gran and Mr. Muckey   (Volume I)

What a Fag!   (Volume II)

Heroes of the Hook.   (Volume III)

The War Poems of a Young Soldier

Main Characters

2nd Lt Peter Blake	One Platoon Commander
Major Richard Lawrence	Able Company Commander
Corporal Smith	Section Commander, One Platoon
Corporal Hale	Section Commander, One Platoon
Private Winston	Private, One Platoon
Private Burrows	Private, One Platoon
Private Edwin Charles	Private, One Platoon
Private Hallows	Private, One Platoon
Paddy O'Hara	Private, One Platoon
Sergeant Miles	One Platoon Sergeant
CSM Ralf	Sergeant-Major, Able Company
Corporal Williamson	Company signaler
Corporal Cross	Company clerk
Captain Nobby Clark	2 i/c Able Company
The Colonel	Commanding Officer, the Rocks
Jackie	Japanese employee HQBCFK
2nd Lt Bartram	Platoon Commander
2nd Lt Goodall	Platoon Commander

Acknowledgment

My very sincere thanks are due to David Chapman-Andrews for design and editorial help and to Christopher Price for editorial help.

Dedicated to the men of 12 Platoon, Dog Company, 1st
Battalion DWR, who distinguished themselves in the
Third Battle of The Hook during May 1953

Please Note

The Dead, the Dying and the Damned is fictitious. Although names of Korean hills, towns and villages, various military units, and real events are mentioned they have often been changed in terms of timings and locations to enhance the story and save possible embarrassment. Likewise, military jargon and procedures have often been simplified for those unfamiliar with military matters. In all respects, the flow and continuity of the story has been placed above everything else.

Also, for various editorial reasons, a few names of minor characters in the first edition have been changed; <u>and in line with current international trends, and for technical reasons, American-style spelling has been adopted.</u> Some events in this novel did not appear in the Cassell's 1956 edition, but all were part of the original manuscript.

CONTENTS

Author's Introduction to the revised and abridged edition of 2013

In Volume III of my fictionalized Memoirs, *Memory and Imagination* (*Heroes of the Hook,* which I recommend you read before this book), I relate my experiences as a National Serviceman between October 1951 and October 1953. The Memoir records how I volunteered for the Korean War in order to gather material for a book, with the aim of sparking off my career as a novelist.

Since I was looking for trouble, I suppose it was only fitting that I found it in abundance. My army service climaxed with the Third Battle of the Hook, a particularly vicious finale to the Korean War; and having survived the Hook I became all the more determined to write a novel recording for posterity the horrific experiences of National Servicemen in Korea.

As a National Serviceman it may have been better had I recounted my adventures and then left it at that. Why I didn't, and instead opted to write a novel in which fictitious events were often less dramatic than the real thing, is something easy to explain. In my youth (although no longer!) I abhorred exaggerating and laying myself open to charges of distortion and aggrandizement. I was also afraid of upsetting the men with whom I had served by relating what really happened; even the possibility of libeling them while describing incidents when things went horribly wrong.

Not infrequently in *The Dead, the Dying and the Damned,* I placed constraints on incidents to make them more believable, often at the behest of my publisher who had a habit of saying, "That's a bit hard to swallow." I was also obsessed by the need to record the thoughts and inner feelings of characters, which necessitated it being fictitious. This delving into the minds of characters was the vogue at the time, the writers' equivalent to 'method acting', but its most notable effect was to slow down the story and complicate matters.

Another reason to opt for fiction was the decline in demand in early post-war years for real-life war adventures. People were growing tired of the derring-do of people like Eric Williams (*The Wooden Horse*) and wanted to know what the ordinary Tommy had been through. The huge success of novels such as *The Cruel Sea, The Caine Mutiny,* and *The Naked and the Dead*, made this all too clear. .

Most of all, in my youth I was desperate to establish myself as a novelist, not merely someone relating a one-off real-life adventure.

On my return from Korea in 1953, I was living with my mother and two brothers in the delightful Surrey village of Elstead and it was there that the bulk *of The Dead, the Dying and the Damned* was written, having started it on my first day on board the troopship Devonshire as we pulled out of Pusan. As explained in **Heroes of the Hook,** I had no idea of how to go about writing a novel and my only form of training or study was to read three novels, *The Naked and the Dead*, *The Cruel Sea*, and *The Caine Mutiny.* I was misguided enough to think that these three very different types of novels would give me sufficient know-how to get by.

Those on board the Troopship Devonshire accepted my writing and unsocial behavior without interest, but once I got home it caused immediate friction. It was deemed by my family that a young, able-bodied man sitting at a desk all day, tapping away on an Underwood typewriter with two fingers, was both unhealthy and unnatural. Also, they dreaded that once I had exhausted my savings I would turn to them for financial assistance. It was therefore inevitable that they demanded that I should lose no time in getting a job--- a proper job that would be seen as a first step towards a respectable career.

It never occurred to them (or me) that my compulsion to write was not only inspired by my desire to make known the exploits of my old platoon, but also by a mild form of combat stress. Amongst my family, what happened to me in Korea was never mentioned, let alone discussed; but my experiences on the Hook and the deaths of so many friends were seldom out of my mind. Nightmares featuring mutilated bodies plagued me. My family knew nothing of them and as far as they were concerned I might just as well have spent the previous year on routine duties at a regimental depot.

I didn't help matters by being terribly secretive about my writing. If ever asked what I was writing about, I simply said: "Oh, just this and that." I also made sure that none of my family got the chance of a sneak preview of my writing. As soon as I put my typewriter to one side, I locked my manuscript into an old suitcase and stored it away in my bedroom, usually out of sight in the wardrobe.

Matters deteriorated further when I began writing deep into the night. The noise of my typewriter became unbearable for them. As a result I was banished to the garden shed. Not that I minded. I bought a Tilley lamp and a Tilley heater and felt quite at home, as though I was back in a Korean bunker, which the shed resembled in many respects.

I made swift progress and the number of pages I churned out was prodigious, yet the story and events were very slow to unfold. I was writing in the third person and with every new character I introduced I felt obliged to give him a potted biography and record every thought that passed through his mind. My manuscript soon outgrew my suitcase and instead I had to store it in my father's old ocean-going trunk.

Weeks passed and then months. The manuscript grew bigger and bigger. It became so big that I had to sit on Dad's trunk to get it to close and eventually even that didn't work and I just let the foolscap sheets pile up on the earthen floor of the shed.

When the pile became knee-high my money ran out and I had no option but to find a job. That was easy in those days, just so long as one wasn't fussy. I simply got in touch with the Public Schools' Employment Agency and they fixed me up with a job in the City of London as a trainee with Harrison and Crossfield, a famous commercial concern specializing in exporting to the far-flung corners of the globe. This meant living in London and I rented a very dingy bed-sit in Bayswater. My first morning's trip to work convinced me that London was not for me. I was appalled at the way human beings were herded about like animals on the London Underground. I saw two young women trapped in closing doors and once, when I missed a train and was left standing alone on the platform, there was a shoe, a scarf, and a bag full of shopping just lying there, abandoned. However, having signed on with Harrison and Crossfield for a three months' trial period I had no choice but to sweat it out.

One thing London taught me was the agony of being a fanatic: the pain caused by being ruled by a passion which left no time or desire for anything else. Every spare moment I had was devoted to writing. I took my writing to work with me. I scribbled away in long-hand while on the Underground and in my lunch hours I borrowed a typewriter from a girl in the typing pool to thrash out at least another four pages. As soon as I got back to my digs in the evening, I had a quick wash and then went down Queensway to a small Greek restaurant and had their menu of the day for five shillings, sitting at a table for four so I could spread my manuscript out around me.

This devotion to my writing cost me two glorious opportunities which later in life I have always regretted. The girl in the typing pool who lent me her typewriter was petite, with naturally wavy hair that hung below her shoulders. She wasn't beautiful but she had a magnificent figure that burst forth for general admiration despite the dowdy clothes her low wages dictated she wore. She lived in a Young Ladies' Hostel in Ealing and was desperately lonely, longing to get involved in something artistic, and she pleaded with me to let her come back to my bed-sit to do all my typing for me. Similarly, in the Greek restaurant there was a waitress who looked like a youthful Anna Maganani, and she implored me not to waste my money on leftover moussaka, and instead to let her fortify me with tagliatelli back at her place. Alas, such was my conceit concerning my masterpiece, and my conviction that nothing must be allowed to delay its early completion, that I brooked no interference from these lusty and compliant females.

I left my job in London as soon as possible and worked instead for a provincial weekly newspaper, The Woking Opinion. This was not a good name for a local paper. Everyone mistook it for The Working Opinion and it was generally assumed by my friends that I had been 'turned' by the Chinese and was now a communist.

Because Elstead was only a few miles from Woking, and I had recently acquired my first car (a 1931 Wolseley Hornet, a 2-seater open-sports), I resumed living with Mum and my brothers. My work at the Woking Opinion was so varied, so interesting, and was so amusing that interest in my novel began to wane. When I eventually finished it I gathered the manuscript together, piled it high, and covered it with a plastic sheet to preserve it from the rain that dripped from the shed's roof. Then I left it there, fully intending to return to it a few months later to give it a final polish, make corrections, and try to do something about the spelling with the aid of a dictionary I'd liberated from the Woking Opinion.

Once no longer dominated by my novel, I returned to what could be called a normal life. I had exorcised my war-time demons. My inner turmoil vanished and I even took to playing cricket again, turning out regularly for either Aldershot CC under John Aston or the Old Blundellians under Ted Crowe.

Then fate took a hand. I went home unexpectedly one lunch time and found Mum clearing out the shed, about to give my manuscript to the dustmen. She often did things like that. Whilst I was in Korea she'd given away my highly-prized collection of Wisden Almanacs to the Elstead W.I. Jumble Sale where all twenty volumes (including the rare 1932/3 Bodyline edition) were sold for £2.17s.6d. On a matter of principle I was not prepared to let anything like that happen again. I threw a tantrum and made all sorts of extravagant claims as to the value of my masterpiece.

Once I'd saved the hulk from the dustmen, I re-read a few passages. Then I read a few more. By the end of the afternoon I'd dipped into pages all over the place; and to my astonishment some of them weren't bad. There was even one passage, where a man got burnt to death, which I considered first-class. Thus encouraged, I decided that I might just as well send the damned thing to a publisher to see what happened. The next question was who to send it to. The only publishers I knew were Collins (because they published so many novels) and Cassell's because I'd recently read *The Cruel Sea.* I tossed a coin and Cassell's won. So I heaved my manuscript off the shed floor and made it into a parcel.

The Elstead Post Office refused to accept it. They said it was too heavy and so badly wrapped that it would never reach its destination. So, since British Rail was on strike (as always), and Carter Patterson was highly expensive, I decided to pile it into my Wolseley Hornet and deliver it by hand the next time I was in the London area.

Unfortunately, the canvas hood of the Hornet leaked more than the garden shed did and the state of the manuscript deteriorated even further. My girlfriend of the day was responsible for this. Such were the difficulties of making love in the two-seater Hornet that when she suddenly stretched out full length, really going for it, the back of her head went straight through the cellophane rear window; and from there on the Hornet might just as well have been a motor cycle. Within a week or two the manuscript, tucked away in a narrow gap behind the bench seat, became soggy and smudgy.

In those days, Cassell's offices were in St Andrew's Hill, East London, and very Dickensian in character. The main entrance seemed to act as the rear entrance as well and I soon found myself standing by a roller conveyor belt on which several large parcels of books were lined up. No one took any notice of me so I put my weighty parcel on the conveyor belt. Then it became obvious that something special was in the air. The staff members were in a state of great excitement.

I soon found out why. A distinguished-looking cluster of men came down a spiral staircase at the far end of the building and started to walk towards the roller conveyor belt. At the head of them, making slow progress and leaning heavily on a walking stick, was Sir Winston Churchill, complete with his traditional cigar and homburg hat. He was, of course, Cassell's most distinguished author, a Nobel Prize winner for literature, and still Prime Minister. He was my ultimate hero and the most famous man in the world. As he walked along he paused to have a word with one or two of the staff. Near to where I was standing was the foreman of the dispatch department. Churchill had obviously met him before and they exchanged friendly greetings. Churchill then raised his stick and jabbed the huge, scruffy-looking parcel I had just delivered.

"And what do we have here?" he asked.

"Don't know, Guv'nor," the foreman answered with Cockney familiarity.

"This youngster's just dumped it here. A novel, I suppose."

Sir Winston glanced at me and then back at my tome. He smiled around at those hanging on his next word. We all knew he would come up with a scintillating witticism; and he did not disappoint. "Then let us hope," he said in the distinctive tone the whole world knew so well, "that, for the sake of those charged with the not inconsiderable task of reading it, this young man's talent comes somewhere near to equaling his industry."

Everyone laughed and he passed on.

A moment I will never forget!

Four months went by. I was so engrossed by my work on the Woking Opinion that I forgot all about my novel. Then one evening at home, the telephone rang. Surprisingly, my brother Derek (better known to readers of **Memory and Imagination** as Brother Nothing) answered it. I say surprisingly because it wasn't until he was out of his teens that he even dared to answer the telephone at all. Even as a young adult his telephone manner left a lot to be desired and to avoid any unnecessary involvement he had the odd habit of answering the 'phone by saying, "Mrs. Hollands speaking." Unfortunately his voice was akin to a double bass which always caused confusion. Anyhow, on this occasion he picked up the receiver and barked down it: "Mrs Hollands speaking … What do you want?"

The person at the other end paused, obviously surprised. "I'd like to speak to Mr. Hollands, please."

"Which one? There are three of us."

"Mr. Hollands, the author."

"No authors here. Wrong number!"

He rang off.

Several minutes later the telephone rang again. "I'd like to speak to Mr. Hollands, please. The author."

"I've just told you. No authors here."

"The writer … Mr. D.J.Hollands …"

"Him! He's not a writer … Not unless you count trying out his signature since the age of six …"

"I'd like to speak to him anyhow."

So it was that I first made contact with Dr. Desmond Flower, the Literary Director of Cassell's, probably the second most influential man in British publishing.

If anything, I proved even dimmer than Brother Nothing. I was so overcome by whom I had been contacted, and flung into such a tizzy that such a person had actually telephoned me, that I was struck speechless. When Desmond Flower said: "I've just read your novel ... And we would like to publish it ..." I just stood there like a dumb cluck.

Eventually, Desmond Flower grew tired of waiting for a response. He asked a couple of time if there was still someone still there, and when he heard odd gurgling noises he went on to explain that he lived only a mile or two down the road from Elstead (at Headley Down) and since tomorrow was Saturday and he would be at home, perhaps I would like to pop down the road in the morning to see him--- to have a drink or two and to discuss publication.

I cleared my throat and amazed myself by replying: "Sorry I can't make it then."

"Any time will do."

"Sorry. I'm playing cricket tomorrow."

"Not in the morning, surely ..."

"It's an away fixture. I'll be off early."

"Then how about Sunday?"

"I'm playing cricket then as well."

"All day?"

"Yes ... An away fixture ... At Coventry. I can't let the OBs down ..."

At that point he gave up. He suggested that if I really was interested in being published, then perhaps I should give his office a ring and make an appointment to see him during office hours.

We eventually met the following Wednesday. Actually, I should have been playing cricket then as well, having just joined the Guildford Wednesday XI, but after a weekend of agonizing over my crass behavior, I at last got my priorities right.

When I settled on a chair opposite Desmond Flower in his small office I noticed that my manuscript was on the floor, propped up against the leg of his desk. We looked down at it, then at each other. "Not a pretty sight," he said. Then he added, rather curiously I thought at the time, "Do you remember how it ends?"

"Yes ..."

"The last 20 pages?"

"Yes ... I think so ... Definitely ..."

"Good! Only at the moment they're completely unreadable. The damp has got to them and the mice as well I think ... Not that it matters. It's the contents that count, despite what you read in the 'How to Write a Novel' books. What you've written has something rather unique about it, something indefinable. It's got its own special spirit which we've never come across before.   As for the presentation … It reminds me of Margret Mitchell's **Gone with the Wind**.   Her manuscript was as bad as yours from all reports.   She wrote it on the back of used brown envelopes she'd retrieved from wastepaper baskets … She used both sides and even wrote over the old addresses.   At least you used paper.   Mind you, your spelling is hardly excusable.   I can't spell either, but at least I could see your mistakes.   And understand them.   That's more than I can say for our Readers.   I've got a bet with one of them.   About a word you use on page 635.   I'll show you."

He stooped down and unearthed the relevant page.   "Here we are, Second paragraph.   What does, 'Allintenesantperposis' mean?"

"Well …Allintensantperposis …"

"Do you mean, 'All intents and purposes'?"

"Yes."

"Oh, good.   I've just won five shillings!" *

We soon put these minor points behind us and got down to the real issues.   He started by telling me that if I so wished, his editorial staff could soon whip the book into shape.   "We've got dozens of hacks who could do it for you," he said.

I declined the offer.   The contents were so personal to me that I couldn't bear the thought of others messing about with them.

"Good.   Glad to hear it," he replied.   "An author should be prepared to stand or fall by his own efforts.   I don't have much faith in editors.   If they were any good they'd be writing their own books."

Dr. Flower went on to say that the most pressing need was to cut the length of the book.   He was adamant that no one would be prepared to wade through nearly 900 pages.   After all, he pointed out, Korea was only a three-year war, not a hundred-year one.   He said it had to be cut by two-thirds.   He saw no difficulty in doing this.   Why, he wanted to know, did I think readers would be interested in how to carry out 'immediate actions' on a Bren gun?   Or for that matter, details of the working parts of a Chinese Burp Gun?   Nor was it necessary to go into the intricate details of firing a three-inch mortar with a footnote reminding readers of the danger of dropping two bombs down the spout at the same time.

Another major problem was bad language.   He understood my desire for authenticity by using army language, but he was adamant that despite the precedent set by **Lady Chatterley's Lover**, the time was not yet ripe for the use

It is only fair to point out that I am dyslexic.   In those days, dyslexia was unknown and those who suffered from it were regarded as retarded.

of the F-word. So it was ruled that all such profanities had to go. He also reckoned that by cutting out all my obscenities I would save anything up to 10,000 words; and if, instead of continually misspelling words, I cut out all those I was unsure of, I would save an even greater number.

"Those two things alone and you'll be halfway there already--- which, incidentally, is one word, not two."

Dr. Flower then laid down what other changes would be necessary. I had to modify my criticism of American and other allied troops. He reasoned that it would be difficult enough to sell the book without me being rude about various armed forces. I also took heed of his advice on military matters, not only because of his experience as a publisher, but because he also held the Military Cross. He said there was a limit to how much blood and guts the ordinary reader could take, and having more than one man shot in the balls would only make readers think: 'Oh no! Not again!'

He also stressed that although it was permissible to mention as many British army failures as I liked, I should avoid making the army, or any part of it, look stupid. Officers could be made to look cruel, aggressive and callous, but never stupid. When I asked him why that was, he surprised me by saying: "Because most of them are stupid!"

Above all, I was to minimize the casualties caused by 'blue-on-blue' incidents. He went on to name numerous other things. There were to be no references to South Korean atrocities; no murder of a Korean attached to a British unit; no scene in which a dog is slaughtered and then eaten by British officers; and no prolonged romance in Japan with an under-age house-girl. The British public simply wasn't ready for a serious romance with a Jap, no matter how beautiful she happened to be. Anyhow, he said, the affair I described was far too long and would make a book in its own right once I'd given the nation time to forgive the Japanese for their brutalities.*

He was also wary about too many sub-plots which, he claimed, would only distract from the main theme of the book. He classified war stories into three categories: personal experiences in the first person (*Ill Met by Moonlight*); adventure yarns which relied heavily on plot whilst still being authentic (*HMS Ulysses*); and novels which were really no more than documentaries (*The Cruel Sea*).

One of the things we discussed at length, and which was one of my greatest worries, was characters. Being a tender nineteen year-old, the only adults I knew well (apart from schoolmasters) were the men I had served with

*He was quite correct and my romantic experiences in Japan later became the basis of my best-seller, **The Exposed**.

in the army and particularly in Korea, so I inevitably drew on them. Readers of both **Heroes of the Hook** and **The Dead, the Dying and the Damned** will see links between many of the characters: Fletcher and Charles; Corporal Smith and Corporal Holroyd; Bertie Mee and Winston; and O'Hara and Animal Evans. The character 'Burrows' in **The Dead** springs straight from the bandsmen I had in 12 Platoon in **Heroes**, especially the devious way in which the army treated him.

There is even a similarity between Major Earl Gray and Major Dick Lawrence. When I started writing **The Dead** I realized just how unlikely it was to have a company commander as ruthless and unfeeling as Lawrence. With Earl Gray there was a clear reason for his behavior: his traumatic experiences with the Chindits in Burma. So when I created the character of Lawrence I strove for a similar influence; yet something a bit more original than combat stress. I decided on a physical ailment which would plague him in everything he did; something that never gave him any respite and so aggravated him that it had a major influence on his behavior. What better than something truly Napoleonic? After all, Napoleon's ailment cost him Waterloo, or so many historians claim.

Unfortunately, a senior editor at Cassell's objected strongly to the ailment I had in mind. She said it really wasn't very nice and not at all funny, and I couldn't convince her that it wasn't supposed to be funny. So in the original version of **The Dead** I was forced to ditch any kind of ailment. This, in my opinion, detracted from Lawrence's characterization even though no one else ever queried it. They were happy to accept Lawrence as a perfectly healthy middle-aged man whose evilness and dastardly behavior was motivated solely by ambition. In this reissued edition of **The Dead** I have reinstated what I considered to be a vital part of Major Lawrence's make-up and it does, I hope, help to bring more authenticity to his character.

At one point during my discussions with Desmond Flower, he became aware of my alarm at all the various complications. He told me not to worry, especially with regard to all the bits I was expected to discard. He said they could always be used in the future novels, and indeed over the years this has come about, even if, at times, it has led to minor repetitions.

Dr. Flower concluded our discussions by taking me out to lunch, a very rare occurrence for an aspiring and very young writer like myself. We went to a local pub. It was even more Dickensian than Cassell's offices, an ancient, oak-beamed hostelry where they still felt obliged to cover their floors with sawdust. We ate steak and kidney pudding, washed down by bottles of claret. I was careful to limit my consumption, remembering my disastrous experience in the Officers' Club in Kure which readers of **Heroes** will recall. Desmond Flower had no such reticence and sank glass after glass, polishing off two bottles if I recall correctly.

We talked in general terms about my book and he assured me I would get a lot of fun out of it which proved a very accurate prediction. Then, as the meal progressed, he reminisced about his experiences in publishing. For me this was fascinating. Cassell's had a long list of enormously famous writers. Quite apart from Churchill they also published Anthony Eden, General Bill Slim, showbiz celebrities such as Eartha Kitt, and novelists such as Nicholas Montserrat, Alec Waugh, Ernest Raymond and countless others; and he proceeded to tell me yarns about all of them, not in the least gossipy, but insights into what made them great people and such wonderful writers.

One of the things Desmond Flower explained to me was the reasons for the phenomenal success of **The Cruel Sea** and he also gave me a fascinating dissertation on the religious philosophizing at the core of all Ernest Raymond's novels. Then he suddenly stopped in full flow. He leaned across the table, removed his glasses, and stared hard at me. Finally, he demanded: "Who are you?

When I told him he called for the bill.

When we got back to his office and I collected my manuscript, I was feeling very depressed. After hearing about all these other great authors I wondered how I was ever going to transform my novel into something that could compete. I had visions of appearing again in three months and being told, "Sorry! It's just not good enough."

What I hadn't reckoned on was help from an unexpected quarter. Whilst we were at lunch, my manuscript had been rewrapped for me by Dr. Flower's secretary. She handed it to me in a smart new carrier bag and then led the way down the spiral staircase and out on to St Andrew's Hill. We shook hands and I thanked her for her courtesy. She clung on to my hand longer than was necessary. Indeed, she ended up clasping my hand in both hers. Then she gave me a flashing smile, as though we were conspirators, the significance of which escaped me. All the way home I wondered about it.

As soon as I got back home I went to the garden shed and opened the parcel. Her handshake and smile were immediately explained. Clipped to one of the inside pages, as though by accident, were the full Readers' reports on my novel; and in those days such reports were not made by odd-bods giving their opinions on the cheap, or young girls fresh out of a second-rate university who thought they already knew it all. In those days they were by established authors in their own right, literary men or women of repute. I

17

read their views avidly.   They pulled no punches and made frequent and often scathing criticisms.   Yet they were also full of perceptive suggestions. They unanimously recommended publication and agreed that amid all the verbiage there lurked a first-class anti-war novel.   Thanks to them, and the comments made by Desmond Flower, and especially the kindness of his secretary, I saw a way forward.

I set to work straight away--- the fanatic once more.   The following is an abridged version (approximately the length Desmond Flower had suggested) of what I came up with.

PART I

GATHERING STRENGTH

1

While most of the country was capped by a glorious blue sky, providing the year's first spell of hot summer weather, the rugged, bleak moors of Dartmoor were still absorbing the heavy rains which fell recklessly from nimbus clouds. It was typical Dartmoor weather, warm yet continually raining in fierce bursts.

In an old army Nissen hut, situated between two imposing tors and surrounded by swaying gorse, sat over thirty youthful and uncommonly fit young men, known to the army as Six Platoon, Baker Company of Eaton Hall Officer Cadet School. At the far end of the hut was a Captain in the Devonshire Regiment. He was talking in a high-pitched voice and referring constantly to a diagram that was pinned on a tired-looking blackboard. Facing him was his platoon, all of them tired and listless.

Officer Cadet Peter Blake--- the son of an ardent and outspoken pacifist bishop--- was cramped uncomfortably against a portion of the rusty wall, his broad shoulders rubbing flakes off the decaying metal as he kept shifting his weight in an attempt to stem the progress of a trickle of water edging its way down his back to the seat of his trousers. His posture was typical and immediately proclaimed him as lazy. Despite the confined space he had contrived to maneuver his large, crab-like frame into a position very near the horizontal and as he forgot his physical discomforts the instructor's voice drifted away and Blake's thoughts turned to other things. He just thanked God his four months at Eaton Hall were over and that in another two days he would no longer be 22594I76 Officer-Cadet Peter Blake of the Royal Signals, but 423600 2nd Lieutenant Blake on three weeks' leave.

So far, leave was the only thing he liked about the army; and he was confident that after three weeks leave spent touring the West Country on his 350cc BSA motor cycle, it would simply be a matter of sewing bright new pips on his epaulettes and then idling around a regimental depot in Germany or the UK, doing little other than repeat: "Carry on Sergeant!" Maybe he would strike lucky and join the King's African Rifles in Kenya, or even a posting to the West Indies.

His thoughts were disturbed by the instructor banging his swagger stick against the blackboard. "And now, gentlemen, I have here what you have all been waiting for: the regiments to which you have been posted. I'll read them out in alphabetical order and then, when we get back to camp, I'll put them on the notice-board so that you can study the details at your leisure."

Blake's name was the first to be read out: he had been posted to the 1st Battalion The Rockinghamshire Regiment, a northern regiment known throughout the army as 'The Rocks'. He knew of them vaguely, but no more. It was hardly a regiment to inspire enthusiasm. Not that he was concerned one way or the other. Regimental traditions and battle honors did not impress him. It was where he was posted to that mattered.

When they arrived back in camp Blake flung his rifle and equipment on his bed, partly undressed and then, when the inquisitive crowd around the notice-board had diminished, he went to find out the details of his posting. His eyes went straight to the top of the list. He was stunned by what he read. In bold type it said: 'P. Blake. The Rockinghamshire Regiment. Three weeks leave prior to embarking for KOREA.'

His first reaction was anger, intense animosity towards the men in the War Office who had decided to send him to the war in Korea, to pitch him into active service without any warning, into a war of which he knew nothing and cared even less.

He turned back to the austere barrack room where other cadets stood about in various stages of undress, discussing their postings. He heard all parts of the globe being mentioned: Hong Kong, Bermuda, France, Germany, West Africa, East Africa, Singapore, and there was even a cadet who had been posted to Okehampton, to the very camp in which they were now living.

Blake was the only one going to Korea. Of all the places in the world, he had to go to Korea. Of all the damned rotten luck! He lay down on his bed, ignoring his damp underclothes, and took fresh stock of the situation: it was no longer a matter of taking three weeks' leave, sewing two pips on his tunic, and drifting about a depot. It had suddenly taken on a far more sinister aspect. He would be responsible for men under active service conditions; he would have to lead them into battle, perhaps even make a platoon attack. (The very thought of it made him shudder.) Men's lives would depend on his smallest gesture or decision.

He stirred uneasily on his bed as his new responsibilities flooded his mind, and he realized that it was a burden he could not regard lightly. Suddenly, he became aware of how little he knew about soldiering. It was hardly surprising. He had joined the army directly after leaving his public school and from the very start he had regarded it as an impudent intrusion upon his private life; he saw no necessity in his being a soldier; he saw no usefulness in it, and he had never for a moment imagined that he would be expected to kill anyone, or be killed.

He rolled over on his bed, conscious of the pungent smell of cordite that filled the room, and watched the other cadets as they cleaned their weapons and packed their kit in preparation for the move back to Eaton Hall, Chester. He sat on the edge of his bed and as he tugged at his wet socks, his mind dwelt on the responsibilities of being a platoon commander in Korea. In truth, he could hardly do the immediate actions on a Bren gun without first consulting the appropriate instruction leaflet and his practical experience of handling men was nil. Yet he was expected to take on what was probably the most difficult man-management job in the world. It was an immense burden for him to shoulder and one which scared him. Yet he knew there was nothing he could do about it. He would just have to make the best of it.

That evening Six Platoon left Dartmoor and accompanied the wet weather as it spread north to engulf the entire country; then, after two days of drilling, they passed out of Eaton Hall OCS as officers. In a speech at the conclusion of the parade the inspecting General said: "You are now ready to go straight into battle. To lead and inspire your men by your personal example."

No doubt it should have been true, but unfortunately it was not.

2

For three weeks Major Richard Lawrence had been sitting about the regimental depot waiting for the battalion to assemble. He lowered himself into the most comfortable chair in the mess and stretched his short, stubby legs out in front of him. His hands started to play with a tumbler of pale ale on one arm of the chair and a gin and lime which was perched precariously on the other. For some peculiar reason, he liked to consume the two drinks in quick succession.

His face was plump, with a rugged, weather-beaten glow about it, and his slightly blood-shot eyes had a hint of sadness as though he was unfulfilled, always in search of something. His face was small and rotund, matching his figure, not the rugby-playing type the Rocks were renowned for; and like so many little men he was sharp and aggressive, always out to prove himself. He liked to think of himself as determined and purposeful, and he took a peculiar delight in being grouchy towards his juniors: it was his idea of discipline.

He drank some of his ale and smacked his lips contentedly. Alcohol was his best friend. Then he twirled his waxed moustache, which was the focal point of his face. It was his hallmark. Everyone remembered him by his waxed moustache. He pretended to be intensely proud of it, yet within his heart he recognized how pathetic it was: to be remembered for an outdated, egotistical growth of facial hair twisted into pointed ends, rather than for having achieved something notable.

He rose from his chair with a heavy sigh and walked towards the central window of the mess, through which he could see a squad of new recruits drilling under the expert direction of the RSM. The men's drill was smart and precise: they held themselves erect, as though proud of the uniforms they wore. Lawrence glanced down at his own body and noticed with sadness his bulging stomach and parched hands, and he wondered whether mess gossip was not right when it said that he was past it: too old for active service and real soldiering. There was also the matter of the minor surgery he should have undergone. He'd put it off for a couple of years and had been on the verge of going under the knife. Now, he was damn glad he had delayed it and not said a word to anyone. He certainly wasn't going to allow a minor ailment to stand in his way.

He was a third generation 'Rock' and it looked as though he was going to be the first in the family never to command the 1st Battalion. He had been commissioned in 1937 and although most people assumed that in his five years of war-service he must have seen plenty of action he had in fact seen very little. It wasn't until the closing stages of the Second Front, on the far side of the Rhine, that he had heard a shot fired in anger.

Now, with the war over for six years, he was well aware that his career prospects were doubtful, to say the least. Field officers left over from the war were two-a-penny and he dreaded being 'bowler-hatted'. As a civilian living on a meager pension he knew he would never be able to maintain the high standard of living to which he had become accustomed. He was a bachelor and he had no home but officers' messes and they provided him with everything he desired.

He heard the voice of the RSM seeping through the windows and saw the squad of men drilling give a smart turn to the right, break up, and hurry from the square. After they had disappeared he continued to stare through the window across the empty parade ground; his thoughts were of the future. Korea was his opportunity, his last opportunity! He had everything to gain and nothing to lose and no one was going to stand in his way. His company was going to succeed in Korea. They were going to outshine all others even if they all had to die in the attempt.

He turned sharply as he heard someone enter the mess. He jerked to attention as he saw the Colonel approaching: a tall, sparse, man who did everything hurriedly and with an air of efficiency. "Morning, sir," said Lawrence.

"Morning, Dick." The Colonel's voice was cold. He was annoyed to see Lawrence still hanging around the mess littering it with empty glasses. "Why don't you do something with yourself, instead of sitting around the place?"

"Wish to hell that I could find something to do, sir. But you know how it is. With a company that consists of a Sergeant-Major, a company clerk and me, there is simply nothing to do."

The Colonel was irritated by the reply. He was only too aware that Able Company was virtually non-existent and that the whole battalion numbered no more than three hundred men. He felt guilty about it, knowing perfectly well that it was a shambles, the only consolation being that by the time they got to Korea the war might be over, with a successful conclusion to the Panmunjom Peace Talks. "Never mind, Dick," he said, determined to look on the bright side. "You'll be getting a subaltern from Eaton Hall very soon and a section of men from Brigade Depot... So you'll soon have something to occupy you."

Lawrence strode over to an occasional table and rang the small hand-bell vigorously. "What's yours going to be, sir?"

"Nothing thanks, Dick. I'll have some coffee when it comes."

"So I'm going to have an officer and a section of men," repeated Lawrence as he went back to his chair. "And I'll bet that none of them have had any previous experience worth talking about. Been in the army no more than a few months, I expect. Still, never mind. We'll soon get them into shape."

The Colonel made no immediate reply. As a waiter came into the mess he asked for a coffee and then went over to the central table to browse through the daily newspapers. Eventually, when he looked up again and saw Lawrence looking as dour as ever, he added: "Don't get despondent, Dick. We'll also be picking up fresh men in Singapore and Hong Kong, as well as inheriting a good number of National Servicemen from the Leicestershire's who still have time to serve ..."

"What a way to go to war," muttered Lawrence.

"Don't worry ... We'll manage."

Lawrence glanced at the Colonel in annoyance, irritated by his casual tone. Although he respected the Colonel for his sharp mind and sound knowledge of soldiering, he had noticed in him over the past three weeks a feeling of apathy towards the approaching job, of which he did not approve.

"Manage!" he repeated. "We're going to do a damned sight more than manage."

3

Lance Corporal Bobby Smith stood in front of the full-length mirror in his bedroom. He was stripped to the waist, in his army-issue 'drawers cellular'. As he twisted and turned in front of the mirror he was pretty pleased with the result of his Charles Atlas Course. His biceps and pectorals were coming along a treat. After he'd flexed them once or twice he got dressed. Then he went back to the mirror to make sure he was smart and presentable. He had made a great job of whitening the stripe on each arm of his tunic and his boots were as smooth and shiny as glass. As for the creases in his trousers, they were knife-sharp.

He would never admit to anyone, but he was really proud of having been made a lance-corporal. It was the first time in his life anyone had ever shown any confidence in him. Usually, all he ever got was ridicule.

"Bobby! You up yet, lad? You'll be late if you're not careful."

Smith winced as he heard his mother's voice. He'd suffered it for nineteen years and he just couldn't wait to get away from it. "Okay, Mum! I'm coming."

The breakfast table was a familiar, nauseating sight, piled high with cereal packets and strewn with gungy jam jars, a large plastic margarine container, and a giant bottle of tomato ketchup. His father was at the head of the table, hidden behind his Daily Mirror. Every morning he sat there in an identical posture, chuckling over the cartoon page.

Smith's mother was never still, up and down from the table fetching and carrying, waiting on everyone. His elder sister's chair was empty. She'd been out until the early hours with her friend Cynthia. Or so she would claim. Far more likely she'd been spread-eagled on the back seat of a Ford Popular belonging to Cynthia's brother. He was a train driver and in and out of Cynthia more often than he was Leeds Central. For a long time--- until they aroused the wrath of Bobby's father by leaving a condom floating in the toilet--- they'd spent their evenings in Cynthia's room, playing records, or (as her younger brother Ronald claimed) breaking records, and none of them of the 75 rpm variety.

When Bobby took his seat at the kitchen table, Ronald was already on his third helping of cornflakes, sucking them out of the plate like a sewerage pump. He was thirteen and knew everything. He looked up and said: "What the hell are you all dressed up for? You look like a bloody dog's dinner."

"Ronald! Mind your language!" shrieked his mother from the gas-stove where she was frying eggs. "Father! Tell him to mind his bloody language."

"Mind your bloody language," muttered the head of the household from behind his Daily Mirror.

Bobby Smith ignored them. He could put up with most things--- all the squalor, untidiness, and cramped conditions of the house--- but the coarseness and stupidity of the rest of the family were just too much. Sensible conversations, devoid of argument, bickering and insinuations, were beyond them.

"Nowt wrong with my language," said Ronald. "I'm just practicing for when I get my call-up into the bloody army. Mind you, I doubt if I'll ever make it to the dizzy heights of lance-corporal. I mean, there are limits to what one bloody family can achieve ..."

Smith ignored him and started on the eggs and bacon his mother had thrust in front of him. They could jeer at him as much as they liked but his single stripe was only a start: once in Korea he would soon be made up to full corporal, perhaps even more if things got sticky in the front line.

He pushed a large piece of underdone egg white to one side of his plate and finished the rest of his breakfast in several gulps. "I'm pushing off now, Mum," he said, getting up from the table. "I'm meeting the others at the station at half past ... mustn't be late ..."

His mother smiled indulgently. "Have you had enough to eat, lad?"

"Oh, aye..."

"No more tea?"

"No thanks."

"Then how about another egg?"

"No thanks."

"Or what about some more toast?"

"No thanks."

"Well . . ."

Smith turned on her abruptly, his face flushed with anger. "Oh, for heaven's sake, I don't want anything else."

"All right, Bobby. There's no need to carry on."

"I'm not bloody carrying on!"

"You mind your language," chirped up Ronald, mimicking his mother. "Father! Tell him to mind his bloody language..."

"Mind your bloody language," muttered the head of the house from behind his Daily Mirror.

Smith snatched his kit-bag from the floor and swung it on to his shoulder.

God, what a relief it would be to see the last of this bloody lot, he thought. He went to the door and paused.   This was the first time he had ever left home for any length of time and he did not know how to say good-bye.   None of them made it any easier.   They couldn't give a stuff that he was off to fight in a war.

"Well, cheerio, Mum," he said at length.   "I'll let you know how things go.   But don't start creating if the letters don't come regular.   Korea is a long way off, you know."

"You're not going right away, surely, Bobby?" protested his mother. "You haven't said goodbye to your sister..."

"You mean she hasn't said good-bye to me.   It's me that's leaving …."

"We haven't been allowed to bloody forget that," said Ronald.

Mrs. Smith grated her teeth and whacked Ronald across the back of his head.   "You hold your tongue.   I won't stand for any more of your cheek." She went over to Bobby and hugged him.   Then she lunged across the table and snatched the Daily Mirror out of her husband's hands.   "Haven't you got anything to say to the lad?   Don't just sit there like a great plum pudding. Don't you realize your son's going off abroad?"

"I know all about that, lass. I went there once myself, in case you've forgotten.   I'll see him off proper, don't you fret.   Come on, lad.   If I were you I'd bugger off quick, like.   Mustn't be late for t' others..."

Smith led the way out of the kitchen and squeezed down the long, narrow hall to the front door.   His father opened it for him and then stood on the pavement, just outside.   He took his pipe out of his jacket pocket and made a long business of lighting it, a declaration that he wasn't going any further. The pubs weren't open, so what was the point.

Once his pipe was belching smoke satisfactorily, he said: "Well, lad... You'll be reet..."

"Aye, Dad.... I'll be reet..."

"That's all reet then."

"Reet as rain, Dad."

Lance Corporal Smith set off down the pavement, along the near-endless line of northern terraced houses, his hob nailed-boots ringing out loudly. Instinctively, he knew that his mother would now be standing on their well-scrubbed doorstep, waving like mad, a handkerchief to her eyes. Neighbors would be peering out from behind their yellowing lace curtains, and his father would be sucking loudly on his pipe, disappearing behind clouds of Gold Flake.   He half-turned, saw them exactly as he had imagined, and gave a wave.

A real hero's farewell, he thought.

4

At the railway station, there should have been five others waiting for him. There were only three. Edwin Charles and Reg Hallows were missing. It didn't surprise him a bit. They were always late for everything. The other three he knew well. He'd been at school with them, going way back, and he still saw them as kids in short trousers, just the same as they saw him. The thought of them trying to be hairy-arsed soldiers fighting the Chinese in Korea was a sick joke.

Of the three waiting there only one was worth more than a casual glance: Jim Hale. He was a powerfully-built, good-looking lad, so blond he had a touch of Scandinavia about him. Since a very early age he'd always been a hit with the girls: they'd fairly thrown themselves at him. Not that he took advantage of them. He was devoted to one, a buxom wench named Betty; far too devoted in Smith's view. Everyone knew the lass would never wait for him.

Smith exchanged a general greeting with them. It amounted to no more than each of them mumbling, "How do?" None of them called him 'Corp'. Not that he had expected them to. A single stripe never made any difference. Lance-corporals had to trade on friendship and being one of the boys. It needed two stripes on each arm before you could start throwing your weight around.

Smith led the way along Platform One and then across the bridge to the second platform. Then they stood around and waited, each of them smoking. Smith fell to wondering about Charles and Hallows. They were a right pain in the arse and no mistake. They always had been and always would be. Hard cases, if ever there were, with Charles leading the gullible Hallows at every turn. It was quite possible that they'd gone AWOL again. There was a second possibility. They may have succumbed to the army's latest piece of blackmail by which any National Serviceman signing on for an extra year got twice the pay and could choose their regiment, and with it a cushy posting. Smith reckoned it was such a crafty bit of blackmail that Charles and Hallows had fallen for it. He'd very nearly done so himself. It was only the basic injustice of such bribery that had stopped him. It was the sort of cheap trick the army would pull and in Smith's view was tantamount to saying that regular soldiers were too valuable to risk losing in Malaya or Korea, so send the National Servicemen instead: nowt but cannon-fodder!

Private Burrows took a final drag on his fag and tossed it on to the track. He was a sorry sight. Compared with Hale, who he was standing beside, he was a physical wreck; his body sagged, his shoulders were hunched, and his ill-fitting battle dress so engulfed him that he looked smaller than he really was. Ever since his first days at school he'd been one apart and instead of improving with age he seemed to get worse, more and more timid and introspective. The way the army had treated him didn't help. He'd started his service as a bugler in the Rocks bugle band and he had already done most of his two years' service. Then, quite recently, he had signed a form agreeing to stay on for an extra six months in order to be transferred to the York and Lancs to take part in a major ceremonial in four months' time. Then the York and Lancs were suddenly posted to Malaya, so the whole thing was called off. In the confusion that followed Burrows was told that his extra six months still stood but instead of being transferred to the York and Lancs he would stay with the Rocks and go to Korea. It was the type of ruling that needed a squad of solicitors to sort out, so naturally enough Burrows just accepted it. He did as he was told and hoped for the best: normal procedure in the army.

The third man in the group was Freddie Winston. He was short and stocky and looked as though he hadn't washed properly since the day he'd been dismissed from one of the Yorkshire pits. His beret was perched on his head at a jaunty angle and thanks to the recent attentions of an army barber no hair showed below the leather band, only scars on the back of his head. He was a cheerful individual, easily amused; the type who, once he got in the mood, rarely stopped talking, but since his verbal diarrhea was usually nothing but moans and long dissertations about everyone else's incompetence, very few people ever listened to him, knowing that if any bugger was incompetent it was him. As far as the others were concerned, Winston's words went in one ear and out the other, and Freddie Winston had so little between his own ears that it never worried him. When others didn't contradict him he assumed that it was because what he said was dead bloody right.

They heard their train approaching so they grabbed their kit bags, shuffled forward, and prepared to board. Smith ushered the others into the carriage first and then looked back anxiously to the bridge. There was still no sign of Charles and Hallows. The bastards!

5

Earlier in the morning Edwin Charles rolled over in his camp bed and looked around the squalid kitchen.   Last night's dirty dishes were still in the sink and the place stank of his mother's mangy old dog.   The bloody animal should have been put down years ago, poor old bugger.   He was nearly twenty years old and did nothing but eat, sleep, fart, and scratch the door to be let out so that he could shit all over the pavement.

Typical of life itself, thought Charles.   For years he'd lived a bloody awful existence; and until recently he'd always accepted it.   As a kid he'd been resigned to the fact that destiny had singled him out for a rough deal. Yet since leaving school he'd become far more adept at looking after 'Number One'.   He'd looked around the slums of Sheffield and decided, "Bugger them all!"   No one gave a shit about him, so why should he give a shit about them?

The army was typical--- more than typical!   As if two years' compulsory National Service wasn't enough, they'd now done a real flanker on him.   He had decided to take up their offer of signing on for an extra year.   It would have doubled his pay and enabled him to join the regiment of his choice--- the perfect chance of spending a year in Hong Kong in the Green Howards shagging 'taxi' girls.   He and his pal Reg Hallows had it all worked out.   Yet the bastards still managed to shit all over them.   They had the gall to tell them that they weren't wanted as regulars; that since they'd both done 28 days in Colchester Detention Barracks they weren't eligible.

They weren't good enough for the regular army, but they were good enough to go and fight in Korea.

He heard the clock in his mother's room strike eight.   He clambered out of bed and he went to the sink and splashed his face with water, cold, of course. Then he turned to his uniform, which lay in an untidy heap on the floor, and started to dress.   He was heavily-built, verging on fat.   His uniform was hopelessly tight on him, but he wasn't worried.   Once dressed, he walked into his mother's room.   She was still wheezing, just as she had been all night, and above the off-white sheets her face was yellow, like old parchment.   Charles pushed her invalid chair to one side, and shook her shoulder.

She opened her beady eyes and smiled at him.   "Edwin dear, you aren't going yet, are you?"

Charles withdrew his hand and stepped back.   "Off in a few minutes, Ma. We're due down the station.   Reg Hallows will be calling in at any moment."

"Edwin dear, please take care of yourself," the old woman bleated. "Keep clear of trouble, Edwin."

Charles smiled down at her with genuine amusement. The poor old bitch! She had been lying in that bed or pushing herself around her two rooms in her invalid chair for the past two years, slowly dying off, and all the time she hadn't the faintest idea of what he was really like, what her lovely, chubby little boy had turned into. Least of all the number of local girls he'd shagged over three years. Shagging crumpet was about the only consolation he had in life and it didn't worry him one iota that he'd put a few in the pudding club. It was their bodies, so let them look after them.

He thought of the last one he'd had, only a few nights before. It had been at an ORs 'Korean Farwell Party' party at the Naafi Club in Minden. Company Sergeant-Major Ralf's sixteen year-old daughter had turned up, determined to show the lads what a good little mover she was on the dance floor. She was a right little show off with a pert bum and bouncing tits, and whilst most of the lads saw her as dangerous ground, best kept well-clear of, being the apple of CSM Ralf's eye, Charles had no such reservations. All tarts who ventured into the Naafi Centre in Minden were fair game in his judgment; and they were all perfectly aware of that.

Charles, despite his tubbiness, was also a pretty good mover on the dance floor and there was a frisson between them from the start: they fitted against each other naturally. In the end he'd treated her to a few drinks, taken her out the back behind the old Panzer garages, and he'd given it to her as good and strong as he'd ever given it to any girl.

"You will keep out of trouble, won't you, Edwin?"

"I can look after myself, Mother," he said. "Like a cup of tea before I push off?"

"Thank you, Edwin."

Charles walked back into the kitchen and lit the gas under a small, black-bottomed kettle. The poor old dear believed every word he told her. She didn't even know that he was going to Korea as an infantry soldier: she thought he was in the Ordnance Corps and going to Hong Kong as a cobbler!

As she drank her tea he sat on the edge of her bed, trying hard to ignore her sucking noises. "Edwin dear ..." she started off in a weak, almost pleading tone.

He knew what was coming. "Yes Ma?"

"Edwin, you will let me have a bit of money, won't you? You know that I can't keep going on just my pension alone."

He sighed deeply and stood up. "Ma, for heaven's sake! You know how I'm off for money in the army.   You know I can hardly make ends meet myself ... But I'll tell you what.   I'll get them to make out one of them regular allowances ... Deducted at source from my pay ... How about that?"   He turned away, avoiding her eyes.   He hadn't the least intention of making any money over to her.   Why the hell should he?   She had a pension, council house accommodation, a disability allowance, and God knows how much assistance from the Social Security.   The days of starving OAPs were over.

Her gums showed as her mouth opened in a wide grin.   "Edwin, you're a good boy."

He shrugged his shoulders. "That's all right, Ma.   I'll manage."

Her eyes sparkled with pride.   "Kiss me before you go, Edwin."

Charles tried to hide his hesitation as he pecked her cheek.   There was a loud knock on the door.   "That'll be Reg Hallows ....   I must be off, Ma. See you in about a year's time ...   I'll write to you each week, so don't worry."

He opened the door and saw Reg Hallows standing there, grinning at him, just as he always grinned--- his big, ugly face split from ear to ear, and his bright eyes sparkling, exuding mischief.   They'd been mates since joining the army together and they had shared so many scrapes, and had so many brushes with authority, and had so many laughs, that they were unable to disguise their delight at seeing each other again.

Their greatest time had been in Germany when the Rocks were in Minden.   Forever short of cash, Charles had struck on the idea of launching his pal as a prize-fighter.   He reckoned that with his magnificent physique, his grim determination and natural aggressiveness, Reg Hallows was a natural for knocking ten bells out of anyone who crossed him.   So they formed a partnership: pugilist and manager.   Charles declared to everyone that Reg was 'My boy!' and they lost no time in touring the markets, fairs, and agricultural shows in nearby German towns during their off-duty weekends, challenging young Krauts to try their luck against 'My boy!'   There was never a shortage of young Krauts (usually ex-Hitler Youth) willing to have a go at a British Tommy, no matter how unlikely they were to win.

The scheme was a real money-earner for Charles and Hallows and it only came to an end when 'My boy!' came up against an ex-paratrooper with an Iron Cross who was as big as Reg and the ex-boxing champion of the Russian front to boot.   'My boy!' was soon in dire trouble and in desperation his manager urged him to hit the Kraut where it hurt most, meaning (as Charles later maintained) a right upper cut to the chin.   Instead, 'My boy!' took him literally and raised his right knee sharply into his opponent testicles, making him collapse and then writhe about in agony.

The long queue of ex-Hitler Youths waiting their turn to fight the Englander jumped into the ring and a contest which was billed as Queensbury Rules soon became a riot with no rules, with watching British troops rallying to their compatriots' support. Finally, Red Caps turned up wielding truncheons and Charles and Hallows ended up with 28 days in the Colchester Detention Barracks.

The loyalty Hallows had towards Charles knew no bounds and everyone was fully aware that when Charles uttered threats like "Watch it, or I'll duff you up!" or "I'll get you if it's the last thing I do!" it was ultimately 'My boy!' they would have to deal with. So Charles, although held in contempt by everyone, knew that metaphorically he could get away with murder. The only thing they couldn't handle was the military establishment. The army was impossible to fight. It always came out on top.

The two men set off down the street in great spirits, all their troubles and hardships forgotten, knowing that in each other's company there would be plenty of laughs; and the first thing to amuse them was that when they reached the station their train was on the brink of pulling out. They barged past the ticket collector, ignored his shouts and demands for their warrants, and dashed across the bridge.

Bobby Smith had secured a corner seat and saw them coming. He went across the carriage, opened the window, stuck his head out, and shouted to the guard, who was just about to wave his green flag. "Just a second, mate. Two more lads are just coming."

The guard waited and Charles and Hallows clambered aboard, breathless and laughing.

"So you haven't gone AWOL after all then."

Charles tossed his kit bag on to the luggage rack. "Not yet, Smudge ... But still plenty of time yet, don't you worry."

6

On the same morning, 2/Lieut. Blake, feeling self-conscious with his new pips up, paused outside the gates of the Rocks Depot. He looked up at the tall tower, towards the regimental flag which bore a long list of battle honors. The flag meant nothing to him and as he walked through the gateway he was far more concerned by the kind of reception he would receive in the officers' mess.

The moment he had been dreading for months was swiftly approaching. More by luck than judgment he located the Officers' Mess sergeant and was shown his small bedroom. Then he walked round the edge of the parade ground to the adjutant's office. It was austere with a few drab sticks of furniture scattered about and a high pile of military manuals stacked on the table. The adjutant's cushioned chair was empty and for a time Blake stood just inside the doorway looking about.

"Who are you?" a voice demanded from behind him.

"Blake, sir. I've just been posted to the regiment."

"So it seems. Don't you usually salute when you enter the adjutant's office?"

"Yes, sir. But as it was . . ."

"I don't want an explanation. I am telling you what to do in the future." He eyed Blake critically. "So you are now an officer?"

"Yes, sir."

"You are nineteen, I assume? Old enough to serve in Korea?"

"Yes, sir. I'll make it by a couple of weeks."

"Good. Then report to Major Lawrence in Able Company."

As Blake approached the Able Company orderly room he saw a section of men standing outside. Lance-corporal Smith called his section to attention and gave a smart salute. Blake returned it casually and passed into the orderly room. The interior was dingy and untidy and sitting just by the door was a scruffy-looking individual with brilliant, unkempt red hair. It was no surprise to Blake when the man spoke with a Northern Irish accent.

"And what can I do for you, sir?"

"I was looking for Major Lawrence."

"He won't be long, he's just popped round the corner," replied the clerk, and then he surprised Blake by adding: "Sir!"

Blake walked to the other end of the room, still slightly fascinated by the term of respect. Waste paper, articles of webbing equipment, clothing and files were lying haphazardly about the tables and chairs. O'Hara, the clerk, tilted his chair back and grinning broadly. "Are you the new officer from Eaton Hall, sir?"

"Yes, I am. Is it that obvious?"

"Not really. It's just that we've been told to expect a new officer this morning."

Suddenly, O'Hara sprang to his feet, nearly knocking the chair over in the process, and stood stiffly to attention.

Blake turned and for the first time his eyes rested on the portly figure of

Major Lawrence.

"Come on, O'Hara," Lawrence snapped. "I told you to get this place cleaned up." He pushed his way past O'Hara and sat behind his desk. He twisted both ends of his moustache with his index fingers and thumbs and greeted Blake with a cheerful smile and extended hand.

"My name is Blake, sir. The adjutant told me to report to you."

"Glad to have you with us, Blake." Lawrence paused: these days he never knew how to greet subalterns. They were always so damned young they embarrassed him. Most of them, in his view, should still have been at school. "You haven't come to much of a company, I'm afraid. I don't mean that the men in it aren't much good, but rather that there are hardly any of them. You are the only platoon commander so far and our only men are those standing outside, and O'Hara here, of course. You're welcome to him. He's bloody useless as a company clerk. Sergeant Miles will be your platoon sergeant, but he's out in Korea already, with the advance party. The only other two in the company are Sergeant-Major Ralf and me."

"When do we get the rest then, sir?"

"Along the way. Two subalterns will join us at Hong Kong. The rest will be posted to us from other units about to finish in Korea. You're One Platoon Commander since you're the first and you can take that section of men waiting outside as One Section. It's a start, even though it's not much else. O'Hara's last task as company clerk will be to get all their documents sorted out."

"Is there anything I can do?" offered Blake, full of enthusiasm

"Yes," said Lawrence. "You'd better introduce yourself to your platoon, such as they are. Then hang around until Sergeant-Major Ralf turns up so you can have a chat with him. You're all ready to leave, I suppose?"

"Yes, sir."

"Good," said Lawrence. He rose to his feet and walked over to the door. "I'll leave you to it, then." He paused and took a sideways glance at his new officer. For a second he felt like a grandfather. He was accustomed to young and immature subalterns, but Blake seemed to be breaking new ground. "What's your Christian name, Blake?"

"Peter, sir."

"All right, Blake. I'll leave you to it."

Shortly afterwards Blake went outside to introduce himself to the section of men. He stood in front of them and eyed them critically. He recalled a lecture at Eaton Hall giving specific instructions on how a subaltern should introduce himself to a new platoon. The approach, he remembered, should be friendly, yet firm; confident, but not assertive; eager but not bursting with enthusiasm; fatherly, but not dictatorial, dignified, but not superior. All a load of nonsense, he decided. They were merely youngsters, straight out of school, like he was, and whether or not they hit it off was simply a matter of luck. One look at them convinced him that they were totally disinterested, just obeying orders, another thing they had in common. That, in itself, might augur well for successful bonding, he thought.

He had a few words with them about going to Korea and it was clear that they had no precise idea of why they were being sent there. Nor did they seem to care. They regarded his questions as pointless.

Finally, he dismissed them and as they marched off to their barracks he felt quite pleased. At least there were no gnarled old regulars among them, men who knew it all and seen it all before.

Blake went back into the orderly room. O'Hara was still there, sucking on a fag so tiny that it threatened to burn his lips. "Okay, O'Hara, you may as well go as well ... Join the others."

"I'm supposed to wait for the CSM, sir. So I'd better hang around."

"How come an Irishman like you is in this regiment?"

"Me, sir? That's a long story. I volunteered to join the Ulster Rifles and serve in Korea, but I was a bit late. The Ulsters were just about wiped out on the Imjin. So they bunged me in this shower."

"What made you volunteer for Korea?"

"Do anything for a bit of a scrap, that's me, sir."

Blake smiled uneasily. It was the one thing he prayed to avoid.

The conversation got no further. CSM Ralf strode in. He had the air of total ownership, as though the whole barracks was his kingdom and everything revolved around him. He had an inbuilt look of disapproval and when his eyes lightened on Blake this expression did not change. For a moment be stared in disbelief. Then he raised his arm hastily, so that his right hand quivered just above his eye for precisely three seconds before being withdrawn to its original position with equal haste.

"Afternoon, sir," he said, finally convinced that the boy who stood before him was an officer.

"Glad to meet you, Sergeant-Major. My name is Blake."

Ralf ignored this information and marched up and down the room looking for faults. He removed his pace stick from beneath his arm and brought it down with crashing force on a pile of books and loose papers, causing a cloud of dust to leap into the air. "Look at that, O'Hara! Just look at that. Do you see all that dust?" He had the usual high-pitched, screaming voice of a Sergeant-Major.

"Yes, sir. I can see it," replied O'Hara, now standing to attention. "Bugger all to do with me anymore, sir. Major Lawrence has put me in One Platoon."

"Really"

"Shall I join them now, sir?"

"Where the hell are they? I distinctly told you to keep them here until I'd seen them."

Blake ceased staring at the floor. "Major Lawrence told me they were my platoon, so I dismissed them."

Ralf suppressed his rising anger. As Company Sergeant-Major it was his job to see all new arrivals before anyone else, to sort them out and tell them what was expected of them, and it incensed him to find that everything had been cut and dried without so much as a word to him.

"I'm sorry. I didn't realize that you wanted to see them."

"That's all right, sir. I'll see them in due course. It doesn't matter." Ralf was amazed at his own politeness. He saluted again, turned about with stamping feet, and marched out of the orderly room, making for the sergeants' mess. As he strode along, glancing left and right in the hope seeing someone malingering, he mumbled to himself about the curse of National Service.

When he arrived in the Sergeants' Mess there was a letter for him, postmarked Minden. It was from his wife. The contents made the short hairs on the back of his head bristle. He cursed National Service all the more vehemently.

7

Lance-corporal Smith stood at the end of a decaying barrack room, pinning a small notice on the wall. He was in 'shirt tail' order--- his drawers cellular being held up by an old pull-through. The side of his mouth was ink-stained, the result of sucking on a leaking biro. He checked the notice for spelling mistakes and then walked down the room, on either side of which his section was lounging on their hard beds. "These are the fatigues for to-morrow. We'll have to do them or the Sergeant-Major will get his knife into us."

"To hell with the Sergeant-Major," said O'Hara. "This bloody place hasn't been touched for at least ten years, so why should we start now? We'd be just as well off in a cow shed."

Smith didn't like the impetuous Irishman who had just joined his section.

He was nervous of him, but he was determined not to be brow-beaten. He stood at the bottom of O'Hara's bed and looked him straight in the eyes. "That's enough of that crap, O'Hara. You'll clean-up because those are your orders. And you're on the center of the floor. Reet?"

"Okay, keep your hair on," replied O'Hara. "I'll do it, but it's a bloody waste of time. Centre of the bloody floor! This is more like a school for old charwomen than a man's army. Anyhow, there is no need to worry about Ralf. He'll never come round here to-morrow morning. I know him better than you fellows do."

"What's he like, then?" queried Charles, who had a pronounced dislike for all Sergeant-Majors.

"Ralf?" echoed O'Hara, "he's the only man in the British army with a marching pace of thirty square inches."

"How do you mean, thirty square inches?" asked Winston.

"I mean that his arse is so broad that there are thirty inches between his legs."

Hallows put aside the webbing equipment he had been assembling for the coming day. He looked at O'Hara and said: "What do you know about this officer of ours, Paddy?"

"Blake?" echoed O'Hara again, as though he had known the officer for years. "He's just like the others, wet behind the ears. He'll be nothing but a trouble-avoider."

Hallows laughed. "That's better than a trouble-maker. So long as he doesn't start volunteering for patrols and platoon attacks I'm all for him."

"You bastards make me sick," growled O'Hara. "No guts, any of you."

There was a howl of abusive laughter. "Don't tell us you're after a gong, Paddy?"

"Sure I am. It's a right marker for me, or nothing."

Winston stopped stuffing his kit into his kitbag and asked: "What's a right marker?"

"A right marker," replied O'Hara "is the one that goes first in the row, the Military Medal. It's a bit of blood action that I'm after. None of this bloody back pedaling like you fellows. Your number is up or it isn't--- it's as simple as that."

No one made any reply and O'Hara looked around the room in surprise. Freddie Winston was still stuffing clothes into his kit-bag. Hallows had resumed assembling his equipment, Burrows was lying motionless on his bed with an inane expression on his bony face, and Charles was picking his nose and then distributing the debris around his bed space. Hale and Smith were playing cards.

What kind of fellows are these, wondered O'Hara.　They looked just about dead.　What an anti-climax after the last week in which he'd enjoyed complete freedom and made the most of it.　A week in which he had been able to lie in bed of a morning as long as he liked, go into the orderly office for a bit, then down town for the rest of the afternoon.　In the evenings it was drinks in the Gay Garter, followed by a meal at the Bistro, and on to a date with some tart or other he'd picked up along the way; then his leg over before returning to his unmade bed.

"Who's coming down town for a bit of skirt?" demanded O'Hara.　"This is our last night in camp, for Christ's sake!"

"I am," cried Winston.

"You're wasting your time, Paddy,' said Charles.　"We're confined to barracks and RPs are everywhere.　Reg and me have already tried, but got turned back."

O'Hara laughed and eyed Charles with approval.　"Never mind, Charlie boy.　Just follow me.　I know my way around this place.　Dead easy getting out of here once you know how.　There's a very convenient hole in the perimeter fence.　Mind you, one of you buggers is going to have to lend me some cash.　I'm broke.　How about you, Charlie?　Lend me a fiver and I'll show you the way out."

A deal was struck and those who intended taking advantage of O'Hara's know-how looked anxiously towards Smith, who was still playing cards, pretending he wasn't listening.　They still did not know how he would react as an NCO.　"How about it, Smudge?" asked Winston.　"Are you coming?"

"Am I hell!　I don't want a dose at this stage."　It was not the true reason, but it was a reaction which indicated he had no objection to them going.　He sensed that there would be trouble if he tried to assert his authority, especially with two dominating characters like O'Hara and Charles lined up against him. Right now, he intended to avoid a showdown at all costs, just so long as it didn't make him look wet and feeble.　There would be plenty of opportunities for asserting his authority in the future.

They got ready to leave camp, but Hale, Smith and Burrows remained unmoved by the prospect of a woman.　O'Hara led the way towards the door. When he reached the foot of Burrows's bed he stopped and regarded him scornfully.

"What's the matter, Burrows?　Not coming for a bit of ass?"

"No thanks."

"No thanks!　What's the matter with you?　Never had one before?"

There was more laughter. They all despised Burrows for his aloofness. Burrows flushed and for some reason felt desperately ashamed that he had never been intimate with a woman. He was a decent youngster and what little knowledge he had of the opposite sex had been gained either through the medium of other men's conversations or fairly innocent tittle-tattle at school. Text books he'd glanced at had been so open and precise that they had made the whole thing sound like a business transaction, which--- with the likes of O'Hara and Charles---- it was, of course. On the other hand men always spoke of it in the most glowing terms, and when they reached the actual description of it even those with the most lurid and imaginative minds faltered for words, as though there was something awesome about it. The whole thing left Burrows confused and frustrated. He wanted to try it--- wanted to desperately--- but his shyness held him back like an unbreakable leash.

As the group of men leered down at him, he wondered whether, if he got drunk first, it might rid him of his inhibitions. "No," he said eventually. "I've never had a woman."

O'Hara guffawed loudly. "Good God, Burrows! You don't know what you've missed. You mean to tell me that you're going to Korea without ever having had a bit? You might never get another chance. Come on, we'll see you get your end away."

Burrows sat up on his bed. That's what he needed, guidance: someone to find a suitable girl for him; a girl who, when it came to actually doing it, would be able to show him how.

As the others made for the door, Burrows stood up, reached for his tunic and said: "Okay. I'm coming. Just wait while I get my boots on."

Before long they had negotiated the hole in the perimeter fence and were in the market-place of the town. They were not the only troops on the loose. As usual, squaddies from the nearby RASC and REME depots were out in strength. It was, after all, a military town, a miniature Catterick, and everywhere, beneath street lamps, tucked neatly in doorways, drinking in pubs, down alleyways, on park benches, and on the banks of the river, troops talked, drank, kissed and made love with the flock of camp followers who had bussed in from Leeds and Bradford earlier in the afternoon; a motley collection of predatory females in various shapes and sizes, all of them anxious to make the most of the generous rewards to be had from a unit about to proceed overseas, it being traditional for all squaddies to leave Blighty stony broke.

O'Hara and Charles were masters of the pick-up. They swaggered down the streets as though they owned them, and had only to raise an eyebrow, or make a suggestive gesture, or say an apt word, or let out an appreciative whistle, and they were accepted without hesitation. In pubs, they barged in so full of confidence that no matter how thick the crowd was around the bar they somehow ferreted their way to the front and secured immediate attention, with spare females sipping Baby Champs in the background watching them, their interest aroused.

Burrows marveled at their nerve. In each bar they visited he had half a pint of shandy and did his utmost to smile and pretend that he was having a great time, laughing at other's jokes even though he found nothing funny in them, or in many cases didn't even understand them. When closing time came and they were turned out of a pub, he found himself standing on the pavement with his mates, on the edge of a group of girls. They were merry and boisterous, just like the fellows, many of them tottering uncertainly on their high heels, others with their arms twined about the necks of their chosen partners.

Burrows felt like a voyeur, a ghostly figure hovering unnoticed to one side. He listened to the jumble of male and female voices, the repartee of the gutter.

"By heck, you boys are out in force to-night... Never seen so many anxious pricks..."

"Got to make the most of the time that's left ..."

"Me and Daisy were going to the flicks, but we'd seen it before, so we thought we'd see what was going on in town. You know, a quick decko..."

"A pleasant surprise for you then ..."

"Well, I'm not so sure about that ... Not yet."

"You soon will be."

"Ooo-er ... Listen to you."

"That's all right, I know a place."

"I thought you might."

"Hullo, Johnny . . ."

The greeting was directed at Burrows. He glanced to the side and saw a girl eyeing him. She was several years older than him, doing her best to disguise her maturity with a thick layer of make-up. She moved right up to him and nestled against him. There was a tide-mark just behind her ears where the foundation powder ran out. Her eyebrows were nothing but black pencil lines and her lipstick was smudged due to most of it being deposited on beer mugs. She had large ear-rings, false breasts, a skin-tight skirt, and an overpowering smell of cheap perfume. He didn't realize it, but she'd been pushed in his direction by O'Hara, a man always good to his word.

"My name isn't Johnny," he said.

"Really! Sorry, I'm sure. What is it, then?"

"George. What's yours?"

"Does it matter?"

"I suppose not.   I just wondered."

"Sorry, Johnny.   It's Vera."

"George.   Not Johnny."

She slipped her arm through his and giggled.   "Come on then, George."

Half an hour later they were some way out of the town by the river, in a copse of pine trees with rhododendron bushes giving privacy.   For a time, despite a lot of fumbling, nothing much happened.   She grew impatient and the damp grass was getting through to her knickers.   "Use your imagination," she suggested.   "Think of doing something really wicked.   Imagine having me against a tree, or pinning me to the ground as though I was a butterfly on a display board.   Here, I'll wrap my legs round you ... Maybe I can kick-start you."

A little later, he asked, "How do I ..."

"Just pull ...."

He pulled and they slipped down to her smooth legs to her ankles where she kicked them away impatiently.   Then, to his amazement, and not really knowing how it happened, he slipped into her easily and sweetly, a sensation so blissful that he knew his first girl certainly wasn't going to be his last.

The Rockinghamshire's Officers' Mess was the height of opulence, situated in a recently renovated Baronial Hall that dated back to the 17th century.   Its grandeur was famous throughout the region and it was the focal point of most social activities among the more notable citizens of the county.   Invitations to regimental functions were highly prized, and never more so than when there was a dining-in night and a Grand Ball prior to the regiment embarking for foreign climes.   If they were off to a war, then so much the better; all the more spectacular the decor and all the more boisterous and dangerous the mess games they played once the guests had departed in the small hours of the morning.

The Ball on the night of September 1st 1952 was hardly on a par with the one before Waterloo, but it was certainly a night to remember.   Blake knew it would be the only occasion on which he would wear his No.1 mess kit which had cost his father so much.   He delayed his entry for as long as possible, worried that he would have difficulty finding anyone to converse with, and dreading that he would end up circulating around the hall, drinking too much to compensate for his lonesomeness.

It didn't turn out like that.   A fellow subaltern had his sister with him and her good looks attracted plenty of others to their group.   When they went into dinner he was amazed by the resplendence: wine glasses sparkled, acres of cutlery gleamed, waiters in immaculate uniforms stood at regular intervals along the enormously long table, down the center of which was a magnificent display of regimental silver, choice items which had been looted in the heyday of the regiment, the center-piece being a magnificent solid silver tiger which had once belonged (and still did legally) to the Maharajah of Baroda. Most impressive of all was that whilst they stood behind their chairs, waiting for the Padre to say grace, curtains at the end of the room were drawn back to reveal a string orchestra, reputed to be the only one in the army.

Blake had the good fortune to sit next to one of the many regimental veterans at the dinner, a colonel whose service went back to the Boer war and included most major battles of the Great War. He was a splendid old fellow with a walrus moustache, three DSOs, a Military Cross, and a Mention in Dispatches. He regaled those around him with endless stories of military triumphs and at the end of the meal, after toasts had been drunk and port was circulating, he singled out Blake for some special advice.

"Don't be overawed by all this glitz young man, nor by any of my yarns. I well remember what it was like to be your age. And I know how anxious you young fellows are about making your way in life ... Being a success. But that's one of the great advantages of fighting in a war. Especially a real war like the one you're going to. It'll make a man of you. Make you mature beyond your age. And after you've done your bit in Korea you'll be able to face up to anything in life. Succeed at anything. Turn you hand to anything. The city, the law, the arts, or anything else you fancy."

The decanter of port came round for the third time. He helped himself to a generous tot. He sipped it appreciatively, wiped his moustache dry, and then added: "Unless you get killed, of course. That will put a very different complex on things."

8

Six weeks later Blake was woken by a cold stream of clammy air pouring unopposed through an open port-hole. He pulled another thick blanket over his bulky frame and just lay there, letting the minutes tick by. On the two bunks opposite, Bartram and Goodall, his fellow platoon commanders in Able Company who had joined them in Hong Kong, were still asleep.

Above, on the promenade deck, Blake could hear the steady beat of gym shoes as the more energetic passengers ran round the decks in an attempt to get fit. Eventually, Bartram and Goodall were woken when their steward entered with their morning tea. "We'll be in Pusan within half an hour gentlemen," he announced.

Blake dressed quickly and after a large breakfast he went on deck to watch the rocky coast line of Korea become clearer. Then Pusan came into sight. Even from the distance it was crumbling and rotten, like a decaying skull.

So this was Korea, reflected Blake. The country where so many lives had been sacrificed in the name of freedom; and where, just to the north, had been the famous Pusan Perimeter which had alone saved the United Nations from defeat.

Blake stayed on deck as they steamed into Pusan harbor, watching the town as it was revealed as a conglomeration of slums. The Rocks lost no time in disembarking. Then they marched to the nearby Railway Station where a train was waiting to take them north to the battle zone. The train was old and very basic, with no toilet facilities and carriages which only had hard, wooden seats. In the officers' carriage several members of the battalion's advance party were present and they were soon expounding on the war that lay ahead of them. As the train started off with deafening rattles and violent jerks, Blake listened to snatches of the conversation between the field officers.

"Hill 355 is the place to watch. It's a massive hill. Completely dominates everything else."

"The Canadians have had a rough time. But it's the Yanks who really catch it in the neck'"

"I haven't had a bath since I arrived …."

"So that's what it is!"

"On the other hand, the Australians are a very different cup of tea. They're reputed to be the best out here."

"Brigadier is quite a nice old chap. Bit of an old woman, though."

"We should be in reserve by Christmas, old boy. With any luck we'll be able to get some grouse shooting in."

"Gunners do a splendid job. No ammo restrictions, just blaze away whenever you want to. Glorious fun!"

"Chinky gets a bit big for his boots occasionally, but normally it's pretty quiet. Glorified training-ground compared to the last do."

"Not many National Servicemen, I hope? Pity! They're going to be a terrible liability."

So it went on. Maps were pulled out and complicated theories were expounded about how to end the stalemate of the war. Blake soon tired of listening and turned his attention to the country through which they were passing. The hills were never ending, rolling into each other like the waves of a raging sea, and between them, making full use of every scrap of land, were terraced paddy fields.

Progress was slow and the train labored up even the most gradual slopes. Stops were frequent and seemingly pointless. At one stage of the journey a coupling broke and the rear half of the train disappeared back down a slope it had taken them half an hour to surmount; and on another occasion there was sudden panic when a young boy, having been refused any 'buckshee' as he ran alongside the train, threw a stone through a window, making many think they were being ambushed by communist guerrillas.

At eleven o'clock the following morning they reached the end of the rail line. The battalion was then bused on to Britannia Camp, a sprawling mass of tents in a broad, open valley where they were to spend the night before pressing on to their training area. It was here that the Battalion was made up to full strength by reinforcements. They were practically all National Servicemen, many of whom had seen service in Korea with other units which were now due to return home.

Sergeant Miles--- Blake's platoon sergeant who had arrived in Korea with the advance party--- stood at the top of the platoon re-entrant in their training area and looked over the thirty six men confronting him. He'd rarely seen such an unpromising lot.

Miles was a thin man, bordering on scrawny. His nose leaned heavily to the right (the result of a bar-room fight) and it gave him a tough, rugged look. He was thirty-seven years old and he'd had enough of soldiering. He had another two years to serve and as far as he was concerned they couldn't pass quickly enough. Yet in those two years he was determined to win promotion to a junior warrant officer: it would make all the difference to his pension, and as married man with a daughter, he needed a good pension.

He scanned the men in front of him and decided there was no point in the familiar tirade sergeants usually gave a new platoon. That was strictly for basic training and these men, young and inexperienced though they were, had already been through that. There was no point in trying to put the fear of God into them. What he needed was their respect and co-operation, and that required something much more low-key. Also, he'd spotted one or two among them he knew of old: Charles, 'My boy!' Hallows, and Paddy O'Hara; and it would be no good trying to intimidate them. He eyed Charles in particular. He was always at the root of any trouble.

"Well, here we all are at last," he began in a tone suggesting humor. "The place where most of us hoped we would never be. Those of you who know me, or have heard about me, know that if you play ball with me, I'll play ball with you. I don't want any buggering about. Just let's do what we have to do. Do it well, and just pray to God that we all come out of it all right. And we'll only do that if we all pull together. I don't want any one being the old soldier. If you do, you'll very soon fall out with me. And I wouldn't advise that.

"We're in reserve for ten days and during that time we've got to do some hard training. We hardly know each other's names yet but by the time we go into the line we've got to be a proper fighting unit ... And another thing ..." Miles paused in order to make sure that the point sank in. "...As far as you are concerned, I am your platoon commander. You take your orders from me and no one else. If you have got anything on your minds or any grievances come and see me." He eyed them severely. "Not go above my head. Anyone who goes above my head, I just don't want to know. All right? That's all."

Blake was at a meeting of the battalion officers and the Colonel and the Brigadier were holding forth. Unlike Miles, they were not concerned with personal behavior--- officers were above such concerns--- but the general attitude towards the war, the need for a truly aggressive spirit. The Brigadier (well known as a master of clichés) made it clear that the one thing he would not tolerate was anyone sitting back and taking things easily.

"No sitting tight!" declared the Brigadier. "No cold feet! No 'After you, Claude! No after you, Cecil!' Anyone found sitting tight with cold feet, waiting for Claude to get in first, will have me to answer to."

When the officers' meeting was over, a temporary bar was opened and there was a minor stampede for refreshments. Blake opted out, strictly a very occasional drinker. He just wanted to get away from the smoke-ridden atmosphere and the incessant chatter. He walked along the track leading back to Able Company, listening to the distant rumbling of shells landing on the front line. Although he could see and hear the war, he still couldn't focus on its reality: he still couldn't see himself as part of it. It was like a distant dream which he still imagined he would be able to wake from and avoid.

In Able Company lines, open petrol fires were blazing and men were behaving as though they hadn't a care in the world. There was a general hum of conversation and frequent outbursts of swearing, but above it all rang out the boisterous voices of Charles, Hallows and O'Hara, singing about a pleasant young lady named Lulu. Blake stood still for some time, absorbing the dim scene, trying to catch some of the words of the song. Then he started to climb the slope towards his tent. As he approached the crest of the hill the shelling became louder and more persistent, with brilliant flashes illuminated the sky and casting momentary shadows across those sitting by their pup tents.

"That's the Hook, sir," said Miles, who had followed Blake up the hill.

Blake turned sharply, surprised. "Is that in our Divisional front, Sergeant?"

"Very much so, I'm afraid, sir."

"Bad as that, is it?"

"Yes, sir. It's probably even worse. It is the traditional invasion route to Seoul. Armies have fought for that piece of ground for God knows how long."

"What's it like up there?"

"Marvelous view," replied Miles, with the trace of a smile. "But that's about all." They paused as they reached the top of the hill and looked towards the Hook. "It's probably the foulest bit of ground in the world. I'd rather be anywhere than there. When the Chinks get lively up there they reckon on getting about fifty killed each week. Unless, of course, there is a big attack, and then it rockets up. When I was on the Yong Dong position--- that's on the Hook's right flank--- we watched a battle going on for three whole days. All the time without let-up. The Hook itself changed hands ten times. It's quiet up there at the moment in comparison, but I don't suppose it will last long. You can't dig there without coming across the remains of some poor bastard. And the rats!"

"Which unit is up there at the moment?" Blake stopped walking as they reached the junction of two tracks, one of which led to the sergeants' mess and the other to the officers' mess.

Miles rubbed his hands together briskly. The night air was bitingly cold. "American Marines, sir. But that's only a temporary arrangement. Our Brigade is expected to move up there when we get into the line."

"Which regiment do you think will actually go on the Hook?"

Miles laughed. "Not us to start with, sir. We're far too green." He noticed Blake's expression of relief in the light of another series of explosions. "Don't worry, sir. The war might be over by the time our turn comes. Why don't you come and have a drink in what passes for our Sergeants' Mess? We haven't got much in the way of drinks. Beer and whisky, if that will do you. And I know CSM Ralf would like a word with you. "

Blake wasn't keen to have any drinks and even less to have a word with CSM Ralf; but he felt duty-bound to accept. They walked on and Miles took the opportunity to mention some things which were worrying him. "How much do you know about the lads in the platoon, sir?"

"Not much. Most of them are new to me. I know Corporal Smith's section best."

"They're the ones to watch, sir. Not Smith--- he's a good lad. And I'm glad you've had him made up to full corporal. But he's still very inexperienced and Charles, Hallows and O'Hara are all real hard cases.... They were nothing but trouble in Germany. And there are a couple of extra snags, as well. There is ill-feeling between Charles and O'Hara over five quid. Charles says he lent O'Hara five quid in Blighty and O'Hara says it was payment for some favor or other. "

"Well they can sort that out, surely," said Blake.

"It goes a bit deeper, sir. Rivalry! Charles likes to be the king of the roost and he sees O'Hara as competition. And he doesn't like competition. What he looks for in others is good side-kicks, men like Hallows and to a lesser extent Winston. There's always a mini mafia in every platoon."

"It sounds all very petty, Sergeant."

"No, sir. It's not petty. It can turn really nasty. You haven't seen anything yet, sir. "

They were silent for the rest of their walk to the mess tent. Miles pulled aside the flaps to reveal a badly-lit interior containing two rustic, home-made beds upon which CSM Ralf and Sergeant Sykes of Two Platoon sat, with a sizable collection of beer and whisky bottles on the floor between' them.

'Good evening, sir,' said Sykes, compensating Blake for the distinctly cold stare from Ralf. "Take a seat, sir. We can only offer you a beer or a whisky in a cracked mug, but I don't suppose that'll worry you. We have to start roughing it now, including the officers."

"I think we all started roughing it in that wretched train," said Blake nervously.

"It's when the bullets start whistling around your head that you start roughing it," said Ralf with typical aggression. He had clearly had too much to drink and it had put him in a belligerent mood. He omitted to call Blake 'sir' in a deliberate attempt to convey disrespect.

Miles plunged his hand under one of the beds and withdrew a bottle of whisky. "Quite a little do up on the Hook," he informed them. "I wouldn't be surprised to see the Yanks catch another packet sooner or later." He succeeded in opening the bottle, and poured some into a cup. "Here you are, sir. Have a tot." Miles could see that Blake was feeling his way awkwardly and he was desperate to put him at ease. The last thing he wanted was for him to take umbrage at Ralf's attitude. "It'll warm you up inside, sir."

Blake took tiny sips and looked about the tent: on top of a cardboard box stood a large, heavily-framed picture of a woman. "Who's the picture of?" he asked Miles.

"That's my wife, sir."

"Any children?"

"A daughter, sir. She turned ten the other day."

"Fellows with family responsibilities shouldn't be allowed out here,' said Sykes. "It's always fellows like you that get it."

"Rot, Reg," said Miles, pouring himself some more whisky. "If a man has got something to live for he'll live through it. Here, come on, sir, have another drink. I should warn you that we speak of nothing but shop up here."

"No thanks, Sergeant. No more for me."

"Now wait a minute, sir," protested Miles, "once an officer comes into a sergeants' mess he does not go out again until he is at least merry."

"Doesn't he?" faltered Blake.

"No sir. He certainly does not."

"Oh, I didn't know that." Blake was uncertain as to whether or not Miles was being serious.

"I always thought that was the first thing any officer learnt," said Sykes, inoffensively.

CSM Ralf's hostile eyes stared directly into Blake's. "It is the first thing an officer learns," he said.

The implication could not have been more obvious.

Later on, after Blake had been prevailed upon to have more drinks, Ralf took him to one side. Miles joined them and it took on the air of an official meeting.

"You've got the rogue platoon in the company," said Ralf. "You might not realize it yet, but you've been landed with the hard cases."

"I'll manage," said Blake.

"Oh, will you ..."

"Certainly. They can't be that bad."

"Don't you believe it. And the one you've got to look out for most is that man Charles. The bastard needs to be put up against a wall and shot."

Blake soon learnt that Ralf had a great keenness for putting men up against a wall and shooting them. There was even a story that out in Burma, when Ralf's men had rounded up some Indian army deserters, that was exactly what he had done. "I know the type of man Charles is, all right," continued Ralf. "And I can tell you this. As soon as things start getting rough he'll do his best to work his ticket. The trouble is that out here he's already suffering the ultimate punishment, so a stretch inside will be like a holiday to him.   So whatever you do, never put him or any of your hard cases on CO's orders .... There are other ways of punishing them … Much better and more effective ways…"

"Put them up against a wall and shoot them," joked Sergeant Sykes.

Ralf glared at him aggressively and Sykes shrank visibly, burying his nose in his beer mug.

"I'll manage, Sergeant-Major," said Blake, trying to relieve the tension. "And with all due respect, I'll command my platoon my way."

"Oh, will you, sir?"

"Yes, I will."

"Then I'd better let you know that I have a vested interest in this man Charles.   Just before we left Minden, the bastard played fast and loose with my daughter.   During the last night celebrations at Minden the bastard forced umpteen drinks into her and then took her out the back and slipped it to her."

Blake was nonplussed.   He had no idea what to say.   He had no experience of things like that.   In a normal, civilian conversation he would have walked away.   And what a revolting expression, he thought.

"So you just make sure he stays in the platoon and does his full stint at the sharp end," said Ralf.   "No bloody cushy options for Charles, Mr. Blake … Understand!"

Ralf walked away with an air of finality, leaving Blake and Miles alone. "Did you know that, Sergeant?"

"There have been rumors, sir.   And Ralf's daughter wouldn't have been the hardest of conquests, from all reports.   Poor kid's been bullied so much at home that it's made her rebellious.   Going to the dance at Minden was her way of stating her independence … Of having turned sixteen …"

"So what am I supposed to do about it?" said Blake.

"Just bear it in mind, sir.   Just go along with everything the CSM says. You'll get nowhere fighting against him.   No one ever beats that bastard."

9

Early the following morning, while moon-shadows still filtered through the re-entrants, the battalion assembled in companies and the calm air was rudely disturbed by shouting voices and the piercing notes of the battalion bugler sounding first parade.   It was obvious from the very start the battalion was going to be worked to the limit of its endurance.

In the morning, while the other ranks erected a double apron of barbed-wire about the company lines, with the purpose of keeping off undesirable Koreans who loitered about the area waiting to steal anything left unattended, the officers scaled a monstrously high hill for a demonstration by the Royal Engineers. They were taught how to build bunkers, weapon pits, tunnels and machine-gun pits; they were told that the main cause of bunkers collapsing was not enemy shelling but the heavy autumn and spring rains: they were taught the correct use of overhead cover, and reminded never to forget a hole in the roof for air circulating and another for the chimney of the winter fires.

In the afternoon they visited the reserve defense line (Kansas) which lay on the southern side of the Imjin, perched on the tops of massive hills which dominated the country for miles around and in themselves presented a major obstacle to an advancing army. In the event of a major withdrawal Able Company was to be responsible for the defense of Gloster Hill, the site of the famous Imjin battle.

When they returned to their reserve position they found that work on the officers' mess had been completed by a squad of Korean porters working under Ralf. Able Company had thirty of these porters under their command, used for carrying stores up and down the hills and doing the most unpleasant and arduous of the laboring tasks. All were short of stature, about five feet five, with fine, thickset bodies and short, muscular legs that enabled them to carry enormous weights on their 'A' frames. None of them spoke English, but they had managed to pick up a few phrases which covered basic requirements, but which were forgotten whenever it suited them. Their clothing had obviously been stolen, or given to them by the troops, for there was no trace of uniformity: some wore odd boots, some with laces, some without, and one character even had large, Canadian-type boots which stretched up to his knees.

They had made a good job of the mess, but Blake soon discovered that there was a lot more to a successful mess than physical comforts. In Able Company none of the five officers had anything in common and a mantle of strangeness engulfed them and showed no signs of lifting. Company officers' messes were invariably a reflection of the company commanders, and Lawrence wasn't interested in socializing with his juniors, only senior officers with influence.

Captain Clark, the company second in command (2i/c), who had joined them at Pusan, was the only one who made any attempt to break down the brittle atmosphere, and on receiving no encouragement he soon abandoned the task. Clark was a solidly-built man and one of the many ex-public schoolboys who on leaving school had gone straight to Sandhurst, not because of any keenness for a military career, but because they could think of nothing better to do. His job as 2i/c was an easy one, nothing but checking stores and ammunition and general supervision.

While in the mess Lawrence generally remained silent, brooding over maps and intelligence reports, many of which were hopelessly out of date but which nevertheless seemed to fascinate him. Only occasionally did he emerge from his shell, either to make some comment on the war or to give them details of their future training.

The three subalterns were, for subalterns, extraordinarily subdued. Goodall and Bartram, although they had known each other for a considerable time in Hong Kong, did not have a great deal of time for each other, Bartram being a very plain man of grammar-school stock with a genuine vocation for the army, whereas Goodall was a snob, an Old Harrovian whose upper-class accent was so exaggerated that men found it painful to listen to. Nor did Blake do anything to enhance things in the mess. At times, when asked his opinion he was far too outspoken; but otherwise he was still timid and finding his feet, worried sick about all the complications that seemed to be piling up on him; most of all wondering why it should be any concern of his that Charles had made love to Ralf's daughter.

During a short pause for a meal between their day and night training, the officers were sitting in glum silence, reading and drinking. Lawrence's Korean houseboy, Kim, entered with their fried bully beef and they left their seats and started on their meal eagerly.

"What kind of condition are the rocket launchers in?" Lawrence asked Clark, through a mouthful of food.

"Not bad at all, Dick. The only trouble as far as I can see is that there is no one in the company who can use one."

"There damned well should be," retorted Lawrence. "They're not all that new, after all."

"Well, actually, sir," offered Goodall, who took the theoretical side of the army a lot more seriously than the practical, "I think you'll find that Nobby is right. Some of these fellows only seem to know how to shoot a rifle. It's simply frightful."

Lawrence looked up sharply. "For your information, Goodall, you don't shoot a rifle. You fire it." There was an embarrassing silence and then Lawrence continued: "If that is the case and no one can use them, you platoon commanders had better see that at least three of your men receive detailed instructions before we go into the line.   And remember, that might be earlier than we expect, so get on with it at once.   I'll make a point of checking up on you."

For a time there was only the sound of their knives and forks knocking against their plates, then they heard someone approach and stop in the doorway.   They looked round and saw CSM Ralf.   The Sergeant-Major saluted vigorously.   "Excuse me, sir, but I was wondering if I could have a man from one of the platoons to act as enemy with me to-night on these practice patrols?"

Lawrence gave him a friendly smile.   "Yes, I think we'll be able to manage that, Sergeant-Major.   Take a man from One Platoon."

"Take Charles," suggested Blake.

It struck him that since there was a possibility that they might soon be related by a shot-gun marriage, the sooner they got to know each other well, the better.

It was almost dark and as Charles fumbled in his pocket for a match, finding it difficult to move in their tiny tent, Corporal Smith leveled an area of earth on which to rest their solitary candle.   After several attempts he managed to make the stumpy piece of wax stay upright and Charles lit it.   Smith lowered himself to his groundsheet, pulled a blanket over himself, and started to suck at a cut on the joint of his small finger the result of handling barbed wire carelessly.   He groaned as he remembered that their day's training was still not complete, indeed only half over.

"Look at this damned candle," exclaimed Charles, fingering the swiftly diminishing stump.   "Ruddy thing won't last five minutes, let alone a whole month.   What a ration!   One candle a month!   They must think we're cavemen, or something."   Charles's face was lined by a dejected frown.   "Just look at this ruddy hole we're living in," he added reflectively.

Smith looked around: it was a hole, pure and simple, covered by a canvas pup tent, about four feet deep, and wide enough for two men to sleep on their groundsheets with a narrow gap between them.   The walls were leaning outwards appreciably and crumbling badly, covering their equipment in dirt.

"It's all right," said Smith.   "Nothing to write home about, I'll admit, but it'll keep the rain out."

"Will it hell!   Don't you remember that time in Minden?   They certainly didn't keep the rain out then."

"So what?   It's not raining yet, is it?"

"Not yet, but by the time we've finished out here it will have rained all right.   Have you thought what it is going to be like living in a bloody hole in the ground for a year?"

Smith had not given it a serious thought before, and as he faced it for the first time he began to realize what it did mean; there was nothing to look forward to; nothing to hope for, and only the prospect of fighting; of learning about death, killing and perhaps being killed. He forced a smile as he realized that as a section commander he could not afford to be despondent. "A fellow I was talking to at the mobile canteen to-day said some of the bunkers in the line are ruddy marvelous. Some of the officers' bunkers are like mansions."

Charles laughed cynically. "I don't doubt that, but what about the ones we'll be living in? Do you realize, Smudge, that I was a damn sight better off doing my year's nick in Colchester than I am out here? Then, I did at least have a chain to pull, a bed to sleep on, and a basin to wash in." Charles sat up and stared at the flickering candle for some time. "Wish to hell I could think of some way of working my ticket."

"You're yellow, Charlie, that's your trouble."

"You're dead right, I am. We all are. Even bloody O'Hara, for all his bluff."

"It's one thing to be scared," said Smith, "but you should never show it. Least of all boast about it. And whether you like it or not, someone has to do the fighting."

"Well whoever does, it's not going to be me, or my name isn't Edwin Charles."

No sooner had Charles made this proclamation than they heard his name being called in the distance. He poked his head out of the tent. "What do you want?"

"Report immediately to CSM Ralf."

When Charles reached Ralf he stood to attention with his arms pressed tightly against his sides. There was a strained atmosphere between them. Charles had visions of the moment he'd had Ralf's daughter, and the CSM was wondering if Charles realized that he knew perfectly well what he'd been up to.

"Did you want me, sir?"

"Yes, Charles. You won't be going with your platoon on the patrols to-night. You'll be acting as the enemy with me."

"What exactly do I have to do, sir?"

"You have to sit in a slit trench with me and fire over the heads of the patrols as they approach. The Bren guns will be firing on bipods on fixed lines, so there will be no danger of hitting them."

"But what about us, sir? Are the patrols going to use live?"

"Of course they are." Ralf grinned. He loved to see the fear in Charles beady little eyes. The temptation of putting the fear of God in him was too much for Ralf. "But we should be all right. We'll be perfectly safe, unless some silly sod decides to start throwing grenades. Anyhow, we've all got to face the music sooner or later. You go out to the training area with your platoon and report to me when you get there. And don't be late."

But Charles's mind was made up. This war was not for him. It was for men like O'Hara and Lawrence: men who wanted medals and glory.

10

In one of the many steep-sided valleys burrowed into the neighboring hills, Able Company prepared to face their first experience of fire initiation. CSM Ralf sat alone in the darkness in the weapon slit, filling magazines, while Lawrence lectured to the platoons on the action to take on being bumped by the enemy, and the best way of laying an ambush.

Lawrence made it clear that he would only accept the highest possible standard. He was appalled by their clumsiness, the way they trod on sticks and tripped over boulders, and the bad control of the commanders; and the cowardly manner in which they clung to the ground as soon as bullets started to fly about overhead. He shouted at them in anger, demanding that they should do things again and again until they had some semblance of cohesion. Men complained bitterly to each other as they reassembled to restart the patrols, but Lawrence gave them no respite. Everything was repeated over and over again until every man knew exactly what was expected of him and had proved capable of doing it.

In the early hours of the morning, when even the distant front line was hushed and sleeping, Able Company trekked back to its lines. Men were tired to the point of exhaustion, but when they reached the end of their journey they were surprised and gratified to find a large urn of tea and containers of hot curry beside a towering bonfire from which sparks and flames leapt high into the clear night air. Equipment was thrown off, weapons discarded, mugs and mess tins produced from nowhere, and an eager queue formed alongside the containers. Shortly afterwards they stood around the fire, some shielding their eyes against the intense glare, some enjoying a sing-song.

Blake was approached by Hale and Smith. "We'll all be worn out by the time we get in the line at this rate," said Hale.

Blake shrugged the remark away with a smile. "It's only because we're not used to it." He was still at the stage where he felt obliged to defend and justify the actions of Lawrence.

As they ate their curry a group of Korean porters walked past with fresh supplies of wood for the bonfire. "What gets me," said Hale "is how we're expected to know the difference between these blokes and the Chinese. I can see that before long there's going to be some nasty mistakes."

Sergeant Miles approached the three men and touched Blake lightly on the shoulder. "I'd like a word with you, sir"

They went to one side, out of hearing of the others. "I've just heard from CSM Ralf, sir. You know that live-fire that Charles was supposed to be helping with?"

"Yes."

"Well he didn't turn up. Cut it. He's spent all night sitting in his tent doing damn all."

"So what do we do about that?"

"Nothing, sir. Not officially. Leave him to me. Ralf has told me to make his life hell."

"That's sounds pretty unsatisfactory ..."

"Don't rock the boat, sir ..."

"I'm not rocking anything."

"Look, sir ... When Ralf tells me to do something, I have to do it. No arguments. Otherwise he'll have my guts for garters. And rather than him make my life hell, I'm going to make Charles's life hell. It's as simple as that."

"How on earth can we fight the enemy properly if we're so busy fighting each other?"

"Wake up, sir. This is the army. Not your local cricket club."

Training progressed: during the mornings they did section attacks up the steepest hills Lawrence could find and during the afternoons they graduated to platoon attacks up the same steep hills. In the late evenings, the nights and the early hours of the mornings, they were back on patrols, with Ralf and Charles firing perilously near the patrols' heads from their slit trench. It was grueling work without a moment's pause. As soon as they had finished one phase of training they were hurried on to the next, doubling everywhere; meals were snatched from mess tins; mail that arrived was read without continuity, a paragraph here, a paragraph there.

For days the same routine continued: section attacks, platoon attacks, patrols; section attacks, platoon attacks, patrols. Commanders lost their voices through shouting; troops began to loathe everyone and everything that taxed their strength, but most of all they hated the country that presented nothing but steep and exhausting hills.

Lawrence gave them no rest. He never allowed them to break off for a smoke or sit idle for a few moments after completing an attack. He was appalled at the time it took them to show any signs of improvement. One platoon was particularly bad. Blake seemed to have no grip over his men and they didn't respond to his half-hearted orders with the speed and enthusiasm that Lawrence demanded.

Instead of charging their objectives with fire and determination they stumbled to the top of the hills, leaning on their weapons, using them as walking sticks, gasping for breath, and then unable to do anything but flop to the ground and point their weapons aimlessly, pretending that they were adopting a proper position of all-round defense.

Lawrence refused to tolerate it; he stopped attack after attack and ordered them to be done again; he singled out individuals and punished them by making them run up the steepest hill in the area; he rebuked officers in front of their men without mercy; and he continued with the training well after all the other companies had returned to their lines.. He pushed them on until they were about to fall, always striving for perfection; there was always a small detail to be corrected, a trifling mistake to be rectified.

"Mr. Blake! For heaven's sake! That attack would have been finished in the first five minutes. You would all have been shot before you were halfway up the hill. Get your men moving. What corporal was in charge of the fire section?"

"Corporal Smith, sir."

"Well, tell Smith to pull his finger out. His bloody section is there to fire its weapons, not admire the view. And who was that man who suddenly decided to stand up and stretch his legs?"

"Winston, sir."

"Well, put him on a charge for idleness."

"Yes, sir."

"Right, Mr. Blake. Take your platoon back down the hill and start again."

"Why don't you go and stuff yourself?" mumbled Hallows.

Then, a few minutes later: "Mr. Bartram, what are you playing at? You know bloody well that you assault with two sections and not just one. And what's the matter with your men? Can't they hear your orders or have they gone on strike?"

"God, what does he expect?" whispered Bartram.

"Perhaps, Mr. Bartram, you might get better results from them if you swore at them a bit."

"Swear at them, sir?"

"That's right. Swear at them. We're training to kill, you know."

"Drop dead," commented Sergeant Sykes.

As days slipped by, Able Company became more efficient. One Platoon began to fear Blake for a violent temper and gradually their legs ceased to feel like lumps of lead and they were able to sprint up the hills with sustained speed. At night, patrols no longer crashed through the paddy fields like an ignorant herd of elephants, but were cats, stalking after their prey, knowing their task exactly and the best way of accomplishing it. Hale proved himself to possess the eyes of an owl and to have an uncanny sense with which he was able to guide patrols along the best routes, avoiding the soft, boggy ground in which they sank knee-deep and finding the bunds that afforded most protection. Miles inspired the platoon with his experience and professional touches, and a reinforcement named Taylor proved himself a capable wireless operator and a batman who had the rare gift of anticipating the wants of his officer.

After ten days Able Company had blended into a sound unit that would be capable of dealing with any situation which might arise. Anyhow, that was what Lawrence told the Colonel. It remained for the future to prove him right or wrong.

PART II

TESTING   THEIR   STENGTH

1

Yong Dong was a quiet part of the line that had seen no enemy action for ten months, and because of this it was the position allotted to 'green' battalions during their first spell in the line.   All four rifle companies were forward with nothing held in reserve, and each was perched on a high hill that dominated the valley, separated from the Chinese by more than a thousand yards.   On the left flank of the position no-man's-land curved sharply to the west, leading to the Hook, which could be seen protruding into the enemy's lines like a peninsular.   Midway between Yong Dong and the Hook, like a clear line of demarcation, was the River Samichon, a sluggish tributary of the Imjin which only became a force to reckon with during the spring rains.

Yong Dong was an area in which men could make mistakes and not have to pay the price for them; where untried soldiers could begin to learn the difference between incoming and outgoing shells, and where old soldiers could forget how they had fought in the desert, or among the hedgerows of Europe, and learn the arts of static warfare; to develop the steel nerves required for four or five patrols a week, to acquire the stealth and cunning which alone could outwit the enemy, and most of all to develop patience, to be able to live on the same hill for weeks on end, waiting for an attack which would probably never come, yet remain ready for it at any moment of the night or day.

The Rocks had a long march down the MSR to Yong Dong and by the time they arrived they were already tired and hungry and proceeded to get themselves into a mess.   Like all change-overs in Korea, it was carried out in darkness and this meant that ingoing and outgoing men were milling about all over the place, all trying to sort themselves out amid confused orders and counter orders.

Blake and his men found themselves standing at the bottom of a steep, elongated hill.   An Australian guide was with them, ready to lead them up the hill. The Australian platoon was soon streaming down the trenches on the reverse slope of the hill, the idea being that only a few Aussies would stay on the hill overnight, with their standing patrol still out in the valley in order to give an early warning of any Chinese activity.   Two of Blake's men were to join them during the night and then all of them return at first light for the routine stand-to.

The guide attached to Blake was the talkative type, and not one inclined to spread comfort. "They say this is the cushiest position in Korea, but in some ways it's also the worst. Rats, mainly. I've never seen so many rats. But you'll get used to them. No one ever thinks they will, but they do. Leave them alone and on the whole they'll leave you alone as well, except for pinching all your tucker."

The Aussie guide wasn't exaggerating. The position swarmed with rats, dating back to the early days of the war when an entire American battalion had been overrun on Yong Dong. The war was so fluid at that time that no one bothered to clear away the dead and wounded, leaving the rats to breed and prosper mightily. When Charles, Hallows and Winston were shown into one of the bigger bunkers it was in total darkness. Winston struck a match and they were immediately confronted by dozens of pink sparks reflected back at them--- rats' eyes as the rodents stuck their heads out of the holes in the walls of the bunker to see what the new commotion was about. Other men had similar experiences and most men in the platoon simply dumped their equipment on the floor of their bunkers and then went round to the CP to complain.

"I wouldn't put my bloody dog to live in there," said one man.

Miles took control. He took a hard line, showing no sympathy. He told them that from now on, that was the norm; that they were hairy-arsed soldiers, not boy scouts on a jamboree. "What the hell were you expecting?" he demanded, "a sea view with all mod cons?"

When it came to 'mod cons' things were just as bad. The latrines the Australians left behind were in a disgraceful state. They may have been the best fighting unit in Korea but they would never have won the Queen's Award for Domestic Science. Every one of the latrines was chockablock and had to be closed down, with new latrines dug as a first priority. Likewise, the cooking facilities were primitive in the extreme and the ACC cook who had been attached to One Platoon spent most of his time chasing the rats away. Men were so convinced they would end up with food-poisoning or something even worse, that they opted to eat American C-rations, which came out of tins.

However, in the weeks that followed, men learnt from their experiences. They discovered the real value of sleep; they became accustomed to being woken at every conceivable hour of the day and night through some idiot declaring a non-existent emergency; and they soon accepted being ordered into the depths of no-man's-land to search for the enemy who were reported to be moving about in large numbers. With time, they learnt to relax; how to fall asleep whenever an appropriate opportunity presented itself, and more important how to jerk themselves back to one hundred per cent alertness.

They learnt to overlook other men's annoying and often revolting habits, to act as a team and realize that it was for their own benefit that they cleaned their weapons, and that their safety lay in their own hands, that if they went to sleep while on patrol they might never wake again. Above all, they learnt how to make themselves as comfortable as the conditions would allow; they developed improvisations that gave them more room in their squalid bunkers.

What they never got used to were the rats.

Nature's gradual conversion of night into day should have come as a great relief to them. Inevitably their first night of waiting and listening, not knowing what to expect, was a great strain, but the relief of daylight proved short-lived. The direct light of the rising sun was hidden by a thick blanket of mist which hugged the ground as closely as any successful smoke-screen; it was poised over the entire valley like a vast shroud and restricted visibility to a few yards. No one could see what was happening ahead of them; it was even more frustrating than the total darkness of the night. It was certainly warmer, which was one blessing, but the mist had introduced a dampness which was already responsible for a slippery layer of mud in the bottom of the deep trenches.

Blake stood in the entrance of his CP, watching the mist with an anxious frown across his youthful face. He was worried about the standing patrol. Because of the mist they had radioed back over their 88-set to say that they would stay out. Blake wondered if he should send out a replacement, especially since the two Australians on it were supposed to have left at dawn. He went round to the front trench, searching in vain for signs of the mist lifting. He was determined not to be prompted from above. He wanted to make his own quick and firm decisions.

He went back to his CP and said to Taylor, his batman and wireless operator, "Tell Corporal Smith to come round." When Smith appeared, Blake told him to take two men down to the standing patrol to relieve Hallows and the Aussies. "Better take Winston and Burrows," he added.

Blake smiled apologetically. He knew that Winston and Burrows were the last men Smith would want to take anywhere, but it was, after all, hardly a dangerous mission, no more than a formality.

Smith led them over the top and then down the zigzag path through the barbed wire and the minefield. Hallows and the two Aussies were glad to see them and after exchanging ribald remarks, Smith's patrol jumped down into the slit trench. They shifted about, endeavoring to find comfortable positions, having no idea how long they were liable to be stranded there.

Right from the start, Smith realized he was in trouble. Winston looked totally unconcerned, but Burrows was clearly terrified. Once settled, Smith looked across at them and wondered if the Chinese had men anywhere near as bad. Then it suddenly dawned on him that he hadn't brought the 88-set with him. What a bloody useless fool! He was just as bad as the rest of them.

"I'm going back for the 88-set," he said. "You blokes hang on here. Won't be long ..." Then he added, even though he realized it was quite unnecessary, "If you see or hear anything, just fire and then retreat, fire and then retreat, like we practiced ... But I'll only be a few minutes."

Winston settled down in the trench. He opened his grenade pouch and lay several of them on the trench wall in front of him. "No point in taking any chances," he said cheerfully.

Burrows had beaten him to it. He already had everything ready, even his Sten cocked and his safety catch off. He could hardly believe that he was out in the middle of no man's land, away from the protection of minefields, barbed wire and the support of the rest of the platoon; just the two of them on their own, with nothing between them and the Chinese. And Winston of all people! He thought how easy it would be for the Chinese to creep up on them and surprise them, or a great gang of them to suddenly appear and overwhelm them, to pounce on them before they had time to react: how he could so easily die on his first day in the front line. He was tempted to ask Winston if he could hear anything, but he resisted the temptation. All Winston wanted to do was go to sleep. He kept on yawning and it soon became obvious to Burrows that it was useless to expect him to pull his weight and keep a proper look out. It wouldn't even be any good telling him to stop making such a racket as he yawned. It would only cause an argument, with Winston going into one of his long and loud tirades.

What really scared Burrows was that when Smith came back neither he or Winston heard him. The first thing they knew he was right on top of them. When he greeted them with his usual, "Aye up!" they very nearly jumped out of their skins with surprise. He had the 88-set with him and he set it up on the trench top, alongside Winston's grenades. Then he sent a message back to platoon headquarters. "Able One. How do you read me? Over."

Smith glanced sideways and saw Burrows staring at him. "Keep your voice down, Corporal! They'll hear you."

"Who?"

"The Chinese!"

"Don't talk bloody wet," replied Smith. "There's no bugger out there. And if I whisper into the wireless no one in HQ is going to hear me. It'll just make them go through all the rigmarole of saying, 'Do you read me, over?' And 'I say again, over ...'"

When Smith received an acknowledgement to his message the wireless crackled loudly and the operator's voice boomed out. Burrows moved sideways and clasped his hand over Smith's earphone, as though it was going to make it quieter. Smith pushed him away impatiently. Then they lapsed into silence, except that Winston, between loud yawns, kept blowing his nose like a trumpet. Each time, Burrows stared at him aggressively. Then he complained to Smith about the noise the 88-set was still making.

"That's static. They always make that noise. You can't do anything about it."

"But it'll be heard miles away ... Turn it off ..."

"If I turn it off we won't hear the buggers telling us that it's time to go in, will I?"

"No ... I suppose not."

Another half an hour passed and the mist continued to swirl about them. "Did you hear that?" hissed Burrows suddenly.

"Hear what?"

"That!"

"What's that?"

"Rustling ..."

"Bollocks!" Smith turned to Winston. "You hear anything?"

Winston blew his nose again, more like the Trumpet Voluntary this time. . "Not a bloody thing."

"Well I did," whispered Burrows. "A rustling sound."

"The wind, probably."

"There is no wind ..."

"No wind!" retorted Winston. "You want a bet?" He leaned to one side and let out an almighty fart. It was so loud it could have raised the dead, let alone alerted loitering Chinese.

Around midday the mist began to clear. Blake's voice came over the 88-set. His tones cut through the still air, very loud and clear, and Burrows immediately made a "Shushing!" noise, as though Blake would be able to hear him.

Blake's told them to return to base before the mist cleared completely and left them exposed. They climbed the minefield path again and when Smith reported to Blake at the CP, he dumped the 88-set on the table and said, "Only one thing to report, sir. Don't ever send me on patrol again with that wimp Burrows."

"Why? What's the matter with him?"

"If he doesn't end up shitting himself, then I'm a monkey's uncle. And I just don't want to be around when he does it."

"Okay ... Anything else?"

"Well yes... That bloody fellow Winston ..."

Blake laughed. "Smudge, you can't exclude everyone."

Smith laughed as well. It was the first time Blake had used his nickname. He didn't mind a bit, but he wondered how he should react. He decided he'd do his best to reciprocate. In future he would always try to refer to him as Mr. Blake, and not the parrot-like 'Sir!'

2

"**A**ren't wasting much time about it then, are we?"

Sergeant-Major Ralf was talking to Corporal Cross, the company clerk. It was a remark of confirmation, for Corporal Williamson, the company signaler, had just said exactly the same thing. It was typical of Ralf. He thought several seconds behind everyone else and had the annoying habit of repeating their more notable remarks.

He was clean-shaven and fresh, being about the only man in the company to enjoy some sleep. He'd already settled into the position. Like most Sergeant-Majors, he had the knack of obtaining more than his fair share of comforts, no matter what the conditions. He had entered the company CP to make sure that all men were washed and shaved. He was determined that no slovenly habits in dress or personal cleanliness should creep in just because they were at last in the line; he was not going to have any of his men end up with lice.

Having satisfied himself that Cross and Williamson were presentable, he listened to them as they discussed recent developments. It was news to him that during the night Three Platoon's standing patrol had reported hearing movement twenty or thirty yards out into the valley; also. that a man in One Platoon had claimed to have heard lots of movement during the morning mist. Consequently, Major Lawrence had decided to send out a patrol that night.

"That's the area where I reckon they must have been," said Cross, pointing at the map of the valley pinned on the bunker wall.

Ralf grunted doubtfully. "Who's going to command the patrol?"

"Don't know, sir. But the major says he's going to send them to the banks of the Samichon."

"Pity they aren't going to cross it," said Ralf, "especially if ..."

He didn't finish the sentence. Lawrence strode in, straight from his morning constitutional at the newly dug officers' latrine. He looked worried and worn out: He had two--- sometimes three--- constitutionals each day and sometimes they turned out to be little more than a damned good scratch.

Ralf jerked to attention and saluted. "Good morning, sir."

Lawrence mumbled an unenthusiastic reply and gently lowered himself onto his chair. He wriggled about for a few seconds, and then said: "I want an orders group right now. Platoon commanders only. Williamson, you go and get some sleep."

"I'm all right, sir…"

"Don't bloody argue. You're going to be up again all tonight … So get some sleep. But before you do, make sure all the platoons fit their 88-sets with fresh batteries."

When Corporal Williamson left the bunker, Ralf said: "A bit of excitement last night I hear, sir?"

Lawrence shrugged his shoulders. "Not really, Sergeant-Major, it's just men being windy. But I'm not going to ignore it. If men make reports, then we'll have to follow them up. And if they turn out to be a load of balls, they'll soon think twice about making other hysterical claims."

"Good thinking, sir. Keep the young devils at it."

The three platoon commanders soon drifted into the CP. They saluted and then sat down wherever they could find room. They were strangely silent. There was nothing cheerful or boisterous about them as there was with most subalterns. It was as though they knew that in Major Lawrence they had drawn the short straw and no frivolous repartee would be tolerated.

"All right, then," Lawrence began. "You will have heard of this alleged contact by Three Platoon and the half-hearted support from a man on the One Platoon standing patrol during the morning mist. God knows why the Chinese should be interested in our neck of the woods, but if there is anything to it, it no doubt has something to do with the attack which is expected on the Hook within the next week or so. That being the case, I propose to send out an ambush patrol."

He offered them an aerial photograph. "Take a look at this recent photo and you'll see what looks like a recently made track going from the Chinese hills to the banks of the Samichon. Obviously a crossing point for them. So we are going to place an ambush on it."

He paused dramatically and searched their eyes eagerly, looking for some kind of reaction. He saw Bartram swallowing hard. Blake kept his eyes firmly on his note book and Goodall had gone very pale.

Goodall broke the silence. "Who is going to command this patrol?"

Lawrence smiled, a trace of gloating in his expression. "Don't worry,

Goodall, not you. Blake, I'm going to give you the first opportunity of putting Able Company on the map." Blake had expected to be chosen, so he made no comment. "The object of the patrol," continued Lawrence "is to ambush the enemy and kill as many of them as possible. That--- although it may not yet have sunk in with you yet--- is what we are here for. Clear?"

"Yes, sir."

"The site of the patrol will be at map reference 324-196 and the composition of the patrol will be one officer, platoon sergeant, and eight men. Leave your best corporal in command of the platoon position. Who will that be?"

"Corporal Smith, sir."

"And take your eight best men. And Sergeant-Major Ralf recommends that Charles should go with you. We want to make sure that we get the better of these Chinks before any of the other companies."

Blake was irritated by the remark. Lawrence was always on about seeing action before the other companies, of claiming the so-called honor of being the first to taste enemy blood. "Why this rush to beat other companies to it, sir?"

"I would have thought that would have been obvious, Blake. We want to create a good impression not only with the Colonel but also with the Brigadier. We want to get ourselves on the map from the very start. The trust put in us for the rest of the campaign depends on it. Now let's just get on with these orders."

Lawrence went through a list of details which had to be seen to in connection with the patrol--- such things as possible artillery DFs, code words and the issuing of bullet-proof vests. Finally, putting aside his map, Lawrence said: "Well, that's all. But make sure you have your signals going better to-night. Blake, don't forget your inspection and rehearsal this afternoon. I want everything to go well this evening. If we succeed it will make all the difference . . ."

"Make all the difference to what, sir?" asked Blake.

"Never mind," growled Lawrence. "Stop trying to be awkward and just get on with it."

It was late afternoon when Blake woke. He stretched out on his bunk and drew his sleeping bag up to his ears, enjoying the warmth. He heard scuffling noises. He opened an eye and saw a rat scuttling along one of the roof timbers. He slid out of his sleeping bag, waking Sergeant Miles who was on the bunk below him. All preparations for the patrol had been completed and now all that remained was for them to have their evening meal and wait for it to get dark. He walked to the doorway and shuddered as he felt the sharp bite of the autumnal air. Soon, the men on the patrol had assembled outside the CP. Blake listened to them as they talked.

"The first bloody patrol the battalion does and it's us bastards that have to do it," said Winston. "It'll be just like this all the bloody time. Just you wait and see."

O'Hara was more concerned about Lawrence. In his view the patrol was so damned pointless it made him doubt Lawrence's sanity. "I'm all in favor of aggression," he said, interrupting Winston's monologue, "but this patrol is just ridiculous. We aren't even going to cross the Samichion."

Blake listened to another tirade from Winston, and then he heard Charles boasting about having had Ralf's daughter in Minden. Blake was surprised that it was actually true, not just a wild rumor, and he felt like telling Charles that he would be well advised to keep quiet about it. Any bragging would be bound to get back to Ralf and would only infuriate him all the more.

Eventually, Blake went out to join them, struggling with his bullet-proof vest. Hallows gave him a hand. "Taken your pips off, sir?" he asked, his face split by a broad grin.

"Of course."

"First time since you were commissioned I'll bet, sir."

Blake smiled. He liked Hallows. Away from Charles he was a different person, the sort who could well make a good NCO.

They waited until the sun had finally vanished and the Chinese hills had disappeared in the haze of falling night. Then they went 'over the top', something totally lacking the drama of the old days in Flanders. They passed through the zigzagged gaps of the minefield and barbed wire, and then down a long spur into the valley; and finally into the paddy fields where their boots made crunching noises on the frosty surface.

They moved in arrow-head formation, Corporal Hale leading the point section. Every thirty yards or so they went to ground and listened. Gradually they drew nearer the Samichon. They could hear the water gurgling beneath the ice as it bounded on its way towards the Imjin. They adopted the formation Blake had detailed and then he went from man to man making sure they all knew their tasks before sinking into his own, central position. Like most men in the middle of no man's land for the first time, they were certain that the enemy would appear.

It was pitch dark, with no moon, and they strained their ears for the first sounds of movement. To start with their concentration was so complete that they didn't feel the cold; but as time slipped by and they heard nothing, they came to realize that away from the hills, stuck out in the middle of the valley, the wind was stronger, colder and more penetrating. Soon, it was chilling them painfully. Within an hour, they were frozen stiff.

Blake looked around him. His eyes were now sufficiently retuned that he could see the frozen river glittering to his front, reflecting what little light there was, and on the far bank were two trees, their bare branches meeting overhead to form an archway through which he thought the enemy might walk. To his left he could see the heads of Winston and O'Hara moving slightly against the dim skyline, while on right his vision was obscured by a small bush.

For two hours the patrol was motionless. Silence reigned supreme as they continued to anticipate the appearance of the enemy. Then, as time dragged on, Blake felt their concentration flagging; men began to move about, snapping twigs and rustling dead leaves as they endeavored to adopt more comfortable positions. Someone coughed and Blake stared angrily into the darkness.

The wind increased appreciably. The bush beside Blake swayed on its thick trunk, and as Blake's shivering became more pronounced he wished to hell he'd taken Miles's advice and put more clothing on. Time dragged on. Minutes seemed to take ages to tick by and there were still no signs of movement. Men became more restless. The voices of O'Hara and Winston were heard to agree that it was bloody cold, as, indeed, it was. Winston started to expand on the point so Blake hissed at him keep quiet.

At 2300 hours the Chinese made it very clear that they had no intention of going near the small patrol that lay shivering halfway across the valley. A terrifying artillery concentration fell with amazing suddenness on the Hook some 300 yards across the far side of the Samichon. The shells crumped into the ground with such loud fierceness that Blake's ears began to throb and his head to ache, while his eyes were unable to see anything but a weird assortment of colored spots and patterns, due to the brilliance of the flashes.

Within thirty seconds of the commencement of the Chinese bombardment, the United Nation's artillery was barking back in reply, like good house-dogs disturbed in the depths of night, and a continuous stream of shells was soon screaming through the air in both directions to fall on and around the Hook. Then they heard bugles, followed by small-arms fire; short bursts and then a continuous flow as Chinese infantry started their assault on the Hook. The Vickers machine guns of the Rocks fired in support, with a glorious shoot along the entire length of the Hook's barbed-wire entanglements. Three tanks, all sitting majestically on the peaks of neighboring hills, fired their 20-pounders and, with a whip-like crack, their shells were flung across the valley and crunched into the enemy lines, shaking the earth for miles around.

All the supporting weapons had soon joined the battle and on their left flank searchlights manipulated by the distant engineers pin-pointed the Hook and beat against the low clouds to create artificial moonlight so that those manning the defenses could see what they were firing at; even the light coughing of the 2 inch mortars could be heard making their feeble contribution.

Above it all came the incessant chattering of small arms fire as the American Marine defenders raked the forward slopes with long, rapid bursts, endeavoring to hold back the enemy. Now, everything was so light that Blake's patrol could see swarms of Chinese infantry sprinting up the slopes of the Hook: tiny, distant figures but quite unmistakable. They could see them struggling through the barbed wire entanglements like battalions of ants. They saw them falling in droves, even though fresh waves of them kept appearing to keep up the pressure on the Marines.

The battle raged on for what seemed hours. Occasionally there would be a pause while the two giants gasped for breath, and then there would be another duel of artillery, and the whole thing would be rejuvenated. In these pauses came the frightening noises of infantry soldiers---the helpless cannon fodder. There were the terror-stricken voices of dying men, cursing blasphemously at their fate, uttering incoherent noises, protesting against their premature and unfair death.

Then, almost as suddenly as it had started, it was all over, snuffed out like a candle. The battle had been decided one way or the other and all that remained was desolation. On the right of the Divisional area, around Hill 355, some mortars were firing, but their noise was relatively soothing.

At 0200 hours the patrol was still lying in the valley waiting for the enemy that they knew now would never come. Their previous tenseness and anxiety had vanished. They no longer attempted to keep quiet. They moved about restlessly, shifting their stiff, half-frozen limbs in an attempt to keep their circulations going. Men stood up quite openly to have a pee. Then, more comfortable, they relaxed and let their thoughts drift into a different world.

Blake thought about his schooldays; about his last year when he had been a monitor in the sixth form. It had been a year of ease and great enjoyment, of comparative idleness in the way of book-work with plenty of free periods and abundant leisure hours in which to concentrate on playing rugby and cricket.

O'Hara's thoughts were simple and very definite. He was reliving the battle he had just witnessed. It was just as he had visualized Korea, with the enemy attacking in human waves: bags of noise, the Chinese blowing bugles and--- as the Yanks loved to say--- all hell suddenly let loose. He couldn't understand why Blake hadn't done something: at least fired their Brens in support of the Yanks. After all, they were within spitting distance and the Chinese attackers were plain enough. Wasn't that what officers were supposed to do--- use their initiative?

Winston slept through the second half of the battle. Having been told to belt up, he thought 'bugger the lot of you!' and nodded off, despite--- or maybe because of--- the cold. Actually, he'd found the first half of the battle pretty interesting: it was spectacular, like a good fireworks display, but it went on too long and lost its appeal as his tiredness increased. He snored quite loudly and every now and then either Miles or Blake woke him and harangued him with vicious hisses; but between these interruptions he dreamt he was installing an electric fire in his bunker. He was like a dog dreaming of a bone, for he cared more about warmth than anything.

Charles didn't find the cold conducive to his usual sexual fantasies and instead he felt only guilt. He was thinking about his mother. Naturally enough, he hadn't done anything about her allowance and he'd already had two letters from the old bitch asking him what had happened. Worse still, now it was common knowledge that Ralf knew what had happened with his daughter, he dreaded to think what the repercussions would be. He decided that the sooner he devised a scheme for getting out of the line and away from the Rocks, the better. He thought hard and long as to what he could do, but no answers came.

It continued to get colder. Men felt their bodies shrinking. They shivered convulsively and their hands and feet lost any sense of feeling. Gloves proved useless, as were all other forms of clothing, and their skin became taut and brittle, like ice. Blake looked at his watch: it was 0300 hours. They had been stuck out there eight hours. It seemed like twenty. Surely Lawrence couldn't expect them to stay out there any longer? He crawled towards Taylor and took the hand set of the 88 wireless from him. He started to contact Lawrence. "Hullo . . ." He had forgotten the call sign. "What the hell is it, Taylor?"

"One Sugar, sir."

"Hullo, One Sugar. Request permission to return from patrol. Over."

The hand-set crackled for a time and then cleared. "Sunray One Sugar. Stay put. Watch your security. Out."

It was an odd thing about the Rocks, though Blake. Whatever one said over the 88-set, and however careful one was, the bloke on the other end always countered with, 'Watch your security'.

Blake crawled back to his position and tried to shield himself from the wind by lying directly behind the bush, but its branches were no protection and only impaired his view. He felt his bullet-proof vest cutting into the flesh beneath his armpits and he realized that it was about the only thing he could feel. The rest of him was numb.

When he looked at his watch next it was 0345 hours. He crawled over to Taylor and took the hand-set from him again.

"Hullo One . . ." He struggled hard to rouse his memory but the call sign had gone completely.

"One Sugar, sir."

"Hullo One Sugar. Request permission to return. Over."

"One Sugar. Say again. Over."

"One . . ." It had gone again. "What the hell is it, Taylor?"

"Sugar, sir."

Blake's request was to no avail. He got another refusal.

Half an hour later Sergeant Miles crawled up to Blake. He had to shake him twice before he got any response. "That bloody fellow Winston is asleep again, sir. And others are beginning to nod off as well. We can't stay out here any longer."

"You're right. I'll contact Lawrence again."

This time he managed to remember the code sign. The message he sent was a straight, unembellished statement that they were returning, with no security at all, ending with a curt: "Over and out!

When Miles roused them and told them to get ready to move, they were so stiff they were like zombies. It took them ages to organize themselves and even when on the move the cold so affected them that they moved in slow-motion. When they eventually got back to their lines men went straight to their bunkers to thaw out and sleep, but Blake went round to the company CP to report to Lawrence.

He found him sitting in his chair, a beer in one hand and a gin bottle poised ready in the other. He had his feet on the table, with a self-satisfied grin across his plump face. The ends of his moustache had been freshly waxed. Williamson was at his side, his earphone clamped over his head and a club-like stick in his right hand, ready to chase off rats.

"No luck, Blake? Never mind. Good practice. It's excellent training for you and your men. Get you familiar with the conditions. You must have had a glorious view of the battle."

Blake's eyes were blood-shot and half-closed with fatigue. It was the instant when his dislike for Lawrence turned into contempt, verging on hatred.

He never thought he would ever feel that strongly about anyone, but he did. He saw him as utterly ruthless and selfish, consumed by personal ambition with never a thought for anyone else: a man he would never be able to respect.

He made no reply, but glanced around the bunker, noting all the indications of his drinking. He walked out of the CP and made his way back through the trenches to his bunker feeling thoroughly depressed, wanting nothing but sleep and warmth. As he lay down on his bunk and closed his eyes, the spectacle of the Hook battle dominated his mind.

He knew now exactly what they had been let in for. It was what Lawrence craved but he dreaded.

3

Able Company had completed its first 24 hours in the front line.

During the three weeks that followed, life on Yong Dong gradually settled into a calm routine; but even so there were incidents and sudden emergencies ('flaps') which cropped up to remind them of how green they were and how much they still had to learn.

Most of the incidents were trivial but others were more serious and claimed a permanent place in men's memories.

On their sixth night in the line patrols from Two Platoon and Three Platoon did their best to destroy each other.

Blake and Miles were relaxing on their beds in their CP. It was their first night without any patrol commitments in no man's land and, apart from a three hours' listening watch each on the 88-set, they were free to get some sleep. Generally, things had settled down a lot and they no longer dreaded another catastrophe every time the field telephone rang or a message came through over the 88-set.

Blake was on the edge of his bunk, his Webley .38 revolver in his hand, ready to shoot a particularly revolting rat that patrolled the beams at irregular intervals during the day and night. Miles was reading through a backlog of letters from his wife. Taylor was also in the bunker, doing the first three hours' listening watch. He was sitting on an old Naafi box, yawning frequently as nothing but a buzz came over the air. Then a message came through and he became tense. Without removing his earphones he said: "It's Two Platoon patrol. They've heard movement on their left." He paused for a moment and then added: "Lawrence has told them to go to investigate."

Sergeant Miles and Blake watched Taylor, anxious to hear further developments. "Three Platoon patrol now," said Taylor. "They've heard the same movement. They are trying to contact the Two Platoon patrol."

There was a long pause in which Blake and Miles exchanged more glances, betraying their increasing concern. They knew that if things escalated they would be ordered out into the valley as an emergency patrol.

"They can't contact Two Platoon so they are going to investigate themselves," reported Taylor. Then he added: "They are closing in now. They both say they can hear the enemy distinctly."

Blake studied the positions of the patrols on his map. "Let's go and see what's happening from the forward trench, Sergeant. We'll completely overlook the patrols from the Browning pit."

They left the CP and walked out into the cold night. They hurried along the trench, looking over the outer wall down into no man's land. There was a bright moon and the valley was filled with shadows, so still and peaceful that it appeared ghostly. Barnes and Collins were manning the American Browning machine gun in the end weapon pit. They were reliable men in their different ways and the only two in the platoon who really understood the American weapon. Miles and Blake had just ducked under the thick head cover at the entrance of the pit when small-arms fire sounded from the valley. First, there were the abrupt explosions of grenades and then the flashes of Stens and Brens. The valley was suddenly flooded with noise. The small arms fire continued for anything up to four minutes, but never the sound of Burp guns or the high, lingering notes of Chinese bugles. Then there was an abrupt silence, followed by human voices. Soon, distant shouts and yells filled the air. The only discernible words were: "You stupid bloody sods! It's us. Two Platoon!"

Before long, Blake and Miles heard men coming up the minefield path. Most of them were quiet and dejected but at the end of the line of men Bartram and Goodall were arguing fiercely as to whose fault it had been. clearly furious with each other.

When Lawrence debriefed them in the morning they were calmer, and Bartram spoke for both of them when he said: "It was a perfectly simple misunderstanding, sir. It could have happened to anyone. And at least there is the consolation that there were no casualties."

That was not the way Lawrence saw it. "Consolation!" he yelled. "No casualties! You lot are so bloody useless that you can't hit a thing. You blazed away all your ammunition and never looked like hitting anyone. You're bloody useless. No bloody danger to anyone, least of all the Chinese.

The next time you decide to fight among yourselves, at least make sure you come back with some casualties to show for it."

Some incidents had their humorous side, even though it didn't seem funny at the time. There was the first time someone in the company spilt blood.

Blake took a patrol out into the valley to inspect the minefield that protected their front, mainly a matter of checking a single strand of barbed wire which bore red triangles every thirty yards or so. The frontage they had to cover was so great that they got lost and were unable to find their way back up the narrow, zigzagging minefield path. As a consequence they were still wandering around no man's land when dawn broke, leaving them exposed to the Chinese. They were soon spotted and shells began to scream over, landing all around them. To start with they escaped unharmed, but when they at last found the pathway and started up it, the shelling became more accurate and a man suddenly cried out, hit in the leg. He went down, screaming in panic, convinced that he was dying. Blake and Corporal Smith bundled him on to the stretcher they had with them and set off as best they could up the narrow, twisting path. The going was slow and for Blake and Smith extremely exhausting. Soon, they were dripping perspiration. Despite all their efforts they got slower and slower. Shells continued to land all around them and it seemed inevitable that someone else would get hit. The man on the stretcher became so alarmed that he sat bolt upright and started to harangue them.

"Get a bloody move on, for God's sake," he kept screaming at them. "What's the matter with you bastards? Move! Move!"

Eventually, the wounded man became so desperate, and so afraid of being wounded again, that he leapt off the stretcher, yelling: "I'm not waiting for you buggers!"

Blake and Smith were left standing there, looking down at an empty stretcher as the man sprinted up the hill like Jesse Owens. He even overtook most of those ahead of him and was among the first back to the platoon and safe under cover.

His wound turned out to be nothing more than a deep scratch. Even so, Blake sent him back to the Company Aid Post (CAP) and he returned within half an hour, a light bandage over his 'wound'.

To add insult to injury, they sent him back on a stretcher.

There was their thirteenth morning in the line when Major Lawrence's jeep driver, Private Armitage, captured a prisoner.

Like so many other mornings, there was a dense mist shrouding the position, infiltrating into every re-entrant, every bunker, and into every small cleft and cranny; and in the midst of this swirling vapor, Armitage was on stag duty in a weapon pit halfway along the trench linking One Platoon and company headquarters. He was alone and due to the poor visibility more than a little nervous. Among other things, he did not consider manning weapon pits to be one of his duties.

All of a sudden he heard someone approaching his weapon pit, along the trench. Everyone was supposed to be standing-to, not wandering about the trenches, so Armitage was immediately suspicious and on his guard. He slipped out of his weapon pit and jumped up on top of the trench wall immediate outside, so that if necessary he could pounce on the man and surprise him, assuming he failed to answer the password.

The footstep drew nearer. They were hesitant and Armitage caught a strange smell. Whoever it was stank to high heaven.

"Halt! . . ." challenged Armitage. "Motor?"

No answer came and the steps stopped. There was a considerable pause and then the steps came on again. "Halt! ... Motor . . ."

"Idawa, Pak Jay Bum ..."

Armitage shuddered as he heard the strange tongue, but he knew exactly what he had to do. As soon as the man's shape appeared out of the mist he flung himself down on him and smashed the butt of his rifle into the man's face, right on the point of his chin. There was a horrible, loud echoing sound of a breaking bone and the man went out like a light. He sank to the ground in a heap.

Armitage was amazed by his own success. He looked down at what he had done with great pride. Then, for several seconds, he stood over the man, gloating. He was an ugly little bugger, a real slit-eyed bastard. The man regained consciousness and became hysterical. Armitage showed no mercy or sympathy. Nor did he take any chances. He thrust the muzzle of his rifle into the man's backside and prodded him along the trench towards company headquarters. Soon, he saw CSM Rolf standing outside his bunker, shaving.

"Sir! Sergeant-Major, sir! Look what I've got, sir!"

"Well, what is it?"

"A prisoner, sir! A Chink!"

Ralf looked up in disbelief. Then he saw the state of the prisoner's face, his jaw already twice its normal size. Ralf was amazed that Armitage of all men could have done such an effective job.

"Christ, you've caught him a blood good one there, Armitage. Well done, lad! Well done!"

Ralf smiled proudly and even considered shaking hands with Armitage.

Then his eyes went from the prisoner's round face and slant eyes to his clothes. The bloke was in rags, any old thing, not a uniform. Ralf's expression hardened. He wasn't even armed. "What have you done with his Burp gun?" he demanded from Amitage.

Armitage didn't reply. He stood there looking puzzled. "Burp gun?"

"Yes! His bloody Burp gun!"

CSM Ralf looked at the man more carefully. Then he pointed a finger at the prisoner. "Who are you?"

"Cooky! Cooky! ... Pak Jay Bum ..."

Ralf turned on Armitage. "You stupid pillock! This is a bloody Gook--- a Korean porter. He's one of those who help out in the cookhouse. Now what the hell did you want to go and do that to him for? Just tell me, Armitage ... Why ..."

"Me ... I ... well, sir," stammered Armitage. "I heard him coming down the trench and he didn't answer the password so I clonked him one. As far as I knew he was a bloody Chink ... He bloody looks like one ... And bloody smells like one ..."

Ralf saw the humorous side of it and laughed. "All right, Armitage. You can't be blamed this time, I suppose. Let the bastard go. And you caught him a real nice one... I'll give you that."

Armitage released the man. He hurried off towards the cookhouse, muttering angrily, nursing his broken jaw.

CSM Ralf resumed shaving. At length he noticed in his small piece of mirror propped up against the trench wall that Armitage was still standing behind him. "Well, what the hell are you waiting for, Armitage? A bloody medal?"

Then there was the first time the company position was shelled by the Chinese. It took everyone by surprise and caught a large group of men in the open, relaxing on the reverse slope. Most of them were slow to realize what was happening. Some were so slow to react that they were well and truly caught. One shell landed right beside a man named Rawlins and he disappeared in a cloud of smoke and dust. Others peered from behind the cover they had found, convinced that Rawlins was bound to have bought it, their first proper casualty, even their first death. Most men thought there would be nothing left of him. However, when the smoke and dust cleared, Rawlins was still standing there, unharmed, except that apart from his boots, socks, and steel helmet he was stark bollock naked. His clothes were lying at his feet in tatters. Everyone stared at him in amazement.

All Rawlins said was: "The cheeky buggers!"

Able Company's first death had nothing to do with the Chinese. It was an accident, the type of thing they soon got used to. In quiet sectors of the front line it wasn't at all unusual for deaths and injuries caused by weapon accidents and bunker fires to be as many as those caused by enemy action.

The first man killed was Private Overton of One Platoon. He was a notable member of the platoon, a chirpy lad of nineteen who had joined the Rocks after serving with the Leicestershire Regiment during their last four months in the line. It was his habit to take the mickey out of his new Yorkshire comrades by imitating their strong accents. It was this which led to his demise. He had been on the second standing patrol of the night with Hallows and Charles. Everything had gone quietly until dawn approached and it was time to return to the platoon. Overton became happy at the thought of getting some sleep and started mimicking Hallows and Charles. They responded in a similar fashion with the result that some innocent horseplay ensued as they made their way up the minefield path. Hallows grabbed Overton's cap-comforter off his head and tossed it to one side. The wind caught it and blew it a yard or two into the minefield.

Since it was so close at hand, Overton ducked under the strand of barbed wire that marked the edge of the minefield. He stepped no more than two yards inside, but that was all that was needed. He stepped on a mine and detonated it. It blew his right leg off at the knee. Hallows immediately retrieved him from the minefield, ignoring the possibility of setting off another mine, and applied shell dressings to his stump which was spouting a fountain of blood. Charles dashed off for stretcher bearers. By the time they got Overton to the Company Aid Post (CAP), he had bled to death.

Gradually, Able Company took proper shape. They learnt from their mistakes and began to behave like a proper front line unit. In the increasingly long hours of darkness men became accustomed to just standing and waiting in their weapon pits and crouching in the narrow slit trenches while out on standing patrols. They went about their routine tasks automatically. Just when they were beginning to feel at home, and were even getting used to living with the rats, they were ordered to move on to the Nae Chon position, further to the east in the Commonwealth Division.

This, Lawrence told his men, was where Able Company's war would really start. This was where Able Company was going to make its mark, where they were going to make an indelible imprint on the map.

4

Captain Nobby Clark described their move to Nae Chon as a disaster, the most chaotic he had ever experienced, despite having gone from El Alamein to the Po; but he hastened to add that it was no one's fault. It was due to the weather. Despite a favorable forecast from Divisional Intelligence, the weather turned very nasty indeed. It was the start of the real Korean winter and as they very soon found out there are few winters more severe than Korean winters, especially when the wind sweeps down from the north east, across the distant wastelands of the Gobi Desert, Manchuria, and Siberia.

The wind turned north easterly very suddenly. They left Yong Dong in clear conditions, but by the time they had marched several miles along the MSR towards Nae Chon the temperature plunged, storm clouds gathered, and they were soon battling into the face of a blizzard, with small, hard pellets of snow stinging their faces.

They plodded along in silence, heads dipped into the wind, with their Parka overcoats covered in scales of snow. Inevitably, men began to grumble, cursing the army for the way they were being treated. "Why can't they lay on some transport?" demanded Charles.

"That would make it too bloody easy," Winston assured him. "But bloody Lawrence will be riding up in his jeep any minute now, just you wait and see."

By sheer chance Lawrence's jeep passed them a few seconds later. Armitage was at the wheel and when he saw his pals Charles and Hallows he slowed down and yelled out: "Keep going, you buggers! There's only another ten miles."

Angry insults were thrown back, but Armitage just laughed and accelerated away, splashing them with mud and slush.

Dissent in One Platoon soon became so vociferous that Blake went back along the length of the platoon. He made a pathetic attempt to raise their spirits. "Come on lads," he kept calling out. "Not much further ... Keep right on to the end of the road ..."

"Get lost, you silly bastard," Charles called back.

Blake didn't know how to respond to such insolence, but Corporal Smith spoke up for him.

"Mind your tongue, Charles, or you'll be on a charge."

"Good! It can't be soon enough for me, Corporal. Twenty-eight days inside would be just the job."

"Well just remember that Mr. Blake is in this, just the same as we are," said Smith. "So keep your insults for Lawrence, if you've got the guts."

"Aye, he's the one to blame," agreed Winston. "I've been saying that all along ..." And off he went on another long dissertation about their company commander.

Burrows listened to it all without saying a word. He didn't have enough energy to get involved. He was quite sure that unless things improved he'd just have to fall out by the wayside and blow the consequences.

They arrived at Nae Chon two hours late, so late that CSM Ralf made them double the last half mile, as though that was going to make some difference. The handover swiftly developed into a nightmare. Troops and vehicles were milling about all over the place, snow-covered figures darting about in all directions, everyone like animated snow-men, no one knowing who others were, or who was in command. There were orders, counter orders, protests, curses, swearing, and constant moans and accusations of incompetence, all being blown away into pointless sounds by the howling wind.

Able Company was in a reserve company position, about half a mile behind the front line. They occupied a hill which towered above all others and, despite being well back from the line, was clearly visible to the Chinese in normal conditions.

Once the Durham Light Infantry Company had vacated the hill, Blake led his men up the narrow and tortuous trench that snaked to the top. The bunkers and weapon pits they inherited offered no comforts. The DLI had (as was the custom) dismantled their improvised space-heaters and carted off their cooking equipment with them. Everyone was cold and wet, soaked through to their skin. Deep into the night, Blake, Miles and the section commanders were still wandering about, trying to sort things out.

When dawn came, the snow-laden wind was still howling across the hills, whipping viciously at bushes and trees, making everything that dared to stand in its way bend and stretch. The monstrous black clouds continued to be low and heavy, drifting from hilltop to hilltop. Snow drifts were already several feet deep. Breakfast was two hours late and stone cold and despite the efforts of NCOs and officers, the men just gave up. They retired to their new holes in the ground, piled on every available scrap of clothing they possessed, and then sat and waited for God's knows what in the driest spot they could find, regarding each other's faces in glum silence.

A few, fortunate enough to find some petrol, lit dangerous open fires and everyone rushed to huddle around them.

For seven days the weather dominated everything. Hostilities dried up. Not a shot was heard or a shell or mortar fired. This was the Korean winter of which they had heard so much. All water points were frozen up and washing and shaving in the morning necessitated the laborious task of thawing snow over one of the petrol fires; the meals which the company cook so valiantly prepared continued to become frozen as soon as they left the cookhouse, and tea, made from icicles which adorned bunkers, was the only thing that seemed capable of retaining heat for any time. It always tasted foul, which was hardly surprising, considering where it had originated.

Of course, some duties still had to be performed and gradually, through sheer necessity, things did improve. Men scrounged around for materials with which to construct more permanent fires, even though they were either feeble and insecure or vast and vicious--- in both cases liable to blow up at any moment. Most of these space-heaters consisted of a 42 gallon petrol drum resting on the roof of a bunker with tubing passing inside, terminating at an old ammunition box filled with earth. On the end of the tube would be a metal clip and by adjusting this they were able to let petrol drip into the earth. There, it was soaked up and when lit formed an effective fire, known to them all as space-heaters.

Men were far too cold to concern themselves with the dangers. Nor did they care that the fires gave off volumes of soot so that they became so engrained in it that they resembled nigger-minstrels. They just had to have warmth. Nothing else mattered.

As soon as the weather improved Lawrence got a grip of the situation. He could not bear to see men huddled up in their bunkers doing nothing all day. It was disastrous for both morale and hygiene and as soon as possible he introduced a digging program. He marked out the site of new trenches and specified others which had to be deepened and improved. The ground was so hard it made digging well-nigh impossible. Every time the point of a pick hit the ground a stinging jar sped up the shaft and tiny fragments of sharp, granite-like soil spat back in their faces, leaving only a minute impression on the ground. Before long, the pointed ends of the picks curled up or became flattened, and after several more swings the shaft would crack and split.

Lawrence and CSM Ralf, annoyed by the lack of any results, visited each digging party regularly and Lawrence took the platoon commanders to one side to tell them how to organize their men more efficiently. He claimed to have solved the problem of breaking pick shafts by cutting them off halfway, and although this did reduce the number of breakages, it also made digging virtually impossible.

At night, sentries had to be maintained, despite their reserve position. Blake cut them to a minimum and had just a pair of men roaming the position and being relieved every hour. These miserable sentries, wrapped up in every article of clothing they possessed, could be seen stamping their way round the platoon, ghost-like in their hooded, shapeless parkas, waving their arms about in an effort to keep warm.

Morale hit rock bottom. There seemed to be nothing to hope for. Conversations lagged and those who did talk rarely received anything but begrudging grunts in reply. Tempers became frayed and men began to fling each other glances of hate over the most trivial points. Practically everyone in the platoon became convinced that he was being victimized. Each thought that he was being made to do more work than others, and they made mental notes of what others did and then compared it with what they had done. Bitter complaints to platoon commanders became more frequent and seldom received convincing answers.

Then the worse thing of all happened: petrol became scarce. The precious liquid, which was virtually their only comfort, the only thing that made life bearable, was, for a time, unobtainable.

Eventually, of course, the weather improved. The wind dropped to a stiff breeze, and weak, insipid rays of sunshine edged through the clouds. Hostilities were resumed and by day plumes of smoke could be seen scattered along the length of the front line, denoting the site of artillery concentrations, while by night small-arms fire was again heard coming from the direction of Hill 355, where, just as before, the Chinese were persistently harassing the standing patrols and forward defenses.

5

Lawrence smiled as he jumped out of his jeep. Battalion Headquarters was just as he had visualized it, and a replica of all other Battalion HQs he had seen in Korea, perched on the top of a hill with the usual cluster of bunkers dug into the hillside. He started the climb enthusiastically but his short legs soon became tired. By the time he reached the CP he was fighting for breath.

The interior of the CP had a smooth and polished appearance which Lawrence had never seen in a bunker before; walls were draped with new blankets, two moderately regulated space-heaters made it comfortably warm, and touches such as ornaments and framed photographs of families gave the place a homely feel.

The Colonel was at the far end of the bunker talking round the stem of his pipe to the adjutant. Beside them, the IO (Intelligence Officer) was working on some maps. "I hope I'm not too early," said Lawrence.

The Colonel continued to listen to the adjutant before replying: "Not at all, Dick. The weather's improved, so it looks as though we might be able to do something. I hope you've told Bartram and Blake to come round as well?"

"They're coming round on foot, sir. I thought it would do them good to get a bit of exercise."

A few minutes later the blanket over the doorway was pulled aside and Blake and Bartram entered, closely followed by a major in the artillery and an officer from the tank regiment. They saluted and on the indication of the adjutant occupied chairs along one of the walls.

The IO supplied the Colonel with the map he had been doctoring and handed round aerial photographs. The Colonel removed his pipe from his mouth. "All right then, listen-in," he said. "You'll all realize that since moving into this position we have not been able to do much, but now things have improved we've got to get down to something. We've been in the country damn nearly two months and so far we haven't achieved anything. I've been in conference with the Brigadier and Major Lawrence, and we have decided that our objective is going to be to capture a prisoner."

He waved his pipe at Blake and Bartram and added: "We've selected these two youngsters as our spearheads and they will be doing the patrolling. Mr. Goodall will be held in reserve. So all we have to do now is decide on the best way of getting a Chink."

The IO unfolded a large wall map and the Colonel pointed at it with his pipe. "We have decided that the best place to concentrate on is Hill 128, or as we shall know it from now on--- the Boot, because that's what it looks like ... It is about four hundred yards across the valley from the right forward company and as far as we can tell it is manned by a Chinese company. We aim to rely on surprise, rather than send over a large raiding party. Now look at your aerial photos. The lie of the land is shown very clearly."

Blake saw a deep trench going around the top of the Boot, typical of all defenses in Korea. At the back of the hill was another trench, stretching down the rear slope to the Chinese living quarters. On both sides of the Boot were narrow re-entrants flanked by much larger hills.

There was a pause of reflective silence and then the Colonel tapped the table with his pipe. "Well, what do think?"

The adjutant responded immediately, as though the question was automatically directed at him. "As I see it the one thing we must do is steer clear of two positions on the Boot's flanks. They are bound to have patrols in the re-entrant between the hills just as we would. But naturally we can't be a hundred per cent sure of that until someone has gone and found out. First step is for Bartram and Blake to probe the enemy defenses with recce patrols. Let them find exactly how the Chinese dispose themselves and then act accordingly."

"Hear, hear," muttered Lawrence.

Blake regarded the adjutant with contempt. His tone had been so positive, so cock-sure, as though the task was perfectly straight forward, even a bit of a lark.

"Anyone other comments?" asked the Colonel.

Lawrence had plenty. This was going to be his 'do', not the adjutant's. "I agree that the first thing is to find out how the Chinese organize their defense, but even if those re-entrants are guarded we'll just have to get through them by stealth alone. After all, the only way we will ever take them by surprise is attacking from the rear. I'm sure that in most cases the Chinese are just like us. I'll guarantee that their sentries watch diligently to their front but would be completely flummoxed if we took them from behind. We'll just have to worm our way through. ..." He demonstrated the process of worming by stretching his arm out in front of him and flexing it from side to side several times.

For over an hour various ideas were discussed and eventually, after much repetition, the Colonel said: "Right, then. I can safely say that we are agreed that the first thing to do is to explore the front of the Boot and the two re-entrants. Then form our plans on the information gathered."

He rose to his feet and knocked his pipe out against the chair, regardless of the ash and clinker that went over the floor. "Mr. Bartram, as the senior, I think you'd better set the ball rolling. Stay on for a bit for a full briefing from the IO. I want you to go up the left-hand re-entrant. Blake, you will, of course, follow up the information he gets."

He picked up his maps and strode from the CP to the even greater luxury of his living bunker.

Lawrence, the adjutant, and the supporting arms officers stayed in the CP to expand on their personal ideas, and since Bartram remained behind to be briefed, Blake walked back over the hills to Able Company alone. He wandered along slowly, thinking of what had just been said. It was not the actual patrols that worried him, but the smugness with which the field officers had discussed them, as though it would be no more than a trip down to the local newsagent on a summer's evening.

As he reached the small collection of bunkers splayed out around the base of One Platoon's hill, he saw the Able Company Medic, Tompkin, lingering in the doorway of the CAP (Company Aid Post). They exchanged salutes. Blake tried to think of something suitable to say. He liked to show an interest in the men; he knew from his own days as a private soldier that if an officer spoke freely with his men he was considered good at his job. "Nobody wounded yet?"

"No, sir. Not a thing. Yong Dong all over again."

"You sound disappointed."

"Not disappointed, sir. Just worried. Unless someone hurries up and gets wounded I will have forgotten all I ever knew."

"Never mind, patrols start in a big way to-night."

"Looking forward to them, sir?"

"I wouldn't say that, exactly. But they've got to be done, I suppose."

He walked on, positive that he had made a favorable impression, and that Tompkin was saying to himself, 'Blake's okay'.

That night Bartram did his patrol as planned. He took Sergeant Sykes with him. It took them an hour to cross the valley, a further hour to explore the front of the Boot, and then two hours to investigate the western re-entrant and return--- four exhausting hours of maximum concentration. Even Bartram, who had previously been keen to do as many patrols as possible, soon discovered that it was no joking matter to spend most of his time crawling around on his stomach.

Blake woke early and after carrying out several routine inspections in his platoon he went across to Bartram for a first-hand account of what had happened. Bartram was sitting on a stool in his CP cleaning his Sten, his batman was waiting for a can of water to boil on one of the few well-constructed space-heaters in the company. Blake looked about for something to sit on and eventually found an ammunition box.

"Come to see if I'm still here?" laughed Bartram.

"That's the general idea," smiled Blake. "Anything exciting happen?"

Bartram shrugged his shoulders. "The re-entrant appeared to be empty. But I heard a lot of movement to the right of the re-entrant in front of the Boot, both on our way out there and coming back. I reckon the Chinese have two or three pairs of men patrolling the front of the Boot. But I wouldn't be too definite."

"And the re-entrant itself?"

"Not a thing. It was perfectly straight sailing. The noise we heard in the front of the Boot was the most significant."

"What's the going like out there?" persisted Blake.

"Sheer hell," Bartram replied. Then he went on to explain how the entire valley was covered by elephant grass that had been blown flat by the wind and then frozen so stiff that it formed a carpet over which one could not help but make a considerable noise. He then stumbled over several adjectives endeavoring to describe the coldness of the stream they had been forced to wade through, the suspense and fear when exploring the re-entrant, and the relief on returning to their own lines. "You heard anything about your patrol to-night?"

"The other re-entrant as per the original idea." Blake looked at his watch. "I may as well go and see old Lawrence about it now. That is if he isn't asleep or drunk again."

"Be fair," chuckled Bartram. "He's only been drunk once. You're far too critical of him. He's only doing his job, you know."

Blake smiled. "Yeah, maybe. I'd better go and see the old devil, anyhow. See you to-morrow …" Then he laughed nervously and added, "I hope. . . ."

He went round to the company CP. Lawrence was sharpening one of his many china graph pencils and Cross was crouching at his feet, picking up the small chips of wood as they fell to the floor.

"Morning, Blake," said Lawrence cheerfully. The past week or two had driven him crazy with impatience, but now he was planning with zest. He considered that Bartram had made an excellent start. If all the patrols went like that they would soon have a prisoner. He also had a good idea about a fresh digging program. He beamed amiably at Blake. "We're going to build an officers' mess, Blake. What do you think of that?"

Blake was puzzled. If the 'we' meant the officers digging their own mess it would be an impossible task, and if it meant the ORs digging it for them, Blake knew that it would only lead to discontent and trouble. "Who is the 'we', sir?"

"The men of course. Officers don't dig."

Blake sat down at the table opposite Lawrence. "Really, I never knew that. At Eaton Hall we never stopped digging. But anyhow, whoever does the digging I can't say I think much of the idea. There are a lot of bunkers that need rebuilding. In fact all the bunkers in my platoon ought to be moved completely. They are in full view of the enemy, even if they are a long way off."

Lawrence flicked another chip off the pencil onto the floor for Cross to clear up. He regarded Blake critically. He was far too ready to speak his mind, always so damned self-righteous. He just thanked God he never had to listen to any of his father's sermons. Blake seemed incapable of understanding that if officers were to maintain their position of authority and respect, they needed suitable accommodation. They needed somewhere to relax among themselves, somewhere they could enjoy a few drinks and entertain officers from other companies. Even from other regiments. Above all, somewhere that wasn't already infested by rats.

Lawrence felt his good mood slipping away. "There's another bit down there, Cross. Pick it up, man." He looked back at Blake. "Well, we're going build one, regardless of what you think."

"No doubt, sir. Your decision... Not mine."

Blake wondered just how much longer he and Lawrence would be able to put up with each other. As far as Blake could see, there was hardly a man in the company who liked or respected Lawrence and on several occasions he'd committed the unpardonable crime of listening to men criticizing him without bothering to reprimand them. He could just imagine the words which would flow when they were armed with picks and shovels and told to build a rat-proof officers' mess so that they could entertain senior officers from other regiments. .

"You've been to see Bartram, I suppose," said Lawrence, "and now you are eager to hear about your patrol."

"Yes, sir." He deliberately didn't elaborate his reply.

Lawrence patted all his pockets as he looked for a cigarette that he knew was not there. "Someone give me a cigarette," he commanded. Cross nodded sternly at Williamson, indicating that it was his turn. Then Lawrence started to explain to his subaltern that it was his task to explore the right-hand re-entrant and the whole frontage of the Boot in an endeavor to find out if Bartram's information about the suspected patrols in front of the Boot had any foundation. Together they went over the various maps and aerial photographs. Eventually, Lawrence was satisfied that Blake knew all the code names, the details of the supporting fire program, call signs, the route, and dismissed him.

When he reached the bottom of his platoon hill Blake saw that Tompkin was again standing around the CAP with nothing to do. They exchanged their usual salutes and went through more casual remarks.. Eventually, Blake mentioned the company digging program. "I don't suppose you've heard the latest. We're going to build an officers' mess."

"What the hell do the officers want a mess for, sir?"

"Search me."

"With respect, sir, that fellow is bonkers. I'll bet ...."

Both of them ducked instinctively as shells passed overhead and landed halfway up the slopes of One Platoon. At the top of the hill men were working on Lawrence's digging program in a half-hearted manner. It was activity the Chinese could see and the reason for the shelling. Then there were more penetrating screams and additional shells landed on the very top of the hill. Men panicked. They threw their tools away and ran for cover. Some flattened themselves on the ground and others made a dash for the cover of their bunkers.

The shells continued to land for several minutes. During a lull, Burrows appeared out of the clouds of dust that had been thrown up. He was sprinting down the hill.

"Work at last," said Tompkin.

Blake watched Burrows approach. His face was pale and grim. Blake became certain someone had been killed. "I'll get my kit," said Tompkin.

Blake's stomach felt empty. This was the kind of crisis for which he was not suited. When it came to blood, raw flesh and broken limbs he was squeamish, faint-hearted and feeble. "It's Lowe, sir," yelled Burrows as he got near. "He got it in the stomach. His guts are completely ripped out. There's blood all over the place."

Guts ripped out! Blake felt faint. If there was one thing he'd hoped he would never see it was a man with his guts hanging out. What did you do with them? Stuff them back in?

They ran back up the hill as fast as the gradient and slippery surface would allow. Burrows led the way into the bunker where Lowe had been dragged. There was an unexpected air of calmness in the bunker and none of the three men at his side was in the least agitated. Lowe was lying there with his front shirt-tail hanging out, wet with bright blood. Apart from that he appeared as fat and healthy as ever.

Miles was one of the men who had hurried to the bunker to give aid and he was now sitting on a sandbag that had been blown from the wall, reading what had once been a glossy magazine.

Blake was mystified. "What's happening then? What's going on?"

Miles waved his magazine at Burrows, as if to indicate that it was his fault. Then he said to Lowe: "Show Mr. Blake what's up."

Lowe lifted the tail of his shirt and revealed a bulging stomach which had a trickle of blood flowing from a small cut just above his navel. Lowe wiped the blood away with his shirt and pointed to a small lump under the initial layer of fat. Blake fingered it cautiously and felt the clear outline of the offending piece of shrapnel. He turned on Burrows. "You told me his guts were ripped out. ..."

"It's all right, sir," said Miles. "I've booked him on a charge for causing alarm and despondency."

Half an hour later, when the sun had vanished behind some clouds and the shelling had stopped, Blake and Miles returned to their CP.   "We will have to get something done about this position, sir," said Miles.   "As soon as we've finished Lawrence's digging program, we'll have to start one of our own, building some new bunkers out of sight of the Chinese.   The next time they shell us someone probably will get their guts ripped out."

Blake laughed bitterly.   "When we've finished this present digging job we start building an officers' mess."

Miles eyed him curiously.   "An officers' mess!"

6

The sun cast a glow of red on the thin clouds above the horizon and it was soon night; there was no moon, but the stars and the flares from the Little Nori area provided reasonable visibility.   As Blake and Corporal Smith cleared the top of the trench in the forward company, together with the three men of the Charlie Company standing patrol, they could see the distinctive, ugly shape of the Boot ahead of them, looking, amid the snow-covered valleys that surrounded it, like an ink stain on a white table-cloth.

The path leading down to the valley had a definite sheen and turned out to be a long sliver of ice. They squatted down so that their buttocks were only a few inches from the ground and slid down it noiselessly, like children on a newly found slide.   Occasionally they had to stand to negotiate the zigzags. After ten minutes they reached the bottom of the hill.   The Charlie Company standing patrol sank into their trenches, and Blake and Smith carried on, into the heart of no man's land.   Apart from their 88-set they were on their own. Now, it was all down to stealth, cunning, patience and, above all, concentration.

Smith reported back on the 88-set to Lawrence that they were about start the patrol, and Blake turned his attention to the ground that lay ahead of them. The paddies were flat, and sparkling slightly with the white frost that covered the flattened grass.   The left edge of the Boot was plainly visible and all he had to do was to head straight for it.

Progress was slow and unavoidably loud.   Blake went cautiously and after every twenty or thirty yards he sank to the ground, head held erect, sniffing the air like a timid animal, straining for signs of any Chinese.

The grass became denser and they reduced their speed accordingly. By the time they reached the stream they were going only a few paces at a time before sinking to the ground to listen again, certain that they must have been heard crashing along.

At the stream they paused for ten minutes rest. The ice looked thick and firm, and although they could hear water swirling beneath it, Blake tried to walk across while Smith covered him from the home bank. His fourteen stone proved too much for the ice. It split then parted, and he went full length into the water. For a moment its coldness paralyzed him and he lay on the bed of the stream like a lifeless brick. Then he floundered and splashed his way to the far bank, completely indifferent to the noise he made.

When the noise of the disturbed water had subsided Smith waded through the gap that had been created in the ice and for a further ten minutes they sat close together on the opposite bank, searching for warmth.

Blake looked at his watch; it was already after ten. He felt the situation slipping out of his control. "We'll be all night at this rate," he whispered. "We'll have to go faster or we'll never be back by daylight."

"It's the grass that is holding us up ..."

"Don't whisper so bloody loudly ..."

"Once we're on the track in front of the Boot things will be much easier, sir."

Blake had already considered this. Originally he had intended to keep away from the track for fear of an ambush, but now, as he looked at his watch again, he decided they would just have to take the risk.

The surface of the track was beautifully hard and solid; nothing crackled beneath their feet as they advanced silently, crouching low. Soon, they reached the area where Bartram had heard movement. They slowed down to only a few feet every minute, putting their weight even more on the outside of their feet in an effort to maintain supreme silence. This was their greatest danger spot: it would be only a matter of seconds before they found out whether or not there was anyone there; only a few seconds before they discovered if they were being watched by slant eyes.

The seconds passed and there was no one there. They were able to continue along the track until they reached the re-entrant in which they had to complete their recce.

It was little more than a long gully stretching about three hundred yards into the Chinese lines. They left the track and crashed through elephant grass again, walking briskly, realizing the futility of trying to keep quiet. First they went up one side, probing several subsidiary re-entrants, and then the other side, until after two hours their explorations were completed. They sank into the frozen grass at the bottom of the valley and relaxed. After the nervous strain they let their minds go blank. Eventually Smith whispered a message over the wireless to Able Company and they started on their return journey.

They were soon on the hard surface of the track again: their task was as good as complete and they were elated, filled by a desire to run back as fast as they could to their own lines. Blake kept reminding himself to concentrate, to take it steadily, to take things a step at a time. Before long they were again approaching the spot where Bartram had heard movement the previous night. Blake slowed right down. Then he stopped and motioned Smith to do likewise.

He had heard something move directly in front of them. He whispered to Smith, asking if he had heard anything. The corporal shook his head. They moved on again. Five yards further on he knew he had heard something. A new batch of flares went up from Little Nori. In their light he saw two figures approaching, both crouching, both looking to each side in turn.

Blake and Smith slithered into the ditch alongside the track. They were well concealed, braced now for a clash with the enemy. Blake peered cautiously out of the ditch. The Chinese were still walking slowly and steadily towards them. Soon, they were no more than ten yards away. Blake could see every detail about them except for their facial expressions: he saw their small peaked caps pulled well down over their faces to protect them from the wind; their short, stubby legs partially covered by long rubber boots; and their well-gloved hands clutching Burp guns.

He heard a metallic click as Smith released his safety catch. Blake followed suit. They raised their Stens to their shoulders and although unable to see the enemy through the sights they covered them with rough alignment. They had the upper hand; they were undetected and ready for action--- ready to kill at a moment's notice. Now, the Chinese were clearly in their sights, only yards away, but still they did not fire. As a recce patrol their orders were to fire only when absolute necessity, when unavoidable.

Blake swallowed nervously as they drew even closer. He gave an involuntary gasp of fear as they stopped directly above them. The two men started to whisper to each other. One of them gave a low chuckle, then they tuned to their right and sat on boulders on the opposite side of the track. They were ideal targets. More flares went up from Little Nori and the enemies' quilted uniforms were shown up in minute detail. Blake was on the verge of firing. It would be so simple, but something stopped him. He repeated in his mind that they were a recce patrol that had to return with its information without incidents.

Then he thought of the advantages of killing them; information from their pockets, identification of their unit, a morale booster for the battalion, and it would put Able Company well and truly on the map. Yet it wasn't that simple. Supposing their Stens had stoppages? They had got wet while crossing the stream so the chances were that they would be frozen up. They would probably just make loud scraping noises, and then they would end up by being shot instead of doing the shooting. He decided to wait.

Time went by: five minutes, ten, fifteen, twenty minutes . . . and still the Chinamen showed no signs of moving. They smoked a couple of cigarettes each.

Blake glanced out of the corner of his eye at Smith. The corporal was shivering convulsively. His clothes were covered by a layer of ice. The grenades attached to his belt were also covered in ice. The pins were no doubt stuck fast. There was even a pear-shaped icicle hanging from the end of his Sten barrel.

Blake's concentration began to falter. He found himself wondering what would be going on in their lines. He could imagine Lawrence cursing them for taking so long, striding up and down the bunker with a gin and lime in one hand and a beer in other, giving a fierce tirade about their incompetence as patrollers; he could almost hear the grunts of Taylor as he sat over his 88-set; he thought of the lone sentry in his platoon area striding along the hill beating his arms about his body; he saw Armitage sleeping in the bunker at the foot of the forward company, waiting to drive them back to the reserve company as soon as they returned.

They were all over there, behind the comparative safety of the forward trenches, laughing, sleeping, drinking, eating, talking, and all of them waiting; and there he was with the enemy sitting right in front of him and he had not got the guts to shoot them!

For the umpteenth time he assured himself that it wasn't a matter of a lack of guts. He would shoot them if he had to, but they could not afford to take risks. Yet it was hardly a risk. It was a dead certainty... Oh, God! he thought. Why didn't the bastards just bugger off.

Another ten minutes elapsed. Then, after looking carefully about them, the enemy rose to their feet and walked off in the direction from which they had originally appeared. Blake relaxed, never so thankful to be able to move his aching limbs.

Smith contacted Lawrence on the 88-set and then they struck out across the valley for their own lines, not daring to keep to the track in case the enemy reversed the position on them. They crossed the stream again, but they were now so cold that the water no longer held any terrors for them. On the home side of the stream Blake soon located the re-entrant through which they had to return; they passed through a clump of stunted trees, over the last paddy field, and then started to talk loudly so that the standing patrol had good warning of their approach.   They were challenged and they answered: it was all over.

Within half an hour Armitage had driven them back to Able Company.   As they entered the CP all other interests were dropped. "We were beginning to wonder if you were ever coming back," said Lawrence, peeping joyfully over the papers and maps that covered his desk.

Blake flopped into a chair and looked at his watch: it was 0430 hours. Suddenly he felt sick.   He rubbed his hands over the crusty blacking that covered his face and wet his cracked lips.   Then pulling off his cap comforter, he scratched vigorously at his scalp.   He glanced across at Smith and they exchanged lame but happy smiles.   He was certainly glad he'd selected Smith as his partner.

Lawrence's debriefing took an hour.   He insisted on having every little detail so that he could give the Colonel a comprehensive report by breakfast time. When he at last finished questioning them it was daylight.   They returned to One Platoon but instead of going straight to their bunks Blake led the way down the reverse slope to a spot where they tested weapons.

When they squeezed the triggers of the Stens nothing happened.   Both automatics were frozen solid, quite useless.

7

It was Winston who started grumbling.

He was standing in a shallow and crudely dug hole, with a pick resting between his feet.   He was the center of a group of men in similar postures. To one side of the hole was a collection of pickaxes and shovels with broken handles, even ones which had been sawn off halfway on Lawrence's orders. It was their third successive day of digging on the officers' mess and they were not taking to it kindly.   They were wrapped up in every scrap of clothing they possessed and despite the presence of Corporal Hale the only time they did a stroke of work was when they became really cold.   Then it wasn't simply an attempt to get warm, like flapping their arms or stamping their feet.

Winston wandered over to a large pile of sandbags and held one open as Burrows prepared to empty chippings into it.   This operation completed, he handed the sandbag to O'Hara, who, by virtue of his dominating character, had secured the easiest job of tying the sandbags up.

"I'd like to know when we are going to do something besides dig," said Winston. "It's never anything else besides dig, dig, dig, and more bloody digging. Anyone would think that we are bloody laborers instead fully trained bloody soldiers. If they've got nothing better for us to do than dig bloody holes in the bloody ground for entertainment of the bloody officers we might just as well bloody well pack up and go home and leave the bloody Gooks to do it. It's about their bloody level."

Winston was essentially a one-adjective man.

"Get on with some work," said Hale, without any conviction. He knew that whatever he said, whatever exhortations he made, they wouldn't take any notice. Nor did he give a damn. They all knew that up to a certain point he was a soft touch. Equally, they knew that when the occasion arose, he was not an NCO to mess around with. They always knew by the tone of his voice when that moment had arrived. Winston abandoned the sandbag. "It's all right for you to stand there with your hands in your pockets, Corporal, but just try making an impression on this bloody concrete."

Hale was hardly aware of what Winston was saying, but he responded automatically. He had a stock reply to anything Winston said: "Shut your moaning hole." This time he added a rider: "You're always telling us how you were taught to dig down the mines ... About the only thing you're any good for is swaggering round in your Teddy Boy suit. If they taught you to dig down the mines I can only say they made a bloody poor job of it."

"They taught me all right, but what you don't seem to realize is that there is digging and bloody digging. And down the mines we weren't given just a quid a week. We were paid properly." Winston looked severely at Hale. "And those that stood around with their hands in their pockets didn't get so much as those that did the bloody work."

There was a ruminating silence as they all considered this. Then Charles decided he was so cold he might just as well try to warm himself with physical exertion. He took hold of his pickaxe, raised it above his head, and then smashed it against the hard ground. It brought no results, simply made him wring his hands in pain. It convinced him against further attempts at digging. "That's my lot," he said with resignation. "Damned if I'm going to do any more digging! They'll have us digging a brothel next, despite the fact that there aren't any whores to go in it. Last thing we dug was a trench. It was six foot deep, a hundred yards long, and two bloody miles from the Chinese lines. We couldn't have wasted our time more completely if we'd tried.'

"Right! Come on! Get on with some work!" said Hale.

Once again they ignored him.

"That's the trouble with the army," resumed Winston. "They're so bloody thick up top. They spend all their time telling everyone how bloody good they were in the past and never get round to admitting how piss poor they are in the present. I'll give you a perfect example ..."

"Get on with some work, Winston!"

At last there was urgency in Hale's voice. They noticed it immediately. Lawrence was approaching, on one of his inspections of the officers' mess.

"That's the last time I'm warning you," added Hale, using the NCOs code for the approach of an officer.

Lawrence was now close at hand. Winston waited until Lawrence was standing above him, staring down into the shallow hole. He grasped his pickaxe, swung it over his head with the effortless ease of an expert digger, and then crashed it against the ground. The handle of the pick splintered like a matchstick. Winston looked up, stared straight into the eyes of Lawrence, and grinned insolently.

"Oh, hello, sir! Nice to see you again. Come to see how we're getting on with your mess? You're just in time to see our last pickaxe go up the spout. Pity about that, but bugger all we can do if the army can't even supply us with decent pick handles."

"Naafi break," shouted Hale. "Back here when some new picks arrive."

They wandered off, leaving Lawrence staring down into the shallow hole, well aware that they'd made no progress at all.

8

That night Bartram did his second recce patrol. His objective was to find out whether the two men roaming about in front of the Boot were a permanent feature of the Chinese defenses. Really, it was more a matter of confirmation than anything else. After four hours of patient and skillful crawling he discovered that they were. He saw the two men twice. First stalking about a paddy field and then sitting on the edge of the track, just as Blake had described.

Lawrence was delighted with the findings. Now he knew for sure and had something solid to go on: he could plan with definite knowledge of the enemy's tactics. He spent the morning in consultation with the Colonel and the adjutant. He had a plan in his mind and although the details were not yet complete he had developed it sufficiently to know that it would be a really good one. Above all, it was going to be perfectly simple. All he needed was one more patrol.

The Colonel and the adjutant were not easy to convince. They were all against rushing things, but eventually Lawrence convinced them to go along with his ideas.

After lunch Blake was summoned to the company CP. Lawrence, who visualized a prisoner being captured and Able Company on the map within a week, was in an uncommonly good mood. "Ah, Blake," he exclaimed as the subaltern entered. "There you are. All set for another patrol?"

"Yes, sir, I don't see why not. How did it go last night?"

"Excellent! It could not have been better. Proved completely what I said to the Colonel the other day. Those two men were at the bottom of the Boot just as you said. Things are going really well, but I want one more patrol out of you and then you and Bartram can go and get the prisoner. Have a drink?"

"No, thanks, sir."

"Really! Oh well ... Yes, I'm hoping to see a prisoner here by Christmas-time. Make a good Christmas present, eh, Blake?" This appealed to Lawrence's sense of humor and he guffawed. "Only ten more shopping days to Christmas. Make a good present, don't you think?"

"Yes, sir. Very nice. But what am I supposed to be, Father Christmas?"

Lawrence gave another loud laugh, missing Blake's sarcasm. He was delighted that his young subaltern was at last entering into the spirit of things. "Getting pretty exciting, isn't it, Blake ..." They sat in silence for a time, Lawrence taking periodical sips at his gin. Eventually, he pulled out the usual collection of maps and photographs and told Blake that the object of his patrol was to go straight up the front of the Boot and into the Chinese main trench that circled the hilltop. He was to find out how wide and deep it was and whether or not there were any telephone wires in it or adjacent to it.

Blake realized at once that this was a far more difficult task than his previous one, and not half so easy as Lawrence's tone suggested. "How about getting past the two men at the bottom of the Boot, sir?"

"You'll just have to go carefully. But it can be done all right. I advise you to go further over to the left, and go into the mouth of the re-entrant and then up the Boot. I'm not pretending that it is an easy patrol, Blake ... Anyhow, what I suggest is that you take eight other men with you and drop six of them off in the mouth of the re-entrant as a firm base. Then, if need be, you can deal okay with the Chinese who patrol in front of the Boot. But don't go looking for trouble. And make sure you take a reliable man up the hill with you. Sergeant-Major Ralf suggests Charles …"

"Charles? Good God, no, sir! He's the last bloke I'd ever take. I'll stick with Corporal Smith. He's the best we've got. Or failing him, O'Hara,"

"As you like."

Blake watched Cross as he filled the major's glass. "Perhaps I should take a bigger patrol, sir? Why not sixteen?"

"Sixteen men would be like taking a herd of elephants. Eight men will be quite sufficient. A Bren group at the front … Another at the back … And you and the man on the recce with you in the middle."

"I've got one query about the exact route …"

Lawrence sat back and laughed. "All right, all right, my boy! Just wait until I've finished my drink and we'll go through it in detail. Never seen you so keen." He patted his pockets in turn, searching for a cigarette. "Someone give me a fag for God's sake."

Again, it was Cross's turn.

9

Blake had forebodings about the patrol. He didn't really see the need of a firm base. They hadn't had one before, so why now? What amazed him was that no one shared his concern. Lawrence took it for granted that they could keep slipping past the Chinese ad infinitum and even the men Blake detailed for the patrol took it calmly. Barnes and Collins, going on their first patrol as point-men with Hale, didn't turn a hair. In fact, they were quite keen to become involved.

The only complication came with Charles. Having turned down Lawrence's suggestion that Charles should be his partner on the recce, Blake was then confronted by Miles insisting that he should go as part of the firm base. "But he's useless," protested Blake. "He's as windy as hell."

"That's beside the point, sir. It's this business back in Minden with CSM Ralf's daughter …"

"Well I'm damned if I'm going to have Ralf tell me who to take on patrol because of his daughter. What happened in Minden is a purely private matter. I'll take the best men we've got."

"It's not as easy as that, sir. Pressure is being brought to bear."

"On who?"

"On me, sir. I'm expected to persuade you to take Charles. And when Sergeant-Major Ralf tells a sergeant like me what to do … Well, you do it … You know how it is, sir …"

"No, I don't. How is it?"

Miles sighed wearily.

Blake had no desire to fall out with Sergeant Miles, but he was damned if he was going to let this silly nonsense escalate. "All right," he said, "this time. But that's the end of it. Any more of this Minden business and I'll take the mater up with Major Lawrence. Understood?"

To try to make things look more normal, Blake included Hallows as well: a logical move, two mates together, and Hallows was anyhow the aggressive type who would be a good man to have around if things turned nasty.

It was a crisp, moonlight night, ideal for a patrol. The subdued coughing of 6o mm. mortars awoke the night as Blake led his patrol up the forward company hill, and they listened to the faint whine of the missiles as they vanished into the distance and exploded. Then the night went back to sleep and all was motionless and calm, as though the cold had once more called half-time.

The patrol plodded along the trenches and after joining up with the Charlie Company standing patrol they slid and slipped down the icy path through the minefield gap. Once again they were on their own. Blake halted the patrol and sorted them out into their respective positions. He told them to keep well spread out, wished them luck, and then watched as Hale, Barnes and Collins, the point section, moved forward on the first bound of the patrol.

As they started on their second bound he turned his mind to the ground ahead of them, their new route. He had studied the valley from the forward company OP and on the air photographs and could remember the pattern of the bunds right up to the last fifty yards before venturing up the side of the Boot to the main lateral trench.

Each time the main body of the patrol closed up on Hale's section, Blake went forward to the corporal and indicated the end of the next bound, and then watched him stalk over the ground like an experienced hunter, followed by Collins and Barnes, two awkward novices who crashed through every bit of vegetation that lay in their path.

They progressed steadily, making good time. They crossed the stream at its narrowest point and this time the ice held. Then they entered the area

Blake wasn't so sure about, well to the left of the route of his previous patrol. They completed two more bounds: shorter ones. He didn't intend to take any chances.

At the back of the patrol O'Hara was being just as vigilant. To his amazement he heard rustling noises in some bushes to their right. He stopped, remained dead still, and allowed the patrol to draw away from him. He crouched down and stared at the bushes but the only noise he heard was the patrol moving forward. He relaxed, smiled to himself, and started to move off. Then he froze completely. Unless he was quite mad, unless his imagination had gone haywire, there were two Chinese looking over the bush, watching him. He rubbed his eyes, not believing what he saw, knowing how the cold could affect a man's mind; but they were still there. He could even see the dark outline of their Burp guns, both leveled in his direction. He hesitated, experiencing fear he never knew existed; the patrol was already some distance ahead of him and he was in danger of being isolated, and once that happened he knew that he would be an easy catch.

He decided to fight it out with them. Wait a few seconds, bring the Bren up to his hip slowly, and then spray the bush with a whole magazine. He brought the Bren up slowly, felt for the trigger....

Bugger! He had forgotten to cock the bloody thing! He felt for the cocking-piece but it seemed to be jammed. In his anger he felt utterly confused. He decided to catch up with the rest of the patrol. He sprang up and dashed off towards them, sprinting recklessly, making an abominable noise, expecting to hear Burp guns and then feel the stabbing sensations of bullets hitting his back.

Neither happened, however, and he reached the patrol safely. Blake moved towards him, hissing at him to keep quiet, indescribably furious. "What the bloody hell's the matter with you, O'Hara? Are you mad?"

"I've just seen a couple of them, sir. They saw us go by. They were behind some bushes."

"Keep quiet, blast you, man! Are you sure you saw them?"

"Positive."

Blake paused. What now? He would have to go back to make sure. He couldn't just take O'Hara's word for it. It would men facing the possibility of walking straight into trouble. His stomach turned in fear. This was the very thing he imagined happening, the very thing he had dreaded.

He went back with O'Hara and they crouched and listened. O'Hara was right. He could hear the Chinese hurrying away, back towards their hill code-named Eden, putting the accent on speed and not attempting to conceal their retreat. Two men, just the same the other patrols had seen. Too well briefed to content themselves with a small kill, they would hurry back to their main defenses and warn them of the patrol's approach. In a few minutes every man on the Boot and Eden would be standing-to, waiting for them. God, what a prospect!

Blake returned to the patrol and lay there pondering over their next move. He knew that if they continued with the patrol they were bound to clash with the enemy. It would be simple for the Chinese to ambush them in the mouth of the re-entrant. Yet how could they not go on? They had a task to fulfill. The fact that he thought they might bump the enemy was irrelevant; they had weapons with which to shoot the enemy so there no reason why they should not continue. That's how Lawrence would see it, anyhow.

He was still debating his next move when loud shouting came from the base of Eden. The Chinese made no attempt to keep quiet, and the voices were shortly replaced by the noise of them hurrying towards Blake's patrol: a lot of men by the sound of it.

Blake decided it was best to wait for them. They had a good position behind a bund. If their exact position had not been noted properly, and the Chinese came forward looking for them, they would have the advantage. So they waited. Half an hour passed and then an hour and all remained perfectly quiet. After the noise the enemy had made getting themselves organized, the patrol heard nothing of them. He wondered what the hell had happened to them. Blake began to worry about the time. Unless they did something soon they would never be able to complete the patrol by daybreak.

Another ten minutes passed. His men were becoming restless and he knew he had to do something positive, and he certainly couldn't return to Lawrence and the Colonel and tell them that he had aborted because he thought they might bump into the enemy. He felt like asking every man on the patrol what they would do. He craved support, sensible advice, yet he could feel their eyes boring into him demanding to know what he was going to do about it. He knew that they would have to continue, despite the danger of the Chinese waiting for them. It was madness to go on, but what other alternative was there?

"Keep going, but take it easy," he whispered to Hale.

The point section edged forward. They completed another bound and as Blake closed up on Hale again he was comforted to hear the corporal say: "I think we must have given them the slip, sir."

He peered into Hale's face and nodded. "Okay. Next one. Not quite so long this time."

They started off, heading diagonally across the paddy field. It was a long one that disappeared into the darkness. Just before they reached the end of it, the point section slid to the ground and waited. As Blake closed up to them he saw a bund directly to their front. Then he spotted another one, running at right angles to it. He told Hale to move forward, to use the facing bund as cover.

When Hale, Barnes and Collins were within about fifteen yards of it, it suddenly bristled with activity. Blake could hear men moving rapidly towards the bund on the right in an effort to outflank them. The noise made their intentions unmistakable. They had been well and truly ambushed. Blake flung himself to the ground and heard those behind him do the same.

They expected Hale to open fire, but Hale just lay there, inexplicably waiting to be outflanked. The rear half of the patrol was badly placed, only being able to fire at the enemy over the heads of Hale's section, but Blake realized that something had to be done. The only way he could gain the initiative was to open fire first. He pulled a grenade off his belt, yanked the pin out, and threw it. He saw it curling away in the air; saw it clear the bund and then heard it explode.

Then everything seemed to happen at once. O'Hara leapt forward, literally pulling Charles with him, to adopt a better fire position; the three men of the leading section all fired directly at the Chinese they could see plainly advancing towards the right flank; and a row of angry flashes from Burp guns stretched out towards Blake. He pressed his head against the ground and heard bullets cracking only inches over his head, while others bit the ground between him and Taylor and ricocheted off with the most terrifying noises, sending up spouts of sharp earth. Everywhere there was smoke, noise, the smell of cordite, and chaos. Shouting and cursing never stopped. They were all fighting desperately for their lives. As another burst of bullets landed beside Blake he concentrated on throwing grenades, knowing that these would get behind the enemy, nullify the cover of their bunds, and help to confuse them. He wrenched the gloves off his hands to make it easier to pull the pins out, and at the same he yelled: "Grenades! Grenades! Throw grenades!"

In the light of battle he could see that the two bunds ahead of them were bristling with men. There were at least fifty or sixty of them making a disastrous outcome inevitable.

Barnes had seen the enemy as soon as he went to ground, but he didn't fire at them, not because he was waiting for orders, but simply because to his right there was a large gap in the bund and he realized that as soon as the Chinese reached that gap they would be exposed, and at his mercy. He lined his Sten up to cover the gap and waited. No sooner had Blake thrown his grenade than they appeared and he gave them a long burst. He felt power and exhilaration as his weapon vibrated in his hands, and he grinned with satisfaction as the Chinese scurried back under cover, leaving several men lying there. Then, as others tried dashing across the gap in small groups, he let them have a series of short bursts. Then he exhausted his second magazine and as he struggled to release another from one of his pouches, he looked up and saw a series of flashes coming from behind the bund.

He slotted in his new magazine but then he slumped forward. Everything came to a sudden stand-still for Barnes. He was dead, shot straight through the head. One second he was alive, in command of the situation, and the next stone dead, not knowing a thing about it.

In contrast Collins had a lingering death, the sort that men fear most of all. He made the fatal mistake of adopting a kneeling position to enhance his aim and the first of the Chinese bullets tore straight through his flesh. He was shot in the groin. At first he felt no pain. He only realized he'd been hit because he was jerked on to his back. It was as if someone had caught him off balance and pushed him back. Then he realized he had been hit and he started to scream. He shook with terror, praying that it was only a Blighty touch, but he was never in any real doubt that he was doomed. Blood was flowing down his legs. Instinctively his hands went to explore the damage. His clothing was shredded and his nerves suddenly recovered and pain seared up from his testicles to engulf his entire body. He lived only a short time, long enough to curse his fate and scream out in useless protest.

A few yards away from Collins, Hale was embracing the earth in a shallow dip that afforded him good cover: he was cool and composed, watching for the flashes of the Chinese small arms and then firing his Sten back at them in effective bursts. He was fighting automatically, his reflexes guiding him, full of grim determination. His mind was possessed by one burning desire: to stay alive. The fate of the patrol, the fate of Collins and the rest of his comrades, and whether or not he was shooting Chinese, were not uppermost in his mind. He only wanted to live through it all. His motivation was a 'Dear John' letter he had received from his girlfriend. The bitch had just cast him aside like a dog and it made him determined not to disappear for her convenience. He was going back, and when he got back …

A burst of bullets landed right beside him, showering his face with earth. He rolled several yards to one side and returned the fire with two long bursts. He became aware that Barnes's Sten had stopped firing and out the corner of his eye he saw him slumped over his weapon, and he was unable to stop the enemy charging past the narrow gap and advancing still further to the right. He saw three men fall under his fire but he knew that it'd be only a matter of seconds before they completed their out flanking movement and swarmed over the bund in a final assault.   Then it would be the end for all of them, and if they were lucky their bodies would be recovered from the valley the next night and the arch bitch would probably greet the news with a momentary shrug before returning to her new passion.

Corporal Smith, O'Hara, Charles and Hallows were lucky.   The positions they had adopted put them on equal terms with the enemy and they were protected from the Chinese bullets by a hollow in the ground.   After overcoming their initial panic, when they all fired wildly in the direction of the enemy, they became more accurate and conserved their ammunition by firing short bursts as opposed to whole magazines at a time.

O'Hara was very much in command.   He had led the way to their fire positions, and he was the first to use his fire properly.   He shouted orders instinctively, telling the others to concentrate on throwing grenades.

Taylor more or less opted out of everything.   He disintegrated as soon as bullets started flying overhead.   He squirmed about on the ground shouting: "Bandit! Bandit! Bandit!' into the mouthpiece of his 88-set.   For a full minute he struggled to pass a coherent message, and gradually he was overcome by a desire to run.   He felt he had to get away from the bullets and exploding grenades; he had to run before it was too late.   He had gone only a few yards when he felt something brush his arm, tearing his combat jacket. He clutched his arm and fell to the ground again.   Eventually, he forced himself to fire his Sten, but his rapid bursts were useless, for he merely held his weapon in the air, with his head pressed against the ground, firing vaguely in the direction of the enemy.

Blake and his patrol fought it out for around ten minutes, but gradually their resolution ebbed away.   With both Barnes and Collins dead, and Hale under increasing pressure, Blake crawled forward for a better idea of what was happening.   As he drew alongside Barnes's almost headless body there was a tremendous bang and flash and he was hurled to one side by a concussion grenade.   His body was winded, his ears filled with a tuneless buzz, and his eyes blinded by an array of colored stars.   He nursed his head in his hands for several seconds, trying to regain his full senses.   He was still half unconscious when he saw the enemy running quite unopposed along the bund to complete their outflanking movement..   He sprang to his feet and yelled: "Hale! Get back! Get back!"

Hale sprinted away and the rest of the patrol, having heard Blake yell "Get back!" took it as a general order and joined Hale in making a run for it.   They ran as fast as they could towards their own lines.   It was full flight.

O'Hara was the first to realize what was really happening.   It dawned on him as he leapt over a bund that he, O'Hara, the man who was going to win himself a right marker, who boasted that he was afraid of no man, was running like a coward. He stopped abruptly and turned, hoping to see the enemy, but all he saw was Blake--- the last of the defeated.

Blake flopped to the ground beside him, his head still throbbing painfully. He looked back towards the enemy but there was no sign of them. The only thing he could see was his own men still running towards their lines.

"Stop running you bastards!" yelled O'Hara. "Get down, you bastards!"

His words had no effect and they kept running until they reached the base of their own hills. Then they stopped, temporarily lost, not know which way to turn next. The patrol action was over and they were safe; that was all they cared about and at once they became careless, flopping to the ground, laughing and thanking God, trying to control their shaking limbs, and wiping away the sweat of fear and sudden exertion which had formed on their brows.

Blake and O'Hara soon joined them. Blake cursed them, shouting at them to get in a position of all-round defense and be prepared for the enemy to strike again. He was almost beside himself with anger and shame. The whole thing had been a fiasco, and they had run as soon as they had been faced by any real danger. Yet he realized he had sparked the whole thing off by shouting at Hale to pull back.

He started yelling at them again. He shouted at Taylor for the wireless. He was about to send a message when it dawned on him that he had not even checked on how many of them were there: for all he knew half of them might still be lying in the valley, helpless with wounds and at the mercy of the Chinese. He tossed the wireless back at Taylor and dashed round the circle of men lying on the ground. There were five of them. Barnes, he knew, was dead, but he could not account for the other man.

"Who is missing besides Barnes?" he demanded.

"Collins," replied Hale.

"Dead?"

"No. Still alive I think."

"Oh, God!" muttered Blake. That was the last straw. To leave a wounded man was unforgivable, and he knew that he had no alternative but to go back to look for him. He sensed that Corporal Smith and O'Hara were thinking the same thing so the three of them sprinted back to the site of the clash. They slowed instinctively as they neared the spot, but they needn't have worried. All that remained were wisps of smoke, the smell of cordite, signs of blood in the patchy snow where the Chinese had dragged away their dead and wounded, and the dead bodies of Barnes and Collins.

They carried the bodies back to the patrol. Then Blake contacted Able Company on the 88-set and requested a concentration of shells on Eden, the hill the enemy had come from originally. Next he warned Lawrence of their premature return, and after listening to the shells landing accurately on their target he led the patrol in single file towards the Charlie Company standing patrol.

"That you fellows buggering about out there?" asked one of them. Charles laughed. They all laughed. Even those carrying Collins and Barnes laughed. They were safe. They were home.

10

The fact that Blake's patrol failed to achieve its objective did not unduly worry Lawrence. On the whole he considered they had acquitted themselves quite well. At least they had returned to the site of the clash and established that casualties had been inflicted on the Chinese and the clash had lasted at least fifteen minutes which, for such an engagement, was quite a time. It meant that the Chinese must now know they were confronted by an enemy who meant business.

The Colonel also seemed pleased. During the de-briefing, Blake and his men gave a perfectly frank and consistent account of the encounter and although the Colonel didn't consider it a text book example of how to fight off an ambush, he was impressed by the patrol's tenacity against such large odds.

When it came to the next step in the process of capturing a prisoner, the Colonel urged caution. He insisted that they should wait several nights before Bartram went on another recce to explore the Chinese trench on the Boot: to discover if they enjoyed telephonic communication. In other words, was there a telephone wire up there which they could cut?

When Bartram went out again he took two men with him and they had another successful mission. They got into the Chinese trench undetected and discovered that there were fighting pits every thirty or forty yards and that these were manned by three men each. They also established that the Chinese relied on field telephones, and the wire connecting all the weapon pits ran along the top of the back wall of the trench, pegged into the ground every twenty yards or so.

It gave Lawrence and the Colonel all the information they needed. It was agreed that the snatch patrol would go ahead on Christmas Eve.

The plan for the snatch was perfectly simple. Both Lawrence and the

Colonel were united in keeping clear of anything overelaborate. They turned down the idea of a diversionary attack on Eden and they were adamant that the Gunners should only be used in the event of things going wrong, and then only as a means of covering the withdrawal of the patrol.

The patrol was to be in two halves; a firm base of sixteen taking up a position in the middle of no man's land and a snatch party of four men. The firm base was to proceed across the valley first, with two scouts going forward to establish when the Chinese two-man wandering patrol had cleared their route and passed on towards Eden. The snatch party would then pass through the firm base and proceed up the front slope of the Boot before lying up in ambush on the lateral trench, halfway between two weapon pits.

The snatch party would then cut the telephone wire and wait, anticipating that the Chinese would send round maybe two or three men to locate the fault and repair it. If that failed, and no signalmen materialized, the snatch party was to remain on the trench in the hope that they would be able to get the better of a small group of the enemy who happened to pass along the trench: maybe an inspecting NCO or a ration party.

Having finalized the plan, Lawrence lost no time in selecting the men for the job. He decided that all three platoon commanders would be involved. Goodall was put in command of the firm base and Bartram and Blake were to form the snatch party with two others. Competition for these jobs was fierce and in the end Lawrence decided upon O'Hara (who wrote a formal note to Lawrence requesting inclusion) and a corporal from Two Platoon. CSM Ralf recommended Charles, but by this time they all knew what motivated him and they took no notice of him. In fact, his suggestion was greeted by groans of derision which didn't please him at all.

During several rehearsals they reckoned the trickiest part of the snatch would be getting past the Chinese two-man patrols that methodically covered the ground in front of the Boot. After much deliberation it was decided that the two scouts should be armed with a reel of telephone wire which they would unwind as he went forward. When they saw the way clear they would give two violent tugs on the wire. That would be answered by two similar tugs and the snatch party would then pass through the firm base and climb the forward slope of the Boot, ending up between weapon pits on the Chinese lateral trench.

Blake suggested Hale as one of the scouts, but when it was mentioned to him, he was strangely indifferent. Whereas a few weeks before he would have gone without hesitation, now he hung back, refusing to say what he thought about it. Blake had never seen him so glum and lifeless and he put it down to his experiences on the ambush patrol, having no idea that he had

106

received a 'Dear John' letter. Eventually, after several other men had fought shy of the job, Corporal Smith volunteered on the condition that he did the job alone, and this was duly agreed to.

Apart from the outcome of the snatch patrol, Able Company's main interest was the approach of Christmas. They intended to make the most of it and the festive spirit was soon in evidence. Friends who a week before had been drifting apart, tired beyond endurance of each other's less attractive personal habits and mannerisms (everything from spitting, farting, belching and blowing their noses without the aid of their handkerchief), suddenly found their friendships rekindled.

Blake was astounded by the way a rebellious spirit that had crept into the platoon disappeared. Men became increasingly cheerful, partly because they knew that with the 'snatch' afoot they would not be required to do any major patrolling, and also because mail from home began to appear more regularly.

Two days before Christmas this spirit was given an additional boost. They were promised an increase in material comforts. Divisional Headquarters produced a Christmas Day menu with a choice or soups, turkey or pork, chipped potatoes and three vegetables, not to mention a host of sauces and Christmas pudding.

Since Able Company was in a reserve position it was decided that a national newspaper correspondent should take them as a typical example of how British troops were spending Christmas. Newsreel shots were to be taken of various activities, ranging from a carol service on the slopes of Two Platoon, Sergeant-Major Ralf and Nobby Clark distributing early morning tea to men in their bunkers, and shots of the Christmas dinner. They would also stage a special mock delivery of mail with Armitage speeding around a bend in the MSR with fake parcels stacked on his back seat and spilling over into a trailer. Sergeant-Major Ralf was then to be filmed tobogganing down one of the few remaining snow-covered slopes dressed as Father Christmas.

Lawrence even suspended all digging projects--- apart from the officers' mess--- and sent Armitage off down the MSR to visit a local Korean village with the idea of acquiring a suitable Christmas tree to place outside his CP. Armitage came back reporting that since the Koreans were all Buddhists they didn't go in for Christmas trees and he would therefore have to extend his search and maybe visit one of the American PX Stores much further down the MSR.

Lawrence sanctioned the trip but became increasingly suspicious when Armitage was away for hours and then reappeared with one of the scrawniest Christmas trees ever seen. Lawrence accused him of visiting one of the many brothels down the MSR, and while Armitage denied this emphatically, subsequent visits to the MO proved it to be true.

Lawrence ordered men to decorate the company lines and as an incentive offered ten shillings for the best decorated bunker and for the most impressive Christmas tree. Men laughed at the stupidity of the orders but they welcomed them, for anything---no matter how stupid--- was better than digging.

Christmas cards began to arrive from home, and in every bunker they were placed well away from oily weapons, patches of crumbling soil and the paper-hungry rats. They also received Christmas cards of sorts from the Chinese, taking the form of a propaganda offensive. Throughout the cold nights an appealing female voice, speaking broken English, boomed through loudspeakers from behind the Chinese lines. The voice drifted across the valley telling the Commonwealth forces that the Chinese troops would be in Seoul by New Year's Eve, and that if they had any love for their families at home and wanted to have the pleasure of seeing Father Christmas coming down their 'chimlies' then they should surrender immediately.

At first, the new form of contact with the enemy alarmed men. They thought there was some kind of trick behind it, but as they became accustomed to it they treated it as a welcome distraction.

Late in the afternoon of Christmas Eve, with the snatch patrol only hours away, Lawrence moved his headquarters to the forward company, knowing it would enhance their wireless communications. As the start of the patrol drew nearer, he grew increasingly anxious and jittery. He never stopped worrying about his plan and kept reading through his notes and making alterations.

By early evening, with only three hours to go, he decided that they should, after all, stage a small diversion by having the Gunners shell Eden and at the same time drop a few stray shells on the Boot--- otherwise, why should their telephone wires ever be cut? When he'd made arrangements with the gunners, and informed the Colonel, he sent Cross hurrying around the bunkers like a call-boy in a theatre telling men to report to the CP so they could be told of the new developments.

Men drifted into Lawrence's control bunker one or two at a time. They were strangely silent and Lawrence realized that, like him, they were all keyed up for the patrol. The bunker was soon crammed with men, the air swirling with smoke. Lawrence eventually finished amending his notes and having explained everything to them he sat there, recuperating from the effort. It was up to them now.   They had to make certain that it succeeded.

"Someone give me a cigarette," he commanded.

O'Hara offered him some, but Lawrence took one look at the dirty and tattered packet and the ragged ends of some half-smoked stubs, and ignored them.   "I want cigarettes, not waste paper," he said sarcastically.   He felt his temper rising.   O'Hara, for all his keenness and aggression, was just the kind of bloody idiot who would make a mess of the whole plan.

Bartram offered him one of his Sobranies out of a silver case.   Lawrence accepted one without comment.   Cross supplied him with a light. "Well, we're all set to go now," said Lawrence.

"But what about all these timings of yours, sir," said Goodall.   "Surely, they'll all be up the spout if Corporal Smith takes a long time making sure that the valley is clear?"

Lawrence sighed deeply.   "Yes, I know!   You don't have to tell me that. It all depends on Corporal Smith.   But we've got to have some plan to work on and try to keep to some kind of timetable.   Otherwise, we'd never get anything done.   So I'm well aware that getting past the warning patrols successfully is the crisis of the whole patrol.   Not the climax, but the crisis."

Smith smiled, thrilled that his importance was at last being recognized. He wasn't such a nonentity after all.   "Don't worry, sir.   I don't anticipate I'll have any difficulty.   I reckon those Chinese patrols go backwards and forwards like clockwork."   He was amazed by the calmness and certainty of his own voice.

Lawrence leaned back, reassured.   "All right, that's everything finally tied up.   Mr. Goodall, you can start off right away, and don't forget that as soon as you are in position contact us straight away----immediately!"

The men filed out of the CP.   Lawrence resumed glancing through his notes.   Smith was the last man to leave and as he passed Williamson the latter said: "Cheerio, Smudge.   It's been nice knowing you."

Lawrence jerked his head up sharply and regarded Williamson in disgust. It was the remark of an imbecile, a man who did not realize what war and death were.

"I wish to hell I could say the same to you, you bastard,' replied Smith.

"Come off it, Smudge, I was only kidding," pleaded Williamson.

"Well keep your kidding for kids like yourself."

When Smith had gone, Lawrence's houseboy, Kim, entered and placed a cup of coffee before him.   He felt hot under the collar and his hair was itching.   Suddenly everything and everyone annoyed him: even the coffee annoyed him.   He was sick of the sight of coffee.   Every night it was placed in front of him and it had become symbolic of waiting.

He picked up the telephone and after a considerable spell of blowing down it he spoke to the FOO who insisted on staying in the OP. He told him that the patrol had left and then he listened as Williamson relayed the same information back to battalion. His eyes wandered around the bunker, searching for something to do, something to occupy his mind and pass away the time. He knew that tonight the waiting would be a hundred times worse than any other night. Tonight, something was definitely going to happen.

When the firm base was halfway across the valley Goodall called a halt. He motioned Smith forward, gave him a pat on the back, and whispered, "Good luck, old boy!"

Smith was alone. He went forward very slowly, reeling out the telephone wire behind him. He took full advantage of the bunds and moved along them in a crouching position. In more exposed areas he had no alternative but to crawl along, field-craft style. After ten minutes he reached the stream, and as he slid across it on his stomach the ice gave out a loud 'crack' but held. When he reached the far bank he rested, shivering, just as much with fear as the cold. Being on his own was a lot more nerve-racking than having Blake with him. When he heard no movement he moved on. As he drew near to the track in front of the Boot an artillery flare went up from Little Nori, exactly what he could have done without. He froze, resisting the temptation to drop to the ground and into cover. He stood there, feeling totally exposed, but still not daring to move. The flare illuminated the countryside for miles around, hanging gracefully, high in the sky, and although he cursed it roundly, it nevertheless made him realize how beautiful the whole scene was. It was totally surreal: that such natural beauty should prevail when he was, in fact, in a perilous situation

Before the flared faded, the gunners laid down their minor diversion on Eden. It was no more than desultory shelling and when they slipped in a few rounds on the upper slopes of the Boot it seemed perfect normal, just usual harassing fire. Finally, as the shelling stopped, the flares faded away for good. Nothing further happened. Smith went a few yards further forward and concealed himself behind a small bush. It was ideal cover from which to observe the track. Now, he just had to wait for the Chinese patrols to appear. He only hoped he was somewhere near where they usually met up for their smokes, before returning to their previous beats.

It was twenty minutes before the first pair appeared. They stopped about fifteen yards further down the track and settled down on the edge of the ditch. He saw sparks of light as they lit cigarettes. They were so careless about it that they obviously weren't expecting any trouble. Their comrades joined them shortly afterwards. Now, Smith knew that all he had to do was be patient. Then, when they parted and trudged off again in their opposite directions, he could summon up the snatch party.

They smoked two cigarettes each before wandering off. He gave them a few minutes and then tugged viciously on his trailing telephone wire. Goodall tugged back with such force that he nearly pulled the reel off Smith's shoulder. Very soon, the snatch party appeared, Bartram in the lead, feeling his way along the telephone wire. He knelt down beside Smith and they exchanged whispers.

"All clear?"

"Yes, sir."

Bartram moved forward swiftly in the crouch position, waving the others to follow him. They slipped across the track silently. Smith watched them and hissed "Good luck" after them. O'Hara was at the rear and Smith suddenly felt great affection towards him. Old Paddy was no bull-shitter! He really did intend to cover himself in glory.

Before he turned away to rejoin the firm base, Smith also had a thought for Blake. What a contrast he was to O'Hara. The Irishman so obviously reveled in it all, but Blake loathed every minute in Korea; yet he stuck it out and even put up with Lawrence's bullying and his outrageously gung-ho aggression; and all because such behavior was inbred in him. He was doing what everyone expected of him: the Public School ethic.

Smith wondered which of the two attitudes was the most laudable.

Bartram knew that to get into the Chinese trench unobserved they needed to take their time. They had no alternative but to crawl on their bellies, if necessary inch by inch. Giving way to any impulse to hurry would be fatal. They all understood that from their rehearsals and he trusted them to take their cue from him.

As they gained height the wind resumed its role as a solitary whistler and over to their right the grumbling thuds and vibrations of the Little Nori battle disturbed the otherwise quiet night. The moon reappeared from behind the shielding clouds and showed up the trench in naked plainness. They could see the dark patch that lay between the two walls, and on the near side they could see the soil which had been flung out of the trench many months before without any effort of concealment. Bartram could also see the regular dark outline of the Chinese weapon pits. He picked out two where the gap between them was the greatest and he made a mental note of the bearing so that if the moon went in they would still arrive at the right point.

As they crawled forward there were areas of dead ground and then they were able to move more freely. Even so, the going was very slow. Ironically, crawling slowly was exhausting and before long they were hot and sweaty, mainly due to the heavy bullet-proof vest they wore. When they got to within ten yards of the trench they stopped and listened. Bartram was anxious not to drop into the trench only to find that there were Chinese walking along it. He went forward on his own and stared down into the trench. It was deep, well over head-high, and the stretch at which they'd arrived was straight, ideal for their snatch. They would have good warning of any wiring party coming along from either direction.

He motioned the others forward and they adopted their pre-planned positions. Blake and O'Hara leapt across the trench to locate the telephone wire on the top of the inside trench wall. O'Hara produced their wire cutters and while Blake held a stretch of it tautly between his hands, O'Hara snipped it. They replaced the wire as they'd found it, close to one of the pegs, and smiled at each other. The trap was set. All they had to do now was wait.

They waited for a hell of a long time. Goodall and those on the firm base wondered what had happened. Those back in the CP could hardly bear the suspense, their frustration compounded by the radio silence that had been imposed. In fact, they waited for over three hours. It was the same old story. At first they felt quite warm, but as time passed the cold spread rapidly throughout their bodies, starting at their extremities, their fingers, toes, and the tips of their ears. Then the cold spread until they were all shivering convulsively. Their eyes ached and their minds felt numb. They started off thinking of all kinds of personal things, but gradually these thoughts faded until their minds went blank. Their initial enthusiasm began to wane and their determination weakened. Their eyelids became increasing heavy. They had to keep jerking themselves back to full alertness. The cold was like a mild anesthetic and the cold went on getting colder and colder.

At approximately 0450 hours another gunnery flare went up from Little Nori. It hung there for what seemed a long time and then, just as it was beginning to fade, Bartram saw three Chinese walking along the trench, coming from their right. He could hardly believe his eyes. The plan had worked. The trap was about to be sprung. There was no mistaking the enemy. They were chattering all the time, arguing by the sound of it; and they kept stopping to inspect the telephone wire. Each time the leading man made the same comment. Bartram could just imagine him snapping: "Bugger all wrong with that!"

Bartram looked around: his snatch group was ready, everyone set to pounce. Out of the corner of his eye he could see the outline of all their heads against the flare-lit sky. Ten yards away from the cut in the wire the Chinamen stopped again. Another inspection: another cynical curse.

They came on forward again. They were now perfectly distinct. The one in front was decidedly ugly and his facial expression suggested that he was sneering at his comrades. When only five yards from them he gave the telephone wire another tug and the cut end reared in the air and then fell into the trench. They all laughed uproariously. They huddled around to inspect it. Two of them started to grope for their tools.

"Now!" yelled Bartram.

At that very moment the flares hanging over Little Nori went out. Everything was plunged into pitch darkness. Chaos descended over the short stretch of trench. Bartram fired his Sten at the leading man, just as planned, but he missed. His bullets splattered against the far wall of the trench, a fraction of an inch away from the man's head.

Blake's muscles were so stiff with cold that he reacted in slow-motion. He flung himself bodily at the man to the right, but instead of his cosh landing squarely on the man's head, it glanced off his shoulder, almost unfelt. Blake flung his arms out and for a brief second grabbed the man's clothes, but it was to no avail. The man, inspired by fear, wrenched himself free and was gone. O'Hara, seeing what had happened, decided to go for the third Chinese rather than shoot him. He jumped on top of him, forced him down, and for a moment had him pinned to the bottom of the trench; but fear and panic made the man wriggle and squirm about so effectively that he managed to break away. As O'Hara still lay in the trench, his opponent had joined his comrades, sprinting down the trench for all they were worth, raising the alarm and shouting for help.

The enemy had literally slipped through their fingers.

Another flare went up from Little Nori. They were left looking into an empty trench, apart from a repair kit left by the Chinese. The very second they had needed light, there was none, but directly before and afterwards it was abundant. The irony was like a slap in the face for Bartram. It was a low, mocking trick. He was beside himself with fury, he just could not understand how he had missed his man, and he began to blaspheme terribly.

While he lashed the air with words the others stood transfixed, mesmerized by the speed with which the enemy had fled. Then they heard voices approaching them, getting louder every second, and without hesitation they ran down the hill and rejoined the firm base.

The plan had worked perfectly, yet they had failed.

It was Christmas Day, but no Christmas present for Major Lawrence.

11

The debriefing the following morning was not a happy occasion. There should have been a double celebration: a prisoner and Christmas, but the lack of the former meant the death of the latter. The predominant feeling in the battalion CP was one of incredulity. How could they have got so near and yet managed to fail so completely? They had not only missed a prisoner, but missed shooting two unsuspecting men at point-blank range.

Lawrence could not credit it. As he kept telling everyone, the conception and planning of the operation had been impeccable, and the failure to press this home meant that the enemy would now be alerted for miles around and they would never get as good a chance of a prisoner again.

Bartram and Goodall said nothing. They hadn't even discussed it with each other, but neither thought they were having a fair hearing. Blake was damn sure they weren't. It infuriated him that Lawrence had the gall to exonerate himself from any responsibility. At the debriefing he waited anxiously for a chance to have his say. Even if Bartram and Goodall were content to say nothing, he wasn't. His chance came near the end. Having listened again to Lawrence carrying on about his faultless planning, Blake interrupted: "Actually, Colonel, what we are failing to appreciate is where the planning went woefully wrong. It was a major error not to realize the effect of the severe cold. Those who spend their time in warm bunkers have no conception of the effect of the cold. If the Chinese had come along within an hour, we would have succeeded, but three and a half hours out there in that cold was simply more than the human frame could stand. It wasn't just one of us affected. It was all of us."

The Colonel, the IO, and the adjutant accepted this as a valid point, but Lawrence regarded it as a feeble excuse and said so in no uncertain terms. His cross words soon became angry and when Blake refused to be intimidated and stuck to his point, the Colonel terminated the meeting abruptly, telling everyone to put the matter behind them, to treat it as a moral victory over the Chinese; and above all not to look upon it as a failure.

"We are about to have a very important visitor over the next couple of days," concluded the Colonel. "And we certainly don't want to give him any bad impressions."

The important visitor was a correspondent of a British national paper. He was to spend two days with the Rocks and write a series of articles on how

British troops in Korea were spending their Christmas.

"It might be a good idea, Dick, if I send him round to Able Company first," suggested the Colonel. "His presence might act as a bit of a tonic for the lads after their disappointment."

"I don't know about that, sir. I'm not concerned with the effect a war correspondent will have on Able Company ... Far more to the point is what effect will the men of Able Company have on the correspondent."

No one quite knew what he was implying, whether he was joking or not, so they were all the more intrigued to see how things transpired.

When Major Lawrence met the correspondent he was appalled. He was a weedy, scruffy, and unkempt individual with greasy hair hanging over his collar. He wasn't even from a respectable newspaper. He was employed by a Sunday muck-raking tabloid; and the final insult was that the fellow admitted quite openly that he wasn't a proper war correspondent. He was no more than a senior 'hack' who had been sent to Korea with instructions to find a new angle, whatever that meant. When Lawrence demanded a clearer explanation, the fellow admitted that his main aim was to investigate the conditions and moral welfare of young National Servicemen on active service. Nothing could have been more calculated to fill Lawrence with contempt.

Under protest, Lawrence followed the Colonel's instructions and took the bounder to One Platoon. He found Blake's men squashed into the biggest bunker in the platoon lines. It was nothing but a large, deep hole in the ground with good overhead cover. The furniture consisted entirely of upturned ammunition boxes, even though there were three crates of free-issue beer in one corner. One of these was already empty and no one anticipated that the other two would last through the night.

As Lawrence ushered the correspondent inside, he couldn't help thinking that this was the Colonel's most disastrous-ever decision. The bloody reporter should have been sent packing with a flea in his ear and a size fifteen boot up his backside. As for Blake and One Platoon, they were never going to impress anyone. Instead of reflecting the true traditions and achievements of the British army, they were far more akin to the rabble which had frightened the life out of the Duke of Wellington.

There was plenty of light from hurricane lamps in the bunker but it was virtually impossible to see more than a yard or two for cigarette smoke: everyone was smoking, even Burrows, who up until three months ago would never have considered such a thing. In one corner of the bunker a space-heater was roaring away full blast, throwing out a smell of petrol that was almost as strong as the heat it was emitting. Lawrence half expected it to explode at any moment. Every one of those inside was covered in soot and there was a lingering tang of BO owing to none of them having had a bath or a proper wash in over a month.

Blake stepped forward to welcome his visitor, but without enthusiasm. He knew this was no place for a Fleet Street journalist. Conversations in One Platoon were hardly edifying, tending to be loud, argumentative and repetitive. As always, Winston was holding forth and dominating things. It was true that he was continually interrupted and abused, and told not to talk such utter bloody rubbish, but that only provoked him all the more.

At one point Winston went over to the space-heater to try to turn it up by increasing the flow of petrol. "For God's sake leave that fire alone, Winston," shouted Miles. "What are you trying to do, roast us alive?"

"Come off it, Sarge. It's no good Mr. Blake inviting us up here to have a drink unless we can keep warm. Trouble is that none of you bastards knows what a decent fire is."

O'Hara shouted back: "Winston, you'll burn to death and that's dead certain. I never saw the fate of a man so clear."

Winston regarded the Irishman with contempt. "Rot! Why the hell should I burn to death? My grandfather died of TB, my father died of TB, and the odds are that I will as well. It's inevitable. Just as it's inevitable that you'll die trying to get your bloody stupid right marker, just like you very nearly did last night."

Blake felt he had to intervene. Already, Lawrence was going puce with anger and the correspondent clearly had no idea of what he'd let himself in for. "All right, fellows," he appealed. "Let's have no more of the morbid stuff."

"Quite right, Mr. Blake," agreed Winston. "Come on, Taylor! Hand round some more bottles. Let's get properly stuck in …"

"As the Bishop said to the actress," cried Charles as soon as the words had left Winston's lips.

For a moment, Blake frowned in embarrassment. Then, to his own surprise, he couldn't stop laughing, realizing that that was what blokes like Charles really thought about the likes of his father. Lawrence watched him, amazed that he should be amused by such a blasphemous vulgarity. He felt like reprimanding him and telling him to pull himself together, but with the correspondent there he restrained himself.

The correspondent watched them all with a vacant, bewildered look. He was wondering how all this fitted in with his request to the Colonel to see National Serviceman in typical front line conditions. How could this be typical? He'd expected them to be in a trench, or in a weapon pit with a machine gun or two at the ready, and with shells exploding, dirt flying, and bullets cracking about their heads. Having deliberately avoided any service in World War II, he had no idea what war was like.

Lawrence excused himself. He couldn't stand any more. "I'm afraid I'll have to be getting back to my Command Post," he told the correspondent. "You stay and enjoy yourself with the men. But come round and see me later in the evening. You'll see how things work then in what you might call the nerve center. And I'll be glad to answer any questions."

Taylor handed around more beers. The correspondent was on his third and was beginning to settle into the spirit of things. He found himself explaining to Blake and Charles about his lack of army service due to flat feet, and how he wasn't really a war correspondent but a specialist concerned with the Social Services.

Charles's eye lit up. "We must have a quiet chat sometime." Having seen all the help his mother got from the Social Services he had long considered the advisability of learning how they could be milked once he was back in civilian life.

"So what exactly do your duties include?" asked Blake. "What do you write about?"

"Well I advise readers on how to claim benefits and their rights, and a column chasing up bureaucratic inefficiencies and telling people how to overcome their difficulties. Sending me out here instead of someone like James Cameron or Sefton Delmer is our paper's way of getting a new angle. My editor thought I might be able to help some of you lads … You know, war pension claims for wounds and shell shock… That sort of thing … Have you seen much action?"

"Seen much bloody action!" cried Winston incredulously. Then, to emphasize his point he repeated: "Seen much bloody action! Did you lads hear that? Have we seen much action! Bloody hell, mate, you must be joking. You've come to the right place if you want to hear about some bloody action. That's right, isn't it, Charlie?"

"Bloody right it is," agreed Charles. "What we've been through will make your bloody hair stand on end. Have a word with Smudge, here… He was up to his neck in muck and bullets all last night, weren't you, Smudge?"

Corporal Smith joined them reluctantly, looking at Blake as much as to say, 'Is this really necessary?' The correspondent was all ears, so Smith told him what had happened. "Mind you, it wasn't half cold out there," he concluded. "Wasn't it cold, Paddy?"

"It was bloody cold all right," agreed O'Hara.

"Cold!" echoed Winston. "Did you hear that, lads?"

"And it was reet bloody scary too," said Smith. "Wasn't it, Paddy?"

"Christ, yes. It was bloody scary all right."

"Scary!" cried Winston. "By Christ, did you hear that, lads? Bloody scary …We were all bloody shitting ourselves …"

"Oh, shut up, Winston!"

"It'll be a long time before they get me out in that valley again," said Smith.

"Or me," agreed Winston. "I've had my bloody bellyful of that valley."

"What the hell are you talking about, Winston," yelled O'Hara. "You haven't stepped outside your bunker in the last month."

Winston's pride was hurt. "I'll have you know, Paddy, that apart from you and Mr. Blake, and Smudge, and Charlie, and Sarge, and Reg, and Lowe, I've done more patrols than anyone in the platoon …"

"Christ, there aren't many left after that lot," said Lowe.

"Standing patrols!" scoffed O'Hara. "That's all you've done, nothing else. They're not even proper patrols."

"Not proper patrols," cried Winston. "Did you hear that, lads? Not really proper patrols …"

Men smiled as they made allowances for Winston's drunkenness. "And we've been in some tight corners as well," Winston continued, flinging a challenging glance around him. "And if you want a good story for your paper mister, just ask me. I'll tell you a thing or two."

"Tell him about that time you captured a Mongolian giant," shouted Miles from his bed.

"He wasn't a Mongolian, Sarge. He was a Manchurian!"

"Bloody Mancunian, more like," corrected Charles.

God, this is horrendous, thought Blake. He couldn't stand another moment of it. He slipped away quietly and headed for Corporal Hale. Often, when he felt like a civilized conversation, he sought out Hale. Now, he was sitting alone by the space-heater, quietly supping his beer, looking very down. They talked of this and that for a few minutes and then Blake asked him why he hadn't wanted to go on the snatch patrol. When Hale told him about his 'Dear John' letter, Blake was highly sympathetic but he knew immediately that when it came to giving advice on women he was out of his depth. He'd never even had a girlfriend, so how would he know how to dispense advice? He wasn't even sure that as a platoon commander he was expected to dispense such advice. It struck him that Hale's best course was to forget her and find another girl when he got home.

"That makes two of you with girl trouble," said Blake.

"Oh, who else, sir?"

"Charles … I thought everyone knew about his troubles …"

"Christ, don't ever equate me with that bastard! He deserves all the troubles he gets. And he'll get his comeuppance soon enough, you mark my words. Old Ralf will never let him get away with what he did. She was three weeks over sixteen for God's sake. My situation is entirely different. In my case …" Hale broke off, realizing the futility of going into details. "Never mind, sir. It'll sort itself out in the end."

Blake had no idea of how to reply and it came as a relief to him when the blanket over the entrance was pulled aside and blast of cold air hit them. Williamson was standing in the doorway. He pulled the blanket back into position and looked around for Blake. When he spotted him he went over to him and said: "Major Lawrence wants you to send over the correspondent, sir. And you've got to send a couple of escorts with him."

"Escorts? But he said he'd come back himself."

"I know, sir," said Williamson, "but he's since discovered that it's dark outside and there might be Chinks about trying to snatch a prisoner. Could you send him down right away, sir?"

"Okay. How are things going at HQ, Corporal?"

"There's a bit of a flap on at the moment, sir. Baker Company caught another Chinky patrol scattering Christmas cards on our wire. You'd think a whole bloody division was coming our way by Lawrence's reaction. He's been tearing the place up something wicked just because the Colonel has stood-to Charlie Company and not us."

"Thank God for that."

Blake told Charles and O'Hara to accompany the correspondent back to the company CP. When they went outside they ignored the correspondent completely and were only aware of his presence because in the darkness, and on the icy surface of the path, he kept slipping over. When they reached the bottom of the hill a flare sprang into the sky like a giant candle and the 25-pounders roared from just behind the ridge. The correspondent glanced sideways at Charles and O'Hara who were staggering along with their arms twined about each other's necks singing at the top of their voices and he wondered if the whole situation was part of an unpleasant dream. For years he had never been more than three miles from Fleet Street but now he was suddenly in this Godforsaken country, trying to make sense of what these young National Servicemen were up to and how they were coping. It was surreal. No other word for it. It was as though they were playing war games. There was the unit's adjutant, gushing over him like a youthful waterfall; the Colonel, so cool and detached that he might just as well have been conducting a tactical exercise at the staff college in Camberley.   As for the company commander, Lawrence, his craving for glory was so transparent that it was no wonder he spent his whole time ruing the failure of some miserable attempt to snatch a prisoner.   On top of that, he seemed to hate everybody and everything.   Then there were the ordinary men, the ones in the One Platoon bunker.   What the hell could one make of them?   He just could not understand their attitude towards the war.   They seemed to have no interest or concern in it, and when they talked of it, it was either with boastfulness or utter indifference.   Few of them betrayed any fear, but neither did they show any enthusiasm.   On several occasions he had asked men what they were fighting for and the answers had always been the same: "How the hell should I know?   Ask the buggers who sent us here."

Yet strangely there was no bitterness, no demands for the right to vote as well as fight--- nothing but calm acceptance.

He began to think of his next cable home.   There was certainly one hell of a good story to write, but would anyone at home believe him?   What would they say if he sent back a thousand words describing how an entire British company in the front line was drunk?   He was amazed by the stupidity of his own rhetoric.   Of course the rag he wrote for would lap it up. The editor and subs would soon convince the great unwashed British public that it was the most sensational National Service story since the Catterick scrubbings that had upset Michael Foot so much.   It would cause a hell of a stink; and after all, having come 10,000 miles out to Korea, to say nothing of the 10,000 back again, he had to come up with something good.

When they finally reached the company CP Charles pushed his way in and called out to everyone in general: "We've brought the newspaper bloke back for you."   He looked about the bunker and saw Lawrence bent over the phone, listening with a grave face.   He noticed that Lawrence was nursing a half-full tumbler of whisky and he felt a sudden bitterness towards the officers.   Even at Christmas they made sure they got the best of everything. They got beer and the officers got whisky.   'Merry Christmas, Major Lawrence," yelled Charles.   "I suppose you couldn't spare a drop of whisky?"

Lawrence strode across the bunker and smiled grimly at the correspondent.   He had every intention of putting the fear of God into him. "It looks as though they're going to have a bash at Hill 355.   They try the same thing every year apparently.   It's a kind of annual fixture."

"Where did you say they were going to attack, sir?" asked Charles.

"Never you mind, Charles.   You just get back to your platoon before we find ourselves up to our necks in it."

Charles ignored the warning, knowing full well it was bullshit. Hill 355 was bloody miles away. He slumped heavily on to a bench and turned his attention to Nobby Clark instead. He liked Clark. He recognized him as one of the few officers who were prepared to treat other ranks as human beings. Now, he couldn't understand why Clark was being so inhospitable. "Can't you spare me just a drop of whisky, sir?" pleaded Charles.

Clark was annoyed, but he made allowances. It was Christmas Night and had it not been for this confounded flap he would willingly have spared time to give Charles a whisky. "Sorry Charlie, but not to-night," he said. "You just push off again."

"But what do you want me to do out there?"

"Oh ... Anything! Go and sing carols." He seized Charles by the collar and pushed him out, together with O'Hara.

They staggered back down the road, once more singing, remaining upright by means of mutual support.

> *"The Chinks are surging all over the Hook*
> *And the Rocks aren't waiting for another look,*
> *We're moving on,*
> *To old Pusan.*
> *We're moving fast and far*
> *Down the MSR,*
> *We're moving on ... "*

As arranged, the correspondent stayed with the Rocks for two more days, during which time he honed his story. Then he submitted it to the Colonel, not because he wanted to but because it was that was one of the conditions of his visit. When a copy of the report reached Lawrence at his CP he was utterly appalled. He'd never read such libelous drivel. He was so carried away by anger that he had an urgent scratch in full view of everyone. Then he got on the field telephone and made his feeling abundantly clear to the Colonel. He was just as displeased as Lawrence and assured him that several offending passages would be struck out and the whole thing toned down.

When the Able Company subalterns turned up at the CP for the usual daily orders group, Lawrence wasn't there, but he had left the journalist's story on his table. They spotted it and had the temerity to read it. Bartram was still holding it, making comments, when Lawrence entered the bunker.

"So you've seen it then," said Lawrence.

"Yes, sir."

121

"Well it won't be appearing like that, I can assure you."

"I should hope not, sir," said Bartram.

"Mind you, sir," chipped in Blake. "If it did appear like that it would at least be certain to achieve one thing …"

"What's that, Blake?"

"It would put Able Company well and truly on the map."

Lawrence eyed Blake with contempt, not for the first time. He was still smarting from his insolence at the debriefing. "Blake, you are sardonic, sarcastic, supercilious, superficial, and supernumerary. And as the son of a Bishop it does not become you."

Bartram and Goodall roared with laughter. It was not the reaction Lawrence had been seeking.

12

Early in the New Year Able Company relieved Baker Company on the forward company position.

Lawrence stood in the doorway of the reserve company CP, a gin and lime cradled in his hands, watching One Platoon as they trudged along the road under the burden of their full kit and all manner of improvisations, such as washing bowls, hurricane lamps, small fires, and lengths of precious rubber tubing, all of which helped to make their existence in their bunkers more bearable.

It was late evening and the mist was filtering through crisp, winter air. The sections of One Platoon were well strung and they were marching at a good, steady pace, singing, not loudly but cheerfully. Lawrence was glad of the move. It gave him greater scope to redeem the failure of his patrols; and judging by the general appearance of the men they also welcomed the change. They liked to be active, not just left to sit around. That always caused trouble. It gave them too much time to drink beer, talk endlessly, and end up moaning about everything.

Lawrence finished his gin and lime and looked out across the bleak country. Directly in front of him Armitage was sitting in the company jeep with Kim perched on the back seat amid a great pile of oddments. One Platoon was almost opposite him now, and he saw the robust figure of Hale leading the first section; a few yards behind him Winston and Charles, two of the less convincing physical specimens in the platoon, were struggling under the weight of their Bren guns. CSM Ralf's insistence that Charles should become a Bren gunner was a bit odd, thought Lawrence, but he supposed he knew what he was up to. The CSM seemed to have Charles on the brain.

Beyond them, only just visible as the hill sloped away, was the half-finished officers' mess. Lawrence smiled bitterly as he lit himself one of Williamson's cigarettes. It was a pity that they'd never finished it. It would have been fun doing a bit of entertaining every now and again, to say nothing of having their meals in comfort; but it didn't really matter. The important thing was that it had kept the men occupied.

"Is that the last of your men?" Lawrence called out to Blake.

"Yes sir. This is the lot."

Lawrence felt compelled to make sure that Blake was working on orders and not his own judgment. "Who told you to move out?"

"Captain Clark, sir."

Lawrence debated whether to ring up Clark and check on it, but he decided against it. Despite Blake's immaturity and general incompetence, and his damned rebelliousness, he had no reason to doubt his word. He joined Armitage and Kim in the jeep. "Right, let's get moving."

They sped across the camouflage road without incident, passing the long lines of marching troops, down the Switch Back road, and eventually to the forward company where they faced the long climb. Armitage changed down the gears until he was in first, forcing the jeep as far as possible up the hill. "That's it, sir. She won't go any farther."

Lawrence climbed out reluctantly. His equipment was bulky and uncomfortable and he knew that by the time he reached top of the hill he would be soaked in perspiration, despite the low temperature. He declined to help Kim and Armitage with any of his accessories piled in the jeep and he waddled slowly towards the crest of the hill. When he reached the main lateral trench he turned and watched Armitage laboring under the weight of his sleeping bag and two kitbags. When Armitage reached him, he laughed: "Hot work, eh, Armitage?"

Armitage groaned and wiped his brow. He felt no resentment at having to carry the kit: he had grown accustomed to doing all manner of jobs for Lawrence and he had long ago realized the futility of complaining.

"Never been up this far before, I suppose, Armitage?"

"I'm no stranger up here, sir," replied Armitage proudly. "I brought Mr. Blake and Mr. Bartram up here when they went on patrol, but I've never actually been in the forward trenches."

"Well leave the kit with Kim and I'll show where Mr. Woo lives." He led the way through the trenches until they were looking out over no man's land.

The trench was narrow and shallow and despite the fading light the Chinese hills looked very clear and near.

"Blimey, sir! Bit near, aren't they?"

Lawrence turned and saw the driver crouching in the trench, peeping nervously over the top. It amused him and he felt very much the old soldier. "Over four hundred yards in actual fact," he said. "You'll be all right in this light."

Lawrence leaned on the trench and pointed out some of the main landmarks. He was enjoying himself and he noticed that the re-entrant between Eden and the Boot was wider than he had previously thought. There was a germ of an idea working in his mind that he might send a patrol through it and attack Eden from the rear.

Crack!

Lawrence's beret was whisked off his head by a sniper's bullet. It had missed him literally by a hair's breadth, and dug deep into the trench wall behind him. Instantly, even though hopelessly too late, he flung himself to the bottom of the trench, his short body trembling from head to foot. For a few moments he remained there. Then yelled to Armitage: "Come on! Get the hell out of here."

Lawrence broke into a labored run, what to him passed as a sprint. In that moment he had lost his nerve. A dormant memory came to life: it was in Germany and a man standing right beside him had been shot straight between the eyes. His whole head had disintegrated into a crimson mess. As Lawrence saw it all again he kept running. Only when they reached the rear slope did he stop to regain his breath.

"That was a near one, sir," laughed Armitage.

Lawrence made no reply. He was still trembling. He made for the CP and ducked down into it. Inside, Nobby Clark and Cross were busy sorting things out, getting the CP operational. They looked up in surprise as Lawrence burst in, grabbed a nearby whisky bottle, yanked out the stopper, and swigged some straight down, not bothering with a glass. Armitage turned away and started toward his jeep. Nobby Clark hurried after him and grabbed his arm.

"What happened?"

"It was a sniper, sir. The bullet missed him by a whisker. Don't reckon he'll be going round there again in a hurry."

Charles was marching at the back of Corporal Hale's section. He had recently been split up from Hallows and put permanently on a Bren gun and he didn't like it a bit. He had made repeated protests about it but it had done

124

him no good and he was now laboring along with the heavy and cumbersome weapon slung across his right shoulder. It was all part of the vindictive plot against him: a plot master-minded by Ralf and Miles. They really had it in for him.

Due to his short legs he was also having trouble keeping up with the others. To make matters worse, his precious hurricane lamp was rubbing against the back of his left thigh each time his right foot went forward. By the time they reached the top of the forward company hill he was exhausted, and he could feel his temper rising, ready to explode at the slightest excuse.

"Okay, hold it, fellows," called out Corporal Hale after jumping on to the top of the trench wall so he could see everyone. "Take a rest while I find out where our bunkers are."

Hale soon reappeared at the end of the trench. "All right you fellows, on your feet. You've got a nice surprise coming to you."

"What do you mean by that, Corp?"

Hale turned his back on them and started to walk back down the trench. "You'll soon see. Come on, get moving."

Sergeant Miles had given Hale a brief preview of the bunkers and they were appalling, to say the least. Miles had also laid down who was to be in which bunker, and that spelt trouble. Miles had ordered him to put Charles in a bunker on his own; in the worst bunker Hale had ever seen or was ever likely to see. It was the last in line along the trench in the most vulnerable spot on the reverse slope. It was such a foul bunker that the previous platoon in Baker Company had left it empty.

Soon, everyone in the section had been allocated to their positions and the only one left trailing behind Hale was Charles. When Hale stopped he pointed down to a small hole at the base of the trench. It was just big enough for a man to squeeze through. There was no proper entrance, just a hole in the ground, leading into what looked like a small, dark cave.

"This one is yours."

Charles looked at it in disbelief. He looked for a chimney, a sign that there was at least room for a fire in it, but there was nothing. There weren't even any visible timber supports. He knelt down and looked through the entrance hole. He lit a match to examine it more thoroughly and in the flickering light he was left speechless by what he saw. All the others had been allocated bunkers that were reasonable; glorified holes in the ground maybe, but still habitable. This was just an overgrown rat hole. He called after Hale as he disappeared down the trench.

"Hey! Corporal! Come back here …"

"What's up, Charlie?"

125

"You might well ask! What is this is supposed to be?"

"Sergeant Miles's orders … Sorry …"

"Well, do you expect me to live in there? It's nothing but a glorified rat hole. There's not even room to lie down in it."

"You'd better have a word with Miles."

"Right! I bloody will, don't you worry."

Charles went down the trench in search of Miles, seething with anger. He didn't give a damn what anyone said---- Lawrence, Blake, Ralf, Miles or anyone else--- he wasn't going to be treated like that. He'd refuse! It would no doubt mean a long stretch in some Detention Barracks, or even a court-martial for disobeying orders and telling them all to get stuffed: but what the hell! There was a limit and he'd just reached it.

When he found Miles, he told him straight. He pulled no punches and took no account of his rank. He told him, man to man, exactly what he thought. "You can do what the bloody hell you like, Miles, but I've just reached the end of the bloody line."

"You reached the end of the line the moment you arrived out here in Korea, Charles. I couldn't give a damn if you do refuse. There's nowhere else for you to go. You can dig yourself a new bunker if you like … That's always your privilege. But as far as I'm concerned, that's your bunker and you're bloody staying there."

"Balls to you, Miles, I'm not having that. You can do what you like … Court-martial me for all I care …"

"Charles can't you get it into your pea-brain that you've already got the ultimate punishment? This is it! There is nothing worse! And I've no intention of putting you on anything … A charge, a court-martial, an accusation of cowardice … Not even high bloody treason. You're here … In that bunker … The ultimate punishment … And that's where you're bloody staying: full stop!"

With that, Miles turned his back on Charles and stalked off. He felt sorry for him. Normally, he wouldn't have put a mad dog in a hole like that, but orders were orders; and as he'd pointed out to Blake on numerous occasions, with his army career at a cross roads, and with promotion meaning so much to him, he certainly wasn't going to cross swords with Sergeant-Major Ralf.

13

Most men in Able Company settled into their new position quickly, even though it was a very different proposition from the reserve company. This was where they really grew up, where they became battle-hardened soldiers. They were no longer able to regard the war as something static, something they only came face-to-face with after a march of half an hour to the forward company; something little more than digging, doing occasional patrols, and putting up with desultory bouts of inaccurate shelling.

Now, the war was right on top of them. There was never any break from it. There were no cushy options. Patrols went out into the valley every night with clear orders from Lawrence to engage the Chinese whenever possible; and those who manned the standing patrols realized they were quite likely to have the Chinese creep up on them to try to snatch a prisoner.

Shelling was frequent and the enemy had an infuriating habit of lobbing over mortar bombs with amazing accuracy throughout the day and night, with the result that casualties soon started to mount in numbers. The sudden and desperate cry for stretcher-bearers became common-place, and hardly an hour went by without casualties being man-handled down the narrow trenches to the CAP; then evacuated, never to be seen again. Above all they became accustomed to death. It was no longer a rarity. It happened every day, very often hourly. They learnt to accept it as part of their daily routine, something which could happen to anyone, including themselves. They learnt to accept death stoically and soon came to value the famous British stiff upper lip. It kept them on an even keel. Even when one of their friends was killed they realized that there was nothing to be gained by ostentatious and exaggerated displays of anger or sorrow.

The Chinese continued with their tactic of sending out numerous small patrols to scatter greeting cards and propaganda on the Rock's barbed wire and outside their minefields. They remained elusive to an infuriating degree and Lawrence increased the number of patrols and pushed them further out into the valley; but they never succeeded in trapping any Chinese and often, the following morning, men looked out into the valley and saw Chinese banners stuck in the very spot where they had been lying for over half the night.

There appeared to be no laws of nature with the Chinese. They seemed superhuman. They were never seen, seldom heard, but they were always somewhere at hand, loitering in the darkness.

Then the weather turned nasty again. If anything it was even colder than before. Men thought that impossible, but it wasn't--- it did get colder. The standing patrols had to be relieved far more frequently. It was well-nigh impossible for anyone to stick more than two hours just sitting there, waiting for something to happen. Men disregarded orders and took blankets out with them to wrap round their legs, and straw gathered from the beer crates was taken out in vast quantities and placed in the bottom of the shallow trenches.

Men felt compelled to smoke and patrol commanders turned a blind eye as they took it in turns to retire beneath one of the blankets and enjoy a cigarette. Burrows found that in this cold he was continually suffering from cramp, and after having been dragged back from a succession of patrols doubled up in agony it was decided that he should go on no more patrols until the weather abated.

Digging all but stopped. Lawrence was reluctant to give way on this and at first threatened to cancel the whole company's Tokyo leave unless they stuck at it; but just as before it eventually stopped because the supply of new pickaxes ran out. Even making a small impression on the ground was a morning's task. The fires in the bunkers were made bigger and better and they glowed red hot both day and night, and the consumption of petrol soared until men seemed to do nothing but heave 42-gallon drums of petrol up the monstrously steep hills.

The worst thing of all was the waiting. It was not just a matter of sitting down and waiting in the ordinary sense. This was the nerve-racking kind of waiting known only to fugitives and infantry soldiers. It combined fear of the enemy, the pain of the cold, the nagging emptiness caused by inadequate food, the dread of death or mutilation, always tempered with the hope and prayers that nothing would happen to them. At nights they waited in their weapon pits or on patrol, in the mornings they waited for the sound of the mortars as they worked on improving the position, and in the afternoons they slept fretfully as they waited for another night of waiting. It was nothing but waiting ... waiting.... waiting....

It was 0100 hours. Blake had just been woken by Miles. He stretched himself and ran his tongue over the yellow film of neglect that covered his teeth. He was still desperately tired. Since moving into the forward company he had been getting by on four hours' sleep a day and the strain was now becoming very apparent.

"Surely to God it's not time already," Blake mumbled as Miles roused him.

"Not quite, sir, but it always takes you about five minutes to wake up."

Miles went to the far corner of the bunker and took a can of boiling water off the fire. He handled it carefully with a handkerchief and made a cup of coffee. "Here you are, sir. This will bring you round a bit."

Blake sat up and drank the coffee. It tasted good despite being gritty. He watched Miles as he stuffed a three day-old letter into his breast pocket. "Anything been happening, Sergeant?"

"No, Sir. Not a thing."

"Good, that's the way I like it. Who's on patrol at the moment?"

"Hallows, sir. He keeps on reporting back every five minutes that it's the coldest night yet."

Blake grunted and watched enviously as Miles slipped into his sleeping bag, having shaken it first in case of any rats being in it. "Who is due to relieve him?"

"Smith, sir. He should be round here any moment."

"Roll on demob," said Blake inconsequently, hoping that Miles would converse with him. He hated just sitting in the CP with only the rats and the 88 set for company; but as always Miles merely turned over on his bunk and went to sleep.

Blake fixed the earphones over his head and started to read a copy of *Men Only*. He turned to the photograph of a semi-naked woman and appreciated it for a time. It was a good picture, he decided, and tearing it out of the magazine he pinned it on a wall alongside several others.

"Hullo, Mr. Blake," said Smith, "won't be any room left for more of those, shortly." He was fully clothed, ready for his standing patrol. "Okay if I start out?"

"Yes, sure. Like any rum to-night?"

Smith laughed. "No thanks, better not. We've got Burrows with us. Don't want to get him tight again." Smith pulled the hood of his parka over his head and walked outside. He could see Charles and Knight, their blankets slung over their arms, leaning against the outer wall of the bunker, and a few yards beyond them Burrows was beating his arms around his chest, trying to stave off the cold. "Ready? Let's get going then."

He led the way along the narrow trench, past the platoon cookhouse and then over the top and out through the barbed wire. They soon reached the standing patrol and after a few coarse remarks about the coldness had been exchanged the change-over was completed. Silence settled over them. They were resigned to two hours of waiting. They hoped that was what it would be. They could well do without the Chinese complicating things.

They had been out there just over an hour when they heard a slight rustling in the undergrowth some thirty yards ahead of them. At first they thought nothing of it. It was very probably their imagination. Men always imagined things towards the end of patrols. Or it might be rabbits or deer, or a wild cat. Then the noise grew louder and it became obvious that it was a party of Chinese; by the sound of it, at least a dozen strong.

Smith picked up the hand-set of the 88 wireless. He hardly dared to speak into it for fear of being overheard by the enemy. "One Peter. Message. Over."

"One Peter. Pass your message. Over."

"One Peter. Bandits approaching. Over."

Blake was dozing when he first heard the message, but instantly he became alert. He shook Miles and then grabbed the field telephone and contacted Lawrence.

"Good boy!" exclaimed Lawrence as though Blake was responsible for the emergency. "Get down there yourself Blake and see to it that you get really stuck in this time. Let's put an end to all these damned posters being stuck around the place."

"Very good, sir," replied Blake, trying not to sound alarmed. He threw the telephone down and turned to Miles. "Take over here, Sergeant. I'm taking out the emergency patrol."

It took Blake five minutes to assemble the emergency patrol. It took them another four minutes to reach the standing patrol, despite the fact that they ran most of the way. Smith's men were still crouching in two trenches: blankets had been dropped and outer gloves discarded to give them greater control over their weapons.

Blake said nothing as he slid in beside Smith, but just listened. The noise was unmistakable. The Chinese were no longer advancing up the hill. They were banging one of their propaganda banners into the ground. They were talking quite loudly, as though unaware of the patrol's presence thirty yards above them.

Blake made a rapid appreciation of the situation, really no more than guesswork. The Chinese were in the hollow of the re-entrant and only the darkness gave them any cover. He decided to send Smith's patrol farther up the hill and round to the right so that they would get the enemy in two streams of fire. After gaining the fire initiative his patrol would be able to charge them. He whispered his plan to Smith.

"Charge them, sir? No need to charge them. Just scare them off ..."

"Yes, okay. You're right." Blake realized he was being overdramatic. He took too much notice of Lawrence's gung-ho demands. If they chased them off they would very likely leave one of their propaganda banners behind; or if they'd already stuck one in the ground they could yank it out and take it back. That would be proof enough of success. What they could well do without was a major clash.

Smith led his men away as quietly as he could, but once off the well-worn track the undergrowth was dense and crackled under their feet like a forest-fire. Above their own noise, however, they could still hear the Chinese driving the wooden legs of their banners into the ground. When they reached the top of the re-entrant Smith felt more confident. He reckoned they had a good chance of taking the enemy by surprise. He switched his Sten to automatic, ordered the riflemen to fix bayonets, lowered himself gently to the ground, and started to wipe away some frost that had formed on his glasses.

Suddenly, before he had time to order his men to open fire, bullets were flying around them. Some were skimming overhead, others bit into the ground near where they lay before screaming off in a new direction. All around them the undergrowth quivered under the impact of Chinese small-arms fire. Without realizing it, they had walked into a Chinese trap. This time, instead of just sending a small propaganda party across the valley, the Chinese had sent a supporting patrol as well. Their banner party was no more than bait.

Smith heard a man cry out in agony. It sounded like a wild beast caught in a trap. It soon trailed away to a distant wail. Smith pushed his head hard against the ground, certain that the end was at hand. When he recovered himself sufficiently, he lifted his head slightly and saw a row of angry flashes advancing up the hill towards them. He looked to either side and saw Charles and Burrows just lying there. He started to fire wildly and yelled at the top of his voice:

"Fire! Fire, you bastards! Fire!"

Stens were soon stuttering uncertainly; then one of Smith's grenades landed among the enemy and sent some squealing like wounded pigs; then there was the solid, old-fashioned thudding of Burrows's rifle; then Charles at last opened up with his Bren gun. The Chinese began to advance up the hill again and Smith wondered what the hell had happened to Blake and his men. Why didn't they catch them from the flank? For a moment the fire fight was evenly poised, on a pinnacle, liable to go either way.

The gap between the two sets of weapons diminished rapidly as the Chinese continued up the hill and just when Smith became convinced that they were about to become embroiled in hand-to-hand fighting, Blake's men opened up from their flank. Their bullets cut straight into the Chinese and brought their advance to an abrupt halt.

Only the Chinese leader continued up the hill. He was screaming out as he sprinted forward, a fanatic who was spraying bullets ahead of him, reminiscent of a Japanese banzai warrior. He was closing in fast on Burrows and as Burrows re-cocked his rifle he felt a series of vicious jolts across his chest. He realized he'd been hit and screamed out in alarm. The Chinese leader was now right up to him. Burrows closed his eyes and thrust his rifle out in front of him as hard as he could. He felt his bayonet sink into the man. He squeezed his trigger and the man fell backwards, rolling several yards down the hill.

Burrows froze in horror at what he had done but the fire-fight went on. Charles went through two magazines on his Bren without the slightest idea of what he was firing at. Blake's group was doing much the same. Above it all, Smith kept yelling out: "Fire! Fire! Fire, you bastards! Fire!"

Then it became evident that the Chinese were in full flight. All of them, including the party working on the propaganda banner, were in disarray, dashing back into the valley. When they had all disappeared and were crashing through the undergrowth midway across the valley, Blake led his party up the hill to rejoin Corporal Smith.

There was general disorder: a mixture of jubilation and concern. Some men were shouting, others laughing, and somewhere two men were moaning in pain. Blake called them to order. He told Taylor to send a message back to the platoon CP and to get Miles standing by with stretchers. Then he checked around everyone to find out exactly what the situation was.

He found Smith bending over Knight. He had been hit in the legs and Smith was applying field dressings in an attempt to stop the bleeding. Another man had been hit in the stomach and a third, who had been hit in his temple, a fraction below his steel helmet, was already dead, just lying there.

An hour later Blake was sitting in his CP, his head resting in his hands. Miles was back in his sleeping bag, asleep; a can of water was simmering gently on the fire. Everything was back to normal. Knight and the other wounded man had had their wounds properly dressed in the CAP, and then, together with the dead man, taken back to battalion. Blake had taken the captured propaganda banner back to Major Lawrence when reporting what had happened. The only thing that remained was for Divisional Intelligence to issue a bulletin in the morning stating that Able Company of the Rocks had had a minor clash with a party of Chinese and inflicted several casualties.

The can of water on the space-heater came to the boil and Blake made coffee for Taylor and himself. He put plenty of sugar in both and then stirred them vigorously with Miles's fountain pen, their tea spoon have been nicked by someone. Then Corporal Smith pushed his way past the entrance blanket, so Blake poured him a coffee as well. The three of them sat in silence for a time, occasionally sipping at their mugs. Eventually, realizing that Blake wasn't going to ask him why he had called round, Smith's face broadened into a smile. He opened up his clenched fist and spread several squashed bullets out in front of Blake.

"We've just dug these out of Burrows."

Blake was mystified. "What do you mean? He came back here under his own steam okay."

"Don't get in a flap, Mr. Blake. He's okay, apart from still shitting himself after bayoneting that Chink. We got them out of his bullet-proof vest."

"You mean it stopped all those?"

Smith nodded. They exchanged glances, but said nothing.

14

Time passed; a week, maybe a fortnight. No one knew for sure; time was completely immaterial. It made no difference to them whether it was the third of the month or the twenty-third: their existence remained the same. There were 'flaps', genuine alarms, numerous clashes with the Chinese in no man's land, and as always the shelling and mortaring. Casualties mounted, more wounded than dead, but each one another retrograde step to their morale. Reinforcements arrived regularly and were absorbed into the company easily enough, even though Blake and Miles had to spend a considerable amount of their time putting them wise to 'wrinkles' which could well save their lives.

There was another cold spell, their third. For another week the wind again swept down from the north but this time it was as though both sides had become impervious to it; no longer was it an excuse to skulk about their positions, ignoring each other's existence.

Warmth was still at a premium and standing patrols became a nightmare. Winston returned from one clapping his gloved hands together as he entered his bunker. He took his Sten off his shoulder and flung it into a corner. He flopped on his bunk and felt it sag under his weight. He hugged himself in search of warmth, but he found none and continued to shiver. "What a bloody awful night. My God, it was cold. The coldest ever!" He looked at Bryant and Ford, the two men with whom he shared the bunker. They were both in sleeping bags on their bunks, trying hard to ignore him. They weren't concerned with what kind of a night he'd had. They had been on standing patrol just previous to Winston's so his mouthing-off didn't interest them one bit.

"Dry up, Winston," said Bryant. "We want to get a few minutes' shut-eye."

Winston made no immediate reply. He was looking at the space heater. The bloody thing was out! Stone bloody cold! He glared at Bryant and Ford. The idle swine! They hadn't bothered about keeping it going once they were in their bunks, even though they knew damned well he'd be coming in later. He always kept it going for them--- the bastards!

"What the hell's happened to the bloody fire?" he demanded.

"It's bloody gone out. Now keep quiet or I'll thump you."

Winston obeyed. Bryant was a big bastard who seldom minced his words. Winston walked across to the space heater and soon concluded that the 42-gallon drum must have dried up. He swore again, more bitterly than ever, and despite Bryant's threat he said: 'Why the hell didn't you keep it going?'

Neither of them replied. Winston grunted with disgust and walk out of the bunker, making towards the platoon CP where spare 42-gallon drums of petrol were kept. He had to struggle hard to roll one back to his own bunker. He swore loudly as he caught his fingers between the drum and the metal picket on which it rested. It was the last time he would ever raise a finger to help those two bastards.

When he eventually fixed the petrol on the roof of the bunker, he went back inside. Bryant and Ford were both asleep. He thought of waking them, but decided against it--- he wasn't a bastard like them! All the same they deserved it. He drew the blanket over the doorway in an effort to keep the cold out, but he only succeeded in plunging the bunker into darkness. Their candle had melted away days ago and now his only chance of any light was to get the space-heater going. He felt for the rubber tube coming through the roof from the petrol drum and placed it in the trough. He adjusted the metal clip so that petrol was dripping through. Then he struck a match and put it to the petrol. For a moment the fire blazed and there was divine warm, but there was some kind of obstruction in the tube and the fire spluttered and then went out. He readjusted the clip and tried again. Once more it flared and then went out.

Winston swore angrily, directing his abuse at Bryant and Ford. He realized that unless he got it alight soon it would be daylight and he would not be able to get any sleep before the morning's work started. He kicked the fire furiously. "Get going, you bastard!" He went through the same procedure of lighting it, but again he was only rewarded by momentary warmth. By now he was almost crying with anger. Why the hell wouldn't the bloody thing work? He kicked it again, so viciously this time that he hurt his foot. He tried to light it again but the result was the same.

He was now so livid that he acted without thinking. He lifted a 2-gallon can of petrol and poured it into the trough. Immediately, there was a great flash, a roaring explosion, and flames leapt back up his arms towards his face; he felt them licking about his ears, heard the faint 'fizz' of his hair singeing. He was momentarily blinded, seeing nothing but a mass of red. His one thought was for his own safety--- to get away from it all before it was too late.

He flung the petrol can away so that it landed beside Bryant's bed and forced his way through the blanket which was already in flames. For several seconds he stood outside the bunker whimpering with fear and pain, beating frantically at his smoldering clothes. Only when he heard a terrified yell from inside the bunker did he realize that the other two were still in there. By then it was already too late: the bunker was a blazing inferno. The entrance blanket had been devoured and the flames were roaring like a monstrous beast. He rushed forward so that the flames curled about him, almost dragging him into the blaze, and he was forced to retire to a safe distance.

He couldn't understand why Bryant and Ford hadn't already made a run for it. "Get out quick!" he yelled.

At first there was no reply. Then there was an agonized shriek. It was not a shriek of pain, or a shriek for help, not even of fear; but one of resignation to a horrible fate. In panic, Winston stared about, looking for something with which to extinguish the fire. He grabbed at an old sandbag protruding from the side of the trench and threw it into the middle of the fire, but the flames were now so sweeping and all-consuming that it made absolutely no impression.

"Help! Help! Fire!"

Winston's voice echoed about the platoon position. Flames were now licking at the main timber supports of the roof; there was a loud crack and a corner of the bunker collapsed. Some .303 rounds exploded and the bullets thumped into the sandbag walls of the bunker. Winston suddenly remembered the grenades. There was a pile of them by his bed. He knew that once they went off Bryant and Ford wouldn't have a chance in hell of surviving. Yet they had to survive. They couldn't die because he had been stupid enough to throw petrol about. He made a third futile attempt to enter the bunker.

Charles appeared down the trench, smiling and highly amused. There had been so many fires in the company without serious consequences that many men regarded them as a joke. "Nice old bonfire you've got going here, Winston."

"They're still in there," gasped Winston, half-choking with smoke. "Bryant and Ford--- they are still in there."

The smile disappeared from Charles's face and he hurried off to get more help. Soon a large crowd of men stood outside the bunker, but there was nothing they could do. The heat was an impenetrable barrier.

Then the unexpected happened. After uttering another shriek, Bryant rushed out from the leaping flames towards the circle of men; he was a human torch, blazing from head to foot. The men recoiled in surprise and horror. Their circle parted, allowing Bryant to dash on down the trench. He slowed with every step, rebounding from one side of the trench to the other as he lurched along. Then he turned through a gap in the trench wall and started to stagger down the hill, some of his clothes falling off and starting small fires in the undergrowth.

"Quick! After him!"

Winston led the chase, sprinting wildly, leaving the flames to satisfy their hunger on the bunker and Ford, who, for a brief moment, appeared in the doorway only to collapse back into the flames. Then the first of the grenades exploded, sealing his fate. The inferno became a roaring, hell-like beast, getting worse as more grenades went off.

Bryant was still staggering down the hill, going forward with the impetus of his initial rush. Eventually, he stumbled into the first belt of barbed wire which surrounded the position and he lay there motionless, everything still blazing except his head, which seemed content to smolder. Blankets, coats, scarves and other articles of clothing were produced and wrapped round him in an effort to extinguish the flames feasting on his flesh; but they were clearly too late. There was already a smell of roast meat and he had ceased to make any cries of protest.

By degrees, the flames were brought under control and extinguished, leaving their victim hanging on two strands of barbed wire, smoke and smell drifting from him gently. Apart from the slight heaving of his chest and the quivering of his red, raw hands he might just as well have been dead. Men hesitated; they waited for someone else to lift him from the wire and expose what they knew would be a horrific sight. The smell was bad enough but what would he look like?

Winston went forward. He was responsible. He had to take the lead. He removed a few articles of clothing which had been wrapped around Bryant and placing his slightly burnt hands under Bryant's chest he began to pull upwards. As he did so he felt flesh falling away like meat falling off the bone of a well-cooked joint.

"He's still alive," said someone who was now helping Winston.

The remark gave Winston fresh hope. Perhaps he would survive. Perhaps, if they got him to the CAP quickly, Tompkin would be able to patch him up. Tompkin would bloody well have to--- he couldn't be allowed to die.

One of the strands of barbed wire Bryant had fallen on had sunk deep into his mouth, cutting through his cheeks to the back of his jaw, almost splitting his head in two. As they took a fresh grip on his body he started to moan with pain and Winston tried to comfort him. "All right, Bryant. You'll be all right when we get you to the CAP."

Bryant gasped weakly as they pulled him from the wire. "Gently, for Christ's sake," said one of the helpers, but although they lifted him as slowly as they could their efforts were futile. As his face left the wire, flesh from his cheeks, jaw, and chin slipped away from the bone, and was left on the wire. The lower half of his hairless head was stripped naked, his cheek bones were exposed and shining with smoothness, only a thin film of watery blood giving them any protection.

As they lifted him into a vertical position some of the clothes fell from his legs. Flames burst into life again, feasting on his flesh with fresh vigor. As Winston beat the flames out and listened to Bryant whimpering, he realized that he might just as well have let them burn.

A stretcher was produced and as Bryant was eased on to it. Winston ran on ahead to warn Tompkin, hoping that with sufficient warning he might be able to save him. When Winston reached the CAP he had to wake Tompkin. "What the hell's the matter with you, Winston?" he demanded. "Why don't you let a fellow sleep in peace?"

"They are bringing in a fellow who has been burnt. You've got to help him ."

Tompkin dragged himself from his blankets. "Oh, for Christ's sake! Not another bloke playing with fire? Someone will kill themselves one of these days. Some people.... Who is it this time?'

"Bryant."

"How the hell did it happen?"

Winston grabbed him by the collar and shook him furiously. "Never mind how it happened. You've bloody well got to do something for him. Do you understand? You've bloody well got to."

When Bryant arrived on the stretcher Tompkin simply stood and stared at him for several seconds. There was only half a man there and the sight nearly made him faint. Tompkin looked about the faces of those who had brought him and realized that they were expecting him to save this man's life. He felt utterly helpless. He had not the faintest idea what to do.

"Well?" demanded Winston.

Tompkin responded automatically. He started to remove some of the clothing, pretending that there was hope. As he took off the clothing next to his skin long strips of human tissue peeled off and in several places there was again that ghastly white gleam of bone being laid bare.

Tompkin stood back. He lit himself a cigarette and blew the smoke out of his mouth in long sighs. Everyone else watched silently. "It's no good," he said softly.

"Tompkin! Can't you do anything?"

Tompkin stubbed his cigarette out and moved forward again. He started to remove more clothing with the same ghastly result.

Winston hurried to the doorway and looked out across the hills, seeing nothing.

Within a few minutes Bryant opened his bare jaw, as though trying to smile, his eyes searching the roof. Then he died, oblivious to everything except relief from pain.

15

Life dragged on like a prison sentence. The war continued to increase in direct proportion to the easing of the cold.

A large part of One Platoon's aggression was directed against the rats which continued to plague them. The cold affected them just as much as it did humans and they became more and more bunker-bound. They were more audacious than ever in the way they stole and scavenged for food. Taylor received a rat trap in a parcel from home and for several days it was passed from bunker to bunker, from man to man, and the number of dead rats in the platoon increased. They were hunted with glee and, sensing the danger, the surviving rats became more cunning and elusive. Eventually, the trap became so over-used that the spring broke and the rats returned, more impudent than ever, knowing that they had triumphed.

In their general depression and frustration, men stared harder and longer at frayed photographs of semi-naked women that they'd pinned to the walls of their bunkers, and they discussed at greater length the finer and more excruciating details of what they were going to do to the first woman they had on Tokyo leave. Coarse minds thrived on the memories of past triumphs and imaginations were pressed to their filthy limits.

More days passed and still the same jobs had to be done, still the same faces to be seen on waking up, or in the darkness while on patrol; still the same meager rations based on corned beef and American C-rations, and still the same unhealthy smell in the bunkers. Men got dirtier and more soot-engrained from their petrol fires and inevitably men became lousy.

"If we don't move into reserve soon, sir, we'll have to dig another of those twelve-foot latrines," said Hale at one of the platoon daily orders groups. "This one is just about full. Another couple of dozen good old British craps and it'll overflow."

The situation was getting serious.

Burrows pushed his head cautiously through the doorway of the Company CP. He entered self-consciously, certain that everyone would be watching him and that no one would welcome him. He was right. "What do you want?" Corporal Cross demanded.

"I was told to report to you, Corporal."

"Oh, yes, Burrows! There's some form or other here for you to sign. Don't make too much noise. Major Lawrence is asleep in the corner."

Burrows glanced across the bunker and saw a vague, ball-shaped figure sprawled in a chair, a dead cigarette hanging from his mouth. His right hand was still resting adjacent to his backside. "Why doesn't he go and lie down on his bunk?"

Cross was fumbling about in a pile of papers, looking for the document concerning Burrows. He chuckled. "Damned if I know. He's always like that, though. Just sits there waiting and waiting, always refusing to get any sleep, always frightened that he'll miss something. Until he suddenly just curls up in his chair, nods off, and sleeps solidly for hours on end. And he's always furious when he comes to. Demands what would have happened if the Chinks had attacked, and then blames me for having let him go to sleep in the first place ... Stupid old sod."

"Why let him go to sleep then, Corporal?"

Cross was amused. The question was so naive. "Believe me Burrows, it is well worth it to have him out of the way for a few hours. You've no idea what bliss it is when he's dead to the world." Cross eventually found the form he was looking for. "Can't quite get the hang of this, but apparently you've got to sign it. It's something about doing another six months service. It doesn't sound your cup of tea, exactly."

Burrows took the form from Cross and studied it. As Cross had said, it had something to do with an extension of service. His mind immediately flashed back to the day on which he had signed on before, and he suddenly recognized the form. He pushed it back to Cross and laughed nervously. "Here, Corporal, you can have it back. I'm not signing anything."

"You've got to--- adjutant's orders."

"I don't care whose orders they are. They aren't catching me again."

Cross stared back, not knowing what to do. Men usually obeyed immediately on the mention of the adjutant. "Well...." He hesitated then added: "I don't quite know . . . Tell you what, I'll go and get Nobby Clark. He'll know what it is all about."

A few minutes later Captain Clark entered the bunker. He recognized the form immediately. There weren't many army forms he didn't recognize. "Well, let me be the first to congratulate you, Burrows. The army is a great life. You're doing the right thing."

"How do you mean, sir? They conned me once into agreeing to another six months' service, so I'm certainly not going to do it again."

Clark gave a friendly laugh. "I think you'll find Burrows that you did not actually sign on for an extension of service. What you signed was an agreement to extend your two years' service when it came to an end. When does it end?"

"Very soon, sir. This month."

"Just as I thought. Technically, you can't extend your service by six months until you've actually finished your two years. But what you did was agree to do so."

An expression of bewilderment flashed across Burrows's face. "You mean that I haven't signed on at all?"

"Not technically. Not yet. But you're going to now."

"Good God," laughed Cross. "I never thought I'd live to see someone actually sign on."

Cross's sarcasm infuriated Burrows. He wouldn't sign on against his will. He would not be fooled again. "Surely, sir, if I only said that I would do it, it doesn't mean that I have to . . . I mean, surely I can change my mind?"

"A bit late for that, I'm afraid. You should have considered everything before you signed the agreement."

"But I signed that agreement to avoid coming here. I was supposed to be transferred to the York and Lancs band. And then stay on for six months extra to take part in a special ceremonial. But then it was cancelled. So they sent me out here instead."

Clark shrugged his shoulders. "That is the position even if you do regret it, young fellow. Take the form away and read the small print. Then let me or Corporal Cross have it back as soon as possible."

Burrows left the CP. He felt like crying with annoyance and frustration. Twenty minutes later he signed the form. It was an untidy signature since he had hesitated halfway through it. Charles watched him with disgust. He didn't really give a damn what happened to Burrows, whether he stayed in the army or not, but to sit there and watch him give way to the army without the least resistance made Charles feel sick. He loathed the way the army always came out on top, the way blokes were treated like shit.

"I'll tell you this straight, Burrows ...You're the biggest bloody fool I've ever met. The only thing they can't make you do in the British army is sign along the dotted line."

"But I agreed to. . . ."

"To hell with that. They didn't think twice about doing the dirty on you. You should still be back in Blighty, blowing your trumpet in the York and Lancs ... Not out here, stopping Burp gun bullets. To hell with them. They can't hold you on an agreement. The only thing they can hold you to is your signature on that of piece of paper."

Burrows looked at it sadly. "But I've already signed it."

"Then scratch the bloody thing out," shouted Charles. He regarded Burrows in despair. For the past few weeks he'd moved into Burrows's bunker more or less uninvited rather than stay in his own rat hole; and he'd come to quite like him, even though he was pathetic. "Why don't you go and see Blake about it? He'll tell you what's best. He doesn't like the army any more than the rest of us."

Burrows smiled. It was the first bit of sound advice he had received. "Thanks, Charlie. I think I'll do that."

"Well before you do anything, for God's sake scratch that bloody signature out."

Ten minutes later he saw Blake. Blake listened to the whole story carefully, asking the odd question to make sure he understood. He found it terribly complicated but it certainly appeared that Burrows had been treated unfairly. Even so, for all his sympathy, Blake had no idea what to suggest. Eventually he turned to Miles, as he had done so many times in the past.

"Can't say that I know anything about it, sir," said Miles. "Try the adjutant. I know you don't get on with him but at least he knows his job and will be able to explain exactly what the position is."

It took Blake several minutes to contact the adjutant over the field telephone, but when he did he was relieved to find him in a cheerful mood. "Hullo, Blake, young fellow. How are you? Everything is very quiet up your end?"

"Not too bad, sir. What I've phoned you about is a man in my platoon named Burrows. He's just turned up with a form which he's supposed to sign, about extending his service another six months."

"I know the case. He was going to stay on in the UK for special band duties with the York and Lancs band for a big ceremonial parade taking place after his two years was up. But there was a major cock-up. The York and Lancs got posted to Malaya instead. So they sent him back to us and he ended up out here--- as you obviously know! And we've got a form he signed promising to sign on for another six months once his two years' is up. You see ... Well let me put it this way... When you only sign on for another six months you can only do it at the end of your service ... Not like National Servicemen extending their service for a whole year, who can sign at any time ... Get it, Blake?"

"Sort of, sir."

"He should be playing in our band, of course. But out here we haven't got one. So he's in your tender care instead. Anyhow, don't worry about the small print. Just get him to sign it and then send it back to me. I'll sort it all out. All his pay and everything ... He'll be getting a handsome rise ..."

Blake picked his words carefully. "I see, sir, but the thing I'm not quite certain about is whether he is actually compelled to sign on."

The adjutant laughed. "Well, of course he could go back on it. We can't force him to sign. He should never have come out here, really. But it's no good crying over spilt milk. He won't know the difference anyhow."

Blake thanked him and rang off. He had found out all he wanted. He turned to Burrows again. "You don't have to sign, but you are expected to. A gentleman's agreement, if you see what I mean?"

"Yes, sir, I see."

Burrows remained standing in the doorway and Blake eyed him curiously. "Is there something else?"

"Well, I don't know, sir. I don't know what to do. What would you advise?"

Blake shrugged his shoulders. "I can't really say. It's up to you. I don't know how you feel about various things."

"Well as I see it, the army has done the dirty on me. I had no idea they were going to send me out of here, instead of staying with the York and Lancs. So why should I sign now, sir?"

Blake still made no reply. His sympathies lay entirely with Burrows.

Yet he also realized that if he told him not to sign it would cause all kinds of ructions: Lawrence, the adjutant, and the Colonel would only ever see it from the army's point of view. They would point furiously to the fact that Burrows had made an agreement and that it was his duty towards his country, his Regiment, and his comrades, to honor that agreement.

Blake studied Burrows carefully as he stood before him. He was more like a boy-scout than an infantry soldier. "I'm not saying that this is sound advice, Burrows," he said, at length. "And I'm certainly not saying that you should necessarily take it. But If I was in your shoes I wouldn't sign it."

Miles said nothing but walked out of the bunker.

"Thank you, sir," said Burrows. "I just wanted to know what the position was and the best thing to do."

Once Burrows had gone, Blake was left wondering if he'd done the right thing. His immediate regret was the rift it had caused with Miles, yet he also felt a glow of satisfaction, a feeling that he had acted correctly, on a matter of principle.

"Stand up, man. Stand up straight!"

It was CSM Ralf's usual parrot cry before he marched anyone into the presence of Lawrence on orders or an official interview. "And don't say a word except when answering a direct question.'

"Sir!"

"Quick . . . march!" Ralf followed Burrows in. "Private Burrows reporting for interview, sir."

Lawrence looked up severely from his chair. He had heard all about Burrows and he was furious that anyone in his company should dare to defy authority. Nothing got a company a bad name more quickly than this kind of outrageous behavior. He was prepared to tear Burrows to pieces if the need arose, but as he stared at the boy's face for a full half a minute without speaking he didn't envisage any difficulty in making him do as he was told.

"Now then, Burrows," he began when he considered that he obtained the maximum effect of silent scrutiny, "I hear that before coming out here you agreed to join us for a further six months at the end of your National Service."

Burrows hesitated. "Well, yes, sir. I suppose so."

"Excellent. I'm very pleased to hear it. We are always pleased to have men of good characters. Mr. Blake tells me that he has a high opinion of you ... Promotion might not be all that far away."

Burrows lowered his eyes in amazement. He had never heard such an obvious lie.

"Look to your front!" barked Ralf.

"I'm especially glad that you are staying with us," continue Lawrence, "because we have a lot of work in front of us and this company has already made a tradition for itself, and that is a lot easier to maintain and improve upon if we all stick together as one unit." He smiled at Burrows, thinking that he had been successful. "Right! And I'll wish you the best of luck in the future." He grinned and groped in his pockets for non-existent cigarettes. Williamson handed him one, already lit.

"Excuse me, sir, but I don't intend to sign." Through his fear and excitement Burrows's words came in sudden jerks.

"Now look, Burrows, I do not wish to have any trouble with you. You know the position. You told me a few moments ago that you have agreed to carry on in the army and a document proving exactly that is held by the adjutant, so just do as you are told and save a lot of trouble and unpleasantness."

Burrows nearly weakened again, but the fact that Blake was on his side fortified him. He knew that he had the right to choose, and he was not going to be frightened into submission. "I know that I agreed, sir. But the point is that I wasn't allowed to sign on before especially so that I might have the opportunity to alter my mind!"

"And who gave you all this erroneous information?"

"Mr. Blake, sir. And he checked up with the adjutant."

Lawrence's moustache twitched as he screwed his face into a tight frown. He jerked forward in his chair, his temper rising. That an officer should openly advise a man not to keep an agreement of this nature was almost unbelievable. "Burrows, I don't take such cases as this lightly. You have made an undertaking with the army and you have got to keep to it. No man in my company behaves the way you are trying to and gets away with it. Do you understand that?"

"I understand what you mean, sir, but I'm afraid that it makes no difference to my decision."

"Really! Well I'm afraid that's not good enough. I'll make sure you face up to your obligations even if I have to take it up with the Colonel or even the Brigadier. Dismiss!"

The Battalion CP was as immaculate as ever. Blake and Lawrence were sitting beside the table, both with harried expressions. Outside the bunker Burrows stood rigidly to attention under the watchful eyes of the RSM and two provost corporals.

The Colonel entered and strode straight to the table without any recognition of the salutes he received. "All right," he said to the adjutant, and finding time to fling Blake a reproachful glare, "march him in."

The adjutant relayed the order to the RSM and Burrows came almost running in and halted on the wrong foot, which brought a stern reprimand from the RSM.

As was his manner, the Colonel came straight to the point. "Now then, Burrows. Why won't you sign on as you should?" Burrows looked back defiantly. With Blake there he felt that there was someone on his side and he was determined to follow the well-tried system of stubbornness and silence.

"I asked you why you won't sign on, Burrows?"

"Just don't want to, sir."

"It is not just a matter of saying you don't want to. I want some definite reasons before I will be satisfied."

"I've nothing to say, sir."

The Colonel's temper rose. Nothing annoyed him more than men who refused to give reasons for their actions. "You must have something to say. You must have some reasons?"

"I've nothing to say, sir, except that I'm not signing."

The Colonel saw that it was hopeless. Some men were as stubborn as mules and he could see that Burrows was one of them. "Very well, Burrows, that will be all. I think Major Lawrence has told you how we feel about your behavior and we will waste no time in getting you out of this regiment."

The RSM marched Burrows out of the CP. Everyone saluted and started to leave. "Mr. Blake, I should like to see you for a moment, please," ordered the Colonel. Blake was not surprised to hear the words. "Yes, sir. Certainly."

"Shall I stay, sir?' asked Lawrence, determined that he should have an opportunity of expressing himself.

"No, Dick, you'd better get back to your company."

Blake stood to attention in front of the table, just as Burrows had done only a few minutes before. The Colonel leaned forward, a gesture that expressed his displeasure. He expected trouble from the rank and file, but certainly not from one of his officers. "Major Lawrence tells me that you told Private Burrows not to co-operate with us. Is that true?'

"Yes, sir."

"So why did you do that?"

"I don't really know, sir."

"For God's sake, don't you start! I can take this 'nothing to say' attitude from private soldiers, but surely to God you have some sensible explanation for your actions?"

Blake explained briefly the circumstances in which Burrows had made the agreement, repeating almost verbatim what the adjutant had said to him. "So when he asked me what I would do in his position, I told him. The army definitely broke its part of the agreement. And they did it first."

"Very good, Blake. That will be all."

Blake remained standing there, hoping that some kind of judgment would be passed on him, that the Colonel would give him twenty-four hours in which to get packed and ready to leave. Nothing of the kind happened, however, and instead the Colonel said: "You don't like this war very much, do you, Blake?"

"No, sir. Not much. But then who does?"

"Oh, quite a few people, you'd be surprised. You did the wrong thing, Blake. You realize that now, don't you?"

The Colonel's change in attitude, and his reasonableness, meant Blake didn't have the courage to prevent the lie slipping from his lips. "Yes, sir. I realize that now."

"All right, Blake. Don't worry about it. It's hardly of earth-shattering importance. Our success doesn't depend on the likes of Burrows. Now you had better get back to your platoon before stand-to."

A week later Burrows was all packed and ready go back to divisional headquarters on the first leg of his journey back to Blighty. To his amazement those not on duty in One Platoon went down to the jeep head to see him off. Due to his triumph over the Establishment he was a hero. Taylor, who was gifted with his hands, had mounted the six squashed bullets dug out of Burrows's armored vest on a wooden butt of a captured Burp gun. In a very rough and ready ceremony, Blake presented the trophy to Burrows.

Burrows was so touched by the presentation that tears came to his eyes. He'd always thought they despised him, but here they were displaying true comradeship. For a moment he felt so kindly disposed towards them that he felt like saying: "Never mind, fellows. I think I'll stay with you all after all."

But he didn't, of course. He knew that would be the quickest way to lose their respect; that they would tell him not to be such a bloody fool and to bugger off quick!

16

It was announced that the entire British Commonwealth Division would go into reserve for the first time, for a minimum of six weeks. The division was to be replaced in the line by the 9th US Division and the change-over was due to take place a week later.

Morale within the Commonwealth Division leapt as never before. It meant, among other things, that every man would be able to take five days R and R leave in Tokyo, something they had all been dreaming about, in many cases quite literally. Everywhere grim faces were split by broad smiles; small parties assembled in the bunkers and reserves of beer were brought out of hiding for celebrations. Whenever two men met there were always hearty greetings and a short conversation which invariably started with the words: "Well, it won't be long now."

In some quarters the aftermath of the Burrows affair lingered on. Major Lawrence was never going to forget what had happened. It wasn't Burrows's departure that worried him; far rather the attitude of Blake. After such blatant disloyalty, he couldn't see how he could continue to have him as a platoon commander. He was firmly of the opinion that the Colonel should have kicked him out of the battalion: indeed, the regiment!

It was Nobby Clark who persuaded him otherwise. He pointed out that when it came to some action, Blake had an excellent record and that someone straight out of Eaton Hall, without the in-depth training of Sandhurst, was bound to slip up when it came to matters of man-management. He had admitted his mistake to the Colonel, so the matter was best left there and forgotten.

In One Platoon CP the atmosphere remained strained. Sergeant Miles never actually came out and blamed Blake, but he was unable to prevent it from forcing a barrier between them.

In the rest of the company the mood was buoyant. A party of Americans came for a day's recce of the position and at the jeep-head heavy stores and weapons kept arriving, all of which illustrated the greater firepower enjoyed by the Americans. Some of the Americans stayed overnight to familiarize themselves with the standing patrols and minefields and Blake, Bartram and Goodall had long sessions with their opposite numbers, generally putting them in the picture about the position and the habits of the Chinese.

The day before the change-over, dawn seemed to come slower than ever before.

Blake watched the faint glow of sunlight spread up over the southern hills. His sloping shoulders were hunched forward his hands buried deep in his pockets and, as he looked down the empty re-entrant, he could see nothing except the naked and gnome-like bushes which swayed gently under the force of the bitter wind that had plagued them for so long. A giant yawn made him gasp for air and he was conscious of a foul taste lingering in his mouth. He'd left the hot and stuffy CP with the express purpose of cooling off but now, as the cold wind chilled him to the core, he hurried back in.

He hadn't slept during the night. It had taken him three hours to show the American officer around the minefields, and as soon as the American departed, Lawrence had called him into the company CP and threatened to stop his Tokyo leave unless there was an immediate improvement in the cleanliness of his platoon area, and unless the new latrine they had started on was completed before they handed over to the Americans. "They won't think much of us, Blake, if we leave them with nowhere to have a shit."

Blake was unable to refute this, so he made sure it was completed.

Blake yawned again as he re-entered the CP. He looked at his watch to make sure it was time to hand over duties to Miles. He shuffled over to him and gave him a firm shake.

"Sergeant! Time for you to take over."

He flopped down bedside the wireless and watched Miles as he rolled off his bunk. He noticed with a sudden rush of anger that Miles was wearing a pair of gym shoes instead of boots, as laid down in orders.

"Why haven't you got your boots on, Sergeant?" Blake realized that it was the first time he had ever reprimanded him.

Miles looked down at his feet, not very concerned. "Oh, sorry, sir. Forgot…"

Blake let the matter drop. It didn't matter a damn what he was wearing.

"Any coffee this morning?" asked Miles as they changed places. Blake laughed. "Oh, damn. Sorry. I forgot." Miles was not amused, but likewise he let it drop.

The blackout blanket was thrust aside and Taylor entered. His narrow face was shining, and large crystals of frost had formed on his eyebrows and several tufts of hair protruded from beneath his cap comforter.

"How did you enjoy being on patrol for a change?" asked Miles.

"Not so bad, Sarge," answered Taylor. "It was quite snug down there with all those blankets. I don't know what they've all been complaining about. Apart from Winston yakking all the time, it was bearable."

"All the patrol in now?" asked Miles. Taylor nodded. "I'll go and stand the sentries down then, sir," added Miles.

Blake settled down on his bunk. He rolled on to his stomach and yawned yet again. He was nearly asleep when an abrupt and violent explosion nearly threw him off his bunk. He tried to ignore it, hoping that it would not occur again, but he knew instinctively that it would. There was something strange about the explosion which spelt trouble. Almost immediately there was another, louder explosion, obviously a lot nearer. Dust and small stones fell from the roof. Then there was a third explosion and the whole bunker was enveloped in dust and rubble. Blake and Taylor coughed and spluttered.

"What the hell is that, sir?" demanded Taylor.

"Damned if I know," shouted Blake above the sound of another explosion. He stayed beside his bunk, stubbornly hoping that the explosions would cease as suddenly as they had started. They did not stop, however. They continued with increasing rapidity. "I'd better go and see what the hell is happening," Blake said.

He only got to the doorway when he bumped into Miles. He stumbled in, a long, deep cut across the length of his forehead, his hair disheveled, gasping for breath, and with one of his gym shoes missing. Blake stared at him blankly.

"It's our own tank on 163! It's firing at us!"

"What do you mean? What are you talking about?"

"That bloody tank! It fired at me as I went into the lateral trench. The tank you can see from Winston's bunker."

"But. . . ."

"Never mind '*but*'. The shell burst a few yards away from me. My head is bloody near bursting."

Blake saw that Miles was badly shaken, but he still found it impossible to accept what he was saying. "Why the hell should one of our own tanks fire at us?"

"How the bloody hell should I know?" stormed Miles. "All I can tell you is that it is firing. I saw the flash of the gun. And I'm damned lucky to be back here in one piece."

"It must be a Chinese support gun. ..."

Miles had reached the limit of his patience. He had respect for rank, but he also had sufficient sense to realize that sometimes this quality was best disregarded. "I couldn't give a bastard what you say. I'm telling you that it came from our own tank, and unless we do something about it bloody quick that whole line of bunkers along that trench will be blown sky-high ... And the men in them."

Blake was still unable to grasp the urgency of the situation.

Miles was desperate. "For Christ's sake pull your finger out," he yelled, catching hold of Blake by the shoulders. "There are men in those bunkers, liable to get killed at any second unless we do something about it. If you don't believe me go and have a look for yourself. I'm getting on to Lawrence." He snatched up the phone and rang it furiously, leaving Blake standing there, bewildered.

Blake decided to see for himself without further delay. He ran through the trenches towards the line of bunkers under fire. There had been no further shelling since Miles had returned to the bunker and Blake temporarily lost his fear and was standing upright. Then he saw the long, pencil-shaped barrel of the Centurion's 20-pounder pointing straight at him. He dived down in the trench and waited a minute or so. When nothing else happened he raised his head and peered cautiously over the top of the trench wall. As was the custom with the tanks, it was perched audaciously on the very top of the hill, and Blake could see a thin film of smoke still drifting up from the barrel of the gun.

Blake stood up, looking about to see where the other shells had landed. By chance he glanced back towards the tank and saw the flash of its gun out of the corner of his eye. He was instantly full length to the bottom of the trench, and before he had time to register a thought the shell landed--- ten yards to one side and level with the top of the trench. The blast was overpowering it rendered him unconscious; his horizontal body was flung into the air, and he disappeared in a mushroom of dust. He dropped to the ground with several large clots of earth and the jolt of his fall brought him round. His eyes were filled with dirt and everything around him was swimming about crazily; he could hear nothing but a high-pitched buzz and he felt a warm stream of blood oozing from his ears and flowing swiftly down the sides of his jaw.

For a few seconds he just lay in the trench nursing his head and trying to recover his full senses. He wanted to run back to the safety of the CP but he realized that there were still men in the bunkers further down the trench and he had to get them out before it was too late.

He started to crawl towards the bunkers, keeping himself absolutely flush with the ground. Soon he reached a position where he could see down the entire length of trench, and outside the last bunker, cringing against the trench wall, was Lowe, his face covered in a thick layer of shaving soap, and a tin, which a few minutes before had been full of hot water, lying empty by his feet. The first shell had landed while he was shaving and the blast had caused him to cut his cheek deeply. It had also scared him so witless that he couldn't move. As he saw Blake emerge from the cloud of dust he shouted: "What the hell's going on?"

"It's the tank! It's the tank!" Blake yelled. "Get out quick and tell those in the other bunkers to get out as well. Hurry up, man! For Christ's sake hurry! Hurry!"

Blake had always realized that Lowe was not the brightest of men, but he did not expect him to act as he did. He ignored the men in the other bunkers, stood erect, and ran as fast as he could down the trench, his arms flaying the air. He literally long-jumped over Blake's prostrate body and then he vanished round the corner in the trench. Immediately, chasing their target, but always a few feet behind, the tank's machine-gun splattered the top of the trench with bullets. Even though they'd missed Lowe, they continued firing.

Another shell landed and Blake resumed groaning on account of the pain in his ears. He wondered if this was going to be the end of everything. He had only to raise his head few inches and he would have been a dead man a hundred times over. He wriggled along the bottom of the trench towards the bunkers, shouting as he went. In the first bunker there was a dead body. It was so mangled up that Blake couldn't even identify it. There was so obviously nothing he could for the man that he went on to the next bunker. O'Hara was full length on the floor, a wooden beam, which had been dislodged from the roof, half across him. He smiled grimly at Blake and muttered a curse. He was shaking with fear, but quite confident that so long as he stayed flush with the ground, he would be safe. "What the hell has bitten the bastards?" he demanded.

"Bloody fools want their heads examined," gasped Blake. "Get out of here, O'Hara. Before the bunker falls in completely." His words were drowned out as another shell landed. They both hugged the ground. "We're best if we stay here," shouted O'Hara, spitting dust. "Let's just lie doggo ..."

"Get out, I tell you! Get out! And for heaven's sake don't stand up. Who else is in these bunkers?"

"Rawlins and Charlie. He's in Burrows's old bunker. And Lowe, of course, that's all." O'Hara freed himself from the broken timbers and crawled away. Blake watched him go, realizing the Rawlins must be the dead man. He went on further down the trench to seek out Charles. He was literally sheltering under the bottom bunk. A rat was sitting there, watching him, no doubt wondering what he was up to. Blake shouted at him to get out and follow O'Hara down the trench. He followed close behind him. As they edged towards safety, bullets were still thudding into the earth a few inches above them. When they got near safety a shell scored a direct hit on Lowe's bunker and reduced it to a pile of rubble.

Once Blake was sure that O'Hara and Charles were under cover in a bunker, and out of the tank's line of fire, he went back to the platoon CP. Miles was still on the telephone, continually pulling exasperated expressions. Blake seized the jar of rum and poured himself half a tumbler of the dark liquid. It steadied his nerves immediately. His ears had stopped bleeding and he could faintly hear what was going on; he recognized the rasping noise coming over the field telephone as Lawrence's voice.

"For Christ's sake, what's happening, Sergeant?"

Miles covered up the mouthpiece. "The silly bastard is calling me all the names under the sun. He says that it must be a Chinese support gun from either Abel or Cain."

"Tell him that we've actually seen the gun firing."

"I have done! He just called me a stupid swine."

"Here, let me have that telephone." Blake grabbed the instrument and ignored Lawrence's voice. "Blake speaking! Now look here ..."

"No! You look here, Blake! Where have you been? And what is all this rubbish Miles has been blathering about to do with being fired on by one of our own tanks?"

"What Miles has told you is perfectly true."

"Oh, for God's sake ... Don't you start ..."

"I've seen the flash of that tank's gun."

"Be your age, Blake. That gun isn't even pointing in your direction. I've been out and looked."

"Well you've looked at the wrong tank. You come here and you'll get your bloody head blown off ..."

"Don't speak to me like that, Blake. Just because you have come under some heavy fire there is no need to become hysterical. Those are enemy support guns from either Abel or Cain."

"I've seen that tank fire and so have three of my men. One of them has been killed. Blown to hell! Another four of us were bloody near killed as well. It's still firing now. At least you check up on it. You've got to stop it."

"Very well! But in the meantime you just remember who you are talking to. And keep those bunkers clear of men."

"There won't be any bloody bunkers left," replied Blake, but his words were wasted. Lawrence had already flung the telephone down, telling everyone in the company CP that he had never heard such insubordination in all his life. He paced up and down the bunker fuming with anger.

"Shall I get battalion on the blower, sir?" asked Williamson.

"Yes, I suppose so." Lawrence was soon speaking to the adjutant. "Look, I'm sorry to worry you at this hour in the morning, but I've had a complaint from this fellow Blake that he is being fired on by the tank on 163. In fact I think it's a Chinese support gun from Cain--- but it might be Abel … I'm not quite sure. But do you think you could check up on that tank, just to satisfy Blake?"

The adjutant turned over in his bunk, trying to recall which hill was Abel and which was Cain. "All right, Dick. You're a confounded nuisance, but I'll get someone to check it out. This fellow Blake is a damned sight more trouble than he's worth." As he prepared to go back to sleep he turned to his assistant and told him to check things out.

"Ah! Is that the duty officer of White? Thanks heavens for that. It's the assistant adjutant of Red here. We've had a report that the tank in your area on 163 is firing at our right forward company."

The duty officer of White turned to the tank's troop commander who, by sheer coincidence, happened to be sitting with him. "Have any of your tanks been firing lately, Tony?"

"No. No, I don't think so. I hope not anyhow, old boy."

"Hullo, Red," said the Duty Officer. "No, old fellow, none of the tanks have been firing."

"Thanks. Sorry to have bothered you, old boy."

"Not at all, old man. Always pleased to be of help. Cheerio."

The message was passed along down the chain of command.

"I've made inquiries, Blake," said Lawrence, "and there is definitely no tank firing."

Another shell landed on the position. Blake groaned with frustration. "There! Surely to God you heard that? I assure you it is firing … I've seen it firing …"

"Now pull yourself together, Blake. Stop acting like a hysterical schoolboy. Not only have I checked up with Battalion, but they've double-checked and if you took the trouble to check your map you would see that you're not in in the tank's direct line of fire."

There was a pause as Blake tried to think of how he could convince Lawrence of the truth. The best he could come up with was, "You come round here and see for yourself."

"Well I'll send round Captain Clark by all means. In the meantime I'd strongly recommend that you get a grip of yourself."

"That tank *is* firing at us!"

Blake wasted his breath. Lawrence had again slammed the telephone down. Blake sat on the side of his bunk. He looked up and saw Miles and Taylor watching him, amazed at the course of the conversation. Blake smiled at them. "Well, I don't suppose I will be with you for much longer, after that."

"What happened?" asked Miles.

"Nothing, really. He's sending Nobby Clark round. When he gets his head blown off, then maybe they'll believe us."

Two more 20-pounder shells screamed in at them. They all ducked for cover as they exploded. Then they heard more machine guns as the tank methodically sprayed the exposed trench and bunkers. "Poor old Nobby," said Blake as the dust and debris settled down. "I don't give the poor bloke a chance."

It was Corporal Hale who broke the stalemate. He had been around the front of the platoon, in the relative peace of the OP. "I suppose you blokes know that that is one of our own tanks firing at us?"

"We are aware of that …."

"I was as safe as houses in the OP, of course," explained Hale. "But it must be a bit hairy being on the wrong end of those 20-pounders." No one replied, not welcoming Hale's facetious tone. Hale shrugged his shoulders and added: "I've got something here that might interest you, sir. It's a bit of shrapnel I picked up on the way round from the OP."

"Let's have a look." Blake took the jagged lump of steel from Hale and examined it. It made him cry out triumphantly. The letters WD and a small arrow were clearly engraved on the metal: conclusive proof that it was a British tank firing..

"I'd like to know what Lawrence will say about this," Blake said, showing it around. He had never felt so relieved. This would show Lawrence! This would make it perfectly clear who the incompetent swine was! He grabbed the field telephone. Lawrence answered. "Tell Nobby Clark not to bother to come round," said Blake quite calmly. "We have all the evidence we need. We've just picked up a piece of shrapnel with WD and an arrow stamped on it."

Ten minutes later the tank fired its last shell at One Platoon. It demolished O'Hara's bunker. Blake sent a runner off to the company CP with the piece of shrapnel. When Blake telephoned the CP several minutes later Lawrence refused to speak to him.

The next contact the two officers had was at the afternoon orders group Lawrence always held. The Major went through his usual routine. When he came to the end, there was a long pause. The issue of the tank and the death of Rawlins was no longer something he could ignore. He took hold of the ends of his moustache and gave them a twirl, a thing he always did when under pressure. He had no idea how to approach the subject. The one thing he wasn't going to do--- the one thing he couldn't do--- was apologize. Likewise he was not going to admit that he was in the wrong. It was vital that it should be seen that he had done everything that could have been reasonably expected of him.

"Now about this tank on Hill 163 ... You're all aware of the incident. I'm afraid I can't explain why it fired on One Platoon in the first place ... Just a genuine mistake, I suppose ... But I can only say that an extremely dim view is taken of it by the Brigadier, the Colonel and, of course, me, especially since it resulted in the death of Private Rawlins. As soon as any information reaches me, and we know why it didn't stop firing when requested, then I'll let you know immediately."

He forced a smile, hoping that Blake would smile back and say 'Thank you, sir,' like any well-disciplined subaltern. However, Blake did not smile back. He was not a well-disciplined subaltern. He just stared at Lawrence, his eyes bulging, orbs of accusation. He was determined to strike while the subject still glowed red hot, before time tempered everything with reasonableness. "I accept that the tank firing on us was a human error, sir. We all know only too well that such things can and do happen. What worries me--- indeed, alarms and horrifies me--- is that Sergeant Miles reported the incident at about five o'clock this morning and it was not until well after eleven that anything was done about it." He waited for a moment, knowing that Lawrence would have no reasonable explanation. "Even a man being killed had no impact on anyone. And it was only because we happened to find that piece of shrapnel that anything was done about it at all. If it had not been for that, the tank would still have been firing now . . ."

His face became flushed and his voice rose in volume. "The worst thing however, was that both Miles and myself were disbelieved, and then told not to be bloody fools. It seems that you don't even trust our word."

"Stop shouting at me, Blake, and control yourself." Lawrence shifted about in his chair. Things were taking the course he had feared. "You made your complaint to me and although I doubted the correctness of what you said, I checked up with battalion. They in turned checked and were told that no tank was firing. So I naturally believed them. What else could I do?"

"Why should you believe them more than me? Surely I should know who is firing at me?"

"There happens to be such a thing as loyalty to your superiors, Blake. If you are told a thing like that you just have to accept it."

"And what about having some loyalty to your juniors? There's no

THE DEAD, THE DYING AND THE DAMNED

damned point in me sitting out there on my own, telling you what's happening, if you aren't going to believe me."

"I checked up with Battalion as soon as you made your complaint. That was all I could do. It was no fault of ours here in company headquarters."

Blake kept his voice as soft as he could. "I'm afraid I can't agree with that, sir. You treated both me and my sergeant as though we were complete idiots. You couldn't possibly have stressed any urgency when you made your investigations. All you had to do to verify the truth was to look across to Hill 163. Then you'd have seen it firing ... Did you ever look?"

"I am certainly not going to be cross-examined by you, Blake."

"No, you obviously didn't. You lied to me! You said you had. I'll say no more. Well, only one thing more. I regard the firing of that tank over a period of hours as entirely your responsibility. And that compels me to ask for a transfer from your company, and as soon as possible!"

Lawrence jumped to his feet. For several seconds stood there, transfixed. He was rigid, struck dumb with amazement. This was something he had never considered might happen to him. It was preposterous! A transfer from Able Company indeed! The sheer arrogance of a junior subaltern demanding a transfer was unbelievable: especially Blake. It was only hours before that he was considering having him thrown out of the Regiment for good, let alone Able Company. Now he had the gall to demand a transfer!

All those present were silent. None of them---Bartram, Gooodall, CSM Ralf, Corporal Cross or Corporal Williamson--- had ever expected to witness such a scene. All eyes were on Lawrence.

"How dare you speak to me like that, Blake?" he spluttered at last. "Do you realize that you are speaking to a senior officer?"

"I'm asking for a transfer. And I'm quite within my rights.'

"Well, you bloody well can't have one."

"In that case, sir, I must insist on having an interview with the Colonel. You cannot stop me having an interview with the Colonel."

Lawrence turned and looked out of the open doorway. What, he wondered, would become of his company if all his officers started putting in for transfers? If Blake went to another company he would be bound to spread stupid stories about him. Lawrence was under no illusions as to what many men thought of him. He often overheard snatches of conversation, noticed fleeting glances, and felt the icy atmosphere wherever he went; but until now it had never worried him. He was a military commander and it was his job to get the best out of his men no matter how he did it. Discipline and toughness were all that mattered. He simply could not allow anyone to act like this and get Able Company a bad name. The Company came before all else. They had established themselves as the best company in the Battalion and the Brigade, and it was going to stay that way, until …

Lawrence turned slowly and faced those at the orders group. He would show Blake: the impudent young puppy. "Very well, Blake," he said evenly, "you can have your interview with the Colonel. By all means … As you say, that is your privilege. But I can assure you that he won't take the matter lightly."

The orders group ended. They left Lawrence wriggling about in his chair, seeking relief from his usual discomfort. They went their ways in silence, chastened by what they had witnessed. Blake was certain the Colonel would have no hesitation in granting him a transfer when he heard what had happened.

17

Following the shelling by the tank, it was with misgivings that One Platoon made their final preparations to move into reserve. The carefree spirit which had existed a few hours before vanished, the elation had gone. The last details were attended to; the new latrine was completed, the platoon area was scrupulously clean, and the bunkers stripped of all personal belongings.

Inside the platoon CP Blake half-listened to a conversation between an American officer and Miles. He hadn't the faintest idea what they were talking about. His real thoughts were miles away. He was going over every detail of the day's happenings, trying to recall the exact words which had been spoken. Nor could he get over the sight of Rawlins's mangled body.

So much seemed to have happened in the past few hours, but somehow it was all totally unimportant. All that really mattered was that he got a transfer to another company.

"The trouble with our men is that they just can't keep it in their trousers," the American was saying. "They go to Tokyo and seem to think that they've got exclusive rights on any broad they happen to see. How about your men, Peter?"

"Yes," Blake agreed abstractedly, "exactly the same with our men. They're sex maniacs, the lot of them." He looked at his watch and stood up. "Come on, Sergeant. It's time for us to depart." He moved towards the doorway and, pulling the blackout blanket to one side, he listened to the battle noises. In the distance, away behind the reserve company, the 25-pounders were banging away with abandon; over to his left he could hear a small-arms battle as patrols clashed by 355, and on his right he could see the searing flashes of shells exploding on the Hook. He stepped into the darkness and saw the sections of his platoon lined up in the trench ready to move off. In the darkness he didn't recognize any of them and he suddenly felt very, very lonely. He realized that he hadn't got a real friend within ten thousand miles. There was not a man in all that distance back to England, not one in all those vast masses, who would give a damn if he was killed. No more than anyone gave a damn about poor Rawlins.

He heard a slight rustling beside him and turned quickly. "Evening, sir. One Section all ready to move off."

Smith appeared out of the darkness, fully laden with kit. As was often the case, he was rubbing frost off his glasses. Blake felt a smile slip across his lips. Perhaps, after all, he had a few friends. Smith was one of them, a really good friend: one of the best.

"Bit of a do on the Hook to-night, Mr. Blake," said Smith.

"Yes. Thank God we are getting away from it all for a bit."

They stood close together watching the Hook. Soon, faint noises developed in the trench leading back to company HQ. American voices became distinct, as did the jangling of digging tools and weapons. Then a clear voice rang out: "How much longer is this goddamned trench?"

Many more American voices followed it. "Shine your light, for God's sake, Sergeant! Let's see what the hell is going on."

A bright torch beam flashed up and down the trench until it reached Blake and Smith at the head of One Section. They watched it with surprise. No one in Able Company had shown a light in such a thoughtless manner since their first night in the line. They said nothing. The Americans obviously had a far more relaxed method of fighting the war.

Blake headed his platoon of thirty-three men along the trench and then down to the jeep-head, past CSM Ralf who was acting as a final check-point on the road. In the moonlight Blake could see the dim, bobbing heads of Goodall's platoon ahead of him, and behind him the steady beat of his men marching along. It gave them a strange degree of unity. They had all had their various differences while in the line: many had hated each other's guts, but now that they were eventually off that drab, stinking hill, and away from no-man's-land, all was well again; their main troubles were forgotten and individual faults brushed to one side.

Soon they were marching along the MSR: the noises of war receding behind them. The shells bursting on the Hook were no more than distant crumps. As they reached the 'long drag' on the MSR O'Hara began to sing, his raucous Irish voice bellowing out. Gradually, one by one, others joined in. Soon the whole company was singing, then the entire battalion. It was the song they had heard so many times during the past winter months. It was, to them, what 'A Long Way to Tipperary' was to the Tommies of the Great War.

> There's a Muma-san coming down the track
> With a titty hanging out and a Kiwi on her back,
> We're moving on,
> To old Pusan,
> We're moving fast and far down the M.S.R.
> So we're moving on.
>
> The Chinks are hiding in the long tall grass
> Playing burp gun boogey on the First Cav's arse,
> We're moving on,
> To old Pusan,
> We've just lost our shacking-up post,
> So we're moving on.
>
> The Chinks are swarming up 355
> And the Jocks are bugging out in overdrive,
> We're moving on,
> To old Pusan,
> They're getting too near my old outpost
> So we're moving on.

Blake was gripped by a dual feeling of sentimentality and pride. He reckoned they'd done a fine job. Why they had done it, and whether it would have any ultimate value was debatable, but in his mind there was no doubt that, give or take one or two disasters, they had done their job pretty well.

PART III

INTERLUDE

FROM

WAR

1

As they marched into the reserve position the sun was already up. They were confronted by a dismal sight. They were some fifteen miles behind the front line, actually out of the battle zone, in a broad valley with very little in the way of natural vegetation; no trees, and not even any bushes, just a series of flat, worked out and frozen paddy fields. As the companies wheeled into appropriate positions and halted, men couldn't believe that this was it, the long-awaited luxury of life in reserve.

There was nothing there. They were going to have to organize everything themselves, from scratch.

The battalion's transport drew up into a hollow square and the drivers crouched on the leeward side of their vehicles, seeking protection from the wind. The rifle companies piled their weapons by sections and just stood about in forlorn groups, waiting for someone to tell them what to do, or even what was happening. There were no tents to erect, no cookhouses or catering equipment to get organized, not even the wherewithall to start digging latrines. The adjutant went from company to company explaining that everything was still in a distant Ordnance Depot, waiting to be brought forward by transport which for some reason had failed to turn up on time.

Men never thought they would miss their bunkers, but they did. They longed to be able to duck down into familiar holes in the ground and sit around their petrol fires.

An hour later O'Hara managed to steal some petrol from an unwary member of the MT Section and several small fires started up in Able Company. Men from other companies came flocking, but were told to bugger off and go steal their own petrol. Very few men spoke. They pulled out their fags and puffed away in silent disgust. It was a terrible anti-climax to their long spell in the line and by noon many were regretting that they had ever made the move. It was hard to imagine anything more likely to turn men bolshie, to search for fresh ways to look after Number One.

It was mid-afternoon when a convoy of trucks arrived with all their requirements. Suddenly, the whole area buzzed with activity. The race was on to get things organized before darkness closed in. Men worked hard. Among other things, it was the only way to keep warm. By nightfall the Rocks had established the nucleus of a reasonable reserve position. Over the following weeks plenty of improvisations and improvements were made, but on that first day they just concentrated on the basics, and when they were established the majority of men in Able Company followed Lawrence's example and got pleasantly tight before retiring to their new camp beds and sleeping as they had never slept before.

During their first day in reserve men were left to themselves. On the second day things changed. Senior officers were anxious to get a proper routine established and senior NCOs were anxious to reassert their authority.

While in the line petty discipline had been relaxed but now everything was back to normal, the 'Depot' mentality took over once more. Everyone was expected to march about like toy soldiers; raucous orders were shouted; salutes went up and down like railway signals at Clapham Junction, and every minute of the day something or someone, somewhere or other, was being inspected. Muster parades were held and men detailed off for completely spurious jobs. Those who were left over were drilled endlessly on the battalion's makeshift parade ground.

Private Charles suffered more than most. Having had such a narrow escape in the blue-on-blue incident he felt he was entitled to at least a degree of latitude, even an apology from someone in authority and certainly a contrite visit from those who had fired at them; but not a bit of it. The Padre held a burial service for the unfortunate Rawlins and the next thing Charles knew was that Sergeant Miles told him he had been transferred. He was to report to CSM Ralf at company headquarters to act as company runner. He knew what that meant. He was to be the company's dogsbody: on duty all hours and given every foul and exhausting job CSM Ralf could dream up.

First of all, as a routine task, Ralf put him in charge of digging the officers' latrine. Even though that was no more than a deep hole in the ground, CSM Ralf found fault with it and gave him extra duties. Then, when he turned up for muster parade with one shirt button undone, Ralf declared him to be stark naked and made him run around the camp perimeter with his small pack filled with sand; and on another occasion, when he was a few seconds late for a parade, Ralf made him join the punishment detail doing early morning PT without gym shoes and only in shorts. It was blatant victimization with no attempt at dispensing proper justice: there was no question of him being put on a charge and being tried by his company commander in the normal manner. Whatever he did, Ralf took one look at him and shouted: "Report to my tent after duty," and then gave him jobs that ranged from peeling spuds for the cooks to helping the Gook porters hump supplies from battalion headquarters around the companies.

When a rumor, emanating from Sergeant Miles, claimed that Ralf's daughter was pregnant, men wonder what would become of Charles when they went back in the line. They all knew Ralf was quite capable of making sure Charles didn't survive. Winston had an alternative view. "He won't do anything as crafty as that. He'll just line old Charlie up against a brick wall and shoot him ... Just like he did those bloody Indians."

These, and several other possibilities, had occurred to Charles. He'd got plenty of other girls in trouble before so he knew how unreasonable even mild-mannered fathers could be, let alone maniacs like Ralf. For a time he could see no way out of his difficulties, but eventually he had the good fortune to come across Private Billings. He was the Rock's oldest serving soldier and one of the finest barrack room lawyers in the army. He could quote verbatim from both The Queen's Regulations and The Manual of Military Law. They met by accident when Ralf sent Charles to battalion headquarters to help shovel the battalion's kitchen waste into a truck destined for a local Korean pig farm. Without ever being real mates, Charles and Billings were on nodding terms as became men with their appalling records. As they went about their work, Billings said: "You're in trouble again then, Charlie?"

"So it seems."

"Ralf's daughter is up the spout, I hear?"

"So it seems ..."

"So what are you going to do about it?"

"Nothing I can do. Old Ralf's going spare as though she had nothing to do with it and it's nothing but my fault. But I'll tell you this. Once she saw what was on offer she was as keen as I was. Now, Ralf's playing it really cunning. He won't even put me on a charge. So there's no way out."

"Come on, Charlie ... You can do better than that. There are always ways out. We have our rights, you know. And even the likes of Ralf can never change that ...You've got two ways out, for sure..."

"Like what?"

"First, you can report sick. And secondly you can apply for compassionate leave. When you go sick you're in the hands of the MO, and when you apply for compassionate leave you're in the hands of the Padre. No one else: not Ralf, Lawrence or even the Colonel. None of them have anything to do with it. It's up to the Doc and the Padre and they're always the softest touches going--- real humanitarians!"

Charles stopped shoveling and looked at Billings with admiration and respect. Possibilities suddenly opened up in his mind. His mother would provide perfect cover for compassionate leave. The old bitch couldn't possibly have all that much longer. As for reporting sick...

"There are snags, of course," added Billings, unable to repress a sly smile.

"In the case of compassionate leave they always--- but always--- make a thorough investigation into your reasons. And that takes time. So that could be a complication. And if you go sick the snag is that you have to have something wrong with you. And it has to be something that even a National Service doctor like our bloke can't see through or dismiss lightly."

"Back to square one then," said Charles, despondently.

Billings's smile developed into a laugh. "What exactly happened when that tank shelled you? There must have been some loud explosions ..."

"Christ, I'll say! They bloody near blew my head off ... I was in the bunker next to Rawlins..."

"There you are then. The perfect way out! There's one thing the medics can't prove or disprove, and that's deafness. With everything else they can give you blood tests or x-rays and prove if you are lying, but not deafness. No one ever knows what you can hear and what you can't hear ... You have to play it clever, of course. But it's perfectly possible. Go sick and tell the MO you can't hear properly ... Because of all that shelling ... Perfect bloody excuse if ever there was. A young doctor like our bloke will know bugger all about ears. You're straight into ENT territory ...... Know what that is?"

"No."

"It is ear nose and throat: really delicate, and deep in specialist territory. I'll even bet there's not an ENT specialist between here and Kure. So convince the MO you've gone deaf and you'll end up in Kure. And once in Kure, they'll never send you back. Even if you recover from your deafness, what doctor in his right senses is going to send you back out here for it to happen again? They'll be too shit scared that they'll end up having to give you a pension."

The corporal in charge of the waste disposal detail suddenly appeared from the front of the truck. He looked in the back of it and yelled: "Right! That's enough. Driver, off you go, mate. You others get back to your companies."

"Think about it, Charlie."

Charles did think about it. For the next few hours he thought about nothing else.

He reckoned compassionate leave was his best bet. It was much more genuine. Also he knew the Social Services set-up in the UK well enough to realize that when some busybody from the War Office went round to his mother investigating, they would be full of sympathy. Sympathy was the backbone of their trade. The complication was time. Like old Billings said, it was bound to be a long drawn out affair, and what he needed was to get away quickly. If compassionate leave took a couple of months to be sanctioned, they could be back in the line, fighting on the Hook. On the other hand, if he decided to go for the deafness pitch, it would be quick and decisive; but the sooner he did it the better. It would be no good reporting sick after a couple of weeks. It had to be done right away, otherwise it just wouldn't make sense.

He went sick that afternoon. He had to inform CSM Ralf and he knew it would be no good telling him that he was deaf. He knew damn well that he wasn't; so he'd have to tell him something else instead. He had the very thing, something that would really put the vertical wind up Ralf. He'd tell him it was for personal reasons: blood tests! Ralf would immediately assume that he had the clap. Charles all but laughed as he imagined how Ralf would react: seducing his little girl, getting her pregnant, and giving her the clap----Casanova's royal flush!

There were only a handful of men waiting to see the MO. As Billings predicted, their Doc was a young National Service doctor who had been thrown in at the deep end and when Charles told him he was still suffering deafness after being shelled by the tank he was immediately apprehensive.
"Let's have a look then."
Charles winced as the MO thrust a small funnel-shaped torch into his ear. He felt it being wiggled about and decided it would be appropriate to wince a little more. "I can hardly see a thing for wax," the MO said as he removed the torch.
"What did you say the matter was, sir?"
"I said it looks like.... Oh, never mind." The MO cleaned a large lump of wax off the end of his torch. "Did you have any bleeding?"
"Any feeling? I'll say! I felt as though my head had bloody near been blown off."
"No, no! BLEEDING?"
"Oh, bleeding! Yes, sir, at the time." Then he added the phrase he'd picked up from Billings. "From my ears nose and throat, sir."
"Ever have trouble with your hearing in the past?"
"Will it last?"
"Trouble in the PAST?"
"Only when I was a youngster, sir. Don't know what it was exactly … Glue-ear, or sticky ear, or something like that. It cleared up okay but when they heard about it at my original army medical they said I'd better go in the infantry … Instead of the Gunners, which I applied for."

The MO gave Charles's ear another examination with his torch. At the end of it he was none the wiser. Deaf ears looked exactly the same as good ears, bar cases where the drum had been split or perforated.

"I think you'd better go back to the Canadian Advanced Dressing Station at Division and let them examine you."

Charles left the tent without delay. Once out of sight, he beamed happily. He had got past the MO! If he could convince him he could convince anyone. He reckoned the glue ear business had done it: complicated past records scared the wits out of doctors. Now all he'd have to do was keep repeating, "Pardon?" or "Sorry I didn't catch that" until they were sick to death with talking to him. Even better, he would have to be ever-ready to come out with rhyming words, as with 'bleeding' and 'feeling'. That was not only convincing, but gave them a laugh and made them more sympathetic.

At the Canadian Advance Dressing Station Charles was relieved of his Sten gun and ordered into a tent where men were awaiting their turn to see a doctor. Charles sat there for over an hour. He didn't worry about that. In fact, he saw it was a hopeful sign. Doctors rushed off their feet would be anxious to clear their backlog of patients, a perfect 'buck-passing' situation.

The doctor Charles eventually saw was a young man, most helpful in that he believed implicitly everything Charles told him. The result was that Charles was sent back to the hospital in Seoul to be examined by a specialist. As he went back to the ambulance, Charles read the doctor's report which he had been told to give to the specialist at Seoul. It concluded: "I know exactly what this man has got, but I forget the name of it.'

The specialist in Seoul turned out to be a specialist in bone fractures. He did, however, have a sense of humor. His report concluded: "I know exactly what the name of this man's complaint is, but I'm damned if I can spell it!"

"What you need is an ENT specialist," he shouted at Charles. "You'll only find one at the Base Hospital in Kure. He'll sort you out."

"Am I on snout, sir?" said Charles. "Yes, sir. I smoke like a chimney."

"No, no … I said … Never mind. You'll go to Kure first thing in the morning on air evacuation."

Charles felt his pulse quicken. Even in his wildest dreams he had never imagined it would be so simple and straightforward. He reported to the hospital and was soon installed in a ward. The only other patient was hidden from view by several high screens, and by the sound of it the man was on his death-bed. Charles undressed slowly, keeping an eye on the screens in case the man should suddenly appear from behind them and turn out to be a 'nut case'. The sheets on the bed were delightfully soft and warm and Charles decided to go to sleep, despite it still being early evening. Sleeping between clean sheets was one of the luxuries he had really missed. He stretched his legs out and turned over on his side.

"Well, well, you're settling down pretty quickly." The voice was soft and friendly and feminine.

Charles looked up sharply, forgot all about his deafness, and smiled brightly at the nursing Sister standing over him. She had a nice figure and long brunette hair. She was a bit old, and a bit plain, but neither too old nor too plain.

"And what's it like in the front line?" she asked as she slipped a thermometer under his tongue.

"Not so bad," spluttered Charles. "It's a bit lonely though. No women up there, you know. And what the hell is life without women?" It was a line he knew all women loved: the need to be wanted. He laid his hand on hers as she felt his pulse. She transferred her gaze from her watch and for a moment her eyes twinkled. "So I've been led to believe on numerous occasions."

She pulled the thermometer from his mouth and, having allowed his hand to rest on hers for a bit, she raised it firmly and placed it beneath the bedclothes. "There, now, you're one of the healthiest patients we've ever had. All you need is to cool off a little. And have a bath!"

"A bed bath! What a great idea ..."

"Sorry. That's a privilege---officers only!"

2

The Colonel had said his piece so he turned his full attention to his pipe. He blew and sucked on the stem with increasing power in an effort to clear it. The company commanders closed their note-books. The Colonel's 'immediate actions' on his pipe signaled the end of the orders group. It had been a long session and the company commanders were not sorry that it was over. He had said some pretty stern things about the lack of discipline in the battalion and the way in which it had to be improved.

Lawrence and the adjutant remained seated while the others departed. The Colonel abandoned all hope of clearing his pipe and said: "Let's get this unpleasant business over as quickly as possible, Dick. Is he outside?"

"Yes, sir, he's waiting."

The adjutant stuck his head out of the door: "Mr. Blake!"

Blake marched in, saluted, and registered considerable surprise on seeing Lawrence. He had assumed it would be a private interview with perhaps just the adjutant present. With Lawrence being there it wouldn't be an interview at all. His presence turned it into a kangaroo court, with Lawrence as the only witness. He dreaded to think of the lies Lawrence had been telling the Colonel. How typical of the army, he thought.

"Now then, Blake," began the Colonel, "your behavior of late has given me grave concern. It has been most unsatisfactory, to say the least. First of all you made a very great mistake over Private Burrows. You advised him not only to defy your company commander and the adjutant, but also myself. On that occasion I was willing to overlook it. We all make errors of judgment and I appreciate that you are very young and inexperienced. But your appalling behavior when you were shelled by the tank on 163 is beyond any kind of excuse."

Blake glanced in Lawrence's direction. "Excuse me ..."

"Quiet!" snapped the adjutant. "You'll have your opportunity to speak in a moment."

The Colonel leaned back in his chair, annoyed by the interruption. "I know the facts, Blake. I know what you said to Major Lawrence and I must say that in all my experience I have never heard of anything so disgraceful. To put it bluntly, Blake, I consider that as an Officer in an infantry regiment such as ours you just don't come up to scratch. I don't propose to give you a lecture on your behavior. It would not only be superfluous, but I doubt if I would be able to do my feelings justice. You don't seem to understand that you are here to comply with orders, not continually question everything." He stood up and walked to within a few inches of Blake, looking him straight in the eyes to emphasize the verdict was about to be delivered. "I've discussed this at considerable length with Major Lawrence and the Brigadier and we've decided that there is only one thing for us left to do. You have got twenty-four hours in which to get packed and out of this Brigade. Have you anything to say?"

Blake opened his mouth to speak, but no words came. What was the point? From their perspective, it was all very true. He had become hysterical, however understandable it may have been; and it would be futile to try to justify his actions. If he put his side of the argument it would only make things worse. The independence of his mind, the way he thought for himself, and the way he spoke his mind openly and often bluntly, were not seen as virtues in the army. If he gave way to his normal instincts he would only end up accusing Lawrence of lying, being incompetent, and entirely responsible for the death of Rawlins. It was all true, but it would never be accepted.

"Your movement order is in the orderly room, Blake," said the adjutant.

Blake saluted and marched out of the tent. He did not mind leaving the regiment. With one or two exceptions, he certainly wouldn't miss his platoon. In fact he'd be damned glad to see the back of most of them, but what really rankled was being called 'useless, disloyal and incompetent.' For all his faults, he wasn't any of those things. Not in his judgment, anyhow.

He wondered how he would ever live down the disgrace, not just in the army and his three years in the TA, but also at home. He would never be able to hide the fact that he'd been chucked out. Even though he had never aspired to be a successful officer, he had never envisaged anything this ignominious.

3

Armitage put his foot down hard on the accelerator and smiled as he felt the jeep leap forward. Jeeps were marvelous little vehicles, versatile and ideal for the front line, but he was still looking forward to getting away from Lawrence and Able Company and returning to driving a 3-tonner. He turned his head and grinned at Kim. "In a day or two you see me no more, Kim … Armitage vamoose…"

"Where are you going, Mr. Armitage--- Seoul?" Kim laughed at his little joke. Several men in the Rocks had already decided that they had had enough of the army and disappeared to Seoul for a few days of debauchery before being picked up by the Red Caps.

"No, Kim. Not me. Me go on tuckson trucks. Number One 3-tonners." He looked at Kim to make sure that he understood. "3-tonners, Number One. Savvy?"

The jeep gave a violent lurch as they went over a huge pot hole. "And Mr. Armitage Number Ten driver," giggled Kim. "Savvy?"

"Ah, dry up, you little monkey."

Kim laughed, loving the banter he always had with Armitage.

When they got back to camp Armitage slowed down and waved cheerfully to the R.P. on duty at the gate. He kidded himself he was on good terms with everyone, but he was soon disillusioned. When they passed the battalion orderly room they heard the unmistakable roar of the RSM. "You… You in that jeep! Stop! Do you hear? Stop!"

Armitage jammed on the brakes, and skidded to a halt. "Yes, sir?"

"Why the bloody hell didn't you salute the adjutant?" Armitage saw the adjutant lurking in the background.

"I was driving, sir. No driver salutes when he's driving."

"Oh yes you bloody do! You salute officers at all times. Have you read orders?"

"Not that one."

The RSM produced a little red book. "What's your name?"

"Armitage, sir."

The adjutant stepped forward. "When was this jeep last cleaned?"

"Last night, sir."

"Why haven't you cleaned it to-day?"

"Because I clean it every night. Like orders say."

"That's not good enough. It must be done every morning. It's a disgrace. Get this man transferred to a rifle company at once, Sergeant-Major. He is obviously not fit to be in charge of a vehicle."

"Sir!"

They left Armitage with his mouth hanging open. "The rotten bastards," he managed to say at length.

Kim, he noticed, had jumped out and slipped off very smartly.

The Colonel, the Adjutant, the Assistant Adjutant, the QM, the orderly officer, the RSM, the Provost Sergeant, and a Regimental Policeman (walking along in strict order of seniority), were doing the weekly inspection of the battalion lines. Trouble was in the air. The water butts in Charlie Company had not been painted yellow as specified in Part II orders; and in Baker Company a man had been seen swaggering along with his hands in his pockets. In Dog Company the cook had been seen dipping his finger into the stew to taste it; and a Gook had been caught urinating against the side of the officers' mess.

Able Company was well-nigh perfect, however. Lawrence had made sure of that. He'd had his men up at the crack of dawn cleaning the company lines, putting another coat of whitewash on all stationary objects, sweeping the insides of the tents, and cleaning their personal equipment. "Yes, Dick," the Colonel said at length, "this looks good. Well done!"

He was about to leave Able Company without having passed any criticism when he noticed two lines of tent pegs. Two long rows of tents had been erected in straight lines, and likewise their pegs had been lined up in perfect dressing. The Colonel stopped, and all the men trailing him stopped. He looked down the line of pegs and frowned. They all looked down at the line of pegs and frowned. "Those pegs! A bit far out into the pathway, don't you think, Dick? Men might trip over them in the dark'"

"I'll get them moved immediately, sir."

"No need for that, Dick. Just get them whitewashed."

"Yes, sir! Sergeant-Major Ralf!"

"Sir?"

"Get those tent pegs whitewashed. Get some men on it."

"Sir!' Sergeant Miles!"

"Sir?"

"Get some of your men on those pegs at once, Sergeant."

"Sir!' Corporal Hale!"

"Sergeant?"

"Detail two men for white washing, Corporal."

"Sergeant! Winston! Taylor! Get some whitewash and paint those pegs."

"Oh God!" cursed Winston. "Bloody roll on demob!"

The urge for discipline eventually subsided. Once it had been firmly reestablished, and all men marched about the camp in constant fear of being charged for hardly any offence at all, the field officers were satisfied and diverted their attention to training.

The Training Officer drew up a comprehensive program but not satisfied with this, Lawrence had Able Company do half an hour's early morning, pre-breakfast PT under the leadership of the platoon commanders. While other companies lay-in, awaiting the first notes of Reveille, they cursed Able Company for the racket they made.

After breakfast, platoons assembled and then started out on route marches of increasing length. Even the keenest of men became depressed; they were soon wilting under the strain, and by the time they graduated from route marches to dashing up and down the steep hills attacking an imaginary enemy, they were completely stale; their one desire was to be left alone for a bit. They wanted time to eat and sleep and time in which to catch up with their mail.

Before long they had progressed through section, platoon and company training and were concentrating on battalion exercises. Able Company was, as usual, leading the battalion in an advance to contact. This was their second big exercise and not only was the Corps Commander due to pay a visit but the Brigadier was going to be in attendance. Lawrence was hurrying along with short steps between Cross and Williamson, feeling rather apprehensive: he was determined to give a good display in front of the Corps Commander but he was worried by his lack of control over the company. The country over which they were moving consisted of very steep hills divided by frequent valleys, which meant that the leading platoons were often out of sight, leaving him dependent on his wireless, a situation he distrusted.

He watched One Platoon, now commanded by Sergeant Miles, plod up the next hill and then disappear over the crest. Then he heard the feeble noise of blanks and the more substantial explosions of the charges the assault pioneers (acting as the enemy) had put down, and at once the whole company went to ground. He started to go through the familiar drill; first of all an appreciation of the situation, a warning order, then a report of the situation back to battalion, and finally a word from them that it would be a battalion attack with Able Company acting as fire company and with Lawrence responsible for directing the fire of the mortars.

Lawrence crawled forward. He pulled out his binoculars and studied the ground ahead of him. All he could see of the enemy position were some tiny whiffs of smoke. He cursed the Colonel under his breath. It certainly wasn't his job to direct the fire of the mortars. Where the hell was their FOO? How could he do it when he couldn't even see the target properly? Then he saw a tree ten yards to his front, and with surprising agility he darted forward and climbed halfway up it. At first the mortars were hopelessly off target but Lawrence was soon calling down corrections so that they were landing accurately on the position which (for obvious reasons) the enemy had now evacuated. For twenty minutes he watched the attack go through the various stages. As he saw the assaulting companies forming up in the assembly area he heard the voice of the Colonel. He looked down and saw him leading the Brigadier and the Corps Commander towards the tree. Then they stood directly beneath it.

"This is Able Company, sir," said the Colonel. "They did very well while in the line."

The General made no reply but looked about for the Company Commander. The Brigadier and the Colonel were likewise concerned as to his whereabouts. "Where is Major Lawrence?" the Colonel asked Corporal Williamson.

"He's up the tree, sir," answered Williamson with obvious relish.

"Up the tree?" chorused the General and Brigadier.

"Yes, that's right, sir," replied Williamson with increasing amusement, "up the tree. He got up it all right. But I think he might have considerable difficulty getting back down again. Whenever he looks down he seems to suffer from acrophobia."

"Here I am, sir," called out Lawrence.

"Say, Major, what the devil are you doing up the tree, for God's sake?" demanded the General.

"I'm directing fire, sir."

"I suppose you can see better from up there?"

"Yes, sir, much better."

"Good thinking ... Come on down and join us."

"Well I think someone will have to get a ladder before I can get down, sir. I'm a bit stuck at the moment."   In his panic he was also itching like hell.

The General took the Colonel by the arm and led him back down the hill. "Tell me, Colonel.   I don't quite know how you Limeys manage your armies, but isn't it just a bit unusual for company commanders to go climbing into trees like Boy Scouts?"

"It most certainly is," said the Brigadier.

"He did very well in the line, sir," said the Colonel.   "Lawrence is my best company commander."

The General stroked his powerful jaw.   "I reckon Major Lawrence could do with a stretch of R and R in Tokyo, Colonel.   Give him a few extra days over there."

"He's done exceptionally well out here so far, sir," the Colonel repeated.

"Oh sure, Colonel.   He probably just needs a woman to give him a bit of stimulation, like the rest of us.   Anyhow, send him off on some R and R. And tell him to try the Laccus Club, Central Tokyo, just off the Ginza.   All the cabs know it.   Expensive, but by Christ they've got some good whores there."

4

Charles had been idling about at JRBD (the transit camp just outside Kure) for several days.   In all his experience in the army he had never known anything like it.   It was a life of complete ease and, to him utter bliss.   Here, he wasn't hounded by officers and N.C.O.s and there was no routine for him to abide by; no checking on his appearance and bearing, no orders being barked at him the whole time, no restrictions to the hours he kept; no one bothered about how often he went into Kure and how long he spent there, and--- most miraculous of all--- no one seemed to bother about how long this situation continued.

Even the facilities in the camp were wonderful. There were a swimming pool, football teams, basketball teams, and a good canteen in which they could buy cheap beer and with Housey-Housey (Bingo) each night, giving a welcome opportunity to win some extra cash if lucky, as Charles just happened to be. He likened it to being the Forgotten Soldier, which was a hell of an improvement over the prospect not long ago of becoming the Unknown Soldier. Somewhere or other the small bundle of papers with his name on it, which he'd handed in at the orderly room, had been temporarily lost; or some obligingly lazy clerk had pushed it to one side to be dealt with later; or a stupid officer, not knowing what to do with it, had stuffed it under his carpet.

Within twenty-four hours of arriving at Kure, Charles knew the town intimately. He knew the names and locations of all the principal beer halls, the best places for meals, where the more refined geisha houses were, with the relative risks attached to each.

On his third night he visited an attractive little beer hall just off the Hondori (the main Street) where he had become attracted to one of the hostesses. She was a kinky little girl; a smart little cookie who was always freshly painted and decorated with her bosom jacked up to maximum elevation and her hair back-combed and brittle with lacquer, dressed Chinese-style with slits up the sides of her long dress which gave generous flashes of stocking tops, suspender belt, smooth flesh and miniscule underwear: the sort of girl with whom Charles felt immediately at ease. She had a dingy little bedsit just off the Hondori and after long evenings of drinking together she would lead him up the rickety stairs and then they would retire to her futon where they had fun and games of an adult nature until morning.

After rising somewhere around midday, she would cook Charles a fish and rice breakfast and then return to the beer hall to entertain early customers while Charles went back to camp to see if there was news of his long awaited medical. When he'd confirmed that he had again failed to feature on orders he wandered about the camp, adopting the old dodge of carrying a broom about with him, as though destined for some duty or other; but after a time he was rather piqued to realize that dozens of other men were working the same dodge. The bloody place was heaving with men with brooms, pick-axes and God knows what else, all pretending to be bound for some duty or other. One enterprising Jock in the Black Watch even carried two full fire buckets around with him and, if challenged as to what he was up to, would break into a run and yell: "Canna stop now, Sarge…. Emergency!"

To Charles, if it had been heaven itself he would not have complained.

Then, without warning, it was snatched away from him. A staff sergeant approached him as he stood outside his barrack block, enjoying the spring sunshine.

"Are you Private Charles of the Rocks?"

"I might be ..."

"Don't give me any lip, soldier. Are you or aren't you?"

"Yes.   Anything I can do for you?'

The staff sergeant waved a piece of paper in Charles's face. "You've got to go and see an ENT Specialist in Kure right away at the Base Hospital.   Go to MT.   The duty truck will take you in."

Charles realized that this was the crisis of his adventure.   It brought him back to reality with a jerk.   He'd almost forgotten that he was supposed to be deaf, but now he'd have to be especially on his guard.   Equally, he knew that he must not overdo things.   Even if the tank had deafened him completely, it would be normal for it to be wearing off by now.   From what he'd been told, men usually got their hearing back within two months.

When he reached Kure Hospital he found the ENT Department easily enough.   There wasn't even a queue.   He knocked on the door and a female voice invited him to enter.   Sitting behind a desk in the outer office was a Queen Alexandra's Nurse.   She was young and incredibly beautiful.   She had a small, pixie-like face with the most perfect complexion Charles could ever recall.   He snapped smartly to attention and saluted as efficiently as he could, a real 'wobbler' as his drill sergeant used to describe good salutes.

He was surprised when she laughed, her face split by an adorable smile, revealing perfect teeth.   "No need to salute me," she said. "I'm only a corporal!"

"Oh, sorry ... I thought all nurses ..."

"No, no.   Only nursing Sisters.   I'm a medically unqualified receptionist cum clerk ... But I'm working on it..."

"Well, well," smiled Charles.   "Just put it down to natural respect.   If you're not commissioned, you certainly should be ..."

"Thanks.   I'll take that as a compliment."

"My name is Edwin Charles ... I was told to report ..."

"Yes, I know, Edwin.   Major McInroe will see you very soon.   Sorry we've kept you waiting around at that ghastly JRBD place for so long."

They chatted for a time and Charles was careful to slip in a few "pardons?" and "I didn't quite catch that?"   It all fitted in well with her questions about Korea and the rough time he'd had with the Rocks.   What he couldn't understand was how such a gorgeous girl could ever end up in such a

175

mundane job. She was real model material or even more; a Rank Starlet if ever he saw one.   Yet there was no side to her, no airs and graces; and straight away she was calling him 'Edwin' as though they'd know each other for a long time; and the ease and confidence with which she chatted away was something he had never encountered in a girl before. He wondered why he had been wasting his time shagging a Jap scrubber when there was crumpet like this in town. Surreptitiously, he glanced down to see if she wore an engagement ring, but she didn't, and she was doing her best to advertise the fact. He suddenly felt really elated.

After about ten minutes a buzzer sounded on her desk. "Ah, that will be the Major ... Ready to see you, I expect ... Hang on a tick and I'll just have a word with him ..."

He watched her as she got up from her desk and walked across to the major's consulting room. His eyes flashed up and down the length of her body, checking her features. He dreaded that she might have jumbo legs, but she didn't. They were long and slender. As far as he could see, she was well-nigh perfect. Her waist was tiny and beneath her tight-fitting skirt the cheeks of her bottom were sashaying about a treat. He had her mentally undressed within seconds.

She was in Major McInroe's office for a good ten minutes. When she returned she apologized for the delay and then ushered him into the major's presence. Charles saluted, stood rigidly to attention and prepared to say, "Pardon, sir," to just about everything he heard. There was no way he was going to louse things up now.

"Sit down, laddie."

The Major's voice boomed out. Charles heard it so distinctly that he very nearly obeyed without hesitation. He took a grip of himself, however. He inclined his head and repeated his old formula: "Pardon, sir?"

The Major pointed to the chair. When Charles was seated he said: "So it would seem you were involved in a blue-on-blue? And were deafened?"

"Deafened, sir? Yes, that's right, sir."

"Okay. So let's have a look. I have to give you a general examination first, to make sure all your parts are there and working okay. Purely routine, just normal army bullshit, really."   He laughed at his witticism. "Okay---gear off ..."

"Clear off, sir? Already?"

"Take your clothes off."

"Oh, right, sir."

Major McInroe went through the usual rigmarole. When satisfied that Charles was all there and sound enough, he turned his attention to his hearing.

He produced what looked like a canteen of cutlery but which turned out to be a box containing a vast collection of tuning forks. He explained the procedure to Charles: that he would strike different tuning forks which would let out a hum and when that hum disappeared, he was to say so. This did not increase Charles's confidence, but as far as he could tell all he had to do was be premature in saying that the humming noise had disappeared. He reckoned it would be easy enough to wait until it was in definite decline, but still there, and claim that it had gone. That would surely prove his deafness. The only thing he wasn't too sure about was whether he should hear the low notes longer than that high notes, or treat them just the same. So he decided to treat them all the same and it seemed to work perfectly.

When it was all over, Major McInroe spent several minutes writing up his notes. Charles sat there and waited patiently. Once Major McInroe had finished, he smiled across at Charles, as though relaxing, as though they'd just completed a very satisfactory process. He even sat forward and leaned across his desk confidentially. He smiled knowingly and spoke softly. There was a definite twinkle in his eye which Charles recognized as the hallmark of a roué.

"Did you notice young Cathy when you came in?"

"Cathy? Yes, sir. Yes, I certainly did."

"A really lovely girl ..."

"Yes, sir."

"She's told me all about what happened to you in Korea. Sounds like you had a rough time."

"Yes, sir."

"Never mind, Charles. Your luck might have changed. In fact, I'd wager a guess that it really has."

"In what way, sir?" asked Charles, intrigued.

"Cathy!" Major McInroe leaned ever further forward and went into a semi-whisper, the way men-of-the-world do when discussing confidential matters about desirable members of the fair sex: "She fancies you! She was bowled over by your respect in saluting her ..."

"Really, sir?"

"Aye! Could be the best thing you ever did."

Major McInroe beckoned Charles forward, to meet him halfway over his desk. Then he added in a whisper: "I'm not a match maker Charles, but you've made a hit. And I don't mind telling you that Cathy is some girl. She might look as though butter wouldn't melt in her mouth, but between you and me she's a right little raver. And she loves men who are well endowed."

"Well endowed, sir? Rich, you mean?"

"No, no, you fool.   Men who are well hung like you."

"You mean with…. "

"Precisely!"

"Eleven and a half inches when on parade, sir," boasted Charles.

"Splendid!   She'll love that."

Major McInroe leaned back in his chair, all smiles, leering like an old lecher.   He tapped his nose and said secretively: "I'll put in a good word for you … Although knowing Cathy she may well have been watching through the keyhole."

Charles laughed and turned to see if there was a keyhole: there was, and there was no key in it.   Bloody hell, he thought. I'm well away here.

"I'll go and have a word with her… Put a good word in for you, shall I?"

"Yes please, sir."

Major McInroe went into the outer office.

He was away several minutes, during which time Charles heard Cathy's typewriter clattering away twenty to the dozen.   When Major McInroe returned he marched briskly to his desk.   He was now a different person: efficient and business-like instead of a gay old dog.   He folded a sheet of paper he'd brought back with him and placed it in an envelope.   Then he handed it to Charles.

"When you get back to the Rocks, give this to your MO.   It's a full report on your condition.   Also included is your movement order back to Korea. I've classified you as medicine and duty.   In others words--- as no doubt you are well aware--- there's nothing wrong with you.   Neither has there ever been.   These tests with tuning forks are a waste of time with men like you who lie through their teeth and refuse to cooperate properly.   They don't prove a thing, as you were obviously aware before you came in.   But when I whisper a whole lot of confidential tosh and you hear and understand every word of it, it tells me all I want to know."

Charles stood up and stared back blankly.

"That's all, Private Charles. You can go, and no ill-feelings.   Don't bother to salute Cathy on the way out."

5

The first leg of Blake's journey back to Kure took him as far as Seoul. It was a slow and at times painful journey, bouncing along the MSR in the back of an empty Troop Carrying Vehicle. He spent two days at a transit camp in the capital with nothing to do but eat, sleep and wander about the city absorbing the atmosphere of dirt, squalor, decay, and tragedy. It looked exactly what it was: a city which had changed hands four times in two years and been sacked ruthlessly each time. Apart from Pusan it was the most depressing place he had ever seen, now little more than a collection of wrecked buildings, what Dresden must have looked like after its bombing.

In contrast, his journey from Seoul to Kure was swift. It was by Air Ambulance, a plane crowded with wounded men on stretchers. At Iwakuni Air Base in Japan, the wounded were taken to the Base Hospital in Kure and Blake was driven to the nearby transit camp, JRBD. When he reported to the orderly room no one had ever heard of him and later, when he saw the adjutant, he was told that since he had been dismissed so suddenly by his regiment it would be a week or two, perhaps even a month, before he was allocated a new posting.

For the first few days Blake enjoyed himself. He had a decent bedroom to himself and the officers' mess was luxurious. He was content to spend his time sitting by one of the huge log fires in the lounge, reading books. It was a delightful change to be able to do as he pleased, to be waited upon, and only stir himself to eat in the well-appointed dining room.

Then the fascination of idleness wore off. He got chilblains on his toes, became tired of reading books, and yearned to do something active. At nights he searched the town for some form of relaxation. He had heard reinforcements who in Korea talked in glowing terms of the night-life in Kure, but after wandering the streets and finding nothing but noisy beer halls and brothels, lousy with posturing tarts and heaving masses of troops, he invariably ended up in Kure's Officers' Club, adjacent to the buildings of Headquarters British Commonwealth Forces in Korea (HQBCFK). Unfortunately the Club was frequented entirely by elderly staff officers with whom he had nothing in common and who often regarded him as an intruder. Likewise, the subalterns he met at JRBD were so preoccupied by their imminent departure for Korea that he found it impossible to make any lasting friendships with them. Consequently he began to view Kure with a jaundiced eye.

Eventually, he took to visiting the adjutant at JRBD on a daily basis, hoping for news of a posting. "What's the matter, bored?"

"Bored stiff," smiled Blake.

"I can always send you on a week's course at Hara Mura, the Battle School. You'll be the only one from JRBD, but you won't be bored, I promise you."

"Okay, I'll give it a try…"

"On your head be it, old boy."

Hara Mura Battle School was an incredible place, the army's best training facility bar none. It was situated in rugged mountains, virtually a replica of what Blake had experienced in Korea. It was unbelievably gung-ho in its attitude. It wasn't so much a training camp as a site for war games. The exercises were highly specialized, and those they held at night were so realistic that Blake felt as though he was again patrolling in Korea. Safety measures were taken, but accidents, even deaths, were not uncommon and were always explained away as the price one had to pay for realism. No one ever argued.

Hara Mura was run predominantly by junior officers who had been singled out for their instructing skills. Living conditions were rough but the over-zealous members of the staff reveled in this, seeing it as all part of the pretense of war. Blake was the only one on his course with first-hand experience in Korea, so he was regarded as a combat veteran and often questioned as to what it was like.

At the Battle School they were expected to play hard as well as work hard. Behavior in the officers' mess after training was reminiscent of the antics of squadrons of the Royal Flying Corps in the Great War, when life expectancy was down to two weeks. It was a hell-raising attitude, a sense of having a last fling before facing the possibility of death. Beer was consumed in vast quantities, and each evening, after protein-packed meals of near-raw steaks, served by the now familiar bevy of attractive girls, port circulated freely, and when the decanter had done several rounds rugby songs were bellowed out around the mess piano, succeeded by games which were often little short of free-fights, with arm and leg wrestling predominating.

The final night of each course was different, something very special which staff officers never stopped alluding to throughout the week. It was known as 'the subalterns' initiation'. Theoretically, it was voluntary, but tradition (if there can be a tradition after only 18 months) demanded that all subalterns entered into the spirit of things, just as public school new boys, university freshmen, and newly elected Masons were expected to.

After the port had circulated and mess antics been completed, the staff officers disappeared, most of them heading off in a convoy of jeeps for a Friday night of heavy drinking in the famous bars of Hiroshima. Only the subalterns remained, appropriately in the care of the assistant adjutant, himself a subaltern.

What happened next was straightforward.. Straws were drawn and the longest went first. The assistant adjutant led the winner to the impressive double doors of the lounge, pushed him through surreptitiously, and then closed them behind him. Standing in a long row in the anteroom like debutants awaiting presentation, were the young Japanese waitresses. What happened next was predictable enough.

Blake drew a fairly short straw. By the time his turn came, and he was eased through the doors, he was feeling highly alarmed. This was not how he had imagined his first romantic tryst. As soon as he was in the anteroom the girl who had drawn the equivalent straw stepped forward. She was a diminutive and cheerful young girl, known among the staff officers as 'the giggler'. She bowed deeply and then took his arm, just as though he had invited her to dance and she was leading the way to the floor. The other waitresses nudged each other and made guttural noises of approval, and Blake had no alternative but to go along with her, heading out of the mess, towards his tent.

The tent next to his was already occupied and he heard predictable noises emanating from it. He turned to face his companion. He was so embarrassed he had no idea what to say. Eventually, in a quiet but firm voice he said: "Not tonight, thank you!"

For a moment or two the two of them just stood there. He suddenly felt a complete and utter idiot. More than that, he also felt a rotten swine. He was so embarrassed he had no idea what else to do or say. The girl continued to stare at him blankly. Then, when she realized she had been rejected, tears flooded her eyes. Her hands went to her face to cover her shame. Finally, she let out a great sob and ran off into the night, her loss of face more than she could stand.

Blake went into his tent and flung himself down on his camp bed. He felt a complete bastard, totally inadequate. For the rest of the night he lay awake, trying to fathom out his conflicting traits, listening---- partly in disgust and partly in envy--- to the intermittent cries of joy coming from neighboring tents.

A week later Blake was summoned to the adjutant's office at JRBD and told that a posting had come through for him. He was to report to Major Hugh

Vallance at HQBCFK to be the Assistant Camp Adjutant.

"A really soft number, Blake," said the adjutant. "I'd make the most of it if I was you."

It was indeed a sinecure, acknowledged as the best job in Japan for a junior officer. Perhaps the best feature was the Commandant, Major Vallance. He was a rarity, an officer who really was a gentleman as well. In fact, he was a gentleman well before he ever became an officer, someone born and bred in the best traditions of the British upper-middle class, an Etonian with the finest trimmings.

He welcomed Blake in a most cordial manner, stressing that he was the 'adjutant' not the 'assistant adjutant'. "There can't be an assistant to someone who doesn't exist," he explained. "It's just the army's way of trying to keep you in your place. As for our duties ... Well, really we're nothing but glorified house-keepers. And the better we do our jobs, the less people notice us. Like good umpires or referees."

Blake soon discovered that this laissez-faire attitude was made possible by two men. One was the Japanese chief clerk and translator, known as Eddie, and the other was the Warrant Officer 1st Class Webber of the RASC who was in charge of admin. The former had been chief clerk at the headquarters when it was the nerve center of the Japanese Navy, which meant he knew exactly what was required, and the latter knew all the idiosyncrasies and foibles of the British Army, especially how to handle young British Tommies in foreign climes.

Both of them were well aware that Blake would have no idea of his duties, or how to handle them, and that Major Vallance was far too preoccupied with his social life in the Officers' Mess and the Officers' Club to instruct him, so they took him under their wing and hand-fed him, RSM Webber making it clear that in return he was expected to be docile and compliant, and never pull rank as his predecessor had.

It turned out to be an admirable arrangement.

Blake's greatest pleasure came from his accommodation. He had his own bungalow. It was of traditional Japanese design, sporting wooden-framed walls with tissue paper stretched across the lattice work, situated down a long drive between two other bungalows. It stood in its own grounds behind all others, giving it a wonderful degree of privacy, with a large garden featuring artistically arranged rocks, stunted conifers, and a pond traversed by an ornate wooden bridge. Inside, the bungalow was light and airy, even though sparsely furnished. It had a western style double bed instead of a futon, but otherwise he was expected to sit on cushions scattered about the tatami mats. He had two house-girls, a mother and daughter combination who looked after him with fanatical zeal and amused him by constantly referring to him as "Officer Peter-san"

HQBCFK was a busy place with dozens of senior staff officers working hard to keep the Commonwealth Division in Korea properly armed, equipped and fed. To help them, there was a host of Other Rank clerks. They were housed in modern barracks, with plenty of facilities, including a canteen, mess hall, a cinema; even a well- appointed library. A Brigadier was in command and there were numerous back-up units, such as MT, Internal Security, a Cinematograph Section, Catering units, and even a newly formed legal department. Indigenous auxiliary staff also abounded, with--- as always--- hand-picked young Japanese girls in abundance.

To start with, Blake was at a loss for anything to do, but Major Vallance was swift to resolve this. "If you're at a loose end, go and inspect something. Anything will do. Just snoop around ... In a friendly way, of course .... It keeps men on their toes. And it justifies your existence. And good exercise, too, to say nothing of helping you to get to know everyone. Look upon it as waving the flag ... letting everyone know that we're on the ball."

As things turned out, Blake soon grew tired of idly wandering around the place and he found several ways to make a real contribution to the headquarters without in any way intruding on the efforts of Eddie or RSM Webber. He concentrated on helping with the social welfare of the Other Ranks. There were over a hundred of them and so far, as far as he could make out, they had just been dumped in their comfortable quarters and left to their own devices. There was no social or entertainments committee and what leadership there was came from a RASC Corporal named Jason. His rough and ready ways, and his foul language, reminded Blake of Charles, and it didn't surprise Blake a bit when---many years later--- he became one of Britain's top trade union leaders.

Corporal Jason persuaded his mates that since they were in a defeated nation still under occupation they could do as they liked. Normal moral and social behavior, such as they abided by in Britain, went by the board.

Most of Blake's information about their behavior came from Sergeant Gemmell, senior cook in the Officers' Mess, with whom Blake soon established a good rapport. He was not only a first-class cook, who specialized in curries, but a mature 40-year old who took a dim view of how the Other Ranks behaved. He, more than anyone else, persuaded Blake that there should be an ORs Social Committee to organize their general welfare and off-duty activities and get them to act like normal human beings.

He also introduced Blake to a Japanese auxiliary worker who supervised the house-girls and waitresses and was the housekeeper for the bungalows.

She was several years older than Blake and at first he was in awe of her, seeing her as a very superior being, the only Japanese female he'd come across who had been entrusted with responsibilities and authority. She was always immaculately turned out in a kimono, obi and geta sandals, and very attractive in a rather refined and formal way. It also struck him as odd that she spoke such excellent English. She didn't even have an American accent, as though she must have had a university education. She had assumed an Anglicized name and introduced herself as Miss Jackie with no surname. She insisted on calling him Mr. Blake, never Officer Peter or, as the house girls and waitresses were already doing, Officer Peter-san.

After several meetings her attitude thawed a little and she became increasingly attractive to him. He began to see her as a fascinating older woman, not a potential girlfriend, but a woman who could, perhaps, befriend him in the sense of guiding him into the world of sexual relationships, albeit platonic ones; someone who could boost his confidence, dispel his gauche ways and prevent him from ever again making a damn fool of himself, as he had done at Hara Mura.

Their friendship gathered pace after he formed a ORs social committee and decided to hold dances for them in their large canteen. The committee was keen on this but Blake discovered to his alarm that Corporal Jason, as secretary of the committee, intended to invite a whole lot of scrubbers off the Hondori. To forestall this, Blake approached Miss Jackie and suggested that she should help him out by persuading the house-girls and waitresses to attend instead. She agreed readily, knowing that it was the very thing they craved. Giving him one of her rare smiles---which he found radiant and longed to see more often--- she said: "What a great idea, Mr. Blake. The girls will all jump at the chance."

Inevitably, it meant that she helped him to organize the dances and whilst they worked together the formality between them thawed and they even got round to adopting first names. Most mornings they met in the mess kitchen and while chatting with Sergeant Gemmel they enjoyed many good laughs. After a time she even became convinced that he wasn't just a junior version of the stuffed shirts who predominated among the staff officers.

The dances soon got underway and were a great success. They held them fortnightly and much to everyone's surprise (most of all Blake's) the ORs all turned up in Teddy-Boy suits, with jackets which reached down to their knees, velvet collars, natty boot-lace ties, pocket flaps with braid surrounds, blue suede shoes with thick crepe soles, and trousers that hugged their legs and exaggerated every contour. They left the girls speechless, realizing that their brightly colored kimonos and obis had been outshone. For their part, the

ORs loved the way the girls discarded their getas and danced in their snow-white tabi socks which had a separate compartment for their big toes.

Blake always made a point of inviting Jackie, making it quite clear that it wasn't simply a way of safeguarding that everything went smoothly. She laughed at his concern and to their mutual relief they found that they were very compatible on the dance floor, with their bodies molding into each other as though they'd been designed for dancing together.

The dances soon became increasingly informal and before long several of the girls invited selected friends back to their homes for partying once the dances had finished at midnight. Blake placed a standing order with MT for two 15 cwt trucks and they would squash into these and drive off into the buraku (slum) areas of Kure. He could hardly believe the squalor that was revealed in the headlights. They twisted and turned along interminable alleyways, squeezing between an assortment of wooden and corrugated iron shacks. Scores of children scampered about with barking dogs at their heels, and ancient street-vendors wandered about like lost souls, ringing hand bells or playing repetitive tunes on their flutes as they sold noodles.

Despite the poverty they always managed to have a great time, but it made Blake wonder if he was taking things a little too far. So many of the couples were becoming so closely attached that there was talk of engagements and ideas were floated about the possibility of girls going back to England as brides; and he realized just how unrealistic it all was, how such ideas were bound to end in tears.

Jackie never invited them back to her home after the dances, and when a group of the lads teased her about this, she explained that she lived with her married sister, whose husband was an Australian corporal and lived in married quarters in one of the Australian Occupation Forces camps several miles towards Hiroshima.

When Blake next met her on one of his mess inspections the subject came up again and to assure him that there was no dark secret behind it she invited him a to a social evening at her brother-in-law's corporals' mess.

"Won't it matter that I'm an officer?"

"Not a bit," she laughed. "The Aussies aren't like you Poms. They're very relaxed about things like that."

"What happens? Do they play 'two-up' the whole time?"

"No. They do that in secret. It's illegal. But they do play Housey-Housey, just the same as your lot do in the Officers' Club. But mainly, being Australians, they concentrate on drinking beer."

"Do you go there often?"

"Frequently. I sometimes help serve behind the bar on busy nights. I have done for two or three years."

Blake went to the social and thoroughly enjoyed himself. Jackie only had a short spell behind the bar and then joined him. She sat with him through the Housey-Housey and became highly excited when she had a small win. He met her brother-in-law but wasn't greatly impressed. He was friendly, like most Australians, but he was only interested in standing at the bar, knocking back schooner after schooner of beer.

The evening became more memorable to Blake when he saw that the mess had an old, upright piano which no one was able to play. He went over to it and managed to get a respectable tune out of it. As soon as he did, he was pressed into service and his popularity zoomed when he played 'Waltzing Matilda'. He then played several more songs with an Australian flavor, helped by the crowd around the piano. They first of all sang them and then he picked up the tunes on the piano. During a pause, when they all prepared to go back into the bar for 'eyes down' at more Housey-Housey, she asked him about his musical ability.

"I suppose you would call it a gift," he said, looking up from the keyboard to face her. "I just picked it up from my mother and I've always been able to play by ear. I don't need music, just the tune. Rather like the joke with the father and his teenage son."

"What joke is that?"

"Oh, it's just an old English joke. A father and his teenage son were trying to maneuver a piano down the stairs when they were moving house. The father was down the stairs pulling at the piano near the keyboard, and the son was a couple of steps above, pushing at the back of it. All of a sudden they came to a jarring halt. Then the son said: 'Dad, do you know the piano's on my foot?'"

" 'No, son, I don't … But you hum it and I'll play it.' "

Normally, she found English jokes totally obscure, but this one made her double-up with laughter. She leaned on him and wrapped her arms about his shoulders, so amused that tears rolled down her cheeks.

When she eventually recovered herself, and they went to join the others for the Housey-Housey, their arms remained wrapped about each other's waists.

6

Back at the Rocks, there was a battalion muster parade at which the Colonel stood on a dais and addressed his men. In ringing tones he told them he was proud to be able to announce that when they went back into the line they would assume full responsibility for the Hook position. He also announced that R and R leave in Tokyo would start immediately and all those who wished to take leave could do so. He added that a pay parade would be held later in the day and that back-pay which had accrued during their time in the line would be issued.

The Colonel had little idea of what he was unleashing. The Hook was regarded by the rank and file as a suicide mission, especially since a Chinese spring offensive was expected at any time; so they were convinced that the R and R and back-pay on offer could well be their last chance to really enjoy life. Consequently, they drew every last penny of their pay and went off to Tokyo intending to have the time of their lives.

Tokyo was waiting for them, ready to accommodate them in any way they chose. It was a city of a thousand delights where men could find the debauchery they craved in their wildest dreams; a city the like of which had never been known before and has never been seen since, where the refloating of a defeated and bankrupt nation was underway, all based on man's insatiable desire for alcohol, bright lights, shady bars, female nudity and sexual intercourse.

It was later disclosed in the American Forces newspaper (*The Stars and Stripes*) that the Rocks had had more men arrested by the military police than any other battalion, bar the one from France.

"Now look here, Colonel," said Lawrence when told of his imminent departure for Tokyo, "let's get this perfectly straight. I don't want any bloody leave, and certainly not three days longer than anyone else. Nor is it right that I should go off before anyone else.."

"It's not a matter of what you want, Dick, it's a matter of what is good for you."

"But what good can I do in Tokyo? What is this---a plot against me? What will my men say when I go on leave before they've all been? And what the hell will become of the company with only Clark in charge?"

"They'll survive," the Colonel replied placidly.

"I doubt that very much. Tokyo is the last place I want to go to. The whole thing is damned ridiculous."

"It's no good arguing, Dick. You're going!"

Lawrence soon found himself in Tokyo. For the first two days he stayed at the officers' hotel in the Ebisu leave camp, drinking solidly at a private bar which remained open all day. On his third day he went into Tokyo because the Colonel had given him specific instructions to visit the Laccus Club, and he was the type of soldier who obeyed orders even when they were easy to avoid.

The Laccus Club was the biggest and best of its kind in town, and it was packed with semi-drunk officers and hundreds of very classy girls in long evening dresses, all of them looking wonderfully demure and innocent, even though they were all available at 10,000 yen for the night. The bar was so crowded there was little prospect of getting a drink within half an hour.

"Not a bad place this, Major," said an American Colonel enthusiastically, as he stood beside Lawrence waiting for service.

"Not too bad" replied Lawrence, trying to be friendly.

"Commonwealth Division, aren't you? I thought so. We support you, Major. I'm with the 39th Battalion of Engineers."

"Really?"

"Sure thing." The American drew a deep breath and extracted a fat cigar from his hip pocket. "Ah, great! Here comes the floor show. How about joining us at our table, Major?"

He led the way to a low table pushed well forward, at the edge of the dance floor. The whole room settled down in anticipation of the floor show. Soon, a Japanese girl appeared and started a tantalizing and skillful strip-tease. Immediately, Lawrence wished that he had remained at the bar. He sat at the table, acutely embarrassed, and when the girl finally slipped off her last flimsy garment to stand naked before them, only a foot or two away, a wave of disgust overtook him.

"Now watch this," said the American Colonel. "This really is cute."

The girl advanced to their table, turned about once so that everyone could admire every aspect of her gorgeous figure, and then borrowed a coin from one of the Americans. She placed it on the edge of the table and then, lifting one leg into the air, she picked it up again.

There was a great roar of applause. "Have you ever seen a woman like it?" the American Colonel yelled.

"Bloody revolting," snapped Lawrence and left as quickly as he could.

Having spent three days in Tokyo, Lawrence had had enough. He'd followed orders and visited the Laccus Club, so now he was going to please himself.

He decided to take a train to Hiroshima--- long journey though it was--- and visit the Hara Mura Battle School, of which he had heard so much.

He telephoned an old friend on the staff of HQBCFK (Bunny Graham of the Green Howards) and soon had the visit organized, with two nights' accommodation at the HQ mess and a day-visit to Hara Mura. Then Bunny would give him a lift to Iwakuni and he'd fly back to the Rocks.

The trip went well and he was tremendously impressed by the Battle School. As he told the school's CO over lunch, it was a crying shame that all units going to Korea didn't first of all do a fortnight at Hara Mura. "God knows, my lot could have done with it," he added.

He then returned to Kure and rounded off a fascinating day by over-eating at the Officers' Club with Bunny Graham and a few of his pals.

The plane on which Lawrence was due to fly back on didn't leave until the afternoon, so he spent a leisurely morning in the mess, reading several regimental magazines which were lying around in the lounge. He'd just been served a coffee by a Japanese flunky when he heard a kerfuffle going on outside and a lot of female laughter and unruly Japanese squawking, as though there was a school playground near at hand.

He got up and wandered across to a window to see what was going on. He saw a large group of house-girls and waitresses, all highly excited and jumping and skipping about. In the middle of them--- the source of all the excitement and reveling in every second of it--- was Blake.

Lawrence could hardly believe his eyes. He listened to Blake as he laughed and joked with the girls, explaining to them in broken English of his own concoction that he was going to give them English lessons every Tuesday afternoon; news that was greeted by hysterical cries of joy, with lots more jumping up and down in celebration.

God Almighty, thought Lawrence. Whatever next! He opened the window and stuck his head out.

"BLAKE!"

Blake looked up in astonishment, recognizing the voice instantly. When he saw the familiar stocky figure, with his ridiculous moustache freshly waxed, and his inevitable aggressive frown, he couldn't help smiling broadly, as though genuinely glad to see him. Now, happily settled in Kure, he could afford to be magnanimous and forget all their past differences: laying on plenty of what his father always termed, 'True Christian spirit!'

"Hello, sir. What are you doing here?"

"On the contrary! What the hell are you doing?"

"I'm on the HQ staff, sir. I'm just organizing some English lessons for the house-girls and waitresses. Hang on, sir ... I'll come on in."

189

A few seconds later Blake entered the lounge. He saluted and after they both assured each other that they were fit and well, Blake explained about his new posting, unable to prevent his enthusiasm bursting forth. As Lawrence listened he became increasingly piqued. Never for one moment did he imagine Blake would end up with such futile and feeble and non-military duties, not only living in luxury but cavorting about with a bunch of amenable and no doubt obliging young girls.

Eventually, Blake asked Lawrence what brought him to Kure. Lawrence told him all about the Battle School and was surprised when Blake told him of the week-long course he had done there. They were agreeing how excellent the school was when Jackie stuck her head through the open window. For a moment she was all smiles, enraptured by the exuberance of the girls still outside the mess. When she saw Lawrence her smiles faded and she bowed formally. "Excuse me, Major! I didn't mean to intrude." Then she turned to Blake and added: "Peter, I'm taking the girls off, so I'll see you later." Then, after another bow, she was gone again, leading off all the chattering house-girls and waitresses.

"Who is she?" demanded Lawrence.

"She's a friend, sir. That is, she's on the staff as well. She's house-keeper for the officers' bungalows ..."

"So what's she got to do with you?"

"Nothing, really ... Except that she also helps me to organize the dances for the ORs."

"Dances?"

"Yes, sir. We have one every two weeks."

"Dances! With girls?"

"Well naturally, sir. You can't have dances without girls ..."

"Jap girls?"

"Of course. There aren't any others."

"Great Scott!"

"All innocent fun, sir."

"Really..."

There was an awkward silence.

Eventually Lawrence said with heavy sarcasm: "Well, don't let me hold you up. You're obviously very busy..."

"Yes sir, I am a bit. There's been a crisis with the laundry girls this morning ... It gets so hot in the laundry that they want permission to work stripped to the waist... Oh, and incidentally, sir, how are things going with the Rocks?"

"Fine!" replied Lawrence. "Everything in the regiment is absolutely fine."

Winston booked in at a hotel which had been recommended to him by a Canadian at the Ebisu Leave Centre. The manager, who was short and fat with protruding yellow teeth, showed him straight to a room, pointing to a double bed with the sheets already turned back. "The lady will be here shortly, sir."

No sooner had he spoken that a sweet little girl appeared behind him. She walked straight into the room, smiled coyly, and without even waiting for the manager to disappear she undressed and jumped into the bed. Winston ripped off his clothes and joined her. Within two minutes of having signed the hotel register he was getting what he had come for.

"This is the country,' he chuckled. "Talk about service!"

"Now if we are going to make the most of our time here," said Hallows, "we'll have to pool our money and plan our budget."

"Fair enough," replied Taylor, throwing a small bundle of notes on the table.

Hallows counted the notes and then announced: "With my lot, we've got exactly twenty-five thousand yen."

"So?"

"It means we can go to a posh hotel for two nights and get some really classy girls, or we can go to a decent brothel for three nights, or we can pick up some girls off the streets and keep at it solidly for all five nights."

"The streets it is then," said Taylor.

O'Hara entered the hotel determined to get the best that money could buy. Once installed in his room he rang for service and when the manager appeared he demanded the best girl he had.

When the manager returned he had a girl with him. "My number one girl, sir. Five thousand yen, okay? You pay?'

"Five thousand yen for that old rat bag!" exclaimed O'Hara. 'Never hatchy! She number ten."

The manager left the room with the girl in tears and shortly returned with another. "Really number one girl, sir. Six thousand yen."

O'Hara looked the girl up and down with obvious displeasure. "Now look here, you old idiot," he stormed, turning on the manager, "I want number one girl." He took the Jap by the collar and towered over him. "Her bloody number ten. Savvy?"

"Okay, sir, okay," the Jap replied nervously. "I get number one girl."

The manager was away a considerable time but when he did return he was beaming with pride. With a series of polite bows, and speaking in courteous tones, he ushered in a ravishing brunette, quite the most attractive girl O'Hara had seen since arriving in Tokyo. O'Hara went forward eagerly to welcome her.

The manager drew him to one side. "Please, sir. Ten thousand yen. She really is my number one girl."

"Okay, okay," snapped O'Hara, and in his eagerness to get rid of the manager he overpaid him by 5,000 yen, but he got his money's worth.

Williamson could still hear movement in the next room and he felt envious of Armitage's stamina. He waited until his own girl was asleep and then tip-toed into the next room where things were at last quiet, with Armitage and his girl also asleep. He woke Armitage silently.

"What the hell's up, Willy?"

"What about the money, you dope?" whispered Williamson. "I don't know about you, but I'm broke."

"How much do they expect?"

"Three thousand yen each."

"I've only got five hundred."

"Well, that settles it," hissed Williamson. "We're going to have to scarper …"

"But I haven't done yet."

"By the noise you've been making you've had a damned sight more than your three thousand yens worth. Come on! Get out while the going is good."

Armitage started to slide out of bed, but the girl beside him woke and clutched him vigorously. "You can see how it is, Willy," he protested. "This is real love."

"To hell with that. Let's get out."

"How about one for the road?"

"Okay. One. But for God's sake make it a quickie."

"Now I know you fellows won't believe this," said CSM Ralf to an enthralled sergeants' mess, "but every word of it is true. It was in one of those night clubs where a couple of girls were doing the usual strip-tease. Only this time, when they finished they didn't run off, but just stood there stark bollock naked. Naturally, I saw my chance and started to dance with one of them. I guided her out into a small garden or courtyard and before I knew what was happening I looked across some artificial bushes and there was the RSM going like a bloody two stroke engine with the other girl."

"What's the matter with you then?" demanded the MO as Chambers entered the RAP

"I think I've got a dose, sir."

"And what makes you think that?"

"It's making itself pretty obvious, sir."

"Um ...I'll say it is. Tell me, when were you last in contact with a woman?"

Mulligan looked up in surprise. "Blimey, sir, I've been in Tokyo. I've been in continual contact for the last five days."

7

Nobby Clark flopped, almost exhausted, into a chair in the mess and drank a glass of orange squash straight off. He stretched his legs out in front of him and, catching the eye of the mess waiter, he ordered another soft drink. "Thank God Lawrence is back," he said to the adjutant, who was the only other officer present.

"What's the matter? Was the responsibility too much for you, Nobby?"

Clark laughed scornfully. "Good God, no! I've managed them all right, but it just isn't my idea of fun. Able Company must be the biggest bunch of rogues in the British Army. Dick Lawrence drove them so hard while they were in the line that they think they can do just as they like simply because they are in reserve. Incidentally, when do I leave for Tokyo?"

The adjutant lowered his paper. "Well I hope you don't mind, Nobby, but I told the Colonel that you didn't particularly want any leave--- Tokyo leave, that is."

"Thanks a hell of a lot. ..."

"Steady old man, I haven't finished yet. The thing is this. A concert party from Blighty is over here and we've been told to supply an officer to escort them around the place."

"E.N.S.A. parties!" groaned Clark. "Still, anything is better than Able Company"

The adjutant sat forward and laughed. "I didn't think that you would mind, old man. It shouldn't be too bad. One of the women is a really good-looker. I've got a picture of her here. I thought it might cheer you up."

Clark scrutinized the picture. "Um, very nice. What's her name?'

"Doris Dawn."

"I've never heard of her."

"Apparently she's an up-and-coming star."

"When does this so-called leave of mine start?"

"You report to a Major Claude at Div. H.Q. first thing in the morning. Collect all the gen from the orderly room. Have a good leave, old man. Don't do anything that I wouldn't."

"That gives me plenty of scope."

Major Claude was a pear-shaped major with a bulbous stomach that tapered up to narrow shoulders, above which were the full red cheeks of a boozer, everything terminating in an egg-like bald head, what he always referred to as 'very fine head of skin!'

As Major Claude and Nobby Clark travelled down to Seoul Station by jeep, Claude talked continuously. "A queer set, these theatrical people, as you'll soon discover. They're all the same, without exception. Conceited, temperamental, hard-working, and just like a lot of kids. The women are always turning on the tap. And some of them are really fast workers as well, old man. Story I heard is that they don't get Equity cards unless they are certified nymphomaniacs. And their shows are nothing but sheer dirt. The troops lap it up, but you won't see a Padre within ten miles of them."

When the train from Pusan arrived at Seoul they had no difficulty in recognizing the artistes. On seeing them, Claude gave a great shriek of laughter and waved excitedly as though he'd known them for years. They were led off of the train by the comedian of the party, Harry Arnold, who for sheer heartiness, unlimited noise, and complete self-confidence, outstripped even Claude. He was small and loose-limbed, like the majority of third-rate comedians; and by way of introducing himself he did a short tap dance there and then on the platform.

"Well, hullo, hullo, hullo," he cried, his exhibition completed. He seemed to think there was a vast crowd there to meet them and added: "How are you all?"

Nobby Clark stood to one side and watched the other artistes as they climbed out of the high, awkward carriage. Doris Dawn appeared in the doorway, a colorful scarf wrapped around her neck: she was undeniably beautiful, tall and slim with perfectly molded features. She wore a thorn colored costume that clung tightly to her body, displaying her curves to their best effect. Her waist was so tiny that Clark felt certain that he would have been able to encircle it with his hands. From beneath the hem of her skirt appeared an exquisite pair of legs which she showed off to startling effect, stretching them elegantly, one at a time, as she stepped down from the train: an extraordinary feat of dexterity which showed off her stocking tops both times.

Nobby Clark hurried forward to greet her and she gave him an encouraging smile. The other members of the party--- a big-busted soprano with several cases of make-up--- and a sleazy little pianist, went virtually unnoticed. Everything, even Doris Dawn's beauty, was overpowered by the fast-talking Harry Arnold. His voice droned on and on. Even the verbose Major Claude could hardly get a word in edgeways.

"I think it would be best if we all introduced ourselves," said Claude eventually. "I presume you are Harry Arnold."

"Well, well, well, how do you like that?" cried Arnold. "Right first time. Such is fame. Now let me introduce you to the others. You might not recognize them quite as easily. Now let me see. This little lady is Doris Dawn."   He gave her a gentle hug which was clearly not appreciated. "And this is Josephine Ramsbotham. And last but not least, Alec Wright."

"Well, we're Claude and Clark," responded the major as though they were a conjuring act. "Call me, Cecil, and my friend here, Nobby."

Claude and Arnold led the way out of the station, and as Nobby Clark walked behind with the others he listened to Arnold's never-ending voice. 'Yes, we've just come in from Honkers! What a marvelous place. You've never seen anything like it."

"I was there for five years, actually," said Claude.

"It really amazed me. And I've been around. Haven't I been around?" He turned to the others. "Haven't I been around?"

"Yes, you've been around," agreed Doris Dawn.

Clark turned to Doris Dawn and asked her what she thought of Hong Kong. "It stank to high heaven" she replied.

During the next four days the life of the concert party was unvaried. With a staff car and a jeep, they travelled round from unit to unit giving their concerts. The troops crowded into small, temporary theatres and despite the tiny stages, the concert party went through their acts.

In the evenings they were entertained in officers' messes, where they were treated royally, with good food and unlimited drink. Nobby Clark divided his time between looking after Doris Dawn and chatting and drinking with his friends in the other units. He noticed, first with annoyance and then with amusement, how most of the officers flocked round Doris Dawn, trying to be perky and witty. Drinks flowed freely and laughter would ring out merrily, but always there, throbbing like perpetual motion, grinding on and on, was the voice of Harry Arnold.

The last concert was at the Rocks, due to Nobby Clark's influence. Afterwards, the officers' mess put on a big party. Doris Dawn stuck closely to Nobby's side, as indeed she had for most of the tour. Occasionally, Clark would introduce her to officers who had edged their way towards them and they were continually accepting drinks from waiters serving a terrifically strong rum punch.

Doris Dawn soon became distinctly tipsy. She began to giggle like a schoolgirl and to sway uncertainly on her high heels, with Nobby Clark only too pleased to steady her.

Late in the party, Doris asked: "Nobby, who is that fat little man over there who hasn't smiled all evening and who keeps eyeing me so disapprovingly? The one with the cute little moustache…"

"Oh, you don't want to worry about him, my dear," answered Clark. "He's my company commander. It's best if innocent young girls like you keep away from the likes of him. He's what we call a DOM."

"What's that?"

"Dirty Old Man." They laughed and a subaltern who had been hanging around them all evening blushed and tittered.

"Oh, good!" she exclaimed. "That's exactly the sort of man I've been longing to meet out here."

"Very well, my dear, then I'll introduce you to him." He managed to catch Lawrence's eye. "Dick!' he yelled above the general hubbub. "Good to see you again. It seems ages since you went on leave."

Lawrence strolled over to them. He didn't quite manage a smile, although he tried hard. "Hullo, Nobby," he growled.

"Let me lift your gloom, Dick. This is my very special friend, Doris. Doris Dawn---Major Dick Lawrence."

Lawrence was not sufficiently impressed to make any comment.

"Nobby has told me such a lot about you, Major. I'm thrilled to meet you."

"Is that so?" mumbled Lawrence. "I'm glad to make your acquaintance as well, young lady."

"How did you enjoy your leave, Dick?" asked Clark after an awkward silence.

"I've never known such a bloody waste of time in all my life. Tokyo is without doubt the most sordid city in the world. I've seen most of the cesspits of this planet, but never anything to equal Tokyo." Doris spluttered with laughter, but Lawrence ignored her and continued: "You can't even go into a bar without some female doing a strip-tease. And they were perfectly revolting. They took every damned stitch of clothing off and then gyrated about the place. One of them …Well, I'm not going into that …"

Clark felt Doris squeeze his hand and he realized she was about to stir things up. "Major, that's awful! Really awful! At the Windmill we were never allowed to move once we were completely starkers. If we did we got the sack."

Lawrence gave her a look of disgust and wandered off, muttering to himself.

"Some dirty old man!"

"Were you really a Windmill girl?"

"Oh yes! You know all those comedians who made their names there? Well I had nearly every last one of them. How else do you think I got off the chorus line?"

"Talent!"

"Oh, Nobby! You are so sweet. I must find a way to reward you." She swayed precariously and Clark steadied her again.

"I think I'd better take you outside for some fresh air."

Outside, the noises of battle coming from the north confirmed that the Hook was taking another pounding. In the light of distant explosions and flares, Clark admired the elegant lines of her face and her high cheek bones. He took her face in his hands and kissed her, and she kissed him right back, passionately, her tongue plunging halfway down his throat, nearly choking him.

"We won't be able to stay out long," he said. "It's much colder than you think."

"Where can we go?"

"My tent …"

"Nobby! What a brilliant idea … I thought it would never occur to you."

He untied the flaps of his tent and ushered her in. He followed close behind, lit the hurricane lamp and started up the space-heater. Then he went back to the flaps and stuck his head out, just to make sure they hadn't been observed. Suddenly a strong torch beam flashed into his face.

"Well, hullo! hullo!" cried Harry Arnold. "If it isn't my old mate Nobby. You can't turn in yet, old man. Come and have a drink. Come on. I've got a really smashing gag I must tell you. It's about Oscar Wilde and the Pope. It's the best I've thought up for some time. Alec will tell you that."

"Sorry, old man," replied Clark, his heart pounding. "But I really must turn in … Got a splitting headache. Tell me in the morning."

"Rubbish, Nobby. I'm not taking no for an answer. Bring Doris along with you. She hasn't heard it either."

"Blast the man," said Clark as they followed the comedian into the mess.

"He really is the end," said Doris.

A week or two after Lawrence returned from Kure it became evident---despite what he'd told Blake--- that things weren't at all fine within the Rocks. Quite unexpectedly, they had a crisis on their hands. They were short of platoon commanders.

At an orders group the Colonel explained to his company commanders that with only days remaining before they relieved the American Marines on the Hook, they were five short. Young Finch of Baker Company had been evacuated with acute appendicitis; Cousins in Dog Company had been granted compassionate leave because his father had died, and Baker and Franklin, of Charlie Company, had been killed in an accident along the MSR. A fifth one, Mason of Baker Company, had been transferred to divisional headquarters at the request of the General.

"We've got two replacements coming over from Japan, but that's all," said the Colonel. "There are dozens of them sitting about over there, but they'll still not yet nineteen."

"Why not just let the platoon sergeants take over," suggested the adjutant.

"No, that's not good enough," said the Colonel. "Platoon sergeants are not commanders. We need officers in charge. Especially while on the Hook."

"We could always call Blake back, sir," said Lawrence.

"I hardly think we can do that, Dick. Not having only just thrown him out."

"We could forgive and forget, sir. I have no objection to having him back. I'm sure he's learnt his lesson. And I have no wish to be vindictive. The last thing I want to do is stand in the way of his army career, even if he is only a National Serviceman. And he is experienced. In fact, he's recently completed a course at the Battle School and Colonel Tatton told me he did extremely well. So perhaps he deserves another chance."

"Well it would certainly help." The Colonel turned to the adjutant. "See if you can trace him ..."

As Lawrence left the tent he said in an aside to the adjutant: "HQBCFK. He masquerades as Camp Adjutant. Major Ward is i/c postings. And don't listen to any old flannel about him being indispensable out there."

198

8

Blake had made what he fondly imagined to be his decision. He was still naïve enough to think that any decision made to cement a relationship was in male hands, rather than female. It was true that during the course of a sleepless night he'd resolved to act, but he had no idea that it was really up to her and that she was still in two minds as to how their friendship should develop.

As it happened, they became lovers two weeks after Major Lawrence had made his visit to Kure. Those two weeks were very good to them, a time in which he assured himself he had fallen in love with her. He woke every morning eager to see her again, to wave enthusiastically as he spotted her in the distance, and then watch her face burst into her gloriously soft smile as they hurried towards each other.

She had also grown terribly fond of him, so fond that she didn't have the heart to tell him that his feelings were not entirely reciprocated, that she still had lingering reservations. Unlike him, she was no stranger to love, and love had taught her the need for caution; that infatuation needed time to mature and needed to be balanced against other factors. She knew also that love could be cruel, often heart-breaking, and therefore not a thing to be embraced easily or lightly. With Peter, she knew they were in an impossible situation, with no future.

Yet she owed him happiness and she quite knowingly joined him in behaving like the proverbial love-birds, with all their friends in the headquarters aware of how close they were. They went on picnic trips along the coast of the Inland Sea in the jeep always at his disposal; and they went across to the sacred and beautiful island of Myajima to see the Itsukushima shrine, making a day trip of it rather than stay overnight.

The dances became ever more popular and when they visited the homes of various girls she always went as well, as firmly a member of the 'gang' as any of them. They had films shows featuring Will Hay and the Three Stooges, and she even laid on an evening of Kubuki dancing by a local troupe from Kure.

They saw the famous Japanese Cherry Blossom at its best and enjoyed the May Day celebrations, especially how the local policeman on point duty on a dais at a busy cross-roads in town was showered with gifts and drinks and became so drunk that the traffic was reduced to chaos, with him waving multitudes of scooter vehicles into each other's paths.

They dined out in Kure and she introduced him to the full gamut of Japanese dishes, having lots of laughs as he struggled to master chop sticks. He had been unable to invite her to any of the events in the officers' mess or the Club, but he delighted in taking her back to his bungalow and got Sergeant Gemmell to send waitresses round with insulated containers of curry, with all Gemmell's usual assortment of side dishes, proving to her that the British army also knew how to eat well.   After these meals he drove her back to her home near the Australian camp and even though she never invited him in to meet her sister, or any relatives, he was never offended, understanding the sensitive nature of her situation, speculating that somewhere in her family was a deep-seated, war-inspired prejudice again the British; or perhaps--- more simply--- it wasn't really her home and therefore not her place to invite him in.

On the morning of his assumed decision, Blake went to the mess kitchen for his elevenses, knowing that Jackie and Sergeant Gemmell would be there. His arrival was anticipated, Sergeant Gemmell having a cup and saucer waiting for him.   For a time the three of them chatted away in their usual manner.   Then they were interrupted by the arrival of a breathless messenger with an urgent message from Major Vallance.   Blake unfolded it and read it. It said, quite simply:
"A new posting has arrived for you.   You are to rejoin the Rocks soonest possible."
Jackie watched him as he read it: she saw blood drain from his cheeks, and then anger and dismay engulfed his face.   He kept swallowing hard, his Adam's apple bobbing up and down in his throat.   Eventually, he read it out to them.   As he did so his voice cracked.   They made no comment, just continued to watch him.   She wasn't surprised when he said: "It's that bastard Lawrence!   He's done this ... And they're already on the Hook!   What a bastard!   My God, what a bastard ..."
That was the moment when she made her decision, the decision that counted.   As she watched his reaction to his news she realized she could never be so heartless as to withhold her love.

She guessed--- a woman's instinct--- that he had already booked a room at the Willows Hotel, a few miles outside Kure.   It was the choice of most officers having illicit love-affairs with Japanese girlfriends of whom they were genuinely fond.   She knew the owners so well that she telephoned them, and when they confirmed that he had indeed booked the room she made sure they gave them their only en suite room and that they generally laid on five-star treatment.

Later that evening they drove out to the Willows. Once inside they crossed a narrow bridge traversing a small pond that formed the center-piece of the reception area and for several seconds they stared down into the clear water, smiling at each other's reflections and watching goldfish dart to and fro without causing a ripple on the surface of the crystal-clear water.

He felt the touch of her hand and she led him into their room. With them there was no 'Oh be joyful!' love-making; no tearing off of each other's clothes and rolling around on the bed as though rehearsing for a wrestling match; no clawing or scratching, love-biting, or overt displays of physical passion. They undressed on different sides of the room, came together in the middle and hugged each other silently. Then they slipped between the sheets and lay there, not saying a word, holding hands.

They both knew that before their love could be consummated he had to talk; that he was a tortured soul and needed to tell her everything: to tell her exactly what he had experienced and thereby let all the horrors and tragedies flow out. Before indulging in love he had to cleanse himself, confess to her all his weakness and all his failures, to make sure she understood all his agonies: only then would he feel able to unleash unconditional love.

So he told her everything. They turned and faced each other, hugged each other, and then, with his lips brushing her ear, he whispered all his traumas away. He even told her things that had never occurred to him before. How brave the lads had been, how most of them never even mentioned their fear, even though it plagued them night and day. How, when they lost their closest mates, they acted as though nothing untoward had happened. How they had endured the agonies of the cold and survived all Lawrence's over-zealous demands.

An hour or so later, when she thought he had quite finished, she took hold of him. She caressed him gently and lovingly, and sliding her body over his she slipped him inside her. She heard a faint, incredulous gasp. "Now we make love, Peter-san."

He surprised her by laughing softly. "No, no. Please! Don't move. Remain perfectly still. Let's just lie still a little longer, as we are: one person. I must tell you the good things as well, the happy times and the funny incidents. It wasn't all bad."

So they lay there a while longer, still one person. First he made her smile and then he made her laugh, and with her laughter came internal movements that became increasingly delightful to them. He made her laugh all the more and he ended up telling her of how the wounded man on Yong Dong had leapt off the stretcher and made a run for it up the hill, leaving Smudger Smith and himself looking down at an empty stretcher while dozens of shells continued to fall around them; and how the so-called wounded man bounded off like Jesse Owns, leaving them to face the music.

That made her laugh so much that her body went into a frenzy of shaking, taking them into a state ripe for unrestrained love. With both of them laughing out of control they rolled and lurched and thrust and plunged, until finally they cried out with joy and relief as they shared their love.

He woke early, his head resting between her breasts, his nose level with the top of the bed clothes, just as the light of dawn seeped through the paper walls of the room. They ate breakfast alone in their room and then had a final love-making. It was a more conventional coupling this time, but none the less satisfying for that.

They took the long way round to Iwakuni Air Base, but eventually they found themselves standing on the edge of the runways, by the doorway of the reception buildings. They found a secluded spot around the corner of the buildings and they kissed and hugged fiercely. Eventually, as other troops leaving on the DC-3 came out of the building and made their way across the tarmac to the waiting plane, they released each other.

"Sayonara," she said.

"Hey, come on! It's only mata dozo ..."

She forced herself to smile. "Of course. Mata dozo."

She watched him board the plane and disappear, but she kept on watching, knowing that he was at one of the tiny windows, unseen but feasting his eyes on her until the last possible moment.

"Sayonara, Peter-san," she said again, this time a whisper to herself. She had known it all happen before. Men went off to war, full of love and high expectations, full of future dreams, never suspecting for a moment that they would never come back, that they would never be seen again.

She was content that she had done her best to make him happy. That, at least, he deserved. Now she prayed that he would return. It was perfectly possible; maybe even likely, but he would never return to her. There could never be any future for them. She didn't have it within her to split her love.

As the DC-3 taxied off, she was already rehearsing the phrasing of her letter, explaining everything.

9

Winston smiled with gratitude as O'Hara handed him a bottle of beer, one of the many he had stolen from the PRI tent the night before when their free-issues had run out.

Winston had only just got back to Able Company after spending twenty eight days in the Seoul detention barracks. It was good to see all the old faces again and amusing to hear what they'd all been up to. There was the fantastic story about Charlie and the ENT specialist in Kure. Another couple of lads had just got back from the Hara Mura Battle School where they'd done a course on Rocket Launchers, weapons which no one ever used. Three others had been in the Pusan Detention Barracks (far worse than Seoul!) after burning down a brothel along the MSR where they claimed they had been overcharged. Smudger Smith had been promoted to temporary sergeant while Miles was acting as platoon commander, and Corporal Harden had lost his stripes for striking a Gook who had refused to give him a bigger helping of potatoes while serving out an evening meal. Now, there was a rumor that Blake was on his way back.

Yes, Winston assured himself, he was certainly glad to be back among friends.

"Bit noisy tonight," he said, as though he was the only one to have noticed it. All the way up from Seoul he had heard nothing but how activity in the line was increasing, with everyone certain that there would soon be another big battle for the Hook.

O'Hara smiled, almost pleased to see that Winston had not altered and was still the same empty windbag. "It's been a lot worse than this before," said O'Hara, nodding towards the Hook. "The Chinks are all bark and no bite. But it'll come sooner or later, and when it does come they'll take some stopping. The mob that's up there at the moment won't last five minutes."

In the corner of the tent, almost hidden behind a cloud of tobacco smoke, Charles stirred uneasily. He feared that what O'Hara said was true. To make matters worse, ever since his reappearance and all the stories about his fiasco in Kure, Ralf and Miles had been picking on him more than ever. The way they were carrying on, it was obvious that as soon as a really dirty job came up he was going to get it. The bastards were just waiting for the chance to write him off for good and all.

"Let's just hope for the best then," he said. "I reckon we could still strike lucky."

No one took any notice of him. They knew he was only trying to kid himself. One thing about old Charlie was that he never lost his optimism regarding personal things. They all knew he'd had another long session with Billings and that another plan was afoot. The old bastard Billings had laughed like a drain when he heard what had happened in Kure, but now he was advising Charles to exercise his second option and apply for compassionate leave; and Charles reckoned that if his mother's letters were anything to go by, and she was knocking on death's door like she kept saying, he might well end up getting it. He'd even seen the Padre and to his amazement he'd been highly sympathetic and promised to set investigations in motion. Now, Charles was praying that they'd pull their fingers out and get on with it before they actually moved on to the Hook.

The din on the Hook got louder and louder. It drove them into despondent silence. It continued for over twenty minutes and then their tent flaps were pulled back and CSM Ralf poked his head inside. "Lot of enemy movement in front of the Hook," he announced gravely, as though they didn't know. "One of you go and tell the rest of your platoon. The alarm might go any minute."

Winston gave an involuntary shudder. As soon as Ralf had disappeared he said: "Trust my bloody luck. First bloody night back and we're straight into the shit."

O'Hara laughed scornfully. "Ralf comes in here and says the same thing every night. He's just got the wind up."

"Who is going to tell the others?" asked Winston, making it clear he wasn't going.

"I'll go," answered O'Hara. "Any of you others go and you'd only cause panic." He pushed his way out of the tent and sauntered towards the latrine. He had no intention of passing on Ralf's message. What the hell was the use of it? They'd heard the same thing every night for the past week. The alarm wouldn't go any more than it had all week.

He lit a match in the latrine and saw two rats scuttle away. He lowered his trousers and settled down comfortably, feeling the bulging muscles on his thighs with satisfaction. Quite without warning a terrific concentration of shells landed on the Hook, vibrating everything, illuminating the sky for miles around, and covering the Hook itself in a great mushroom of dust, smoke and rubble.

Almost simultaneously the alarm went. The whole camp resounded with the noise of bugles and fire alarms being beaten. At Able Company headquarters, Ralf screamed his head off at men to hurry, and nearer at hand, in the platoon tents, men bustled about, swearing at each other as they grabbed their weapons and equipment and hurried down the hill.

O'Hara pulled his trousers up and rushed madly towards his tent, cursing at his stupidity. There was no one left in his tent and he even heard the first of the trucks revving up, ready to take them to the base of the Hook as the counter-attack company. He heard the metallic clanging of men clambering aboard. He cursed himself as he thought of all the times they had rehearsed loading on to the trucks, and he'd been caught with his trousers down!

He reached the One Platoon truck just as it was pulling away. He flung his equipment in the back, grabbed the tail-board, and dragged himself aboard. "Who the hell is that?" demanded Miles.

"O'Hara, Sergeant."

"Why are you so late?"

From the back of the dark mass of faces Charles called out: "He was in two minds whether to come at all, weren't you, Paddy?"

"Shut your moaning hole, Charles. Or I'll do it for you."

Charles was not deterred. "Not quite so keen on the old right marker when it actually comes to getting it, are you, O'Hara?"

Several men laughed. O'Hara was furious, but he managed to control his temper and he mumbled to himself: "I'll get that right marker, don't you worry about that."

Miles was quaking with dread. He was still in command of One Platoon and it was a definite part of the plan that if a counter-attack was required One Platoon was to lead it. To make matters worse, he had just received a letter from his wife when the alarm sounded, and he now realized that he might never get the chance to finish reading it. The very thought chilled his marrow. He stared hard at the outline of O'Hara's head and his temper flared. "Why the hell were you so late, I asked?"

"Because I was on the shit-house."

"You great Irish turd! You'll be sorry for this if you come out of to-night alive." At once he regretted his words. It had been a direct threat.

"Call me a turd again, Sergeant, and it's you that will be sorry." O'Hara sat down, wiping the sweat from his brow, and apart from the grinding of the engine and the shelling, nothing could be heard. Soon, shells began to fall nearer the truck and it rocked so violently that it almost overturned. Then the convoy came to a halt. Men started shouting frantically. "What the hell's the hold-up?"

"They've been hit, sir."

"Well, get them out of the bloody way."

"But they're all badly wounded."

"I couldn't give a shit. Get them off the bloody road."

Winston stared out of the back of the truck as they moved on again. He saw a bunch of men huddled together in the monsoon ditch, some of them moaning, others lying silent, one of them pleading for help, and all of them wet with blood. "Poor bastards," he said, but he felt more sorry for himself than them.

"Always the same in the bloody army," explained Johnstone. "I can remember when I was attached to the Grenadier Guards for a parade. A couple of fellows fainted and they just left them lying there until the whole bloody thing was over, and then they threw both of them straight into the guardhouse. The army just couldn't care less about individuals." He glanced at the dark outline of the others, lurching heavily with the movement of the truck. "Look at us! We're just like a lot of bloody cattle being driven to the slaughter house. Except that we know about it, and cows don't. I mean you can't tell a cow, can you ..."

"Oh, for Christ's sake shut your mouth," yelled Miles. The very sound of others infuriated him. "It's a bit late to start bitching about the army now."

Johnstone shuddered as he saw O'Hara attaching his bayonet to his Sten gun. Someone had once told him that there were always at least fifty per cent casualties on the Hook and he had thought about it so much that he had eventually resigned himself to the fact that he would be one of them. He knew that he would not have the courage to face the Hook and that within a few minutes would disintegrate into a nervous wreck. He tried to expel everything from his mind by talking. "I wasn't bitching, Sergeant. All I was saying is that you can't tell. ..."

"Shut your bloody mouth!"

O'Hara looked at Miles's dark face. "You're nervous, Sergeant," he said placidly, determined to even his account with him. His dislike of Miles went way back, to when they first arrived in Korea.

Miles slipped his hand into his trouser pocket and felt his wife's letter. "Of course I'm nervous, and so would you be if you weren't such an inhuman turd ...."

"You've used that word again, Sergeant! You really are going to be sorry."

No one else spoke and it became obvious that they were very near the Hook. The truck seemed to leap off the ground every few seconds as it was caught by blast. Then it came to a halt and, climbing out of the trucks with frantic speed, men dived into the monsoon ditches for cover. Further up the road there was a piercing scream as another stonk fell, and a voice kept yelling: "Spread out, spread out!" until it dissolved into a pitiful scream.

"He's been bloody spread out and no mistake," said Winston.

Johnstone couldn't help laughing. He was lying in the ditch with Winston's big feet practically in his face. He was comforted by Winston's presence and for some crazy reason he moved right up to him until his forehead was touching his boots. "What do you reckon will happen, Winston?"

"How the hell should I know! Just hope to hell we stay here."

"Do you think we will?" Johnstone desperately needed reassurance.

"How the hell should I know? Stop asking bloody stupid questions."

'But do you think we will?" Johnstone demanded, as though it all depended on Winston's opinion.

"I reckon so. But I hope not."

"Oh, Christ," moaned Johnstone.

A mortar bomb landed in the road only a few yards from them. For a moment Johnstone was numb all over, unable to see or hear a thing. He was panic-stricken and screaming. As he calmed down, hope replaced panic, hope that he was wounded, hope that there was a small piece of metal in his leg which would prevent him from moving. He felt his legs, searching for blood, but there was none and he had to resign himself to the fact that he was unharmed.

A hundred yards farther up the road, in the same monsoon ditch, Williamson was listening to his wireless set. For the first time since arriving in Korea his face was deadly serious, his mind concentrating entirely on his job. "Right, sir. They've just given us the word."

"Send One Platoon up then," Lawrence ordered.

The message was sent back. Taylor removed his headphones and turned to Miles. "That's it, Sarge. Up we go."

Miles had little difficulty in getting his men to follow him. They had rehearsed it so often that it was second nature to them. They were sprinting along the road automatically, crouching low and praying hard. Soon they were at the morgue, where there was a collection of burnt-out ambulance jeeps which had tried unsuccessfully to evacuate some of the wounded. Inside the morgue three or four Tilley lamps burnt brightly and two medics struggled frantically with the mass of wounded men who were laid out on stretchers in two long lines, the slightly wounded near the door, the serious in the middle and the dead and the dying at the end.

When One Platoon reached the base of the Hook they entered a long trench that stretched to the top of the hill, twisting and turning like an alpine pass.

Hale was leading the platoon, not knowing what to expect. He edged forward slowly, wondering whether, in fact, the Chinese were in complete possession of the hill or just a part of it, or whether they had been sent up the hill simply as reinforcements in case things got worse. He could only see a few yards ahead of him. The sky was brilliantly lit by flares and the searchlights of the tanks and the Engineers, but dust and smoke swirled around him. The only indication of the enemy's position was the continual rattle of Burp guns some distance ahead of them.

Hale reached a trench junction and branched left along one that was uncomfortably shallow, the walls having collapsed under shelling. Over the trench wall he could see the line of another trench stretching out towards the forward platoon, where most of the small-arms fire was coming from. He stopped on orders from Miles and peered over the trench again. Lower down the hill he could see bodies hanging limply on their barbed wire entanglements, some of them complete, others incomplete. Nearer the top of the hill two Chinese were stumbling about as though drunk. Hale ducked down hastily, possessed by the urge to survive. Then he got a grip of himself. He raised his Sten to his shoulder and brought his sights to bear on them. He was about to fire when a shell landed right beside them. When the dust and smoke cleared the Chinese had vanished.

The platoon remained in the trench, waiting for orders. They flinched every time something exploded near them or as a stream of bullets cracked loudly overhead and whined off into the distance. Lawrence was waiting halfway up the Hook with the rest of Able Company, also waiting for further orders. He was getting mad with impatience at the lack of real action, and eventually he decided to go forward to find out what was happening. Together with Williamson, he crawled forward until they reached the trench in which One Platoon was crouching.

"What the hell is happening up here?" he asked Miles.

"Don't know, sir. Haven't seen a thing yet."

"Have you had a look, man?"

"As soon as we came up, sir. But the hill was deserted. Just a lot of firing from the forward platoon and from the right."

"Christ, they must be somewhere," exclaimed Lawrence. Then he declared: "I'm going to have a look." He raised his head above the trench wall and for several seconds scrutinized the hill for signs of life, but all he saw were heaps of rubble and dead bodies. He ducked down into the safety of the trench again.

"All right," he said to Miles. "This is what I'm going to do. As I see it, the Chinese are still being held by the forward platoon, but if they overrun them we'll have to hold them from here. It'll just be a matter of sticking your heads up, firing and hoping for the best. If they do come they'll come thick and fast."

"Okay, sir."

"But the thing is this," continued Lawrence. "You'll have to send two men down the trench leading to the forward platoon as scouts. They'll have to give warning of any Chinks coming up that trench and force them up on to the top of the hill so that we can shoot them down from here. You know what that means. Send your two best men. Their job will be to stop the Chinks from getting up that trench."

Miles was now numb with fear. "Yes, sir." He watched Lawrence crawl away again. He turned to Hale's section, which was nearest him, wondering who to send; wondering how he could expect men to face what would inevitably mean death; wondering whether he ought to go himself. That thought brought him back to his senses. He certainly wasn't going, that was one very definite thing. He was married, with a daughter.

The whole platoon had heard what Lawrence had said and they were all waiting, quite certain that Charles's name would be the first to be called out.

"Charles. . . ."

"I'm not bloody going."

"That's an order."

"I said I'm not going."

"Yes you bloody are ..."

"No I'm bloody not."

"That's a direct order!"

"I don't care if it's the eleventh bloody commandment. I'm not going."

"I'll go, Sergeant."

Miles stared at O'Hara with hate, flinching as bullets sent up small spouts of earth in front of the trench. He remembered the threat he'd made and realized that he could not possibly send him. If O'Hara was killed and someone remembered that threat ... O'Hara was just the man for the job, but he couldn't possibly send him. With Charles it was different altogether.

"Charles!"

"I said I'd go," repeated O'Hara.

"You're not going," snapped Miles.

"Why the hell not?"

"Because I want the two best men in the platoon and you're not one of them." He searched up and down the line of faces as deathly shadows flickered across them, and eventually his eyes rested on Johnstone and Lowe. Lowe turned his head, pretending that he wasn't there like some comic turn on a music-hall, and Johnstone just stared back blankly, as though past caring.

"You two, then! Johnstone and Lowe! Get going down that trench. As soon as you see anything let them have it. And don't come back here until you've shot the lot. Force them up on top …"

"But Sergeant," protested Lowe.

"Get going! You heard me!"

Johnstone stood erect so that his head and shoulders were exposed: he was working by instinct; he knew quite well what it meant, but he was unable to register any protest. He was like a robot; army discipline, born on the Guards' parade ground, had clicked in.

"Get going!" shouted Miles again, and with Lowe bent double, swearing at Miles, and Johnstone following him blindly, they made their way to the trench leading to the forward platoon.

The rest of the platoon was temporarily buried as soil was showered over them by a fresh Chinese artillery concentration. The man beside O'Hara was killed outright, and another at the end of the trench had the end of his nose sliced off by shrapnel.

"I'm going with them," shouted O'Hara as soon as the dust cleared.

"You'll stay exactly where you are."

"You mind your own bloody business, Miles. You can stay here and get killed by shells if you like. Die groveling in the bottom of a trench like the coward you are. I'm going with the other two."

For a moment they stared at each other defiantly, and then O'Hara walked off down the trench, soon to be hidden by more flying soil as another mortar bomb landed. It was not long before he joined Johnstone and Lowe. They were crouching nervously, huddled together halfway down the trench leading to the forward platoon. He squatted down beside them to consider the position. A few yards in front of them, lying face down in the trench, was a dead Chinaman and beside him a decapitated Briton, and above them, on either side of the trench walls, were more Chinese, all of them very dead.

O'Hara decided to go further down the trench and find out exactly what was happening. If necessary he would go right down into the forward platoon. He seized Johnstone by the collar and shouted at them: "Come on! We're going further forward."

To his surprise they followed him. Now they were being led they didn't mind. The further they went the more intense the shelling became, and they could now tell that the small arms fire was coming mainly from the area of the covered trench and the entrances of the tunnels. They could distinguish the cries and orders of the defenders, and bullets being showered down on the position by the Vickers machine guns on their DFs were thudding into the ground and ricocheting off again. The only thing that was missing was the enemy. They didn't appear to be anywhere.

Then O'Hara stopped abruptly. There they were! Hundreds of them! A fresh wave of them were swarming over the top of the covered trench, heading straight for them. O'Hara knew what they had to do: engage them for as long as possible, drive them on to the top of the hill, and thereby give the rest of the platoon good warning of their approach and enable them to shoot them down.

O'Hara pulled the pin from a grenade and threw it. Then he hurled another, and then another, so that soon he had three in the air all at the same time. Johnstone and Lowe were following his example and as their grenades exploded among the enemy they started to empty their Sten magazines into the mass of advancing men. Scores of them were falling dead only yards ahead of them but they still surged on, until eventually one was standing directly above them. O'Hara shot him dead at point blank range. The Chinese hesitated and then plunged forward again.

O'Hara's magazine was empty and he was halfway through changing it when he saw two more Chinese above them; Johnstone was lying dead in the bottom of the trench, the back of his head chopped off by a massive hunk of metal, and Lowe was fully occupied holding back the enemy advancing along the trench. O'Hara saw one of the men above him drop a grenade into the trench. There was a terrific explosion. O'Hara was rendered unconscious with a deep abrasion above his right eye. Lowe was killed instantly by a piece of shrapnel that ripped through his throat.

The Chinese advanced on up the hill, but Lawrence's idea had worked. The three men had halted the enemy briefly, and the full fire-power of One Platoon was now pouring into the enemy.

Two hours later Lawrence was able to hold a brief orders group in a bunker on the reverse slope of the Hook. The battle had been won. The shelling had practically ceased and dawn had already broken. All was now comparatively safe with a smoke-screen surrounding the Hook and the Ronson, Green Finger, and Warsaw standing patrols in place and ready to give warning if the Chinese tried another attack.

Lawrence looked up at his platoon commanders, the gleam in his eyes a mixture of triumph and anxiety. "Where is Mr. Goodall?" he asked Sergeant Ford of Three Platoon.

"He's had it, sir. He was hit by a bit of shell in the stomach."

Lawrence showed no signs of concern. "You will, of course, carry on in command of the platoon, Sergeant. How about other casualties? One Platoon?"

"Six, sir," answered Miles. "All of them killed except O'Hara. He's got a slight head wound."

"Two Platoon?"

"Four, sir.   Two of each."

"Three Platoon?"

"Nine, sir.   Including Mr. Goodall.   Four of them are dead."   Sergeant Ford was fumbling awkwardly as he tried to light a cigarette.   "When will we be pulling back off the hill, sir?"

"Not for some time.   We're taking over on the Hook until further orders. Baker and Charlie Company will be on our flanks.   This other unit has just about had it."

When the orders group ended, and all arrangements about platoon positions and responsibilities, ammunition and evacuation of wounded had been decided upon, Lawrence turned to Miles.

"Incidentally, Sergeant," he said, "those men you sent out to the forward platoon did a splendid job.   It was the turning point.   I'll make sure they get rewarded."

"They are both dead, sir."

"Was it just two you sent?"

"Yes, sir.   Just two."

PART IV

CANNON FODDER

1

Blake stood forlornly on Seoul railway station. The journey from Pusan had been comparatively comfortable, but now he was at a loss as to what to do. His movement order merely told him how to get to Seoul and no further. He looked about the station to see if there were any other British troops getting off the train, but the only other troops in sight were some Americans and a group of Turks, heavily laden with equipment, bayonets attached even in the city. He wandered down the platform until he eventually found himself standing in the main entrance of the station.

Away from the noise of the station, and with the warm sun flooding the broad street, he felt a bit happier. Even if he was going back to the war at least he would not have to contend with the terrible cold. Soon, he spotted a Commonwealth truck draw up outside a loading bay. Grasping his kitbag and his suitcase, he hurried across to it. The driver told him it was a ration truck, forbidden ever to give lifts, but after a long argument he agreed to take Blake to the British Commonwealth transit camp. Half an hour later they came to a halt outside three scarred buildings that were surrounded by heaps of rubble.

Blake jumped out and made his way along a corridor at the end of which there was a small office where a clerk was engrossed in a comic. He dropped his kitbag and suitcase wearily. "I want to get to the Rocks," he said.

The clerk grinned. "They're on the Hook, sir. I wouldn't be in a hurry to get there if I were you. They've been having a rare old bashing."

Blake felt his temper rising. He was sick to death of hearing and reading about the Hook. "I didn't ask for an intelligence report, Corporal. I asked you to get me to the Rocks."

"I'm afraid you're asking quite a thing there, sir. No transport going up to-day. I could get you on the mail van to-morrow evening. But if you wait around you might miss the attack."

"I'll take the mail van," said Blake.

The following afternoon, having eaten a good lunch and retired to his bed for a rest, Blake was aroused by the noise of chanting voices. He remained on his bed for several minutes, trying to ignore the noise, but eventually he got up and wandered into the street to see what was happening. About thirty yards down the road, outside one of the few remaining buildings where the Stars and Stripes fluttered above the doorway, was a mob of Koreans. They were shouting madly, waving their national flags frantically, and holding up massive banners.   The few in English read: 'Yankees, get on with the war and fight,' another said: 'Unite Korea and free our people,'   A third read: 'Every Korean must fight further north for freedom!'

Blake watched them for some time, growing increasingly resentful. He wondered why he should be expected to fight for these people who were so obviously determined to extend the war.   When a wrinkled old man in national costume, including a small top hat with a chin strap, was hoisted shoulder high to lead the crowd in chanting, Blake gave up and returned to his bed to wait for the mail van.

It was dusk when he arrived at the Rocks battalion headquarters, about half a mile behind the actual Hook.   The driver urged his vehicle recklessly into a re-entrant and, looking anxiously at Blake, said: "This is it, sir."   He knew the Hook well and wanted to get away from it as quickly as possible.

Blake felt nervous, not so much with having arrived at the fringe of the Hook, but rather at the prospect of having to report to the adjutant.   He took his kitbag and suitcase from the rear of the vehicle and looked about the main re-entrant of the headquarters.   There was the usual collection of bunkers dug into the sides of the hills with sturdy timber supports and dozens of wireless aerials stretching towards the sky from sandbag roofs, and likewise there was the inevitable touch of bull in the form of whitewashed posts and highly colored signs outside each of the bunkers, announcing what went on inside. Yet there seemed something essentially wrong.   It was like a ghost town: no movement, no activity, and most of all no troops.

Blake walked up the hill to a bunker which had a notice proclaiming it to be the Battalion CP.   He stepped inside, but apart from a narrow ray of the sinking sun, in which thousands of particles of dust flittered to and fro, he could see nothing.

"You still don't salute when you come into my office, do you, Blake?" The adjutant's voice came from behind a desk which Blake could now see. "I'm sorry, sir, but I didn't. . . ."

"It doesn't matter.   Glad to see you back.   I only hope that we will be able to make better use of you this time."   He paused for at least a minute, finishing off paperwork.   Then he looked up, regarded Blake very seriously, and added: "Look, Blake. I think it would be best if I made it clear that what is past is past.   However, we are not going to give you command of a platoon right away.   The Colonel wants you to get settled back in first.   But you'll be with a rifle company so you will have plenty of scope . . . . Anyhow, I don't suppose it will be long before we give you a platoon again."

Blake felt like telling him that he didn't want a platoon, and the last thing he had any desire for was plenty of scope. All he wanted was to tick over quietly in some safe place until the end of his two years approached and he could go back to Kure. He was disgusted when he heard himself say: "I'll do my best, sir. I hear that it is getting rather sharp up here."

"It is a bit more than sharp, Blake. Still, you'll soon know all about that. You'd better stay here for the night and then go on to the Hook to-morrow morning."

"Which company will I be joining, sir?"

"Able Company, of course. All right, that will be all. Come back here first thing in the morning."

Blake saluted and walked out into the cool evening. There were still no signs of life anywhere and he looked around with a lost expression, wondering where he would be able to spend the night.

"Hi, Blake! You young bastard! Why are you wandering around out there like a lost sheep?" It was Renshaw, the signals officer. His head was stuck cautiously out of the doorway of his bunker.

"Hullo, Ted," responded Blake, his gloom lifting at the sight of a familiar face. "I've just been posted back to the Battalion."

"Well, if you don't get under cover right away you'll get posted back in no uncertain manner----shell mail. Get under cover, for Christ's sake. The milk round is due any second."

"The what?"

"Milk round. You remember. A barrage that comes round the same time each day. Look, Blake, for God's sake get under cover."

Blake hurried into the bunker. No sooner was he in than the milk round arrived. Shells cascaded down. Everything shook violently and dirt fell down from the bunker roof. He sat down opposite Renshaw, flinching every time a shell fell particularly near and brought down more debris.

"It's like this day in and day out," Renshaw said above the noise. "You've come back to a bloody awful existence, Peter"

"Everyone keeps on telling me that. I've heard so many stories about the Hook that I don't mind telling you I'm scared stiff."

"They weren't exaggerating. There have been heavy casualties lately. There is hardly an hour of the day when they aren't clearing some poor devil back to hospital in helicopters."

A tall, slim youth with a spotty face dashed into the bunker. "Hullo, Hawkins, you've survived again. All the others okay?"

"Yes thanks, sir. The crack in our bunker wall has opened up a bit though. I'll make the tea if you like, sir. Will you want an extra one for Mr. Blake?"

"Yes please, Hawkins." Blake declined Renshaw's offer of a cigarette and noticed that when Renshaw lit his it was with a trembling hand. "How long have you been up here?" Blake asked.

"A couple of weeks or so. Don't really know for certain. I've lost all check of time." Renshaw leaned back and raised his feet to the table with a loud grunt. "The last unit took a hell of a bashing up here and we had to help them out with a counter-attack. If it hadn't been for Dick Lawrence's lot we would probably have lost the hill altogether. There was practically nothing left of the defenses afterward, just one bloody great heap of rubble. There wasn't a line working anywhere, so you can imagine that I had my work cut out. Those first few days were hell. There still aren't any shit-houses in the place. On the Hook itself they have to shit into sandbags. Then it's stored up and sent back to B Echelon."

"Oh God!"

"You'll get used to it," smiled Renshaw. "You get used to everything in the end. Seems you've arrived just in time for their spring offensive. We got a prisoner the other day. According to him the Chinks are going to launch a big attack in the next week. Things are steadily warming up, no doubt about that."

There was silence in the bunker for a time as they took their mugs of tea from Hawkins. Then Blake suddenly leapt to his feet as he saw a rat crawling up the sandbag wall only a few inches from his face. The others eyed him with surprise; they had come to accept rats as such an integral part of their lives that unless they made a real nuisance of themselves the vermin were allowed to go their own way. Blake blushed: he was completely out of touch with this life. Things here were very different to what he'd known before. Even the rats were different--- twice the size of anything he'd previously encountered. He changed the subject, trying to cover up his revulsion at the sight of the rat.

"Many new faces in the battalion?"

"Quite a few. You're one of several new subalterns. A fellow called Dean has taken over from Goodall and a chap called Mallet has got Ron Green's platoon."

"What the hell is old Goodall up to then? Don't tell me that he has got one of these cushy jobs?"

Renshaw smiled uneasily. "He bought it the first night up here."

"And Green?"

"He was blown up by one of our own mines about three nights ago. It's one of the Chinks' favorite tricks. They know exactly where all our minefields are and where all our patrol routes are, and somehow they manage

217

to take the mines from the fields and put them on the patrol routes. We've lost several like that so far."

"Sounds as though we're taking a hell of a bashing," ventured Blake.

"I wouldn't say that," said Hawkins. "I wouldn't be over the other side of the valley for all the tea in China. For every shell we get, I reckon they must get three. The lads on the Hook are killing off a tidy few, as well. Do you remember Charlie, sir?"

Blake grinned for the first time since entering the bunker. "Yes, I remember Charles all right."

"Well, old Charlie got three of the bastards the other night, and if Charlie can get three I reckon the others must be getting flaming hundreds."

Blake chuckled. He could just imagine Charles blazing away at the enemy in a blind panic, yelling a flood of filthy abuse at them.

He was aroused from his thoughts by another rat scampering down the sandbag wall towards a small cupboard in a corner of the bunker. Hawkins and his officer exchanged glances. "Better get rid of him, shall I, sir?"

"May as well," answered Renshaw.

Hawkins drew a long Australian bayonet from a scabbard and moved quietly towards the rat as it gnawed at the wooden door of the cupboard. He lunged like a fencer and there was a loud squeal. "Got you, you bastard," cried Hawkins.

As Hawkins went to the doorway to dispose of it in the usual way--- in flaming petrol---- the rat was still struggling on the end of the bayonet. Some blood ran down its tail and fell on Blake's hand. He wiped it off with deep repulsion, seeing it as symbolic.

2

Blake spent the night in the signals bunker but he didn't sleep well. There were always shells landing somewhere near, or the sound of men shouting, or trucks being loaded and unloaded, and the constant droning of Hawkins's voice sending back messages to Brigade over the 31-set.

Hawkins woke him at dawn. He shaved, borrowed a steel helmet, reported to the adjutant for final instructions, and then went round to the transport pool to pick up a jeep.

He was soon on the final leg of his journey, bumping along the crater-strewn road. The driver kept glancing at Blake, hating him for having dragged him back to the Hook. As they drew near, his foot went to the floorboards and even when they were right up to the jeep-head he didn't slow down.

"Hadn't we better wait for this shelling to cool off?" suggested Blake.

"You've never been up here before, have you, sir? It's like this all bloody day. It never cools off. We've perfected a quick turn-around. Even the Yanks couldn't improve on it. I dash up to the morgue---- I don't stop but simply crash her into reverse. While I do that you jump out and dash straight into the morgue. Then I reverse straight out again and before you can say Harry Pollitt I've gone. . ."

It was just as the driver said. Blake found himself standing in the entrance of the morgue, his kitbag and suit-case heaped at his feet, watching the jeep as it disappeared in a cloud of dust.

The morgue was a big American-type bunker, dug deep into the ground. Its main timber supports were, of necessity, massive, and capable of taking a tremendous strain. Inside were two long rows of stretchers, covered with blood-stained blankets. At the far end of the bunker he saw two men bending over a stretcher, applying a shell dressing to a wounded man. He watched them for some time, noticing the smell of antiseptics and the large number of old dressings littered about the floor; they were working swiftly and silently, taking no notice of the man's moaning. When they finished they remained squatting beside him, wondering if it had been worth the effort.

Then one of them stood up. "He's passed out. It's no good, Jock, he won't make it." Blake recognized Tompkin's voice, but he said nothing and continued to watch them, appalled by the situation.

The other medic, a Scotsman named Andrews, made no reply but continued to stare at his patient as though in a dream. He was a tall, wiry youth with a haggard face. His shirt sleeves were rolled up to his elbows and some congealed blood matted the hair on his forearms. He wiped his nose with a dirty piece of rag, smiled unobtrusively and said: "Tommy, you'd never make a doctor. You're too bloody pessimistic. The lad's still breathing. There's still a hope. Let's get all these dressings back in the box and have a cuppa before something else crops up."

Tompkin turned and, on seeing Blake, his face lit up. "Well I'll be damned, Mr. Blake! What the hell are you doing here, sir? I thought we'd seen the last of you."

Blake grinned back. He remembered Tompkin well from their days at Nae Chon. It was good to see one of the boys again, even better to be welcomed back as a friend.

"I heard that you fellows were having a pretty thick time of it up here, so I thought that I'd better come and give you a hand."

Tompkin chuckled. "Like hell! No one comes up here voluntarily."

Andrews strolled up to join them. "You were right, Tommy, he's snuffed it. He turned to Blake. "Do you know, sir, that's the first one that has died in here over the past three days. Mind you, plenty come in dead, and plenty die before they get to the RAP. But we pride ourselves on keeping the living alive while they're here."

They talked on for some time, exchanging gossip: how Lawrence was still driving them, and Blake's impressions of Kure and the reason for his return. Then more stretcher-bearers burst into the bunker. Blake judged it was time for him to leave. He went up the main trench on the reverse slope and soon came to the Able Company CP. Inside, the bunker was cramped, but well lit by three Tilley lamps which were suspended from the roof by old boot laces. At the far end of the bunker, stretching across its entire width, were Corporal Williamson's wirelesses and telephones. He raised his head as Blake entered and a faint smile flickered across his face, but then he resumed its former expression of deep concentration as he listened to a message coming through his earphones.

No one else stirred. Nobby Clark was stretched out on a bench snoring peacefully; a runner sat beside him reading a tattered **Blighty**, waiting for orders; and sitting at the main table, on which the usual collection of maps and information boards were scattered about, was Lawrence, his moustache left waxed. He was engaged in a telephone conversation. The whole bunker reeked of stale breath.

"Yes, sir. . . . Yes, sir. . . . I know all about that, sir. What you say is probably true, but if I am to hold this hill I must have them. I know all about them being expensive and hard to get, but if you don't mind me saying this isn't the time to think about expense. You will. . . . ? Thanks very much, very kind of you. Cheerio, sir."

He tossed the telephone to the table and made his usual gesture of annoyance by pulling on his moustache. Then he said to himself: "Don't know what the hell these bloody fellows think they're up to. They must think that we're playing some kind of game up here. Bloody idiots make me sick." He buried his face in his hands, relaxed against the back of his chair, and sighed deeply.

"Blake, sir ... They told me to report to you."

Lawrence hesitated before turning to face Blake. Then he forced a smile, obviously embarrassed. For a few seconds they stared at each other, both well aware of what the other was thinking. Eventually he took a piece of paper off his desk and handed it to Blake. "That's the Hook layout," he said.

"Study it and memorize it."

"Quite a dominating feature, sir," said Blake after a brief examination.

"Yes ... Well never mind that. I want a few words with you, Blake. You others all clear off for a bit." They all left except Nobby Clark, who went on snoring. "Well, Blake, we'd better clear the air. You probably resent being brought back, and I suppose that's only natural. But we had no choice and your first duty is, and always will be, to the Rocks. The point is this, what's happened has happened, so we must make the most of it." He looked Blake straight in the eyes for the first time. "This company of mine has been through a hell of a lot since you've been away, and although I say it myself the men are bloody nearly worn out. You'll see that when you meet them all again. We've been up here three weeks now, which is longer than any other company ever has, and a damned sight longer than any company should be. The Brigadier has promised that we shall be off the hill after another two or three days, so you can take that as more or less definite."

He paused, searching for the right words. "The thing is this, Blake. We're desperately short of officers--- the right kind of officers. . . . Dean. . . ." He broke off, realizing that he could not discuss the faults of other officers with Blake. "There is an attitude in the company of let's hang on for another day and then we'll be in reserve. It's a defeatist attitude and they all think that so long as they keep out of sight of the Chinese they'll be all right. It's your job, together with the platoon commanders, to crush that and instill the men with an aggressive spirit. It's still likely that we will have to take the brunt of a major attack, and it will be your job to lead men ... To inspire them to do their duty ... That's what officers are for. Do you understand that?"

"Of course, sir. You don't have to tell me all that."

Lawrence looked down at his map board and fingered it nervously. "I'll be frank with you. Forget our past differences and if you really get down to it and display some real leadership ... If you really play ball ... Then I'll see to it that you are properly rewarded."

Blake felt numb. He could hardly believe it. The bastard was offering him a Military Cross if he gallivanted around the place like a madman. It was sometime before he replied. "You mean a Military Cross! Well, I couldn't give a damn about a Military Cross. You can give me a bar as well if you like, but I'm just not interested in gongs."

"That's enough of that, Blake. I'm not offering you anything specific. Just remember that you've come back to war, a real war. So I don't want any more of your damned hysteria."

He turned away and gathered up some papers, regretting that he'd ever tried to be conciliatory. It had made things worse, not better. "Just let's get on with the job in hand.   So long as we stay on this hill you will not act as a platoon commander.   The platoons will stay as they are until we're in reserve purely on account of administrative problems.   When we get in reserve you will, of course, resume command of One Platoon.   While up here your job will be in this CP under my direct command.   I will use you mainly as a reinforcement officer which means that you will lead any counter-attacks that might prove necessary and take out patrols.   You will be ready for action at any moment of the day or night.   Is that clear?"

"Yes, sir."

Lawrence had not expected Blake to respond like that about the Military Cross, and it put him off his stride.   Usually such an offer---- by no means unheard of--- was enough to capture the full support of any subaltern.   Now, he was determined to be stern with Blake, to keep him in his right place and make him do some bloody fighting: to earn his crust!

"Incidentally," Lawrence added, "before I give you the full details for the routine in the line I'll make it quite clear to you that our orders up here are to hold until the last man.   The only person who can authorize any kind of withdrawal is the Brigadier.   Do you understand?"

"Yes, sir."

"Right, then," continued Lawrence, "here are the details for the daily routine: sleep will be confined to exactly four hours a day, no more and no less. At least two-thirds of the company has to be alert at all times.   All officers will be on duty all night and every night. . ."

3

It took Lawrence half an hour to complete Blake's briefing.   Then he called Corporal Cross back into the bunker and told him to give Blake a tour of the Hook.   When they reached the right-hand platoon position, occupied by Three Platoon, they ducked into a small weapon pit, and drawing back some crudely made curtains that were draped over the actual weapon slit, Cross said: "That's Warsaw over there, sir.   The Chinks hold that, but I don't reckon they have many up there until they are about to attack.   I wouldn't be surprised if it is full of the blighters now."

To Blake Warsaw was alarmingly near, so near, in fact, that he would have almost thought it part of the Hook. It was without doubt the baldest hill he had seen in Korea.

"That ridge coming towards us from Warsaw is Green Finger, sir," continued Cross. "That's the route the Chinks always use when they attack. This is one of the key weapon pits here, sir. It's where Mr. Goodall was killed. Better not stop here too long, sir. Chinky snipers are pretty hot these days."

They walked on down the trench, past a group of men repairing shell damage. Occasionally they passed more weapon pits, most of them occupied by two or three men curled up on the ground asleep. In other pits men were cleaning their Bren guns, or peering through the weapon slits, scrutinizing the Chinese hills through binoculars. Living bunkers were non-existent: men existed entirely in their weapon pits; they fought in them, they slept in them, they ate in them, they excreted in them (sandbags), and not infrequently they died in them.

They reached the forward platoon at the same time as a stonk of mortars and they flung themselves into the nearest weapon pit where Harden and Corporal Smith were lying against each other, asleep. They both looked five years older than before. They stirred in their sleep but did not wake.

The stonk was a short one and they were soon on their way again. Smith's bunker was the last one facing out towards Warsaw and a few yards down the trench they turned left into a long covered trench stretching across the actual front of the Hook, facing out on to Ronson, a small feature only occupied at night and then generally alternately by the Commonwealth forces and the Chinese, depending on who got the better of the patrol clashes. They stumbled along the covered trench feeling their way because of the darkness, except around the entrances of the weapon pits.

Halfway along the trench they turned off into a tunnel leading back into the hill--- a tunnel filled by the revolting smell of decaying bodies. To Blake, the tunnel seemed to go on forever, twisting and turning every few feet so that he continually bumped against the rough sides. It was almost unbelievable that this had been the home of some of his men for the past three weeks. Eventually, they reached the end and emerged into the fresh, warm air. "Thank God we're out of there," he said.

"There's another down the trench, sir. It's not quite as bad as this one, though."

After walking along the trench leading to the rear left platoon--- the trench in which Lowe and Johnstone had died--- they entered the second tunnel. "How do you fellows manage for sleep? Can you really exist on four hours?"

"We manage, sir. On the Hook no one ever goes to sleep while on duty, no matter how tired they are."

223

As the afternoon wore on and the sun began to sink, and as the clammy evening mist settled down a few feet above the ground, the Hook became more active. Men emerged from their weapon pits after their sleep, and the shelling increased. Small-arms fire periodically raked the forward trenches and men began to prepare for the coming night, hurrying along on various missions, checking their ammunition, and blacking their faces.

An hour before stand-to Lawrence held his daily orders group. As the platoon commanders and others concerned entered the CP Blake found them an interesting study. CSM Ralf was the first to arrive and to Blake's surprise he was bright, breezy and seemed to be in his element, still clutching his trusty Lee Enfield. During the winter Blake had always thought him to be ultra-cautious but now, with the call for harsher discipline and unlimited scope for throwing his weight around, he was nearer to being the archetypal Sergeant-Major than ever before.

Bartram was relatively unchanged; tired and anxious, perhaps, but seemingly content with his lot. Sergeant Miles's face remained long and cheerful, but he lacked vitality and after smiling at Blake in surprise he slipped unobtrusively into the background of dirty sandbags.

One by one they drifted in. Lawrence glanced at his watch and turned to Ralf. "Sergeant-Major, where is Mr. Dean? He knows very well what the time of the O group is."

"I don't know where he is, sir. It's not my job to keep trace of the officers--- everyone else is here." There was a hint of defiance in Ralf's reply, as though the same thing had happened many times before and he was fed up with it. Reluctantly, however he put his steel helmet on and wandered a few yards out into the trench. "That bastard Dean," he mumbled to himself. "Why can't the yellow swine turn up on time?" He walked to a nearby bunker. "Corporal Cross! Corporal Cross! Go and get Mr. Dean for the orders group."

A few minutes later Cross burst into the CP. He was out of breath and shaken. "Well?" demanded Ralf. "Where is Mr. Dean?"

"His bunker has just been blown in, sir. He's been buried alive."

"Well go and get the bastard dug out then," yelled Ralf, temporarily forgetting himself.

"He has been dug out, sir, but he's resting." Over by the telephone exchange Williamson groaned with despair.

Lawrence uttered an oath and buried his face in his hands. He was sick to death of Dean's cowardly behavior. The man was so scared that he had been nothing but a bloody nuisance since he first joined the company. He controlled his anger and looked to Cross. "Go and tell Mr. Dean that we sympathize with him, but he must break his rest and come round here immediately."

Blake had met Dean at JRBD. He remembered him for his Sandhurst accent, his self-assurance, and the way he boasted of his desire to get to grips with the Chinese. At length, he shuffled into the bunker. He remained in the doorway for a time. Then, when all eyes were on him, he announced dramatically: "I've just been buried alive."

Everyone ignored him except Williamson, who sniggered. Blake could see that Dean was a broken man. He just had not got what was required. His face was pale, lined heavily with fear, and he was thin and limp, looking as though he might drop in exhaustion at any moment. He obviously should not have been within ten miles of the Hook.

"Now we can get on with things," said Lawrence. Men waited in hope and dread of his orders. A shell landed nearby and a Tilley lamp flickered and went out. "The first thing," began Lawrence, "is that they have just intercepted another Chinese wireless message which indicates that the attack might be coming to-night."

Bartram sighed loudly. "That's happened every night for the last week, sir."

"I know that, Bartram. But we must be prepared to face the fact that one night it will be true. The last thing we must ever do up here is to settle down for the night thinking that we're safe." He consulted his notes for a space and then announced: "Patrols for to-night. As usual Green Finger patrol and Warsaw patrol will be supplied by the flanking companies. Ronson will consist of one officer and four men. Mr. Dean, you will be in command."

"Me, sir?" shouted Dean incredulously, his limpness disappearing as he jumped to his feet. "But I've just been buried alive."

"Yes, we know that."

"But an officer on standing patrol, sir? Surely it would be sufficient to send a senior NCO... A sergeant if need be?"

"I'm afraid not," answered Lawrence coldly. "You'll have to do it."

"But, sir, I won't be able to command my platoon properly if I'm on patrol. Wouldn't it be better if..."

"You're going on that patrol whether you bloody well like it or not," yelled Lawrence, realizing his mistake in not having sent him on a Ronson before. "Other officers do standing patrols so there is no reason why you shouldn't." Out of the corner of his eye Lawrence saw Williamson grinning, and he refrained from shouting at Dean again. "Yours will be the first patrol, Mr. Dean. Your duties will be the same as always. Namely, if you are approached by the enemy you will engage them with small-arms fire and hold them off as long as possible. If you can't hold them completely you will come back to our trenches having given the code word first over the wireless."

Dean flopped back on the bench and sat there like a ghost, his mouth sagging open a little, not bothering to take any notice of what Lawrence was saying. "Your patrol will be relieved by one from Two Platoon," continued Lawrence. "Sergeant Sykes, you will be in command, and Mr. Blake, you will also go on it with the purpose of getting familiarized with the surroundings."

The orders group was interrupted as Williamson suddenly called up from his wireless that enemy movement had been spotted on Warsaw. They waited until the FOO had consulted his maps, contacted his Battery CP by wireless, and brought down some effective fire. Lawrence then went through a long list of administrative details before coming to his last point.

"To-morrow," he said, "the Brigadier will be paying us a visit and I want everything to meet with his approval. You all know what I mean. We don't want to blot our copybook right at the end. I've been told on good authority that we will shortly be moving off the hill, probably after the next two days...."

Lawrence broke off, waiting for the spontaneous relief to wear off. "I don't want you to tell your platoons about this yet, since it is not absolutely definite. So keep it under your hats and your fingers crossed. After three weeks in this place I think we can honestly say that we've earned a rest. Just see to it that we do as well in the last two nights as we have done already."

He smiled at them for a second and then, realizing that the time was not yet ripe for praise, he adopted his previous stern manner. "All right, that's all." As they stood up and started to file out he called after them: "Make sure that all your wireless operators and telephone orderlies keep alert all night. I'll court-martial any telephone orderly who does not reply within five seconds of me blowing down the receiver."

Soon, it was dark; the Chinese lines faded until only the faint outline of their hills remained; men walked about the trenches as little as possible and when they did the password was constantly on their lips, ready to respond to a challenge; and on their left flank, in the American Marines sector, flares were already hanging in the sky trying to expose the marauding enemy. Every man was at his post waiting expectantly, itchy fingers coiled about their triggers, dank palms gripping the butts of their automatics. This was the danger hour, the hour that shattered strong nerves, the hour in which the Chinese were most likely to attack.

Dean was lucky, for the first half of the night was comparatively quiet,

with only a few intermittent bursts of shelling.   None of the patrols had any
contact with the enemy.

Blake was nearly asleep when Williamson nudged him and pointed to his
watch, indicating that it was almost 0100 hours.   Blake looked about the
smoke-filled bunker.   His eyes were aching, his stomach was uncomfortably
empty and he was yawning repeatedly.   Everything was quiet except for the
FOO relaying messages back to his Battery.   It was the moment Blake had
hoped would never come, the moment he had been dreading since arriving on
the Hook.

He picked up a mug from the table and emptied it with one deep swallow.
He looked at himself in a bit of broken mirror to make sure that the blacking
had not worn off his face, and then, standing up laboriously, he put his
bullet-proof vest on and gathered up his Sten and ammunition.

"You off now, Blake?" asked Lawrence.   "Remember what I told you
about this patrol.   Just leave everything to Sykes.   He's the best Ronson man
we've got.   I don't suppose you'll have any trouble to-night, though.   If they
don't come in the first half of the night they don't generally come at all."

Blake suddenly felt almost happy.   If they got through tonight he would
be all right.   Then there would only be one more night to wait through and
they couldn't possibly send him on patrol two nights running.   He walked
towards the door.   "Okay, sir.   I'll remember everything.   See you at
breakfast time."

"Oh, incidentally," added Lawrence. "Tell Dean that he is to report back
here as soon as he returns.   And another thing, if you see Captain Clark
wandering about in the trenches, tell him to go to Three Platoon.   They
missed my signal over the 'phone.   Tell him to find out who the telephone
orderly is and put him on a charge."

"Yes, sir."   Blake left the bunker and walked to Two Platoon, where he
had arranged to join the rest of the patrol.   "Sergeant Sykes?"

"Ah, there you are, sir.   All set?"

"Well, I'm a bit out of touch with this kind of thing.   You had better give
me all the griff.'

"I know what you mean, sir," laughed Sykes.   "It's a bit thick when
you're sent from a place like Kure straight on to a Ronson.   You have my
sympathy, sir.   Still, if you keep at the back of the patrol I think we'll manage
all right.   You act as a kind of rearguard, sir."

The idea of staying at the back appealed to Blake, but he had heard so
much about officers leading from the back, so many snide remarks about
officers watching others doing all the dirty work, that he felt that he could not

accept Sykes's plan. "I know what you mean, Sergeant, but wouldn't it be better if I was up the front . . . with you. ...?" He felt his cheeks coloring again. "I mean wouldn't it. . . ."

Sykes laughed, as did two of the men. "You don't want to worry about that, sir. The back is the worst place of the lot. I'd better tell you exactly what happens before we go out. It's like this: we go out as an ordinary patrol but when we get out there we split into two. The main part stays on the reverse slope of Ronson and two men go on to the forward slope. When the fellows in front see the Chinks coming they nip back and tell the rest of us and we all wait for them to come over the crest of the hill. Then--- Bob's your uncle. If there are hundreds of the devils we give them a burst and then run like hell back to the trenches, having given the code word on the 88-set." Sykes paused and chuckled. "That's invariably when the last man gets it. He's expected to cover the others before he makes a run for it."

"Poor bastard," said one of those on the patrol.

Blake felt a sudden pang of temper. He wanted to lash out at this damned fool sergeant who thought it was such a joke. The bloody idiot talked as though it didn't matter a bit whether they returned or not. "It's nice to know, anyhow," replied Blake coldly.

"Come off it, sir," appealed Sykes, "it's no good being gloomy about things. It's not so bad once you get used to it. Anyhow, sir, if anything does turn up and we have to make a run for it I yell, 'Piccadilly' just as we approach our trenches, to let the lads know that it's us coming, and when the last fellow gets back in the trench he yells, 'Haymarket.' As soon as he's yelled, 'Haymarket', One Platoon belts off at the Chinese and Lawrence gets the five-mile snipers to bring down a bloody great stonk on Ronson. Nothing to it, really. After the gunners have finished plastering the place we just go out again. And pick up the bodies, naturally."

Blake shuddered. "We'd better get going, hadn't we?"

Sykes led the way through One Platoon and along the trench leading out of the position to Ronson. They were in no-man's-land again: the narrow strip of ground where men crawled for hours on their bellies trying to out-maneuver their foes, where shells fell in their tens of thousands, altering the very shape and nature of the earth, where bullets screeched through the air on an unholy mission, many labeled with someone's name, where victors roamed the crumbled soil unmolested, and where the vanquished ran in terror for their lives, or lay still and dead, mangled into a hundred different shapes.

Blake kept within touching distance of the man in front of him. He could not forget the words of Sergeant Sykes. He was the last man. One of the bodies they always picked up afterwards. He trembled. He prayed silently, knowing in his heart that it was stupid, that it would make no difference; but he still did it. 'Please, God, make it a quiet night. Or if something happens spare me, just this once. I'll never sin again. And I'll never ask for more'.

He cursed himself for being so pathetic. Then when he stopped his silent prayers he had visions of the life he had just left: the pleasant hot sun beating down on the smooth mountains surrounding Kure, the ORs dances, all the lovely little Japanese girls, and most of all the love and companionship of Jackie.

They reached Ronson and settled down swiftly. Ahead of him Blake could discern the crest of the hill over which the advance section of the patrol had already vanished. To his right Sykes and another man were in a shallow dip. Visibility was down to a few feet, bullfrogs croaked loudly in the floor of the valley, and mosquitoes, invisible attackers that descended in silence, bit through their clothing, heedless of the foul smelling repellent that covered their sweating bodies.

An hour later a fresh flare went up and Blake noticed that the man beside him had become rigid, his eyes protruding unnaturally. He also saw that Sykes's Sten was pressed hard against his shoulder. Then they heard men running towards them and a few seconds later the scouts from the forward slope appeared. "Thirty at least," said one of them as they dropped to the ground into fire positions.

As another flare rose into the sky two Chinese appeared on the crest of the hill, silhouetted perfectly, but they held their fire, knowing more would soon show up. Presently the whole Chinese patrol was a sitting target. "Fire!" yelled Sykes and simultaneously five Sten guns fired magazines of twenty-eight rounds without hesitation. The Chinese cried out as they were hit; some ran straight into the flaming Stens; some ran away; others groveled on the ground; but the majority were level-headed veterans of patrol actions and returned the fire with amazing rapidity.

As Sykes felt his Sten cease firing he snatched the pin from a grenade and flung it. As soon as it exploded he shouted: "Beat it, fellows!"

This was the tricky bit, the moment when Blake delayed his own retreat to cover the others--- and then get shot in the back as he too ran off. Already the others were on their feet, running. Blake fired off his second Sten magazine. Soon, as the Chinese closed in on him, he too was on his feet, sprinting for all he was worth. A burst of bullets sent up small spouts of earth ahead of him. He heard more bullets cracking just above his head. He tried desperately to sprint even faster.

Everything was going well; the trench was looming up swiftly. Sykes had almost reached it and the Chinese fire seemed inaccurate; then the man in front of Blake was hit, a burst raking across his broad shoulders. He went down like a log, quivering with pain and yelling his head off.

Blake stopped and knelt beside him, not knowing what to do: the man was still very much alive, but as he pulled at his arms Blake was unable to move him. He put his hands under the man's shoulders and felt the blood seeping through the bulletproof proof vest; he tried to lift him but he was big and awkward and still struggling. He let him drop to the ground again as more bullets landed beside them. He heard the cries of the Chinese commander, and as another flare lit the sky he saw them advancing towards him in an extended line. He noticed the clear whiteness of the wounded man's eyes against his blackened face, and watched him as he tried in vain to stand. He tugged desperately at the man's shoulders in a final attempt to save him, but he only succeeded in moving him a few inches. The Chinese were almost on top of him.

Blake panicked: he leapt to his feet and ran off, leaving the man to meet his fate alone, screaming hysterically.

"Piccadilly!" shouted Sykes.

Blake struggled on; his legs felt like lumps of putty, the trench never seeming to get any nearer. The faster he tried to go the less progress he seemed to make. The brief seconds it took him to reach the trench were like those in a nightmare when escape from a disaster is impossible. Then, at last, he made it through the gap into the covered trench: "Haymarket!"

Immediately, One Platoon fired their weapons hopefully into the darkness. The whole hill became a line of leaping flames as bullets were spat out at the enemy.

Blake joined the rest of the patrol further down the covered trench and flopped down beside them; they were shaken, scared stiff, sweat flowing freely down their chests and backs. One or two uttered exclamations and curses, and the wireless operator passed messages between Sykes and Lawrence. Two-inch mortar flares went up from Two Platoon and there was a sudden increase in the volume of small-arms fire as One Platoon spotted more of the enemy.

Chinese shells began to land accurately about the forward trenches, trying to silence the weapons, and the patrol moved down the covered trench into the first of the tunnels. Someone lit a match and in the flickering light Blake noticed that their blackened faces were streaked by sweat. He scrutinized the face of the youth beside him: the boy's face was uncommonly smooth and round, almost feminine. A faint smile twitched across his face. Presently the smile became a laugh. "Bloody hell! That was a close one. I saw the whites of their eyes that time all right, Joe."

As the match was replaced by the glowing end of a cigarette Blake lost sight of the boy's face, but he knew instinctively that Joe was the man he had left behind.

"What do you say, Joe? I thought we'd had our lot then. One blighter wasn't half a size. Didn't half come down with a wallop. How many do you think you got, Joe? Joe?"

There was no reply to the frail and excited voice.

"Where is Oaten?" demanded Sykes.

"He didn't make it," said Blake. "He was shot in the back."

"Why didn't you drag him in?" The youngster's voice was accusing.

"Because he was dead, shot in the back!" snapped Blake. He hated himself for not having tried harder to drag the man in.

"But he was alongside me. I don't believe it! Not Joe!" The youth sprang to his feet. "Come on, we've got to get back out there, quick. Quick! Qu... ick!" His voice cracked as he screamed at them.

Sykes grabbed the youth's arm. "Shut up! Shut up, I tell you! He's had it. It's no good now. Do you hear? It's no good now."

The shelling subsided. Small-arms fire withered away. The wireless operator took another message. "Lawrence says go out there again now."

Sykes struggled to his feet, looking at his watch. "Only another three hours. We'll make a search for Joe Oaten, first."

They found Oaten. His body was a mess. He'd not only been shot in the back but bayonetted several times for good measure.

4

The dawn was never more welcome. Blake watched it reveal a clear sky and details of the Chinese hills. He smiled as Sergeant Sykes led the way back to their own lines. When they reached the covered trench Blake saw men of his old platoon still bent over their weapons watching their front. He left the patrol in Two Platoon, watching them with sympathy as they ducked down into their weapon pits for a few hours' sleep. In the company CP everything was exactly the same as when he had left, except perhaps for a slightly more spent look on men's faces. He relaxed on the bench beside Williamson, and ran his hand through his knotted hair, scratching vigorously.

"We've just got back, sir," he told Lawrence as the major finished talking on the telephone.

"Right! Good. Get the hang of things okay? You'll be taking out the second Ronson tonight."

"Again, sir?'

"What do you mean---again? Of course it's again. And another thing, I think you could have made more of a fight of it ..."

Blake suppressed his anger. "Easy to say that when you're sitting in here, sir ..."

"Come off it, Blake," laughed Lawrence. "It was about the quietest night we've had."

Clark looked up from the company nominal roll which he had just finished altering. "It may have been quiet, Dick. But we're getting a bit thin on the ground now. Four killed last night and the only wounded who have come back are O'Hara and Joslin."

Lawrence didn't seem particularly concerned. He glanced through the roll and then turned to Blake. "I suppose you want to get some sleep now?"

"If you don't mind, sir."

Lawrence glanced at his watch. "All right. Off you go. But be back here by nine-thirty. Better hurry or you'll get caught in the milk round."

Blake was caught in the milk round. He had only just left the CP on his way to a small, disused bunker situated off the trench leading down to the morgue, when shells cascaded down in their usual numbers. He dashed down the trench and flung himself head first into his bunker. A rat scampered off his sleeping-bag and squeezed its way down a hole, disappearing for a second and then poking its head out again, as though to make certain that Blake intended to stay.

He brushed rat droppings off the sleeping-bag and, using his bullet-proof vest as a pillow, he settled down, keeping an eye cautiously on the rat hole; for some inexplicable reason he feared the rat more than the shells.

The shelling continued for a long time. They kept thumping down one on top of the other. Always another ear-splitting explosion until his head felt about to burst. There was never any respite, never a minute that was not shattered by a shell landing close at hand, never a quarter of an hour without a stretcher being man-handled down the narrow trench to the morgue.

Eventually, tiredness overwhelmed him and he slept. He felt something knock against his shoulder and for a moment he thought he had been hit by a piece of shrapnel. He looked up sharply and saw Corporal Cross standing over him. He closed his eyes and rolled over, but Cross was persistent. "Major Lawrence wants to see you, sir."

232

"You must be mistaken. He's just told me to get some sleep."

"No, sir. He said you all right."

"God! Tell him he can go to hell."

Cross laughed and remained there for a time, not knowing what to do. "He said that you've got to go up there at once, sir. It's got something to do with the Brigadier's inspection."

Blake looked at his wrist-watch; it had just gone half-past eight: not two hours sleep. "How the hell do we stick the man Cross, that's what I'd like to know." He zipped up his bullet-proof vest. "Tell him I'm on my way."

Blake's job for the first part of the morning was to make sure that all litter lying about the company was cleared up, so that the Brigadier might be 'suitably impressed'. It was a ridiculous task, for men were either fast asleep or too busy maintaining their weapons to bother about clearing out the trenches. Blake realized the futility of it and spent most of his time talking to Miles in the small platoon CP situated in one of the rear tunnels. Apart from the smell, it was like a disused coal mine. Taylor was lying on a sleeping-bag that stretched across the entire width of the tunnel and Blake and Miles sat opposite each other, separated by an old beer crate on which a candle flickered.

Blake listened with interest to a brief review of what had happened since he left the platoon. Miles told him of the troubles he had had in reserve; how, at one time, a fifth of the platoon was in one or other of the Detention Barracks; how others had been arrested in Tokyo; how they held off the Chinese attack on the Hook and had then been given the command of the forward platoon.

Finally, he told Blake about O'Hara's peculiar behavior since returning from the field hospital with a head wound which quite obviously had not healed properly. "When he first came back, he seemed just the same as before. You know, sir. Always boasting and shooting his mouth off. But it soon became plain that there was something wrong with him. He brooded all day without saying a word, and would then all of a sudden fly off the handle. I had to report him to Lawrence twice for causing trouble, but Lawrence just stopped some pay and left it at that.

"Then one night Winston came dashing in here and told me O'Hara had disappeared. He certainly wasn't in the platoon area and we thought that he had been snatched by the Chinks. I mean, you can never be sure in a place like this, can you? Anyhow, sir, to cut a long story short about three in the morning he turns up in front of the Ronson patrol! He'd been out in no man's land all night looking for Chinks to have a go at. Winston says he's been off his head for some time, and I reckon that he's right. He had a nasty head wound, even though it doesn't look much."

Miles laughed softly. "All in all, sir, I'll be bloody glad when this change-over comes. I don't mind my share of this place but I draw the line at having a bloody nutcase in the platoon. You're welcome to them as soon as we get back in reserve, sir."

"Why don't you tell Lawrence about him if he's that bad?"

"Do you think I haven't? But you know what that bastard is like. He won't let go of anyone, no matter what condition they are in. They had a young kid in Two Platoon not so long ago. He came straight off the boat. Turned nineteen the day he arrived in Korea. He just couldn't face it up here. Used to shit himself every time a shell landed near him. He was a pathetic case. We laugh about shitting ourselves, but this poor lad really did. But Lawrence wouldn't do a bloody thing about it. Not a bloody thing. He died in the morgue three or four days ago, more through fear than anything else. He only had a couple of small pieces of shrapnel in his shoulder. It would have been the perfect Kure touch for anyone but him."

"I don't see why the whole Corps artillery could not have their DFs around the Hook," said Lawrence.

The FOO smiled indulgently. "Well, I think that's aiming a bit high, sir."

"Good God, man, if we don't insist on the absolute maximum we won't get any more than we've got at the moment."

"Well, we could try, sir."

"Try!" cried Lawrence. "Damn it, man, we've bloody well got to insist. If the Chinese do come there will be a hell of a lot of them. The last attack will be a probe compared to this one that is coming. I wouldn't be surprised if they outnumber us thirty to one."

During a short silence Kim entered, carrying a collection of chipped enamel mugs on an old chromium-plated tray which, despite several bare patches, was highly polished and Kim's proudest possession. He beamed at them cheerfully, displaying a mouthful of gold teeth. "Tea, gentlemen," he announced.

"Good old Kim," said Williamson. "I don't know what we'd do without you."

Blake watched Kim as he went from man to man in strict order of seniority. Blake envied him, for he was so calm and unruffled; to him the whole war was just a matter of course, something which had been going on for nearly three years and which was likely to continue for many more. In all probability the peace talks meant nothing to him. He probably did not even realize that but for Syngman Rhee the whole war might well have been over.

He probably wasn't concerned with the war, content with his present life as the slave of Lawrence.

"Hullo, Kim," said Blake as he took a mug. "What do you think of this place?"

The frail youth grinned and then a frown crossed his brow. "Very different to when I was last here, sir."

"When was that?"

"With the Americans. Then the Chinese used to attack regularly twice a week, but there wasn't all this shelling. The Chinese used to be able to take the hill any time they liked. But they were never allowed to keep it. The Americans always took it back with a counter-attack. But now we just stay here no matter what happens."

"Thank Christ there is someone around here who has got the right idea," said Lawrence.

5

Life was not without its moments of humor.

Later that morning Lawrence turned on Corporal Cross aggressively. "What about that latrine I told you to get ready for the Brigadier's visit this afternoon?"

"It's all ready and waiting, sir," answered Cross. "We were wondering if you would like to christen it for us when you have your constitutional before lunch, sir?"

Lawrence was suspicious. "Why do you want me to christen it?"

"Well, sir, we thought that you, as company commander, should have the privilege of using it first. After all, it makes a good change from sandbags."

Lawrence was convinced. He loathed using sandbags. Having a good scratch over sandbags was damn nearly impossible. "Has it got a comfortable seat?"

"Yes, sir. It's a damned good shithouse. We just thought it would be in accordance with your position, just like the Queen opens Parliament."

Lawrence smiled at the comparison and agreed to perform the ceremony.

Half an hour later, on Cross's instigation, a small group of men assembled around the new latrine, waiting to see Lawrence christen it. They gave him a muffled cheer as he appeared in the trench. Lawrence strode into the restricted area made private by an old piece of canvas, and, having lowered his trousers and made himself comfortable, he called out: "I now declare this latrine open!"

No sooner had the words left his mouth than there was an ominous cracking of timbers as the rotten supports of the latrine gave way. Lawrence's steel helmet, which had just been visible above the canvas, disappeared. He let out a cry of despair and it was followed by a dull, sloppy thud.

With an animal noise of disgust Lawrence hauled himself from the hole and walked away from the latrine holding his trousers about his waist, his arms and legs covered by excrement. He paused, turned to the small group of men, and said: 'Someone has already christened it."

There was a terrific guffaw from the men.

"Corporal Cross, you're on a charge! In fact, I'll have you bloody court-martialed."

6

The Brigadier arrived shortly after lunch and it was plain from the start that he intended his visit to be a short one. He burst into the CP sweating profusely through hurrying up the hill, and he lowered his heavy body into a chair as everyone stood up. His clothing was immaculately clean, his creases knife sharp. He dabbed his forehead with a handkerchief and grinned at Lawrence. "Hullo, Lawrence. Bloody steep hill you've got here."

Lawrence simpered, all sweetness and gushing. "Yes, sir, it's the worst thing about the position."

"How are things going then, Lawrence?"

"Fine, sir. Absolutely fine. Last night was about our quietest yet."

"And the men?"

"Very good indeed, sir. Morale could not be higher, considering."

"Excellent. What's the shelling been like this morning?"

"The milk round was one of the heaviest we've had, sir, and went on for most of the morning, but it has only been spasmodic for the last couple of hours."

"Jolly good. Is it wise for us to have a look around now?"

"Yes, sir. I think so."

They went into the trench, with Lawrence leading at a brisk pace. He stopped at the first weapon pit facing on to Warsaw and ushered the Brigadier in. The Brigadier pulled the small curtains back very cautiously, and peeped out of a tiny corner of the slit. He continued peeping for well over a minute, trying to find his bearings. Eventually he was compelled to turn to Lawrence. "Which hill is that one, Lawrence?"

"That's Warsaw, of course, sir."

"Oh, yes. I remember now. The name just slipped me for a moment."

They sped on down the trench again, pausing once in Three Platoon to speak to Dean. Like Lawrence, he was bright and cheerful in the Brigadier's presence. Then they turned into the darkness of the forward tunnel. "Can't you do something about this smell, Lawrence?"

"Not really, sir. The bodies might be anywhere and beyond moving."

They reached the open trench again and continued rapidly back towards Two Platoon. A mortar bomb landed only a few yards behind them and they broke into a shuffling trot. They turned a corner in the trench and were directly confronted by O'Hara. He was urinating into a small hole which had been dug into the side of the trench for that purpose.

The Brigadier had not been impressed by the Hook, but he had said nothing on account of the sharpness of the position. However, O'Hara's condition was so appalling it demanded comment. His brilliant red hair had been toned down to a rusty color by a thick layer of dust and his face was filthy, with dirt concentrated about his nose. His clothes were in a shocking mess, covered by a multitude of tears, and his trousers hanging over a pair of gym shoes out at the toes.

O'Hara finished urinating in his own good time and then, seeing that attention was focused on him, he said: "Good morning, sir."

The Brigadier turned to Lawrence. "Just look at this man, Lawrence. He's in an appalling state. I expect to see men like that in the South Korean units, but certainly not in my own Brigade."

Lawrence was unable to make any reply. He was equally shocked.

"Have you any idea what you look like?" demanded the Brigadier.

"A fair idea, sir."

"Well great Scott, man, why don't you do something about it? Have you got no self-respect? You're a revolting sight." The Brigadier ran his eye up and down O'Hara with final disapproval and turned to Lawrence. "This just won't do, Lawrence. I appreciate that it's difficult up here, but this man is simply foul. Once men are allowed to get like this they will get completely out of hand. Get on to his platoon commander. It's his responsibility."

Another mortar bomb landed near at hand and they hurried on, leaving O'Hara staring after them.

On returning to the CP they consulted a map together with the FOO to discuss Lawrence's ideas about new DFs and the use of air-burst shells.   At first, the Brigadier did not consider any changes were necessary and, like the FOO, doubted if things could be added to so dramatically at such short notice; but Lawrence was so persistent that the Brigadier eventually agreed.

"Very well," he said.   "I'll see what can be done, but I still think you'll find that you don't need them.   I saw the General last night and the picture looks a lot more cheerful at the moment."

He looked at the other men in the bunker and smiled at them, trying to inspire them with hope.   "There is still a lot of enemy transport moving about, of course, but according to intelligence everything points to the attack coming off on Bunker Hill.   Another thing in our favor is that rain is forecast. I think the Chinaman has more sense than to attack while there is rain about."

"Rain stopped play," quipped Williamson in the background.

The Brigadier regarded him sourly. "Yes. Something like that." He stood up and prepared to leave.   "Well, Lawrence, keep your end up, old boy. If there is anything you want urgently just let me know."

7

O'Hara was sitting on two beer crates which he had pulled together and affectionately called his bed.   He had washed since the Brigadier's visit but it had been to little effect, and if anything he looked even more revolting, with tide-marks encircling his big face.   The evening was drawing in and the bunker was almost in darkness.   O'Hara leaned forward and stared at the back of a month-old Daily Mirror which Smith, who was sitting directly opposite him, was reading.   There was nothing on the back page which interested him and he waited impatiently for Smith to turn over so that he might be able to read the cartoons.

Blake pushed his way into the bunker.   He nodded at O'Hara but made no mention of his confrontation with the Brigadier, which was now well known throughout the company.

Smith lowered the newspaper and greeted Blake with a friendly smile. "What's the latest news, Mr. Blake?   Any hopes of the armistice being straightened out?"   He let the paper drift to the floor and kicked it towards a corner where other periodicals had received the same treatment.

"Mind that paper, Smudge," shouted O'Hara, making a sudden grab for it.

"I haven't seen the bloody cartoons, yet. Hand it over before you rip it to pieces."

Smith retrieved it for him and the Irishman settled down behind it like a contented child. "What's the news then, Mr. Blake?" repeated Smith.

"Haven't heard anything fresh about the armistice, but I wouldn't pin any hopes on it if I were you. It'll drag on for a year or two yet."

"Makes you sick, doesn't it?" said Smith with feeling. "If those bastards had to do a bit of fighting they'd bloody soon sign the thing."

Blake laughed. "No need to get morbid. Haven't you heard? To-night is our last full night up here. The Aussies are taking over then."

Smith forced a smile. "Yeah, I know. Sergeant Miles has just told us. But I'm not counting my chickens."

O'Hara, having studied the cartoons without any amusement, let the paper drop to the floor. All this rejoicing over the fact that they were going to be relieved annoyed him. He still needed that chance to prove himself, to do something he could be proud of in the future; and he wanted things to happen quickly, before his dizzy spells got worse. "There's still time for the Chinks to come yet. For all you two know they might be preparing for an attack this very moment. Queer thing, you know, but they might have a whole division ready to attack, and we don't know a damned thing about it." He laughed at this idea and added: "I'll bet they bloody well have, too."

"Not much danger of that," replied Blake. "I heard it straight from the horse's mouth this afternoon that the possibility of an attack is now practically nil."

O'Hara snorted with disgust. "Well, if you're talking about the same horse as I think you are, sir, it isn't a hell of a lot to go by. Bloody Brigadier came careering round here this afternoon and all he could bloody well do was bawl me out for having a dirty face. He said that if he had a clean face I should have as well. Silly bastard! He has a bloody batman to wipe his arse, let alone wash his face. Anyhow, I'd like to see anyone keep clean up here. It's a waste of time trying."

Smith regarded him unsympathetically. "None of us is perfect, Paddy. But you were ruddy foul this afternoon, and there's no getting away from it."

"Holy Mary! Don't you start, Smudge. Anyhow, what are you on this evening?"

"Just ordinary stag."

"Same here. What about you, Mr. Blake?"

"The second Ronson."

"We'd better get ready for the night then," said O'Hara. He leaned over to the corner where there had once been a fire and, covering his hand with soot from the chimney, he smeared it over his face until it was jet black, except for a small area around the wound on his temple. He pulled a tattered cap comforter out of his trouser pocket and placed it carefully on his head. He picked up his Sten and made sure that all the magazines were loaded, and then stepped into the doorway.

Then he stopped and said: "You blokes really know what I'd like to do? I wish that when I stepped out of here it was straight into Trafalgar Square instead of that crumbling trench."

"Trafalgar Square?"

"That's right. Trafalgar Square, with all those lights and pigeons." He grinned as though in another world. Then he steadily himself by grasping one of the timber supports and added: "I've only been to the Square once, and then it was only for a few moments as I was passing through, but I thought it was the most beautiful place I'd ever seen. I was at the top end by the art gallery and I was leaning against that damned great wall--- you know the one that overlooks the fountains. Those fountains really got my eye. I'd never seen any as big as that before. We've got some in Belfast, mind you, but none to compare with them."

There was a pause as O'Hara sought a more vivid mental picture of the fountains. Blake glanced across at Smith and saw that he was staring down at his boots, clearly embarrassed.

"As the water came down," resumed O'Hara, "the wind blew it in a fine spray all over me. I didn't mind because it was raining anyhow. And I had my mack on. There were a lot of other people there. Just looking down at the fountains the same as me. And everywhere about us people were dashing backwards and forwards, hurrying along the pavements, knowing exactly where they were going and what they were going to do when they got there."

O'Hara slammed a magazine on his Sten, looked at Blake, and added: "You know, sir, when I've finished with this lot I'm going to stand in Trafalgar Square and watch life as it goes by for hours on end." Then he stumbled out into the trench.

Blake smiled sadly. "What the hell is he on about Trafalgar Square for? I'd have thought that it would have been the Irish peat bogs with him."

Smith grimaced. "The poor devil has been like that for some time now. Sounds quite sensible the first time you hear it. I mean we've all got something we'd like to see, even if we don't talk about it. But after the fourth or fifth time of him saying all that, you realize that he's not quite all there. Always the same thing. All that drivel about the fountains. And the people, the spray blowing over him. ... The bloody mac he's wearing. The only thing to do with Paddy is give him his right marker--- and God knows he already deserves it--- and then send him on leave. Come to think of it I reckon we could all do with some leave. Heaven knows, I've been thinking of Sheffield a lot lately so I'm probably on my way round the bend as well."

"Wish to hell I was back in Kure, for that matter," said Blake.

"Don't tell me you had a woman in tow?"

"You bet."

Blake took out Jackie's photograph but before Smith had time to study it, a terrific artillery concentration fell on the Hook. The entire hill shuddered as shells showered down like raindrops. Blake and Smith were flung to the ground as the bunker received a direct hit: a main timber support snapped with a horrifying report, smaller timbers fell on them as part of the roof caved in, and Smith's glasses fell from his nose and were shattered.

Blake was unconscious for some time, his body covered by rubble. When he came round he nursed his head and wiped away a stream of blood flowing down his cheek. He saw Smith squatting in the corner with a wild glint in his eyes. Shells were still pouring down on the hill. "You all right, Smudge?" he yelled.

"Yes, but I've lost my glasses. Can you see them?"

"They're just beside you. But they've had it. They're smashed."

"What do I do now? I can't see a bloody thing without them."

"We'll just have to stay here until this is over. Better get out of that corner. It looks as if it's going to collapse."

But the shelling did not pass over. Instead it became more intense. It became indescribable, just one long roar of explosions as thousands of shells landed. It was one of the greatest concentrations of the Korean War, and did not even let up as hordes of Chinese infantry emerged from their caves and forming-up areas and started their assault.

After three weeks of waiting for the attack, Able Company was taken by surprise.

8

It was a night of utter chaos. At no time did anyone know the true situation. Each man had his own personal dramas. All of them were reduced to tunnel vision, seeing only what was going on directly ahead of them, not even aware of things happening several yards away.

Most men in Able Company survived, even if wounded or mentally scarred.   Some were heroes, some were not.   Some men died well, others not so well.

Private Hallows died accidentally, the victim of another blue-on-blue.   He was on the Green Finger patrol so he was among the first to die.   Really, he should never have been on the patrol.   A man from another platoon became a casualty and Hallows was ordered to replace him.   He did not like the idea of the patrol from the start.   He had a feeling that something would go wrong, simply because he had no faith in the patrol commander.   He knew him well, going back to Minden.   He was a greaser, a man who got his stripes because he always went out of his way to agree with those who mattered: the kind of imbecile who told his men openly that he intended to make a run for it as soon as things became difficult.

They were clear of the Hook when the shelling started and they got to their patrol position unscathed.   Then they watched their front keenly, each of them knowing what to expect.   Hallows was beside the patrol commander, glancing at him occasionally, well aware of how he kept turning his head to measure the distance back to the trenches.   Soon after the shelling started, flares went up and the searchlights were brought into action, giving them good visibility ahead.

And there they were!   A mass of them: a solid wall of men advancing up the spur.   "Christ, just look at that lot," hissed the corporal.   "Come on, lads! Beat it!"

Hallows lunged at him and caught him by the arm.   "Wait!   What the hell do you think we're here for?"

"I couldn't give a damn why we're here.   I'm not staying to fight that many.   We don't stand a chance.   Come on, lads!   Bug out!"

Hallows watched with disgust as the rest of the patrol sprang to their feet and ran for the trenches.   He raised himself to his knees and hesitated, not knowing whether to follow them or stay.   He watched them run into the shelling and saw several of them perish.   He decided he had as much chance trying to fight the Chinese off as anything else.   He settled down behind his Bren, the weapon in which he had so much faith.   He was sure he could hold them off long enough to at least give One Platoon good warning.   "I'll show the slant-eyed bastards," Hallows mumbled to himself.   He squinted down his sights and picked out the man in front, their leader.   "Now," he whispered to himself and squeezed his trigger.

Nothing happened. The piston group was stuck firmly in the body of the gun.   He cocked the gun with desperate speed and pulled viciously at the trigger again, but still nothing happened: the gun he had pinned so much faith in was useless. He started to go through the first 'immediate action' to combat a malfunction; but he knew it was far too late. He felt for his grenades and thanked God he'd brought several with him. Swiftly, he lined them all up in front of him. He pulled all the pins out, one after the other as quickly as he could. He then had about five seconds in which to throw them all. He had never moved so fast in his life, but he managed it. By the time the Chinese were within twenty yards of him they were all gone, the first ones exploding with the others still in the air. He realized he could do no more so he jumped up, leaving his Bren where it was and made a run for it. He got through the barbed-wire gap and the outline of the covered trench appeared. He was within a few yards of it when he heard a piercing cry: "Here they come, lads! Let them have it! Fire! Fire!"

He shouted back, realizing too late what was happening: his words melted away in the noise of battle and he felt a sharp jabbing pain as .303 bullets from his favorite Bren guns ripped through his body.

O'Hara confirmed himself as the true hero of the Hook, even though no one else was aware of it. He had just reached the weapon pit he was sharing with Winston when the shelling started. The blast hurled him against Winston and for a few seconds they stood swearing at each other, arguing stupidly as to whose fault it had been. Eventually, they realized that the shelling was a softening-up process before an attack, and they knew they were not ready for it.

"Get that bloody Browning mounted, for Christ's sake," yelled O'Hara.

"Okay, Paddy. But you keep your eyes skinned for them. If this is it they'll be right in with the shelling."

O'Hara peered frantically out of the narrow slit of their weapon pit but there was so much dust and large clots of soil being thrown up in great spouts that he could hardly see a thing. He abandoned the task and after helping Winston mount the Browning he hoisted his Bren gun up beside it. Then they stood there, leaning heavily against the parapet, not saying a word, hardly conscious of the tremendous din as they waited for the enemy. One of the timber supports of the weapon pit cracked ominously.

Then they heard faint cries from the right and a series of grenade explosions. These were followed by small-arms fire; slow at first, in sharp bursts, but within a few moments a continuous stream being poured out.

"Right! This is it!" cried O'Hara. He started firing, spraying bullets across their narrow arc. Winston followed suit with his swifter Browning, shooting hopefully at nothing, blazing away into the flare-lit night. Mines went off, adding to the incredible din. Then O'Hara saw them struggling through the barbed-wire and for a long time they held them off. They simply sprayed their weapons backwards and forward, with the Chinese falling in droves. Even those who managed to get through the barbed wire fared no better: they just went on falling until a mound of dead bodies formed in front of One platoon.

Gradually, as the Chinese closed in on them, their fire became more accurate, sweeping across the weapon pits, often going straight through the apertures to kill men. O'Hara's Bren was wrenched from his shoulder as something hit the bipod. He heard Winston give a short gasp. He looked round and saw the Browning swinging gently across the arc of the slit with Winston slumped over it, an ugly crimson hole in the back of his neck. O'Hara lifted Winston's head, but it sagged backwards and there was already a glassy stare in his eyes.

O'Hara looked out of the slit again and saw some vague shapes moving about only yards away. He glanced at his Bren and saw that the barrel was bent and the gas regulator useless. He grabbed his Sten from the floor, fixed his bayonet, and hurried along the covered trench until he reached a gap leading out on to the forward slope.

He was beside himself with rage; he did not know what he was doing, he was conscious of nothing but the fact that Winston was dead. Winston, the man with whom he had shared so much, who at times he had hated, yet to whom he had become attached, was dead. He was filled with loathing towards the enemy; he wanted to get at them and tear them all apart, one by one. This was his moment at last, and he was going to sort out the bastards if it was the last thing he did.

He burst out of the gap leading on to the forward slope as though he was the hero straight out of a Hollywood war film, a giant figure spraying bullets from the hip as he rushed forward. He saw a group of fifteen to twenty Chinese running up the hill towards him. He slammed in a fresh magazine and felt delight and omnipotence as he charged straight at them, his Sten shuddering in his hands. They were not slow to respond. A few bullets from their Burp guns flattened themselves on O'Hara's bullet-proof vest. The number being fired at him decreased as four of the enemy fell under his fire, and then he felt bullets tearing through his flesh. He knew that it would only be seconds before he was dead, but he was faintly aware of a feeling of delirious fulfillment and it drove him on, kept him blazing away when lesser men would have collapsed. Soon, he was right among the Chinese, still firing. He even managed to clip on another a fresh magazine. Within seconds he was firing again and he kept on firing until eventually he was able to look around and see all of them lying on the ground around him. It was only then that he too fell to the ground and died among them.

Edwin Charles died taking a reckless gamble. He and Armitage had been in their weapon pit all day, for most of the time with his old mate Hallows who always made a point of visiting them. Hallows had only just left with the Green Finger patrol when the bombardment started. For a time they just crouched there, hoping the weapon pit wouldn't collapse under it all. They joined the rest of the platoon in firing hopefully down the forward slope of the Hook. When the surviving Chinese suddenly appeared just in front of their weapon pit, Armitage and Charles turned to cover the entrance. They just stood there, their weapons trained on the doorway, ready to shoot anyone who tried to enter.

Charles began to curse and swear and then, quite suddenly, without any warning, the noise of the shelling and the prospect of the Chinese lobbing in grenades or satchel charges proved too much for him. He cracked under the strain. "We've got to get out of here," he yelled. "The bloody place is collapsing. I can hear the wood cracking."

"We're all right here, Charlie. It won't collapse."

"We'll be buried alive. Let's run for it. I'm not staying here. We'll make for one of the tunnels."

"Don't be a bloody idiot, Charlie. You'll get cut to ribbons out there. You won't stand a chance."

"I can't stand the noise. I'm getting out before I'm buried like a rat."

"Charlie, for Christ's sake!" Armitage jumped across into the doorway and barred it.

"Get out of my way, or I'll brain you."

"You'll never get through that shelling I tell you, Charlie."

He pushed Charles back against the far wall, but Charles had reached the stage where nothing was going to stop him. He flung himself at the doorway and tried to pass Armitage. They struggled for a time and then Charles raised his knee as hard as he could into his friend's groin, and as Armitage sank to the ground in agony he burst out into the trench and started to run.

He went about ten yards before a harpoon-shaped piece of metal killed him outright.

Simultaneously the bunker collapsed and Armitage was crushed to death.

Corporal Hale died stubbornly. His section was given early warning of the enemy's approach by the premature retreat of the Green Finger patrol. "There is at least a brigade of the buggers coming," the patrol commander shouted as he hurried passed Hale, making for his own platoon.

Hale shuddered. His hand went to his breast pocket where he kept his 'Dear John' letter. Lately his mind had been dominated by the determination to survive. He wanted the satisfaction of seeing her again, of confronting her with her treachery.

He joined Harden at the weapon slit and watched for the first signs of the enemy. He kept wondering what would happen if they could not hold them. How would he escape if they were overrun?

"This is it!" shouted Harden. He could see something moving faintly in the dust. "They're coming," he yelled again.

Hale stepped back into the entrance of the weapon pit and shouted as loudly as he could down the covered trench: "Here they come, lads! Let them have it. Fire! Fire!"

Harden had already put half a magazine through Hallows, and all around him other weapons were opening up. He turned to his number two on the Bren, a young reinforcement who had recently arrived on the Hook. "Come on, get those magazines ready. I'll never keep them off the rate you're going."

Hale went along one of the open trenches to see how the others were getting on, and to spur them on. He had only gone a few yards, and was between weapon pits, when he saw a Chinaman standing above him on the trench wall, quite plainly silhouetted against the sky, bristling with weapons and satchel charges, and covering him with a Burp gun.

Hale stopped abruptly. The Burp gun was pointing straight at him. For a few ridiculous moments they just stood looking at each other. The Chinaman was small, with a round and wrinkled face, and he was looking down at Hale with a gloating air. Hale raised his Sten and fired a long burst, spraying his enemy across the chest; but the Chinaman had also fired and Hale was spun round in a tight circle. He clutched his wound, groaning, expecting more bullets to thud into his body. He was on the floor of the trench, but nothing else happened. He glanced up and saw that the Chinaman was dead. Hale had shot him straight through his wrinkled face.

Hale realized that once he reached the morgue he would be all right. In his condition he could no longer do anything to help the others, but with luck he might be able to reach the morgue. He could feel blood flowing freely. He clutched his numb shoulder and pressed on it, as though that might stem the flow of blood and then he stumbled along the trench, half expecting to be confronted by more Chinese as they spilled into the position. He got back to another weapon pit and glanced inside. Both men were dead, slumped against their weapon slit. Hale carried on down the trench and, just as he had feared, he heard Chinese advancing towards him. He lay down again and

246

watched them as they stopped outside another weapon pit in which a Bren and browning were still firing. They tossed grenades in. There was a terrific explosion and the automatics went silent.

Next, Hale heard Chinese approaching from the opposite direction, and he realized that he was trapped. He had no way out. A few more seconds and he would be dead. He felt his legs buckling up beneath him. He collapsed completely and lay motionless on the trench floor. He buried his face in his left arm and remained motionless. He felt the vibrations of the Chinese boots as they approached. He heard them shouting at each other, some of them laughing. Then he realized that they had met and stopped directly above him. One of them gave him a savage kick. He bit into his lip and stopped himself from moving or crying out. There was a pause as he could feel them all watching him. Then there was more chatter and they moved on towards Three Platoon.

He stayed in the trench for a time, trying to muster up enough courage and energy to move. He wanted to stay there and hope for the best, but he could still feel blood flowing. Eventually, he got to his feet and forced himself along. He was more determined than ever to get to the morgue. He wasn't going to let himself die. He crawled on by sheer guts. His strength waned with every foot he went, but the weaker he got the more determined he became. He staggered on through Two Platoon. There were dead lying all over the place---most of them Chinese--- ripped apart by the shelling. Occasionally he recognized some of his colleagues, often just by their clothing.

When he reached the trench junction leading off to the company CP, he finally became unconscious through loss of blood.

He was one of the few men picked up by stretcher-bearers that night and two hours later he regained consciousness on a stretcher in the morgue. He looked at the long rows of wounded men on either side of him and then noticed his own blood trickling from beneath his stretcher down the slope to the center of the floor.

Slowly, everything became dimmer and quieter; it was bliss to have the pain diminishing and the noise of the shelling fading into a distant rumble. Nothing mattered any more. All he wanted was peace and to hell with the lot of them. The last thing he was aware of was a face peering down at him, talking to him as though far, far away. There was something familiar about the face, something that made him want to smile back. He tried to speak but a clot of blood formed a constriction in his throat, and he was only able to splutter for a few seconds, dribble some blood, and then die.

Sergeant Miles died because he 'froze' at a vital moment: he seized-up when an instant reaction might have saved him. For greater safety he had moved out of the platoon CP and into the main tunnel, together with Taylor and the platoon runner. As soon as the attack started he busied himself, contacting the sections over the 88-set, encouraging them and getting the latest situation from them. Every now and then he sallied forth into the covered trench at the front of the platoon and urged them on as they cut down the swarms of Chinese advancing up the hill. When things became desperate and it was clear that the Chinese were going to overrun them, he returned to the tunnel and ordered the others to do likewise. They set up barricades and prepared to hold off the Chinese. Miles went deeper into the tunnel and sent back messages over the 88-set, letting company HQ know what was happening. Then out-going calls failed and he got nothing but demands from Lawrence as to what was happening. Eventually, he turned to the platoon runner. "You'll have to try to get back to company and tell them what's happening."

Hammond obeyed meekly. He twisted his way along the tunnel and squeezed his way through the make-shift barrier. He paused, summoning up courage. Then he made a wild dash for it. He'd only gone twenty yards when he saw a group of a dozen Chinese advancing up the trench. He gave them a burst with his Sten and then ducked inside the nearest pit as they returned his fire. When they disappeared down the trench, he dashed back to the tunnel. He was challenged by Miles. "It's okay, Sergeant. It's me--- Hammond."

"What the hell's happening, then? What are you doing back here?"

"They were right on us, Sergeant. I had to run for it. They were blowing up the weapon pits as they went along."

Miles turned to others sheltering a few yards down the tunnel. "Well, don't just stand there. Get down to the far end and help the others hold them off in the entrance. Taylor, Hammond! We'll stay this end and do the same thing. We've got to keep them out at all costs."

Hammond had only just got to the tunnel entrance when he heard, and then saw, a group of Chinese dithering uncertainly in the entrance. He crouched behind the zigzag, leaned around it, and fired into them. Soon a battle was raging, all of them lying on the ground firing wildly.

Miles and Taylor rushed forward to join Hammond. Taylor handed grenades to Miles from a small pack. For a time they kept the Chinese at bay, but every grenade Miles tossed forward around the zigzag brought down a substantial fall from the roof, behind which the Chinese were able to shelter.

Eventually, the Chinese tried to rush forward. They brushed past the make-shift barrier and their leader managed to throw a grenade around the

zigzag. It went past Hammond and two other men and landed at the feet of
Miles and Taylor. At that moment, Miles's right hand was in his map pocket,
clutching his wife's letter. In the split second it took him to extract his hand,
the chance of grasping the grenade and throwing it back disappeared. It was
too late. He actually got hold of the grenade and it was leaving his hand
when it exploded in their faces, killing him and Taylor.

Blake and Corporal Smith survived. As the shelling started they huddled
together in the corner of the bunker which seemed least likely to cave in.
They hoped there would soon be a respite, but none came. Blake knew
Smith could do nothing without his glasses, but he had to get back to the
company CP. He hesitated in the doorway and then dashed down the trench,
crouching as low as possible, blind to everything as he defied the shelling.
His luck held and when he got inside the CP most of them were trying
unsuccessfully to establish wireless contact with various outstations. Apart
from the FOO only Williamson was actually in contact with anyone, and he
was relaying Lawrence's messages back to battalion, where the Colonel was
in a state of terrific agitation. Lawrence looked up sharply at Blake.
"Where the hell have you been?"

"The forward platoon, sir."

Lawrence's attitude changed. "Good lad! What the hell's going on up
there?"

"Don't know for certain, sir."

"Good God, man, you must have some idea!"

"Well, the Chinks are there, sir."

"Are we holding them?"

"So far..."

"What the hell's the matter with all the wirelesses up there?"

"No idea ..."

"Christ!" bellowed Lawrence. "What a bloody war! All these bloody
gadgets and only one works when they're most needed! Williamson, tell
battalion that so far we are holding them. But I want reinforcements standing
by."

Williamson passed the message and then said: "The Colonel wants to
know what strength they've attacked in."

"How the hell should I know?" stormed Lawrence. "Tell him that they're
in brigade strength ... No, make it division ... Make it sound as desperate as
you can."

Lawrence paced about the bunker. "Cross, go round to the forward
platoon and find out what the hell is happening. I want to know everything.

Any questions?"

"No, sir … Not that I can think of… But give me a chance and I'll think of a few!"

"Get going!   Williamson, leave that bloody useless wireless.   Take a couple of your signalers and go and get those wirelesses in the platoons working.   Take plenty of spares with you."

"You want me to go as well, sir?"   Williamson sounded amazed.

"Yes, you!   Now get a move on.   I want to hear your voice coming from one of the platoons within ten minutes.   Blake!   You go down to the morgue to meet the counter-attack platoon.   When you meet them, tell their officer to bring them halfway up the hill and keep them there until I give further orders. On no account are they to wait at the bottom of the hill because of the shelling. As far as they, and you, are concerned the shelling is non-existent."

Blake's only hope was speed.   He left the CP and sprinted along the rear trench.   In places, where shells had scored direct hits, the walls had collapsed and he was forced on to open hillside.   He was halfway down the hill when a mass of shells passed overhead, destined for the area around the jeep-head and morgue.   He stopped, peered over the broken timber behind which he had taken cover, and saw a short convoy of carriers drawing up, jammed tight with the counter-attack platoon.   He saw them take the full might of the shells. The carriers were reduced to hunks of useless metal, around which bodies were scattered, most of them still and dead, many mutilated.   Those who survived ran for cover in the monsoon ditch, ignoring the cries of the wounded lying helpless in the road.

Blake ducked as more shells screeched overhead.   Then he pressed on down the hill.   Back in the trench, he came across some stretcher-bearers struggling along with two wounded men.   They were making painfully slow progress and Blake cursed at them, trying to force his way past them.   When they reached the open stretch of ground before the morgue he sprinted ahead of them and dashed inside.   "Are there any reinforcements in here?"

Andrews, the medic, was leaning over a stretcher, halfway down the morgue.   His entire body was soiled by blood.   He looked up sharply and waved his arms at the two long rows of wounded men.   "Yeah," he yelled back sarcastically.   "Breach up the wall with our English dead."

Blake made no reply.   He stood there trying to believe what he saw: it was appalling.   There were at least fifty men all waiting to be evacuated back to the RAP, but the jeep ambulances hadn't got a chance in hell of getting through to them.   It was a nightmare; a concentration of revolting wounds, of split skulls, gaping bowels, broken limbs and severed blood vessels; and just a handful of army medics to deal with it all.   It was a futile situation, but no one would admit it. The wounded kept appealing for help, refusing to believe that they were near their end, and the medics continued to apply shell dressings and then say: "You're okay, mate. You're lucky--- a Blighty touch."

At the far end of the bunker a man with the voice of a bull was shouting: 'I can't see. I can't see." Others were moaning softly. Only the dead lay quiet. Blake walked further into the morgue and noticed with a start that Hale was lying on a stretcher near his feet. He hardly recognized him. His hair was no longer fair and flowing, but blood red and clotted, and his skin, which had been so smooth with a ruddy complexion, was now ingrained with filth and taut across his cheeks, while his blue eyes were buried in deep cavities. Blake crouched beside him and for a moment, as their eyes met, he thought Hale was going to speak; then the Corporal's head rolled gently to one side and came to rest at a peculiar angle.

Blake turned round and blood seemed to be everywhere: the blankets covering the wounded were saturated by it, the walls were bespattered by it, and the ditch in the middle of the floor, which had originally been designed to drain water in the rainy season, was now full of it, flowing towards the doorway.

The poor light of the hurricane lamps cast ghostly shadows and as he walked back down the bunker he felt that life no longer mattered. What if he was torn to bits by a shell? What did it matter if his brains were dashed to the ground? It was happening to everyone else, so why not him?

As he paused in the doorway he was pushed aside by Captain Jackson, the 2 i/c of Baker Company. Jackson marched up the line of stretchers, staring down into men's faces, trying to recognize them. At length he stopped at those he was looking for and glared down at them. "So here you are," he bellowed. "I thought I told you stupid fools not to bunch. The first thing you did was get together like a bunch of old whores. If ever ..."

Andrews stopped work and eyed Jackson narrowly. "Captain Jackson," he said quietly, "just leave those men alone. They're wounded and fighting for their lives."

Jackson did not bother to face Andrews. "If they'd done as I told them, they'd still be fighting for other people's lives and not just their own."

"What do you think these men are," yelled Andrews, "cannon fodder?" He threw a shell dressing angrily to the ground. "The only thing that matters with these men is that they recover. And the way you're behaving they certainly won't do that."

Jackson made no reply. Andrews walked to within a few inches of him and scrutinized the officer's face hatefully. He jerked his thumb towards the doorway. "Get out! Or I'll thump you."

For a time they stood toe to toe, then the medic's clenched fist landed with a resounding thud. Jackson reeled under the blow, and he nursed his jaw as he recovered himself. As he pushed past Andrews he said meekly: "You'll hear more of this, my man."

"I hope I do," answered Andrews as he resumed bandaging a man's leg. "I bloody well hope I do."

Blake followed Jackson out of the morgue and started to organize what was left of the reinforcements. He came across their platoon commander, a short-service officer named Savage. He was in a bad way, clearly in deep shock, but Blake's presence stirred him, making him realize that they couldn't just sit there. Between them they got the surviving men together and led them up the back of the Hook.

Blake stopped about three-quarters of the way up, just short of a stretch of trench that had been blown in, and left them there to await Lawrence's orders.

He went on alone. As he reached the junction where the trench branched off to Two Platoon he heard heavy footsteps, those of a fatigued man in a hurry. He pressed himself against the side of the trench so that he would be able to take the man, whoever he was, by surprise. He was shaking with fear but fought the temptation to run back down the hill.

The footsteps became louder and louder and then a dark shape flung itself round the corner; the man swiveled round instantly and fired rapidly down the trench he had just left. Blake was about to shoot, but he recognized Williamson. He shouted at him, but Williamson did not hear and sprinted down the trench towards the CP. Blake was about to follow him, but he heard Williamson's pursuers coming. He smiled grimly as he anticipated shooting them at point blank range. The first one appeared and the second was close on his heels. Blake timed his effort superbly and they both fell to the ground under his fire. One of the bodies continued to quiver, so Blake emptied another burst into him just to make sure; then he stood there for a few seconds looking at what he had done with a queer feeling of satisfaction.

He looked down the trench to make sure that there were no others following, and then, stepping over the two bodies, he ran to the CP. As he entered there was loud shuffling as men grabbed for their weapons. Clark challenged him loudly. Everyone in the bunker had their weapons trained on him. Even Lawrence held a .38 revolver unsteadily in his hand; they were all cocked and the slightest slip would have killed him. "Okay. It's me," he said.

Someone laughed, others apologized. "Sorry! But there are lots of Chinks roaming around out there."

"I know. I've just disposed of both of them."

"I thought you said there was at least a platoon of them, Williamson?" demanded Lawrence.

Williamson was sitting in his normal place, the only signaler to have returned; every part of his body was jerking and twitching beyond his control. He tried to smoke a cigarette but he couldn't find his mouth, and he ended up by tearing the cigarette so that tobacco fell to the ground. "I thought there were more than that, sir. Honestly I did."

"Never mind," mumbled Lawrence, handing him a bottle of rum. "Here, take a swig of that."

Williamson drank greedily, spilling a lot in the process.

"Now then, Blake" said Lawrence, "are those reinforcements all waiting in the trench?"

"Yes, sir."

"Right, then. We'll bring down the V.T. as soon as possible." He turned to the FOO. "Your fellows ready with it?"

"Yes, sir. I'll give them the word."

Lawrence picked up the headphones to contact battalion. "Hullo One. Mike One Able is overrun. Am bringing down Sugar One now. I say again. Am bringing down Sugar One now. For figures one zero minutes. Over."

"One. Say again, over."

"In plain bloody English," yelled Lawrence, reaching the limit of his patience, "One platoon has had it, and I'm going to counter-attack as soon as the VT is over."

"One. Roger! Watch your security. I say again, watch your security. Out."

Lawrence flung the headphones across the table. "To hell with security." He was livid, tugging at his moustache.

The FOO finished relaying his orders to his battery and they sat and waited for the VT. It arrived within a minute. The massive shells hurtled towards the hill and then, while still some distance from the ground, exploded with a mighty roar, each shell a great ball of fire, flinging out red-hot splinters of metal over the entire hill, leaving anyone still in the open to be shredded.

As the VT was about to finish, Lawrence turned to Blake. "Right, you can do your little bit now, Blake. Get down to Savage and get that hill cleared between the two of you. Don't hesitate! Go straight in. And for God's sake keep in wireless contact. Right, move!"

CSM Ralf survived because he was a canny old soldier. He had know-how, which gave him confidence, and he knew that--- just as the Rocks motto said,

'Fortune Favors the Brave'. All night long he disregarded his personal safety and remained positive and decisive in everything he did.

At the start of the battle he was sitting in a bunker at the bottom of the hill awaiting the arrival of the ammunition truck. He was sharing a bottle of beer with Cook-Sergeant Pounder who had arrived several minutes before in the Rations Truck, well-stocked with provisions for the next day. Even now, his truck and its driver were waiting outside and he was anxious to get away, but Ralf insisted that they should share a beer. As soon as the shelling started, Ralf said: "By heck, this is it, mate!"

They glanced through the doorway of the bunker, stunned by the ferocity of the shelling. Pounder saw his driver leap out of the Ration Truck to make for proper cover. As he did so, the truck took a direct hit and burst into flames. The driver lay alongside it, also a mass of flames, as dead as mutton due to shrapnel wounds. Ralf put a hand on Pounder's shoulder. "Nothing we can do, Sergeant. Just keep away from the doorway."

Sergeant Pounder, being a cook, had never contemplated doing any actual fighting. He'd served in many combat areas in Europe, but he'd never seen anything like this. "What will it mean, sir? Will we be all right here?"

Ralf finished his bottle of beer. "I don't know. All in God's hands now. If you've been good, Sergeant, then you're in real trouble. Only the good die young. So my hunch is we'll both be all right. Mind you, if those lads can hold them off on the Hook it will be a bloody miracle. And they won't stand a chance if the bastards from battalion don't get a move on with the ammo. There's hardly any Browning ammunition left in Two Platoon. Did you see anything of them when you left battalion?"

"I saw them loading the truck. But when we left they were still mucking about."

"Ah, the bastards make me sick. The bloody RSM needs to kick their arses. He's too bloody soft. They'll learn a thing or two when I take over."

Ralf paced the floor for several minutes, waiting for the familiar noise of the 3-tonner grinding along, rattling like an old Bull-Nose Morris; but all he heard was the continuous row of the shelling, vibrating everything, only interrupted by more damn-fool questions from Pounder, which he ignored.

Eventually, as the shelling slackened off a little, he peered out of the doorway, towards the morgue, where he knew the company jeep was always parked, ready for instant use. He waited another minute or two and then made his decision. "Right, Sergeant! You and I are going back to battalion to see what the hell has happened. We'll go and get the bloody stuff ourselves." He zipped up his armored vest, snatched up his rifle, grabbed Pounder's arm, and led him out into the open, dashing towards the jeep.

They were soon driving along frantically, away from the Hook, heading for battalion headquarters. They hadn't gone far, and were rounding the only bend in the road linking them to battalion, when they saw the ammunition truck. A shell had blown it into the monsoon ditch. The cab of the truck was smashed and in flames. The driver and his mate were both dead, hanging out of what had been the windscreen, flames feasting on their clothing. Ralf didn't bother to check them over. He drove the jeep straight up to the back of the truck which was sticking out into the road. He stopped the jeep but kept the engine running. He jumped out, shouting at Pounder: "We're going to unload some of the Browning ammo. The long, grey boxes with US markings. "

"But the truck could blow up any second …"

"Then get a bloody move on."

They worked feverishly, heaving the boxes into the back of the jeep. Flames from the cab were advancing towards them all the time. The heat was becoming intense. When they'd transferred two or three dozen boxes, Ralf said: "That'll do. Let's get out quick!"

They did a swift three-point turn and sped away. Very soon they were back at the jeep-head, by the morgue. The shelling had tailed off a little and so far there was no sound of any small-arms fire coming from the top of the hill. The Chinese assault hadn't yet started, but Ralf was in no doubt that it soon would. He glanced back at the ammunition boxes. Usually, it was the job of the Korean porters to take up ammunition on their jikkay frames, but when there was shelling and danger they disappeared very smartly.

Ralf went into the morgue. Things were relatively quiet. He sought out Corporal Andrews. They didn't get on, but Ralf knew he could rely on him. If necessary he'd bribe the bastard. He'd offer him a couple of bottles of whisky. Being a Scot he'd never be able to resist that. Ralf soon found him and explained the position to him.

"We're going to pile the ammunition boxes on stretchers and take them up to the platoons—Two Platoon in particular. They're desperately short of Browning ammo …"

"You and who else?"

"Some of your lads…"

"Now wait a minute …"

"It's got to be done. They're doing bugger all else at the moment. Just one trip up there, then I can get the platoons to send men down to get the rest. There's a couple of bottles of whisky in it for you."

"Oh, okay. But just one trip. We could be inundated any time now."

It took them half an hour to load the stretchers and climb the hill to Two

Platoon. They left the stretchers in the trench and all piled into Bartram's CP to avoid any more shelling.

By the time they reached Bartram's CP the Chinese assault was well underway. The CP also acted as a weapon pit and Sergeant Sykes was leaning over a Browning, firing long bursts. Bartram's batman was behind him, ready with another box of ammunition. They were accounting for more of the assaulting Chinese than anyone in the company. The barrel of their Browning was glowing red hot. Bartram was in a corner, trying to get some response out of a wireless set. He looked up as Ralf entered. "Hullo, Sergeant-Major, this is an unexpected visit."

"I've brought some Browning ammunition for you, sir, and some grenades."

"Thank heaven for that. We were wondering if we would get any. Not before time."

For the rest of the night, Ralf adopted a roving commission. He was here, there, and everywhere: company headquarters, helping in the morgue, rescuing wounded, carrying stretchers, and generally marauding around the hill looking for Chinese to kill. At one point he turned a corner in a trench and came face to face with Blake. Blake looked at him in amazement: the CSM's clothing was torn and smothered in blood..

"Have you got anyone with that rifle of yours, Sergeant-Major?"

"Two so far, sir. Cold steel both times. They don't like that. Stuck both of them straight up their Jacksies ..."

He hurried on, leaving Blake to wonder what and where was a man's Jacksie.

The counter-attack led by Blake and Savage was a failure. When Blake rejoined Savage's platoon it was only to find that they had suffered more casualties. They were so thin on the ground that they only had three Bren guns between them. Nevertheless, they advanced along the main trench towards One Platoon as soon as the V.T. was over.

They soon met the enemy. Their dead were scattered about all over the hill. The relative few who had survived the VT were wandering about, seeking out resistance and looking for more weapon pits to destroy. Savage's men engaged them from the trench, and although they had some initial success fresh Chinese appeared and forced them to withdraw.

Savage consulted Blake as they crouched in the trench. "What the hell do we do? There're too many of them."

"It wouldn't be so bad if we could get out of the trench. We're so hemmed in. And we're sitting ducks all strung out in this trench."

"You're right," said Savage. But what about the shelling? We wouldn't last a minute on top."

"We'll have to risk it. There is nothing else we can do."

Savage turned to his platoon, strung out behind him. "Okay! We're going up on top. Spread out in an extended line. Right, move! Now!"

They scrambled up from the trench, into an extended line. As they advanced along the hill towards One Platoon another stonk fell. Some men jumped back into the trench. Others ran forward and disappeared in the dust. The platoon was in complete disarray. Savage had lost all control. Then, as a final act of confusion, a fresh wave of the enemy appeared, coming over the covered trench in One Platoon. Those still with Savage and Blake held them off for a time, inflicting heavy casualties on them as they ran straight into their fire, but eventually the reinforcements were forced back, badly mauled.

Savage was in the trench, his steel helmet tipped over the back of his head, sweat pouring down his face. Eventually, he said: "We can't stay here any longer. We'll have to get back."

His remaining men followed him meekly, dragging their wounded with them, until they were on the reverse slope. Blake and Savage went into the CP. Lawrence stared at them with fiery eyes. "What the hell's been going on? I haven't heard from you once."

"The wireless operator was killed early on, sir," said Savage.

"All right, all right. But what's happening?"

"We were forced back in, sir," replied Blake, helping himself to a tot of rum. "As always there were too many of them. They were all over the place. Just wandering around. At the moment they're in possession of the hill. The top part at least"

For a time Lawrence remained motionless in his chair. Then he wriggled about in discomfort, as they'd seen him do so often in the past. "What the hell now," he muttered.

"Go ahead and have a good scratch, sir," suggested Williamson. "That always inspires you."

Lawrence looked across at his signals corporal: the cheeky bastard, he thought. Had it been that obvious all the time? Suddenly he jumped up, as though awoken from a nightmare. Scratch or no scratch, he'd bloody show them! "Right," he shouted. "If they're still wandering around on top, we'll blast the bastards to kingdom come. We'll give them such a bloody great wallop that they won't know what's hit them. We'll just keep at it. No time limit. By Christ, I'll show them!"

He turned to the FOO. "Bring down all the V.T. you can get. The whole bloody shooting works. Do you understand? The whole bloody lot. Every bloody gun you've got. All in VT."

"Roger, sir. The whole lot in V.T."

Lawrence grabbed Williamson's head-set and contacted battalion again. "Hullo Sunray! I am bringing down V.T. on Mike One Able again. Require more reinforcements to stand by immediately. Over."

"One. Roger. One Queen on way now. Watch your security. Out."

"Watch your security, be damned," responded Lawrence. "Watch your security. That's all they can damned well say. Kim! Get me another drink. A gin, and a beer as well."

"How long do you want the V.T. for, sir?" queried the FOO. "Same as last time?"

Lawrence looked at the FOO with exasperation. "For Christ's sake man, I've just told you! I want every bloody thing you've got in the entire Corps. And just keep going. No time limit! Every gun to fire VT until you run out of shells or the gun barrels melt. Is that clear? Or do I have to get on direct to your CRA and tell him myself that we need everything---- but everything. Now is that clear?"

"Reasonably, sir. I'll see what I can do."

"Just bloody do it, man. Never mind see what you can do!"

Shortly before dawn Savage and Blake led in the second counter-attack. They met no real resistance. The CRA at division had done his stuff and earned the DSO which he was later awarded. The Corps artillery gave it everything they had and the sheer weight and viciousness and duration of the VT--- which even veterans of World War II had never seen or heard the like of--- virtually wiped out all the Chinese on or around the Hook.

By 0530 hours the battle was over: The Hook was a complete and utter shambles, having received over 50,000 shells on it in the course of a few hours. Dead bodies were littered everywhere. There was hardly a space between them. Trenches throughout the hill, which had been anything up to eight feet deep, had all been leveled.

When the counter-attack had been completed a thick smoke screen was laid down over the hill and it wafted to and fro in the gentle summer morning breeze. A company of Royal Engineers, together with a handful of Able Company men, still with sufficient energy and guts to work, dug furiously at the entrances to the two tunnels in One Platoon and among the collapsed weapon pits.

For a time their work seemed to be in vain, but by degrees it became more hopeful. A Sapper corporal digging in the main One Platoon tunnel swung his pick, brought it down viciously, and as it landed he heard a ripping of clothes.

"There's someone here," he cried, and immediately there were two or three men with him, clearing away the powdery soil. They dug in silence, exercising care, as though there was still some chance for the buried men, and it was not long before they extracted the bodies of Miles, Taylor and Hammond.

Beyond the three bodies the tunnel was practically undamaged and the Sappers advanced rapidly. After some fifteen yards they came to a feeble barricade consisting of a few cross-pieces of wood with blankets draped over them. The Sapper corporal was careful and flashed his powerful torch beyond the barricade; he heard some shuffling and soon picked out a small bunch of men huddled together. They were shielding their eyes against the sudden light.

"Who is it? Who are you? For God's sake who are you?"

"It's okay, mate. You are all right now. It's us. You're safe."

"They're here fellows!" the same man screamed. "They're here! For God's sake, you stupid devils! They're here! We're all right!"

When certain there were no more living to be rescued, Blake returned to the company CP. He sat on a couple of ammunition boxes and stretched out, his eyes closed. He sighed contentedly. It was all over. He had lived through a night of hell which he would never forget. He was still in one piece and free to go on living. The whole world seemed to throw itself open to him. After that, he could do as he liked, go where he liked, the future held no worries, everything was now perfect, plain sailing, and delightful. They would go into reserve now ... Probably for at least a month and then, within a week or two he would be due to sail for home; and they always went back via Kure! He conjured up a vivid image of Jackie running towards him, her arms outstretched in welcome ... He could feel her warmth and softness as she lay beside him. . . .

"Blake! Blake ! Wake up, man!'

He sat up and rubbed his eyes. "Sorry, sir."

"You'd better have a drink."

"Thanks, sir. Mind if I have some of your gin?"

"What's the matter with your rum?"

"We've finished all that, sir."

"The whisky?"

"The Sergeant-Major took that down to the morgue."

"All right then.   But leave some for me."

Two hours later the change-over was under way; the morgue had been cleared, a small token force had been established on the Hook, the smoke-screen had been thickened, and the 25-pounders were laying down heavy concentrations on all known enemy forming-up places.

The 2nd Battalion The Royal Australian Regiment started to take over the position a section at a time.   As some of them passed the remains of Able Company, who were lying in the monsoon ditch opposite the morgue, they regarded them in amazement.   They were a harrowing sight.   The Aussies had never seen men look so totally spent.

Without warning 25-pounder shells passed overhead with their usual screech.   In the monsoon ditch the remains of Able Company ducked for cover.   One of the Australians called out: "It's all right, lads!   They're ours!"

Another yelled across: "Good on yer, Pommies!"

Another addressed himself to CSM Ralf: "Fine bloody mess you've left us to clear up, mate!"

Ralf, looking old and flabby, grinned.   In fact they all grinned or laughed or called back cheeky remarks.   Now, they could face any banter anyone threw at them.   They'd achieved something out of this world, and in their hearts they knew they were up there with the best of them, even though it was something they would never claim.   They had upheld the regimental traditions of nearly 400 years.   Not that they were under any illusions.   No one back in Blighty would give a toss.   To most people they were still what they always had been: the latest edition of Tommy Atkins.   They'd been paid a quid a week to do a job and they'd done it: well done, say no more!

9

Able Company arrived in their reserve area in the early afternoon.   The first thing they did was to have a muster parade.   The officers--- Lawrence, Clark, Blake and Bartram--- stood on a small hillock, watching CSM Ralf and Sergeant Sykes organize men into their respective platoons.   Then Ralf pulled out his company roll book.

"Answer you name when your name is called out.   Just answer "Sir!"

Officers are on parade."

He called the names out alphabetically and whenever a name was met by silence someone called out either "Dead, sir!" or "Wounded, sir!" or "Missing, sir!" Then there was a pause as Ralf made his entry. There was gentleness in his voice, a distinct lack of his usual swearing. He progressed steadily.

"Carmen?"

"Sir!"

"Carter?"

"Sir!"

"Cartwright?"

"Dead, sir!"

"Cavendish?"

"Dead, sir!

"Charles?"

"Dead, sir!"

Ralf paused: only his eyes moved as he searched the company for a reaction. "Poor old Charlie! Confirmation of his compassionate leave came through last night ... What bad luck ... Cheeseman?"

"Wounded, sir! He got hit in both legs ..."

"No speeches ... Chester?

"Sir!"

"Chilvers?"

 "Sir!"

And so on, until eventually Ralf closed his note book, did a smart right turn, marched over to Major Lawrence, saluted, and then reported: "Fifty seven on parade, sir. Thirty-eight dead, forty two wounded and one missing."

Their small re-entrant was ideal as a reserve position. It was some way from battalion headquarters and out of the glare of criticism, and it had a magnificent view straight down the Imjin valley. It was quiet and peaceful, and during the hot summer days that followed the shelling along the front line dissolved into a distant rumble.

Training was down to an absolute minimum and Lawrence's aim was merely to keep men occupied; and there were no counter-attack commitments hanging over their heads as there had been during their previous spell in reserve.

Tent accommodation was good, drink was plentiful, and they were able to relax. They sat about doing nothing without the fear of being chased or chivvied; they caught up with their mail and devoted more time to reading the newspapers which reached them in dribs and drabs. The war ceased to worry them. It became a detached interest and the latest state of the Test Matches against Australia became the most eagerly sought news.

Evenings which had previously been spent in weapon pits, or on patrols, were now spent drinking in a marque that served as a canteen, and when men did eventually totter back to their tents, their heads reeling, they lay naked and slept peacefully beneath new mosquito nets which protected them from the tormentors that had previously made life at night so unpleasant.

In the mornings they rose late, ate breakfast at their leisure in the sun, and then had a muster parade, at which they were detailed off for routine chores. In the afternoons they bathed in the Imjin, splashing about with freedom and basking in the hot sun so that everyone developed a rich, nut-brown tan.

It was war at its best: no hardships, no responsibilities, and very little work. The contrast was so great and so sudden that all the deaths, mutilations, and general destruction began to fade. After a week a basketball pitch was completed and the game became so popular that an inter-platoon league was formed. Then a rifle range was completed and shooting was added to the league. Finally, canoe-racing on the Imjin was to have been added, but the three canoes, constructed under the critical and supposedly expert eye of Lawrence, sank as soon as they touched the water, with the result that the three men were nearly drowned; but since they weren't it became a huge joke.

Reinforcements arrived from Japan. Among them was Blake's new platoon sergeant, an experienced NCO named Nichols. In command of the draft was Second Lieutenant Ray Fuller, a tall youth with a great shock of fair hair and a ready smile which gained him many instant friendships. He was a bright, witty product of Blundell's and Eaton Hall and his youthful exuberance was infectious. The small officers' mess took on a novel air of cordiality and Blake loved it when they dined together al fresco and ended the meal with liquors, looking down the Imjin into brilliant sunsets.

Mail was delivered regularly. Blake received a mixed bunch: anxious enquiries about his safety from numerous relatives and old school friends and a long letter of relief from his parents, to whom he'd sent one of the army's express letter-forms designed to let next-of-kin and relatives know that they were safe after a major battle.

His most surprising letter came from Jackie. When he saw the Kure postmark he knew it could only be from her. It read:

"Dear Peter,

As you will see, I am better at talking English than writing it.
I have heard of your big battle and can only pray that you are OK.
If you are OK you will get this letter OK. If you are not OK then
this letter will not matter. I write to send you my love and
to say sayonara. Yes, really sayonara. I have not always
been honest with you. I have a daughter, a little girl aged three.
She is everything I live for. Her father was an Australian.
When Korea happened, he was one of the first to go and
he never came back. He was killed in the north, near Sinanju.
It happened to many men just like him, and a lot of them left
behind Japanese girlfriends like me, and sometimes with babies,
like mine. Think about it, Peter, and you will understand
why I wanted us to be lovers. I just had to do that for you, in
case the same thing happened to you. It was my gift to you.
But a gift is all it can ever be. If that sounds bad, remember
your English saying: 'More happiness in giving than getting'.

But we are in a situation that has no future. We have different
lives. I have my daughter and you have a future in England among
your own people. But let us always remember each other, just like I
remember my daughter's father. If you write back, just say that you
are okay and that you really did feel love for me, as I did you.

That will make our memories good ones.

Love and sayonara, Jackie."

His own 'Dear John'! Now he would be qualified to comment, even though his was a far cry from the one Corporal Hale had received. Blake's was based on sound reason, not fickleness. As he re-read Jackie's letter, tears formed in his eyes. It wasn't so much as what she said, more that its finality brought into focus all the emotions he had bottled up within himself whilst serving in Korea: regrets and sadness bursting free. The things he had been able to talk to her about. He wondered if he would ever again be able to talk like that with anyone else.

After he had indulged his emotions he went to the company orderly tent and got another of the army express letter-forms from Corporal Cross. He ticked the box marked 'I am safe and well' and then, in the box marked 'Message, ten words only', he wrote: "Yes, I really loved you. I will never forget, Peter."

He counted the words to make sure there were only ten. Then he addressed it and slipped it in the mail bag, knowing that that was the end of it.

Several of the letters Blake received were from relatives of the dead he had written to. Private Potter, his new batman, brought him the first one when he was stretched out in front of his tent sunning himself after a particularly agreeable lunch. The envelope was type-written, which was unusual. In fact, it wasn't from a relative, but from the social workers looking after Mrs. Charles. Politely, using civil service jargon, it deplored that Charles had not been able to take advantage of the compassionate leave granted to him. It said that Mrs. Charles had now lost all will to live. It made Blake question exactly what had happened: just how long before the battle started was CSM Ralf aware that Charles had been granted compassionate leave? He considered asking a few pertinent questions at the battalion orderly room, but he didn't. He couldn't believe that Ralf would have been that much of a bastard, even if his daughter was pregnant. He decided that one day, when everything had calmed down, he would ask Corporal Cross: he would know.

A number of men noticed there was something wrong with Bartram, but Lawrence was the first to mention it. "You're ill, Bartram," he said as sat in the mess after dinner, at which Bartram had hardly eaten a thing. "You look like a ghost."
"I just feel a bit feverish, that's all, sir. It'll soon pass."
"Nonsense! Go sick first thing in the morning."
The next morning it was about all Bartram could do to get to the RAP. At first the MO thought he was drunk. His legs were so feeble that he was rolling all over the place and when he spoke it was with a pronounced slur. The MO examined him and soon realized it was more than drunkenness. Within an hour Bartram was installed in a hospital in Seoul.
That evening, in the Able Company officers' mess, Lawrence told them: "According to this message from battalion, Bartram has got Songo fever."
"What on earth is that, sir?" asked Fuller. "It sounds more like a dance than an illness."
"Well I'm afraid it isn't. It's serious. Apparently it's caused by the fleas off rats." He turned to Blake and Fuller. "You two had better take tomorrow afternoon off and visit him."
When they got to the hospital Bartram was delirious with no idea of what was going on around him. He didn't recognize them. They left, desperately worried about him, and two days later he died. It was among their worst deaths in Korea.

Then followed an incident Blake was destined to see as among his most bizarre in the Korean campaign. Just as they had got into the swing of the easy life they received orders from battalion that, together with Baker Company, they were proceed by TCVs to an area in South Korea near Taegu.

At their briefing, they were told that in a tactical ploy to sabotage the peace talks in Panmunjom, President Syngman Rhee had ordered the release of around 25,000 prisoners of war--- men who had no wish to be repatriated to North Korea or China when the war ended. The South Korean guards had simply opened the gates and allowed them to walk out and they were now wandering around the countryside in ill-disciplined gangs, some real desperadoes among them. Korean civilians were being encouraged by their government to sustain them, whereas the Americans were determined to round them up again and incarcerate them as before so that the peace talks could be resumed.

Able and Baker Companies were ordered to be ready to move in two hours, with a journey south estimated to take 24 hours. They left their company lines exactly as they were, taking with them only arms, ammunition and C-rations.

When they arrived south of Taegu they found a critical situation. There had already been armed clashes between some of the released prisoners and American units. The Rocks bivouacked in open countryside and at dawn they set off into a range of hills which the Americans warned them were thick with bands of escapees. Blake's platoon headed the force of some 200 men, all strung out in extended line across the hills in a giant sweep.

In early afternoon Blake's men climbed a steep ridge and then looked down into a giant col formation, an area of dried-up paddy fields. Below them was a group of around 500 prisoners, a clearly disorganized rabble heading straight towards them, about to climb out of the col. Blake ordered his men to ground and studied them through his binoculars, then he lost no time in contacting Lawrence over his 88-set.

Lawrence, Nobby Clark, CSM Ralf and the Baker Company OC soon joined him. They lay down and studied the POWs for themselves. They were indeed a wild-looking lot without any obvious leadership, split into several large groups, just wandering around with no apparent purpose other than maintaining their freedom. Lawrence knew exactly what they had to do. They had to round them up and return them from whence they'd come.

"Right, here's what we'll do," said Lawrence. "Keep our men in extended line. Bring them up to this ridge, quietly and unobserved. Then, on my order, they all stand up on the skyline, weapons at the high port."

"Like Red Indians in a cowboy film," laughed Blake.

His flippancy was ignored. "We must show them that we're armed, mean business, and they have no escape. In fact, once they're aware of the situation we'll put of burst of Bren over their heads. They won't dare to run, knowing we can mow them down."

"A lot of them are armed," said the Baker Company OC, still studying them through his binoculars. "They've got American carbines by the look of it."

"Not that many of them," said Lawrence. "They'll just stand fast, not knowing what to do."

"And then what?" asked Nobby Clark.

"Someone will have to go down and parley with them. Persuade them to lay down their arms and be taken back."

None of them made any comment, but they looked around at each other, all of them knowing that it had to be someone of substance, of authority, and above all rank. It was not a situation for delegation.

"You're senior to me, Dick," said the Baker company OC. "You'd better do it. We'll cover you."

Lawrence knew his moment had come. He had avoided ever going into no man's land, but now he had no escape. It was a job he alone could undertake. He turned to CSM Ralf, a marksman and a regimental Bisley shot. "Sergeant-Major, when I give the word, order the men to stand up … All at the same time … Maximum impression. You and Mr. Blake stay down, covering me. Mr. Blake with a Bren."

When the two companies stood up, the result was spectacular, just as anticipated. The POWs stopped in their tracks. Their faces were upturned as they gaped at what confronted them. Lawrence started down the hill, unarmed apart from his Webley which was still in its holster. He headed for the largest group and as he neared them a man came forward to confront him. He was armed, holding an American carbine. Tension became increasingly tangible; metaphorically every man was holding his breath. The two men met, face to face. None of those in Able and Baker companies could hear what was being said. Yet they talked, obviously understanding each other. Very soon their voices became raised. Lawrence was heard to shout: "That's an order!"

A fierce argument developed.

"Stand by for trouble," said Nobby Clark. "Have you two got the major covered?"

CSM Ralf and Blake said they had. The bipod of Blake's Bren was firmly embedded. CSM Ralf had his trusty Lee Enfield pressed against his shoulder. The only snag was that for the most part Lawrence was standing directly in front of his adversary, obscuring him. The argument continued and became more agitated. Lawrence started to gesticulate, a sure sign that he was losing patience.

"I don't like the look of this," said Nobby Clark.

The POW suddenly raised his carbine. He cocked it. Lawrence started to fumble with his holster, trying to extract his Webley.

"The bastard is going to shoot him!" exclaimed Clark.

At that moment, as Lawrence ducked his head to see why he couldn't get his Webley out of his holster, Blake and Ralf at last had a clear view of the POW. Ralf had him lined up to perfection. He squeezed the trigger of his Lee Enfield. The noise of the single shot echoed around the col. The bullet struck the POW straight between the eyes. It knocked him backwards, flat on his back, stone dead.

"Move!" yelled the Baker Company OC. "Down the hill! Move! Move!"

To a man, the two companies ran down the hill, yelling wildly. Blake fired off a Bren magazine over their heads. The POWs were so stunned by the dramatic death of their leader and the resolution of the troops sprinting down the hill that they stood stock still, mesmerized. They raised their hands and dropped their weapons. Within a few minutes they were rounded up and their carbines collected.

Corporal Williamson radioed back to the parent American unit and called for additional help and guidance.

That night, Able and Baker companies were billeted in a local village. The men were in various village huts. They enjoyed a riotous evening with plenty of locally brewed sake to wash down their C-rations, to say nothing of a few romantic encounters with the more flirtatious of the local girls.

The officers were billeted separately. They were in the village school and two American majors joined them, which made it rather a special occasion. They were served a hot meal by village girls dressed in national costumes. It was goat stew and one of the Americans cause great amusement when he said: "Let's hope the goat was female ... Not a Billy goat ..."

"Why's that, Major?" asked Fuller.

"Because in Korea, when they cook stew they use the entire animal. Private parts as well. Like the Arabs do. So it's not just the eyes you have to look out for ... It's the bollocks and a dick as well ..."

"Oh dear," sighed Fuller. "And just in case it's a female goat, I'll keep an eye out for an udder as well." Then, with corniness that didn't really do him credit, Fuller added: "Any udder advice you can give us, Major?"

It was a measure of the ambience that already existed among them that they laughed as though it was hysterically funny. However, it didn't stop them eating their stew with great care.

As the evening wore on, things became increasingly jovial and relaxed. Being a dozen in number was ideal, especially since the Baker Company officers were well known as a lively lot. Fuller was in particular good spirits. It was his first Korean adventure and he had been thrilled by it. If that was war, then he was looking forward to plenty more of it. He also amused everyone by becoming increasing tight, rolling out a flow of witty remarks and more audacious puns.

There was a pause in their conversation as one of the Americans passed King Edward cigars around. When Lawrence had his underway, he leaned back contentedly and said: "A very interesting operation this morning. Very gratifying …"

"But hardly text book stuff, sir," said Fuller. "I don't ever recall them covering that scenario at Eaton Hall. Although come to think of it there was a lecture on how to quell native riots. In Cairo I think they set it …"

"And what did they tell you to do?" asked one of the Americans.

"Can't recall for sure, sir   I didn't take too much notice, since I never thought I'd be in Cairo, let alone have to face a riot … But I do recall that they advised us to keep our swagger sticks firmly under our arms, be damned careful our monocles didn't drop down, and face them squarely … And Bob's your uncle … Exit the locals, full of respect. Not like today. As Blake said at the time, it was just like a scene out of a western … Tell me, sir," added Fuller, turning to Lawrence, "when you confronted that Chinese communist chappie, did you raise your hand and say 'How!'"

They all laughed, including Lawrence. He was enjoying himself as much as anyone, entering into the spirit of things in a manner that would have been a revelation to those who had only known him since arriving in Korea. His usual dourness and grumpiness had vanished and he was full of bonhomie, really chuffed to be presiding over a gathering celebrating a first class performance in which he had played the heroic role.

"No, Fuller," he replied. "If you must know, I ordered him to stand at ease and to pay attention …."

More laughter, at the end of which Lawrence added: "To tell you the truth, that's not an experience I would want to go through again. That bullet Sergeant-Major Ralf fired literally skimmed over my head. I even felt the wind of it …"

"Wow! You really must have got the wind up, sir," quipped Fuller.

They laughed louder than ever and Lawrence grinned tolerantly.

"Maybe, Fuller, but certainly not the vertical wind-up I can assure you."

"Of course not, sir … It was strictly horizontal because of the angle it was fired at …"

Blake then made the mistake of trying to enter into the repartee, even though it was not a situation for which he was suited. In a carouse such as they were enjoying he should have sat back and enjoyed it: been a listener, not a participant. As he spoke for the first time, attention focused on him, everyone wondering if would be able to match Fuller's wit.

"It really was a very perilous situation," he said formally. "I don't know if you realized it, sir, but the whole time you were talking with that man you were standing directly in front of him, obscuring him from our view. Most of the time all we could see was the back of your head."

"Christ, you could easily have shot me!" exclaimed Lawrence, pretending to be highly alarmed. It was a good piece of acting that brought more guffaws. Blake waited for it to subside and then said: "Yes, sir, you're right. We were well aware of that. Ralf said as much to me, but I told him not to worry. That if things became really serious he'd just have to take a chance on it and try for the man anyhow… That it was a risk well worth taking."

Blake was amazed when there was no laughter. He had intended the remark to be flippant and amusing, but whereas they'd been laughing at everything Fuller said, no one found Blake's remark in the least jocular. The tone of his voice carried no humor. It came across as perfectly serious, as though he really had been prepared to see Lawrence shot and not the prisoner.

The expression on Lawrence's face changed instantly. A man being shot between the eyes right in front of him had not been a pretty sight. It had thoroughly unnerved him and reminded him all too clearly of the man who had been shot by a sniper in Germany. As he reflected on these two things he wasn't at all amused. He glared in anger at Blake. The two Americans sensed a dramatic change in the atmosphere and became embarrassed. The others searched for a way of changing the subject, desperate to get things back on track. They all knew that Blake had dropped a brick of major proportions.

"Just joking, sir!" added Blake in desperation.

That only made matters worse.

"Oh yeah …" said Lawrence sourly. "Many a true word said in jest!"

At a stroke, the improved relationship between Blake and Lawrence since the Hook battle vanished. The deep-seated and personal rancor between them was rekindled.

10

The afternoon before the Rocks were due to move back into the line it rained. It really rained: great black clouds rolled slowly by, shedding their tremendous loads of water. Stinging rain swept over the hills, through the valleys and across the plains. Streams sprang up in what had previously been shady nooks, streams became rivers, and rivers plunged and roared as they swelled like straining blood-vessels.

Men sat gloomily in their tents watching the rain with a morbid fascination, wondering at its power and cursing at its effect. Within a matter of minutes everything was sopping wet. The Imjin began to climb dangerously near the base of the Teal Bridge; monsoon ditches, which had been so carefully maintained throughout the year, proved pathetically inadequate and many long stretches of road were washed away; transport came to a standstill and brigade majors informed their battalions that the situation had been declared 'Red'.

In the front line the weather forced a cease fire. The enemy hills were barely visible, and the likelihood of any form of aggression from either side was nil. Bunkers began to collapse as water simply washed away badly constructed walls. The Rocks's move back into the line was postponed.

When the move eventually came it had a familiar ring to it, with men wondering what the new bunkers would be like, how active the Chinese in front of them would be, and--- most of all--- would the rat situation be better or worse.

The sun reappeared and it became intolerably hot. Everything went moldy. Enemy shelling resumed and at night their patrols were active, small ones at first, just probing, testing out the new unit confronting them; and then, after several patrol clashes in which Able Company lost three men and claimed to have got six, the Chinese became far more aggressive. During their second week on their new hill, Two Platoon was involved in a fairly major engagement. Small-arms fire raged for over an hour in the valley and at the end of it all Two Platoon had lost six men, even though they claimed to have accounted for at least twenty Chinese. They brought back no evidence of their success, so Lawrence discounted their claims.

Activity along the entire front continued to escalate. Apart from their days on the Hook, the war had never been more real or menacing. Each morning men sought the latest news of the Armistice talks, and each morning they were inspired with hope. The daily paper issued by the Americans---

The Stars and Stripes--- was always wildly optimistic. Men told each other that it could only be a matter of time, but there was always just one more snag, one more objection from President Syngman Rhee which put things back to square one.

Casualties mounted and platoons started to become thin on the ground. The activity was not confined to one area as it had been on the Hook, but instead the whole line was aflame from coast to coast. The Chinese succeeded in pushing back two South Korean Divisions several miles and inspired by this success they increased their efforts elsewhere. In front of the Rocks even the smallest of re-entrants were probed; minefields were tampered with; gaps cut in the barbed-wire, and standing patrols attacked despite the heavy casualties inflected upon the Chinese.

At divisional headquarters puzzled intelligence officers discussed among themselves the enemy's intentions; bewildered Brigadiers conferred with their Colonels, and the Colonels played safe by telling all their companies to expect an attack; and in the companies, where the fighting would be done, men watched and waited, fearing the worst, back to praying for the best.

Blake stretched his legs and scratched vigorously at his groin, thinking to himself that it was about time he had a good wash in the stream running along behind the platoon, as had become popular with the men whenever there was a lull in the shelling. Yet he kept putting it off, never knowing how long the lulls would last, and refusing to take any risks.

Their freshness after a month in reserve had soon disappeared. The reinforcements who had joined them felt the strain most. They were unable to adjust themselves to sleepless nights and the rough living conditions. Lawrence didn't help matters. He drove them as hard as ever. An additional drag on morale was that a sizeable number of men in Able Company, including Blake and Smith, were nearing the end of their two years as National Servicemen. They were due to catch the Troopship Devonshire at the end of July. Blake tried not to let his increasing nervousness show but it didn't go unnoticed. He seldom went out of his bunker unless he had to, and when he did he hurried through the trenches, always with his steel helmet on and his bullet-proof vest zipped up, something that was supposed to be routine, but which very few men ever took any notice of, and which Blake had never previously adhered to.

Blake held a platoon orders group and at the end of it, he asked: "Any questions?"

No one answered so they dispersed, leaving Blake alone with Sergeant

Nichols. "Do you want me to do the first stag tonight, sir?" Sergeant Nichols asked him.

"No, Sergeant. I'll do the first one to-night." Blake always chose what stag he did according to how he felt.

"Doesn't make any difference to me, sir," said Nichols. "They are both as bad as each other. They're real bastards, first or second."

Nichols lay down on his bunk, but he didn't seek sleep. He watched Blake moving about the bunker. Eventually, he went to sit by the doorway, but not in the actual doorway. He always did that and Nichols wondered what was on his mind. Nichols reckoned that he was praying. Being a devout atheist, Nichols never understood men who suddenly turned to prayer when they found themselves in the front line. Blake was so typical: the kind of well-educated young fellow who would pray out of habit and hope, rather than any real conviction.

Blake opened his eyes, his prayers over. "What's the matter, Sergeant?"

"Nothing's the matter with me, sir."

They glared at each other for a few seconds, knowing that the dislike was mutual. Potter came into the bunker with a new battery for the 88-set. "You ready for a spell in the OP with me?" Blake asked.

"Yes, sir."

He gathered up his weapon and equipment and followed Potter into the trench. They hurried along and scrambled into the small O.P. just as another stonk landed. Across the valley, in the gathering haze, tucked away in the Chinese hills, a loudspeaker was booming out propaganda. Blake listened to a female voice telling them to lay down their arms and stop being the Yanks' cannon fodder. "Got that repellent with you?" he asked Potter.

"Yes, sir. The mosquitoes aren't out yet, though."

"That doesn't matter. Get some on you before they are."

Potter produced a small tube of the repellent and they smeared it liberally over the exposed parts of their bodies. When darkness closed in the two standing patrols came over the 88-set stating that they were in position. Their long, nightly vigil started. The mosquitoes were soon out in their buzzing millions, hovering around infuriatingly near their faces despite the repellant, selecting suitable spots to suck at before being squashed to death as one of their hands lashed out in anger. It was a maddening process that went on minute by minute, hour by hour, and night by night.

In the valley, despite the blaring Chinese loudspeaker and the croaking of the bull frogs, it somehow remained hushed with expectancy: patrols lay with their blackened faces streaked by sweat, listening for a clue of the Chinese approaching: the breaking of a twig, an increase in the frogs' croaking, the sudden bolting of a hare, or of a pheasant taking to the air.

Blake and Potter had been in the OP for two hours when they heard the blowing signal over the field telephone. "Hullo. Blake here."

Lawrence spoke, his voice full of urgency. "We've just had word from Three Platoon standing patrol that there is a Chinese patrol coming along the valley towards you. They estimated at least twenty of them, possibly more. They may be heading for Two Platoon but keep your fellows keyed up in case they go on to you. You may have to lend a hand, anyhow."

Blake swallowed hard. "I see, sir."

"Be on the ball, Blake. I can't see them sending out many more probing patrols. This might be something more serious."

"Okay, sir." Blake slapped furiously at mosquitoes which had settled on his forehead. He told Potter to go and get the emergency patrol ready and then he warned the standing patrol over the wireless what was happening.

The noise of the Chinese loudspeaker, over which Bing Crosby was now singing 'Alexander's Ragtime Band', made it impossible to hear anyone until they were right on the position. He wondered why Lawrence always refused to try to knock the loud speakers out with shelling. Others did, even though it never succeeded. His thoughts were interrupted by several long bursts of small-arms fire from the Two Platoon standing patrol. Burp guns seemed to go on firing forever; Stens merely stammered in reply. Then the shooting stopped as abruptly as it had started. It was replaced by confused shouting: "Over here, quick! Stop arguing ... Get a move on for Christ's sake . . ."

The shouting was disjointed and meaningless, but Blake realized that the patrol was making a hasty withdrawal. He could hear them crashing through the undergrowth. He blew down the field telephone, hoping to find out what had happened. No one replied so he gave up trying. Several minutes later a blowing signal came over the telephone. He snatched it up.

"That you, Blake?"

"Yes, sir. What's happened?"

Blake was amazed to hear a soft chuckle, the kind he associated with Lawrence when he'd been drinking. "This is a great day, Blake. They did it. We've got one!"

"Got one what, sir?"

"A prisoner! After all these months..."

Blake was genuinely elated. "That's terrific, sir. How did they manage it?"

"Sergeant Sykes says two Chinese suddenly appeared out of the darkness, so he hit one on the head with his Sten butt and he fell to the ground like a sack of potatoes. The other one ran off. As soon as they realized that they had actually got a prisoner, they hurried back in ..."

"That's terrific, sir."

"But it doesn't alter the fact that they are still out there, Blake. We mustn't take any chances. Understand? I'll let you know of any further developments."

The prisoner changed everything. First of all he was interrogated by Lawrence with the help of Kim and then he was sent back to battalion where he faced similar questioning. Finally, he was questioned by a divisional intelligence officer at brigade headquarters. On all three occasions he stuck to an identical story and gave identical answers. It convinced everyone that the information he gave them was accurate and of great value.

The following morning Lawrence held his orders group a little later than usual. He was in an ebullient mood. Everything was now settled. He explained to his platoon commanders that the prisoner had painted a dark picture with respect to the enemy's numbers, and their aggressive intentions. Their prisoner, who was a junior officer, claimed that it was all part of the Chinese determination to influence the peace talks. "But we have no need to worry ourselves with these bigger issues," said Lawrence. "Our only concern is what directly confronts us. The Colonel and the Brigadier were in conference most of the night and they are adamant that our first task is to stop, or at least delay, any attacks on our positions. We have to take the initiative. And quickly! Within the next few nights."

He paused, as though giving them time to think of what the plan might be. Then he referred to the map again. "From what we've been told, all the Chinese patrols operate through a firm base which is situated at the end of the re-entrant which faces directly on to Three Platoon. That explains why Three Platoon gets the most contacts." He lit himself another cigarette, supplied by Cross this time. "The Colonel and I consider that if we can wipe out that firm base we will disrupt their patrol system. That will at least delay their attack, even if it does not stop it altogether. Are you all with me so far?"

He studied their faces in turn: Sykes was as unperturbed as ever, knowing that he would not be directly involved; Fuller looked distinctly worried, as though it was all just a bit too ambitious for him, and Blake's expression had a trace of boredom in it; he was going back to Kure in two days' time so the patrol obviously wouldn't be his responsibility.

"Okay so far," answered Sykes.

"Our problem is to surprise them, yet at the same time send out a patrol that is sufficiently big to do the job thoroughly. For that reason I have decided to send an attack patrol of 20 men ..."

"Excuse me, sir," interrupted Fuller, "but which platoon will be doing the patrol?"

Lawrence glanced up: he remembered Goodall once asking exactly the same question. "It's all right, Fuller, you won't be doing it." Lawrence looked down at his map. When he spoke again his throat was dry and his voice was little more than a croak. "Mr. Blake. You will command the patrol, drawn from One Platoon."

Lawrence didn't look up, knowing how Blake would react.

For a few seconds Blake didn't react. He regarded Lawrence with total disbelief. Then he demanded: "Me? But I'll only be in the line two more days."

"That's all right then," replied Lawrence. "No problem. The patrol will take place tomorrow night."

Blake's face was pale and grave. He went all hot and had a sudden attack of prickly heat down the length of his spine. "That'll be my last night in the line. I'll be leaving for Kure the following day."

"So you said."

Blake's eyes watered and hate burnt deep into his heart. He had disliked Lawrence from day one, and it had grown all the more bitter with all the incidents that had occurred; but now he didn't just hate him: he loathed him with all his heart. Only a complete and utter bastard would send a man out on a suicidal patrol on his last night. It was even worse than having dragged him back from Kure to face the Hook: that had been callous, but this was positively fiendish.

"You don't honestly think that you're going to get me out in that valley on my last night, do you?"

"Why not?"

"Because it's my last bloody night in the line, that's why not."

The others were all watching them, expecting an even more explosive outburst from Blake, but he just continued to stare at Lawrence, still hardly able to believe what he had heard. He knew it would be pointless to say anything else. He could protest as much as he liked, but he knew it wouldn't make any difference: not with Lawrence.

The rest of the orders group was agony for Blake. He listened to the details Lawrence reeled off and the more he heard the more he realized how futile the patrol would be. Even if they did meet with success there would be nothing lasting about it; the Chinese would soon replace a firm base of forty men, and the following night everything would be exactly the same.

Exactly the same? Would he still be alive? Or would he be like all those men who had died on the Hook, condemned to perpetual darkness?　Nothing!

When Lawrence concluded his orders group, he said:　"I'd like to have a word with you alone, Blake."

The others walked out into the hot sunshine.

"Yes?"

"I want you to be here first thing to-morrow morning so that we can tie up the final supporting fire program with the gunners."'

"Right, sir."

Lawrence hesitated.　He opened his mouth to speak, paused for a second, and then closed it again.　Of course he did not have to give Blake an explanation.　Last night in the line or not, he was there to do a job the same as anyone else and he could not expect favors.　The fact that he happened to be the most suitable man for the task was just the luck of the draw.　To send out Fuller or Sykes would be totally irresponsible.　They were there to do a job to the best of their ability.　There were soldiers, British soldiers, and there was no room for sentimentality.　If he gave an explanation it would merely strengthen Blake's feeling that he was being harshly treated.

"All right, Blake. That's all."

11

Blake left the CP and wandered back through the trenches sullenly, his hands in his pockets, his shoulders hunched forward in dejection, and on reaching One Platoon he went straight to the OP.　He studied the ground over which he would be moving until his eyes were aching and he was familiar with every paddy field, and every bund, and every tree and every small bush.　He noted the long distance to the final objective, and the massive bund behind which the Chinese firm base was reported to exist.　The only consolation was that the valley was full of shell craters, affording a certain amount of cover.　He tried in vain to find a route across the valley which was not obvious but however good some were, they all ended up at the same spot where the bund was high and thick, like a natural fortress, with two smaller bunds on either side.　He imagined them trying to outflank the enemy, only to be caught in withering fire.

He buried his head in his hands, sick to death with the whole thing.

"Something big coming off, sir?" asked the OP man.

Blake glanced at him wearily.　"Yes.　Something that is a damned sight too big." The word 'big' echoed in Blake's mind. Was it really something big? A twenty-man patrol with small arms and a few grenades was not anything big; it was just a token gesture, and a damn silly one at that. He took a final look at the valley, noticing how formidable the Chinese hills were, imagining how they were crawling with Chinese, all of them hidden away like rats in a sewer, just itching to spill out. He left the OP and went straight back to his CP. Nichols was sitting in the doorway, stripped to the waist, fitting the wireless sets out with new batteries. He managed to smile at Blake. "Nice evening, sir."

"Um," grunted Blake. He stopped just inside the bunker and watched Potter as he sat there reading a magazine. Suddenly, he lost his temper and snatched the magazine from Potter's hands.

"Here! Steady on, sir," cried Potter. "I was reading that."

Blake crumpled the magazine in his hands and threw it to the floor. "Never mind about that, there's work to be done. You can't just sit on your bloody arse all day. Go and get the platoon around here. Everyone except the OP man."

"What's up, sir?"

"Never mind what's up. Just do as you're told."

Nichols watched as a very disgruntled Potter left the bunker. Then he glanced at Blake. He looked on the verge of tears. "Anything wrong, sir?"

"We've got to send out a large patrol tomorrow night."

Nichols tried to be cheerful. "Well, it had to come sooner or later." Blake ignored him and they remained silent until the platoon had assembled outside the bunker. "Are you going to brief them now, sir?" asked Nichols.

"No. I'm just going to give them a warning order. An idea of what is happening."

Blake regarded the assembled platoon with sympathy. They were a fine-looking bunch: their bodies, mostly stripped to the waist, rippled with muscles and were burnt deep-brown after many hours of toiling in the sun; their biceps were bulging and hard, their stomachs flat and muscular, their eyes clear and healthy. They were laughing and joking, just like his old platoon had been when he took out his first patrol on Yong Dong. It all seemed a very long time ago.

"All right! All right!" yelled Nichols. "Keep the noise down and listen to Mr. Blake."

Blake hesitated, not knowing where to start, or how to put it. "I've got you here," he said eventually, "to give you a warning order for a patrol which will take place to-morrow night." There was a general groan. "The patrol will be twenty strong.   So it will include most of you.   Corporal Smith and his first Bren group will stay behind as a token force."

"Lucky bastards!"

"All right, you can cut that out," yelled Nichols.

"We'll leave here around 2200 hours tomorrow night," continued Blake. "So there will be a weapon and equipment inspection tomorrow afternoon. You'll have a full briefing then.   All clear on that?   Right, that's all."

"What exactly is it all about?" asked a man.

A cynical smile spread across Blake's face.   What was it all about indeed! That was ripe.   As calmly as he could, he replied: "The object of the patrol is to disrupt the existing Chinese patrolling system..."

"That's a bit of a tall order, isn't it, sir?"

"You don't need to tell me that.   According to the Chinese prisoner Sergeant Sykes nabbed, the Chinese have a firm base patrol of about forty men near the base of their hill directly opposite Three Platoon.   Our job is to attack it and make them disperse ... Make sure they realize they can't just sit there, dominating things."

"How the hell are we supposed to do that, sir?"

Blake laughed in a tone that matched his smile.   He wanted to tell them exactly what he thought: that they were a mere gesture, cannon fodder with little prospects of returning.   He managed to restrain himself.   "It's just another of these army jobs we've been landed with.   There's damn all we can do about it.   Any more questions?"

"Yes, sir.   With some of us it will be our last night in the line."

"I know that.   I'm one of them, as you know.   But rest assured that I'll make sure that those on their last night stay behind with Corporal Smith--- he's another of them, of course."

"Couldn't we wait and see what happens with the peace talks, sir?"

"I'm afraid not.   Major Lawrence has no faith in them.   Our prisoner reckons this activity of the Chinese is their way of influencing things.   What you might call jockeying for position, or if you like, strengthening their bargaining power.   So we have to do something about it."

He watched them as they moved off.   Now, there was no laughter; they were glum, discussing among themselves what they had just heard.   When the last of them had disappeared into the network of trenches, Blake went back into the CP.   Nichols was already there, pacing the floor and smoking. Blake ignored him and lay down on his bunk.   It was no surprise to him when Nicholas spoke.

"You don't give two pins for our chances to-morrow night, do you, sir?"

Blake turned his head slowly.   "No, not really.   A few might straggle back in ..."

Nicholas sat down and looked Blake squarely in the face. He had nothing but contempt for him. In all his service he had never seen anything so disgraceful as Blake's warning order. "You told them as much."

"I simply told them the truth. What else could I say?"

"It's not as simple as that, sir. There are hundreds of silly things we have to do. But there's no point in telling the men that. Men have faith in officers. They expect leadership from them, but to be told they haven't got a chance in hell ..."

Blake said nothing further. He sank back on his bunk; his eyes watered, his cheeks flushed and he resumed staring at the roof. He had made a complete mess of the whole thing. Nicholas was right: it only made things worse by letting his men see his fear.

Nicholas started to check over the wirelesses again. "Are you doing the first stag to-night, sir?" he asked eventually.

"Who did it last night?"

"You were going to, sir. But when that prisoner came along I took over for the rest of the night."

Blake sighed. He was absolutely worn out. He felt incapable of even getting off his bed. "You'd better do the first one to-night, Sergeant. What with this patrol and everything else I'd better get as much sleep as possible."

Nicholas regarded him with disgust. "I'll go round see that the platoon is stood to then, sir. You needn't bother yourself."

As Nicholas left the bunker he dragged the blackout blanket across the doorway, leaving Blake in darkness. It also cut off any fresh air and he was soon pouring with sweat. The mosquitoes were beginning to bite him, but he had not the energy to rig up his mosquito net. He sat up in bed, and after removing his shirt he wiped himself down with an old towel. Sleep still eluded him and he twisted about in frustration. He saw again the time when he'd stood in front of the Colonel, Lawrence and the adjutant and been told that he was incompetent, useless and of no further use to them. So what? Maybe he was all those things, but why the hell should he worry? What had it all got to do with him, anyhow? He had never asked to be sent to this filthy, stinking country. He was just a civilian dressed up in uniform.

He rolled over and buried his face in his sleeping-bag.

12

Blake was woken not long afterwards by Corporal Smith. His new glasses were hopelessly too big and he had to keep pushing them back up his nose. "This patrol is a bit of a bugger, Mr. Blake."

"Yes, I know."

"The lads on their last night were thankful for what you said, sir. But we've worked it all out and we don't quite see how you're going to manage it. One of them will have to go..."

"You're wrong, actually …. I'm only going to take nineteen, regardless of what Lawrence says. I don't suppose he'll notice the difference… Just one bloke light won't make any odds."

"It could do. Especially if he's a Bren gunner."

"Yeah, well … Bad luck."

"There's no problem really. What I've come round here for is to volunteer to be the one who goes with you."

Blake sat up on his bunk. "Don't be damned silly, Smudge. You're the last bloke I'd take out there on your last night."

"I want to go."

"Oh, why?"

Smith gave a short, embarrassed laughed. "A matter of pride really. Ever since what happened on the Hook I've been feeling pretty sick about things. I mean the way I just sat in that bunker and did bugger all, while the rest of you were charging about like maniacs."

"We both know the reason for that …"

"Maybe, but it doesn't alter the facts of it. I feel awful when I think about the lads who snuffed it--- blokes who were good mates of mine. Like old Charlie and Hallows. And like I say, it is a matter of pride … Being able to live with myself."

"Sorry Smudge … No deal."

"Well that's not good enough, Mr. Blake … I'm bloody coming."

"Oh, are you …."

"Yes, I am. And there's another thing …"

"What's that?"

"You need me. Although I say it myself, I'm the best Bren gunner in the platoon … Not saying much, maybe, but I am. And if you're thinking of having Sergeant Nichols in charge of a Bren group, you want to be careful. You've never been on patrol with him, but when he takes us out he's like a bloody old woman. He dithers about and we spend more time lying on the ground listening than anything else. He's got cold feet, sir ..."

"We're all shit scared Smudge, for God's sake."

"Yes, maybe we are, but there is a big difference between being scared and having cold feet."

"You mean he can't be trusted?"

"Well, I wouldn't go that far. It's just that he's not dependable. If anyone gets back, it'll be him. Just you wait and see."

Blake laughed at the way Smith had put it. If there was one man he knew he could depend on, and didn't have 'cold feet' it was Smith. "Okay then Smudge, if that's what you want. One problem solved, at least."

That night there was a lot of action: nothing major, just one small incident after another, each one threatening real trouble but never developing into anything of any consequence. It was a great relief to them all when dawn came and the standing patrols were back in safely. Blake posted a list of all those who would be on the patrol on their notice board. Those named retired to their bunkers to try to get some sleep.

The afternoon inspection went well. It incorporated a rehearsal during which Blake explained the tactics he intended to us. He selected Rivers and Chambers as the point men to go ahead of the main body of the patrol; and he selected the two Bren groups to go on the flanks of their arrowhead formation. With twenty men at his disposal he was able to place two Bren groups at their rear, with Nichols and Smith in charge of them. He then explained that the aim would be to get as near as possible to the Chinese bund without being detected and then be the first to open fire, thereby gaining the initiative. To start with, they would use nothing but grenades, and they had to make sure they landed behind the Chinese. That meant the Chinese would not only have no protection from the bund, but it would also take them by surprise. If a dozen or so grenades suddenly exploded behind them, they were bound to panic, wondering what had hit them. Blake also ordered the main body of the patrol to take as many grenades as possible and concentrate on throwing them while the two rear Bren groups would come forward and all of them direct their fire at the bund, keeping the heads of the Chinese well down. What would happen after that, Blake didn't say. He had no idea. So much would depend on how the Chinese reacted and how many of them there turned out to be.

They spent a considerable amount of time practicing throwing grenades, aiming to achieve a distance of thirty or forty yards, with Blake insisting that they should be thrown from a standing or kneeling position, never lying flat on their stomachs.   Finally, he took them round to the OP three at a time to study through binoculars the ground they would be covering, pointing out the shell craters that were dotted about and which would afford them a degree of cover.   His idea was to 'leap-frog' from one crater to another until they were within grenade-throwing distance.   When he'd shown the last group in the OP he had a final word with them all, telling them to return to their bunkers to try to get some sleep.   He knew he'd never be able to sleep and he doubted if any of the others would either.

There was no moon that night, low rain-filled clouds making it inky dark. Blake saw that as a big advantage.   He had the lay-out of the valley so clearly etched in his mind that he had no doubt that he would be able to close in on the Chinese position accurately.

They set off at 2300 hours.   Those remaining on the position gathered to see them off and wish them luck.   They picked their way down the pathway through the barbed-wire and around the minefield.   They dropped off the stretcher-bearers at the standing patrol a short distance into no man's land.

They progressed well, covering bounds of some thirty yards before going to ground to listen for any movement ahead of them.

At the back of the patrol, Sergeant Nichols and Smith were careful not to lose sight of those directly in front of them.   In the pitch darkness it would have been all too easy.   Occasionally, Nichols would hiss across to Smith: "Okay?" to which Smith would hiss back, "Okay!" wishing that Nichols would keep his mouth shut.   Even whispers were liable to travel a long way in the eerie silence of no man's land.

Then, every time the patrol went to ground to listen, Nichols would crawl across to Smith with some other comment, either that he didn't like the look of things, or it was too bloody quiet for his liking, or he thought he'd heard something--- always some inane remark which betrayed his nervousness. Smith wasn't surprised.   He'd known it happen before with Nichols and it was exactly what he had warned Blake about.

Before long, Nichols comments became far more concerned: "He's going too bloody fast," he whispered to Smith. "He's rushing things. I'll go forward and tell him to slow down."

"Just let him get on with it," Smith whispered back.

"Bugger that!   I'm not letting him rush us head long into a trap.   I'll go forward."

He crawled off and when he located Blake he got short shift from his platoon commander.   "Just stick with us, Sergeant.   I'll shorten our bounds, but there's no point in hanging around for no reason."

When Nichols got back to his position we whispered to Smith: "We'll have to watch this bloke, no doubt about it."

"Just let him get on with it," repeated Smith.

After a couple more bounds, Smith realized that Nichols was slowing down the whole time and the distance between them and the main body of the patrol had widened. On several occasions Smith couldn't see any of them at all.

Then, when the point men were some fifty yards away from the Chinese position, Nichols went to ground on his own initiative. He signaled across to Smith to do the same. As Smith and his number two squatted down, Nichols pointed to his right, jabbing his arm out. "Heard something!" he hissed urgently.

Smith crawled across and together they listened. Smith heard nothing. There was nothing. He was absolutely positive. It was Nichols, up to his usual bloody tricks. Smith went back to his number two. "Have the others stopped?"

"No, I don't think so. I don't know. They've disappeared. Still going forward as far as I know."

"Oh, Christ!" cursed Smith under his breath. "What a bloody cock-up."

At the front of the patrol the point men were crawling from crater to crater, getting really near their destination. The large bund was quite clear, even in the darkness; it was a solid wall stretching across in front of them, nearly waist high. They stopped in a shell hole. Chambers peered backwards and waved to Blake, motioning him forward. Blake joined him. "Next stop and we'll be within throwing distance, sir," said Chambers.

"Right," he whispered back. "I'll get the grenade party all in line. Another short bound ... Take it easy ... And remember to all throw together."

Blake got the grenade party to move forward. Then they crawled on, rejoining the point men. They were in a series of craters which were very handily strung across the paddy. Blake crawled into the crater beside Chambers. He was all excited. He kept pointing at the bund, mouthing something Blake couldn't understand. Then Chambers held his nose and mimed with such exaggeration that Blake at last realized what he was saying: he could smell the Chinese. Blake couldn't, but Chambers was insistent. Then Chambers went rigid, held his head erect, listening. He pointed over to their left flank where there was a low bund. This time Chambers whispered: "Over there too, sir. Voices! Quite definitely!"

Blake hadn't reckoned with the Chinese being on their flank, as well as ahead of them. He glanced around, as though seeking a way out. He could see all his men in line abreast, their heads protruding above the lips of the craters, awaiting his next order. He realized that they'd walked into an ambush, with Chinese on two sides of them. No doubt they'd seen them coming and were biding their time, waiting for the whole patrol to move forward. Blake lost no time. He knelt up and mimicked activating a grenade. He saw arms being raised in acknowledgement. He pulled the pin from his grenade. He waited three seconds, and then hurled it as hard as he could to make sure it cleared the bund in front of them. The others followed his example and soon a dozen or more grenades were soaring through the air. Blake heard distinctive, dull thuds as they landed. Then the explosions came like a vicious artillery concentration, a cacophony of violent eruptions. Vivid red, yellow and orange flashes leapt up.

Almost simultaneously, the Chinese opened fire on them. Burp guns blazed away at them from both their front and from their left flank. They ducked into the shelter of the shell craters and Blake kept yelling: "Keep throwing! Keep throwing!"

He glanced to each side and saw men's heads and shoulders bobbing up and down as they threw more grenades. Then their two flanking Bren guns opened up, spraying the two bunds.

"Keep throwing! Keep throwing!" Blake yelled again and again.

Well to the rear, Nichols and Smith's Bren groups were nowhere near the action. Now, with grenades bursting all the time, and the flashes of small arms, they could see exactly what had happened, how Blake had led them into an ambush.

"Quick! Get forward," shouted Smith.

"Hang on," responded Nichols. "Just bloody hang on until we can see what's happening."

Smith took no notice of him. He could already see exactly what had happened. Furthermore he realized that the Chinese were not aware that there were two more Bren groups loitering at the rear, free to deploy without danger. He could see the flashes of the Chinese all along the flanking bund and it suddenly struck him that here was a perfect chance to set up his Bren at their end of the bund and shoot straight down the line of Chinese on Blake's flank. Not knowing he was there, they would be at his mercy, and he had no intention of giving them any.

He jumped up and yelled to his number two: "Come on! Follow me."

It only took them a few seconds to reach the end of the bund. In the light of battle Smith could see the Chinese leaning against the side of the bund, blazing away as hard as they could at Blake and the others. There were about twenty of them. Smith and his number two dropped to the ground and set up the Bren on its bipod. Then they opened fire, straight down the line of the flanking Chinese. It was a crucial moment. To Smith the result was almost comical. Some Chinese jumped up in confusion, wondering what had hit them. Others ran off or fell to the ground, while a few just looked around, trying to make out what was happening. They were so surprised that they were soon in complete disarray. A few even climbed on top of the bund and were immediately shot down by either Smith or one of Blake's Bren groups. Most of them darted about like mesmerized rabbits.

As Nichols realized what was happening he rushed to join Smith. He set up his Bren and the increased fire-power soon cut the Chinese to ribbons. There were shouts and screams: an assortment of orders, counter orders, warnings, cries for help and the usual yells and screams men make in the throes of death.

To Blake's front, the Chinese small-arms fire had likewise tailed away as they too tried to fathom out what was happening. They were shocked to a stand-still. Blake hurled his fifth grenade and all around him others were doing the same. Within a matter of minutes around thirty grenades had landed among the Chinese.

Blake decided it was time to pull out. He saw his two point men half turn, ready to make a run for it, so he yelled at them to do just that. They jumped up and sprinted away, both doubled-up as low as they could, heading for the rear. Blake turned to the others and yelled: "Pull out! Pull out!"

It was a crucial moment. They had to turn their backs and run, with no covering fire, an easy target for those Chinese still firing from behind the main bund. As they ran, they zigzagged crazily. Blake collided with one man and they both went sprawling, but in an instant they were back on their feet and away again. Another man went down, right beside Blake. He stopped to help him. He hauled him to his feet and dragged him along. Another man went down. He kept yelling: "I'm hit! I'm hit!" Two others went to his aid and dragged him forward.

When they reached the end of the paddy field they scrambled over the bund and into relative safety. The point men were already there, fighting for breath. Blake did likewise and as he recovered himself he peered over the bund. The Chinese were no longer firing. They were totally disorganized. The Bren groups of Nichols and Smith were still thudding away, now on their third magazines.

Then they heard shrill bugle calls, sounds they associated with Chinese attacks; but this time they were making a hasty retreat, all discipline gone. The noise they made as they withdrew to their hill was quite incredible.

Smith and Nichols stopped firing and Blake shouted out to them, guiding them in to join the main patrol. He took out his Verey pistol and fired off a green flare, the signal for the gunners to bring down a concentration on the base of the Chinese hill.

Blake had two things left to do: first, check the casualties and then do a search of the site of the clash. The casualties amounted to three men seriously wounded and four missing. They did their best to put shell dressings on the wounded men and Blake sent a man back to get the stretcher-bearers and send a message back to the platoon for more to come out. Then he detailed Sergeant Nichols and two men to go back to the shell craters to look for the missing men and bring them back, whatever their condition. Finally, together with Smith and Chambers, he searched the area which had been occupied by the flanking Chinese.

A search was never popular. It invited trouble if any of the enemy was still there and only wounded, but it was the only way of proving their success, and he knew Lawrence would never be satisfied unless he did one. He edged cautiously along the bund where the Chinese had been. There was abundance evidence of the havoc Smith's Bren had caused: dead Chinese were sprawled about, each shot several times. There were tracks of blood where their wounded had been dragged away. Weapons, items of clothing, and bits of equipment were lying around. They picked up two Burp guns and some blood-stained Chinese caps. They moved on until they were looking behind the main bund which had faced them. There were tell-tale signs of casualties, but no bodies. They had been dragged away, leaving the flotsam of war.

Blake reckoned they'd hung around long enough. He could still hear the Chinese withdrawing, trying to reorganize themselves, and he realized that at any moment they might call artillery down on the area.

As it was, they had no difficulty getting back to the patrol. He gathered everyone together and made for the standing patrol. Stretcher-bearers were still seeing to the wounded, or carrying them back up to One Platoon.

Eventually, they reassembled outside the platoon CP, together with the rest of the platoon and a few from other platoons as well, even Cross and Williamson from company headquarters. There was great excitement and a general feeling of relief, despite their casualties, which totaled four killed and three wounded. . They had expected things to be far worse. Potter distributed mugs of hot coffee generously laced with rum. Whilst men drank and lit up fags, Blake went amongst them, praising them and thanking them. The survivors all had a feeling of having been born again.

Sergeant Nichols joined Blake. "A good effort despite the losses, sir."

"Yes. I would have settled for that, given the choice."

"I think I was right to hang back with the Brens, sir ... I was being tactical, like."

"It was a brilliant move that saved the day. Well done."

Early the following morning Blake went to battalion headquarters with Lawrence to be debriefed by the Colonel, the adjutant and the IO. Potter went along as well, carrying two Burp guns as evidence of their success. Blake was thankful that the entire patrol hadn't been called upon to recall what had happened, as was normally the case. It was necessary to get the debriefing over quickly: Blake and the others returning to the UK were due to leave for Kure at 1400 hours. Had the whole platoon been interviewed it could have gone on for hours, and had Sergeant Nichols been present it could well have developed into a long and embarrassing wrangle. As it was, Blake was now well aware of what had really happened and he had worked out a way of explaining the initiative and bravery of Corporal Smith without in any way being critical of Nichols.

The debriefing was about to be concluded, when the assistant IO came in with a message. The IO read it and smiled, but made no comment.

"Well, a very good effort, Blake," concluded the Colonel. "Capital! I think that should help to re-establish a proper balance in no man's land."

"Actually, sir," said the IO in his usual smooth manner. "It won't make the slightest difference."

They all looked at the IO in amazement. Normally, he would have been the last person ever to contradict the Colonel. Then, having allowed himself the pleasure of a soft chuckle, he added: "A message has just come in direct from Divisional HQ to all units. The armistice has been agreed. It comes into effect at 2200 hours this evening."

Lawrence and Blake walked back to Able Company together. Potter followed them, relieved of their trophies, now destined for the Rocks Regimental Museum. He noticed that the two officers didn't speak. In fact, they couldn't even march along in step.

When they reached Able Company Lawrence at last broke their silence. "Well, there we are, Blake. The war ends and you go home, and all on the same day." He tried to make a joke. "It's just as you once said ... 'All a risk well worth taking'."

So that was it, thought Blake: his own words thrown back at him. Lawrence had never got over that ill-fated remark and probably never would.

Four dead and the three wounded, and all a risk well worth taking! Not for the first time Blake realized that their attitudes to war was, always had been, and always would be, diametrically opposed and totally irreconcilable.

PART V

THE REWARDS OF DUTY

1

The officers' mess commanded a magnificent view across the Imjin River. It was perched on the summit of a lush green hill, surrounded by densely leaved trees and bushes, in which unseen birds sang cheerfully. The sides of the mess tents were rolled back to allow a cool breeze from the mountains to sweep through among the delicately arranged chairs and tables to give some measure of relief from the intense heat.

Lawrence, who was mainly responsible for the selection and development of the site, paused at the bottom of the hill and wiped his face with a handkerchief. Then he sighed and started on the laborious climb. There were several officers ahead of him and by the time he reached the mess they were sitting about in the armchairs, drinking. They were mostly junior officers and Lawrence noticed that the magazines and papers were already scattered about the mess, with tables and chairs disarranged.

He selected the most recent paper left and settled down in a chair. For some reason he could not concentrate on reading and he began to worry about the demonstration Able Company was due to give to the entire division in two days' time. As yet they had had no rehearsals, and now that Blake was probably more than halfway home, his only subaltern was Fuller and--- nice lad though he was--- he was seldom a help.

He felt sweat trickling down the back of his neck and with a sudden pulse of irritation he looked round the mess for a waiter. There were none to be seen. "Waiter! Waiter!" he yelled.

A waiter, immaculately dressed in a white jacket and stiff collar, soon appeared. "Yes, sir?"

"Get me a beer. And make it snappy."

"Yes, sir."

"And a gin and lime."

"Of course, sir."

Lawrence looked up keenly a few minutes later as he heard someone enter the mess, but to his disappointment it was Fuller and not the waiter. As Fuller approached him Lawrence watched him with impatience. "Well, what is it?"

"The Colonel is looking for you, sir. He's on his way up here now, sir."

Lawrence groaned softly. "All right, Fuller. I'll see him."

Presently, the Colonel appeared in the doorway with the adjutant. They were both sweating after the climb, but they looked uncommonly pleased with themselves. Everyone in the mess stood up and Lawrence walked towards them.

"Ah, there you are, Dick," cried the Colonel so that everyone could hear. "I've been looking for you all morning."

Lawrence was immediately apologetic. "I'm sorry about that, sir. I've been trying to get this wretched demonstration into some kind of shape. It'll be all right, of course, but they might have given us a bit longer than two days."

"Yes, well never mind about that, Dick. I've got some good news for you. They've just rung up from Brigade to say that it's come through. You've been awarded the DSO. Congratulations! You deserve it if anyone ever did."

Lawrence was stunned for a moment and then a smile of simple joy spread across his face. He wanted to give a great whoop of triumph, but all he could do was utter a few words of thanks to the Colonel and shake hands with him. Then he shook the adjutant's hand, and then someone else's, and then someone else's ... Suddenly the mess seemed full and he was thanking each of them as they congratulated him.

"Waiter!" he yelled excitedly, "drinks all round. Come on, man, don't dither about. Get the drinks flowing and don't spare them, either."

He watched the drinks circulating with a radiant smile and then joined the Colonel at one of the occasional tables.

"I expect you were wondering what had gone wrong, weren't you, Dick?" asked the Colonel.

"How do you mean, sir?"

"You know ... It being so long in coming through."

Lawrence roared with laughter. "I didn't even realize that you had put me up for one, sir."

There was a wild cry of disbelief from several officers sitting nearby. "Honest to God," protested Lawrence, "I had no idea."

"Come off it, Dick," said the Colonel. "After the Hook battle you were bound to get one. A company commander who can hold off a Chinese divisional attack isn't born every day, you know."

"That's a bit of an exaggeration," smiled Lawrence, twisting the ends of his moustache.

"You wait until you've seen the citation, old man,' said the adjutant, "I'm only surprised you didn't get a VC."

When the Colonel eventually rose and led the way into lunch, Lawrence remained seated. He wanted to be alone to think. So he had got a DSO. By God, what a relief it was. And it had been worth the struggle. The war was over and he had a DSO--- what could be better? He felt immensely secure. Major Lawrence, DSO. That sounded good. It sounded bloody good.

He went into the dining tent and joined the Colonel. As they started on their Brown Windsor soup, the Colonel said: "Another thing, Dick. And this will really make your day. The powers that be have decided that now I'm retiring, and we've got another demanding posting in Kenya to sort out the Mau Mau, my successor had better be someone resolute. So they're going to appoint you."

Lawrence could hardly believe it. He'd half expected the DSO, but CO of the Ist Battalion of the Rockinghamshire Regiment, that really was a surprise. Lawrence abandoned his soup and strolled around the mess, eventually looking out over the Imjin. He chuckled like an excited schoolboy. Lieutenant Colonel Richard Lawrence, DSO ...

All he had to do now was get his hemorrhoids fixed and shave off his moustache. Then life would be perfect.

2

Blake and Smith stood in the main doorway of a Piccadilly store, watching the crowd hurry by in a typically English summer drizzle. It was the first rain they had encountered since leaving Pusan over a month before, and after the intense heat of the Red Sea and the Mediterranean they felt cold.

It was good to be back, but with everything so normal and ordinary it held little excitement; in fact, it came as an anti-climax. They had planned to spend their first evening celebrating in London, but on docking in Southampton they altered their minds and decided to get up to town and take the first train going north.

They remained in the doorway watching the crowds pass by for some time and then, after looking into the sky to see if there was any likelihood of the rain abating, Blake said: "Come on, Smudge. I'll show you Trafalgar Square before we catch that train, even if it does mean getting wet."

They joined the crowds and made their way across the Circus to the Haymarket, down the Haymarket and eventually into Trafalgar Square. They crossed the road in front of the art gallery. Then they leaned heavily on the thick stone wall, looking down into the Square.

In the glare of all the lights, the fountains rose gracefully into the air to join the drizzle, and then drifted in a fine spray in the grip of the squally wind. Directly beneath Blake a couple sheltering in the shadow of the wall were indulging in the pleasures of each other's lips, and behind him he heard the constant beating of shoes on the wet pavement as people trudged off to God-knows where. The surrounding buildings were slightly blurred by the rain and the buses hissed on the roads as they lumbered towards traffic lights that blinked from color to color. It was a comforting but dismal scene.

As Blake stared down into the Square he found himself thinking of the past year; so much had happened that it was difficult to get things into the right sequence. There had been their first night in the line, their first patrol, the patrol on which Collins and Barnes had been killed; Christmas Eve, when they had been so near to capturing a prisoner, the move into reserve after those horrible, cold winter days, the blue-on-blue with the tank, the rows with Lawrence and the Colonel; then there had been Jackie. Now, with Kure over ten thousand miles away, he realized that with Jackie it was all for the best. It could never have been otherwise, just as she had said. Yet he would never forget her and always be grateful to her.

He half-turned and watched Smith sucking hopefully on his dog-end. "No more free fags," said Smith gloomily.

Blake laughed. "Never mind, there are consolations. I shouldn't really tell you this, but you've been put up for a Military Medal. Not that I expect a gong will matter to you."

"You're wrong there," exclaimed Smith, his face beaming. "I think that's terrific. It'll put my bloody kid brother in his place--- good and proper! Something I've been trying to do for years."

They were silent for a time. "What about you, Mr. Blake? Are you getting anything?"

"Good Lord, no! For me, it's just been part of the University of Life ... And it will probably turn out to be worth all the degrees under the sun."

There was another lengthy silence. Then Blake asked: "So what do you think of Trafalgar Square?"

"Not much, to be truthful." Smith paused and wiped his glasses as though to get a better look. His mind was on the Hook. "Do you remember the night of the Hook battle when we were in that bunker with O'Hara? I'll never forget how he was going farther and farther round the bend. Do you remember the way he kept cracking on about the fountains?"

"Yeah ... He kept saying they were the biggest he had ever seen, and how beautiful they were."

"He must have been nuts," smiled Smith. "In fact, he was nuts. Poor old Paddy. He never was found, was he, sir?"

"No.   Still up there, I suppose."

"You know, Mr. Blake, if there was one thing I would like to have seen in that war it would have been Paddy O'Hara coming out of it with his right marker up.   He was a clueless bloody soldier, but he tried like hell."

"So did all the others," said Blake.

Blake watched Smith replace his glasses and then give his dog-end a final, despairing drag before throwing it down and crushing it under his boot, realizing it had died a natural death.

Blake placed a hand on his corporal's shoulder.   "Come on, Smudge. Let's catch that train and get home."

The End

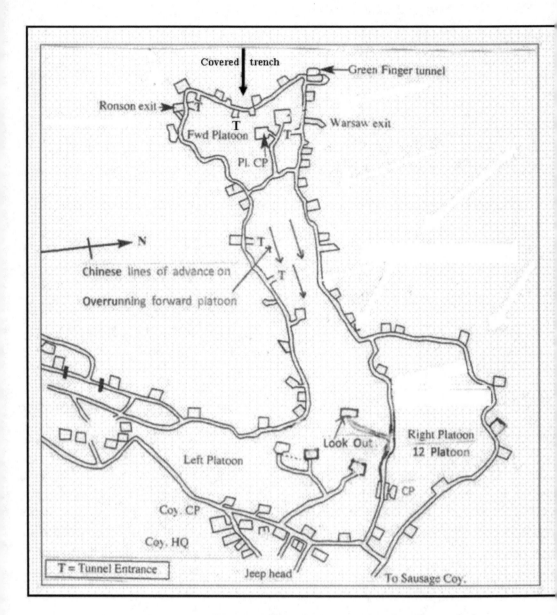

Over the years the fortifications on the Hook varied.
This was the layout in May 1953.
Not to scale

<u>Glossary</u>

CP	Command Post
OP	Observation Post
FOO	Forward Observation Officer (artillery)
Sten	Light automatic weapon
Bren	Light machine gun
Blue-on-blue	Friendly fire casualty
RSM	Regimental Sergeant-Major
CSM	Company Sergeant-Major
2 i/c	Second-in-command
VT shelling	Air burst shells
Bunds	Embankments around paddy fields
Recce	Reconaissance
RAP	Regimental Aid Post
CAP	Company Aid Post
C-Rations	American tinned food
JRBD	Japanese Reserve Base Depot
Point men	Forward patrol scouts
TCV	Troop carrying vehicle
MSR	Main Supply Route
DF	Defensive fire
Stonk	Short artillery concentration
MO	Medical officer
Housey-Housey	Army's version of Bingo
CRA	Commander Royal Artillery
Vickers Machine guns	Heavy machine guns, used on fixed lines
Burp guns	Chinese hand-held automatics
TA	Territorial Army
88-set and 31-sets	Wirelesses used at company level

Acclaim for The Dead, The Dying And The Damned (Able Company)

"The character studies in **The Dead, the Dying and the Damned** are masterly… A genius like Hollands writes a book in which people behave like human beings… A brilliantly angry first novel and Hollands is the only 'Angry Young Man' with anything to be really angry about! Some may ask for its suppression, but I would say this: it is only when people as courageous as Hollands dare to write the truth about war that the miracle will come about when it will be no more."

Nancy Spain, Daily Express

"**The Dead, the Dying and the Damned** stands alongside *All Quiet on the Western Front* as the best war novel of all time."

Paul Wigby, Associated Press

"Admirably done! Sincerely, conscientious and factual."

Marie Scott Thomas, Daily Telegraph

"This book is a truly brilliant piece of writing."

Evening News

"The Korean battles are magnificent and the whole book an incredible achievement for a young man of twenty."

New Chronicle

"It is in the school of the **Naked and the Dead**, but much better written."

Reynolds News

"A truly remarkable first novel. It is bound to become a best-seller."

Yorkshire Evening Post

"A genuinely moving book. There is no mistaking the strength of emotion, pity, indignation and resentment that has driven him to seek an outlet in words."

Peter Quinnell, Daily Mail.

"As fiction, it is grippingly impressive.   As a document it is frightening."
Birmingham Gazette

"It should be read by all politicians."
South Wales Echo

"Impressive and rewarding."
New York Herald Tribune

"The best novel of the Korean war."
New York Times

"The battles scenes are perfect!!
The New Yorker

"An exceptionally fine novel"
Columbus Dispatch

"It rests with such classics as *From Here the Eternity* and *The Naked and the Dead.*"
American Literary Guild

"The best novel to be written about the Korean war."
Chicago Sun-Times

"Magnificent!"
Chicago Tribune

"Hollands allows his characters no privacy, but probes each man's thoughts to the roots.   He has created a very real group of people who gain the complete sympathy of the reader… A novel that ranks with Remarque's *All Quiet on the Western Front* and Sir Phillip Gibbs's *And now it can be Told!*
Robert Barr, Boston Globe

"I have read *The Dead, the Dying and the Damned* many times.   The many well-drawn characters, the humorous descriptions of army life, and the masterly battle scenes make it one of the best war novels ever written.   It is, without doubt, the definitive novel of the Korean War and, as such, should be made readily available to everyone and then read by everyone. ”

Cyril Coombes, Hawker's War

"The battle scenes are well-nigh perfect and make the book a classic."

Chatanooga Times

"This is a brilliant, whopping-sized version of the British side of the Korean war."

Thomas Ripley, Atlanta Journal

"Addicts of war stories will like *Able Company* without too much trouble."

Victor Yanitelli, Fordham University

"This is the novel of the Korean war that had to be written. *Able Company* is exciting, seen through the eyes of Tommy Atkins."

Jim G. Lucas, Pittsburgh Press.

"It is tough-fibred, cleanly written, and grimly true,"

Tom Walker, Salem Journal

"Easily the best novel to come out of the Korean War"

Tom Murray, Boston Herald.

"All of *Able Company* becomes glorious as you read it."

C.E.K.

"An exceedingly able piece of work… It is so well written. The author does a fine job in making his experiences come alive. He has done it quite excellently."

Cameron Rorke, Columbia Dispatch

"Able Company is outstanding among the chronicles of the Korean War: a distinguished novel and a big novel in every sense. The final battle scene is the greatest ever portrayed by an author.

Carl Baldwin, Louis, Post Dispatch

"Hollands writes with power and feeling with many very fine scenes. The descriptions of the confused and bloody battles are sharp and gripping."

Newark News.

Acclaim for other books by John Hollands

The Gospel According to Uncle Jimmy

"Of its type, the funniest book I have ever read.
>> Dr. Desmond Flower, Cassell's

"An hilarious book.   As satire, it leaves *Catch 22* standing.
>> Neil McCallum, Actor

"The best book of its type I have had the pleasure of reading.
>> Adelaide Librarian

The Exposed

"I found *The Exposed* moving and extremely convincing. George was a wonderful character, brilliantly real and fresh, and the Japanese heroine (Katsumi) tremendously likable and convincing.   The evocation of the era and the eye for detail of that time were most impressive.
>> Maeve Haran, *Having it All*

"A wonderful story, superbly told, crying out to be made into a film."
>> Guy Bellamy, *The Secret Lemonade Drinker*

"This is a work of genius!   One of the most moving, wonderful, happy-sad books I have ever read.
>> Trevor Hunt, *Ibiza Shorts*

"It's a superb piece of work with marvelous characters."
>> John Pawsey,   Lit. Agent

"The development of the love affair between George and Katsumi is delicately and beautifully handled.   As a love story it works superbly, with all

299

the right ingredients."

Bernard Boucher, *Opalesque*

"*The Exposed* is absolutely brilliant in all respects: plot, setting, characterization, humor, all superb and most perceptive of human nature."

Peter Brooke-Smith, Oxon

"A fascinating read. The love story is touchingly told: very funny and ultimately very moving. At times it takes one to the depths of despair but, in the end, its profoundly inspiring message is dramatically and effectively revealed... A very fine piece of work indeed!"

John Hogston, *Hawker's War*

Katsumi is, of course, wonderful...the whole thing is simply first class.

David Bolt, *Author's Handbook*

"John Hollands has written *the* most superb novel. His easy style and well-drawn characters will make it a sure-fire winner. The wit and charm of the novel, together with the special treatment of the story, make you want to read it in one sitting.

Ken Fisher, English Bookshop

"Really impressive... The character of Katsumi is utterly enchanting... It is a real achievement.

Jeremy Firth Eng. Lit. Oundle

"The best book I've read for a very long time. This is a book which will be read over and over again."

Brian Warden, Cornish Libraries.

"It is a beautifully written and intelligent novel, with fascinating characters. It is also very funny and hugely insightful."

Amazon critic

"A beautiful novel, crying out to be made into a film...Characters you really get to know and care about... If only the publishers would reprint his earlier novels! There are few better writers today."

Amazon critic